THE
SHOPKEEPER'S
DAUGHTER

Lily Baxter lives in Dorset. She is the author of *Poppy's War*, *We'll Meet Again*, *Spitfire Girl* and *The Girls in Blue*. She also writes under the name of Dilly Court.

Lily Baxter
THE SHOPKEEPER'S DAUGHTER

arrow books

Published by Arrow Books 2013

2 4 6 8 10 9 7 5 3 1

First published in Great Britain in 2013 by
Century
Random House, 20 Vauxhall Bridge Road,
London SW1V 2SA

www.randomhouse.co.uk

Addresses for companies within The Random House Group Limited can be found at:
www.randomhouse.co.uk/offices.htm

The Random House Group Limited Reg. No. 954009

A CIP catalogue record for this book
is available from the British Library

Typeset in Palatino by Palimpsest Book Production Limited,
Falkirk, Stirlingshire

Penguin Random House is committed to a sustainable future for
our business, our readers and our planet. This book is made from
Forest Stewardship Council® certified paper.

MIX
Paper from
responsible sources
FSC® C018179

Printed and bound in Great Britain by Clays Ltd, Elcograf S.p.A.

For Tricia, a friend in need.

Chapter One

East London, June 1944

Ginnie had risked leaving the safety of the air raid shelter when Fred Chinashop suffered one of his funny turns. Despite her father's protests she had returned to the small office at the back of their furniture store, and was about to add a generous spoonful of her precious sugar ration to a cup of tea when she heard the dreaded rasping buzz of the doodlebug. The cup rattled on its saucer and the floor beneath her feet started to vibrate.

The deathly silence when its engine cut out made her hold her breath, closing her eyes as she prayed that the bomb would fall on fields or wasteland, anywhere but on the crowded suburban streets. The explosion when it came was too close for comfort, and she felt the repercussion of the blast shaking the foundations of the building. Large flakes of plaster fell from the ceiling and the air was thick with dust. Her hand was trembling as she picked up the cup and saucer. They had been lucky this time, but somebody somewhere must have bought it.

The all clear siren was blasting out its monotone

wail of relief as she let herself out into the back yard. Sidney Travis emerged from the Anderson shelter red-faced and bristling with anger. 'You stupid girl. You might have got yourself killed.'

'I'm all right, Dad. How's Fred?'

Her father shook his head. 'He'll live, but you could have been dead and buried under the rubble if there'd been a direct hit.' He gave her a clumsy hug. 'Give the silly old devil his tea. I'm going inside to see if there's any damage.' He hurried indoors and Ginnie could hear him exclaiming in annoyance, and cursing the Jerries. She hesitated, gazing anxiously at the surrounding buildings, and breathed a sigh of relief when she realised that the parade of shops in Collier Lane had escaped the worst of the blast.

Purpose-built before the war, the box-like units had been designed with living accommodation above and a functional but drab service road at the rear. The concept, Ginnie had always suspected, might have looked stylish and ultra-modern on the architect's plans, but surrounded by a hinterland of small factories and uniform streets of Edwardian terraced houses in one of the poorer suburbs of East London, the Utopian dream had rapidly deteriorated into a shabby mass of concrete and glass. Most of the windows were now criss-crossed with sticky tape and sandbagged, but Sidney had steadfastly refused to have his shop boarded up, declaring that it was bad for business, and Hitler and his Luftwaffe could take a long walk off a short pier for all he cared.

Ginnie knew that they had been lucky this time. They had survived, and she could only hope that no one had been killed when the bomb landed. She hurried into the shelter, wrinkling her nose at the pervasive smell of damp and sweaty bodies. Fred Chinashop was still sitting on the wooden bench looking pale and dazed. She gave him his tea. 'I hope it's sweet enough for you.'

He managed a wobbly smile. 'Ta, love.'

Ginnie glanced anxiously at the only other occupant of the shelter. Ida Richmond lived in a flat above the shop and had been administering her version of first aid to Fred, which consisted of making encouraging noises and fanning him with her handkerchief. 'Is he all right, Mrs Richmond?' Ginnie asked in a whisper.

Ida nodded vigorously, causing her hairnet to slip over one eye. She adjusted it with a practised tweak of her fingers. 'It'd take more than a Jerry bomb to finish our Fred Chinashop.'

Fred nodded in silent agreement and sipped his tea. His real name was Fred Brown but Ginnie's dad had a penchant for giving people nicknames. Fred Brown had become Fred Chinashop in order to distinguish him from Fred Harper, also known as Fred Woollies, the manager of the Woolworth's store situated a little further along the parade. 'I'm fine now, ducks.' Fred raised the cup in a toast. 'Sweety, weaky and milky – just how I like it.'

'He's all right now.' Ida picked up a willow pattern plate piled high with her latest attempt at baking.

'Nelson squares. Try one of these, Fred.' She wafted the cakes under his nose. 'You need building up, love. You're all skin and bone.'

'I won't say no.' He took one and bit into it. 'You're too good to me, Ida.'

'I was just using up the crusts of bread and some dried fruit that had been on the shelf since last Christmas. My hubby doesn't have a sweet tooth and I have to watch my figure.' She beamed at him through the thick lenses of her horn-rimmed spectacles. 'You bachelors don't know how to look after yourselves properly. I dunno why you never got married, Fred. You must have been quite a good-looking feller years ago, before you went bald and lost all your teeth.'

He swallowed the last morsel and took a mouthful of tea. 'I feel better now, Ida. Ta very much, but I'd best get back to my emporium and see if there's any damage. The blast might have shattered what little stock I've got left. It's hard to get hold of decent crockery these days.' He put his cup and saucer on the wooden bench and struggled to his feet, steadying himself with one hand on the wall. 'Thanks for the cuppa, Ginnie.'

'Any time, Fred.' She stood aside to let him pass as he made his way out of the shelter.

Ida rose to her feet. 'That man needs a wife. He lives on tea and toast. No wonder he hasn't got any stamina. My Norman is twice the man he is. He'll scoff this lot in one go.'

'It's very kind of you to share them with us, Mrs Richmond,' Ginnie said, smiling. She was fond of Ida, who had always taken a motherly interest in the Travis family. With no children of her own to care for and a husband who worked long hours on the railways, Ida had nothing to do other than clean her tiny apartment and she was always popping downstairs with samples of her cooking.

'But you haven't tried them yet, love. Norman won't miss one more.'

Ginnie shook her head. 'No thanks. They look lovely but it's nearly lunchtime and I'll be in trouble if I don't eat everything on my plate. Mum will have been slaving away all morning to make something tasty out of next to nothing.'

'You're a good girl, Ginnie. It's a pity your flighty sister isn't a bit more like you.'

'Shirley's all right, Mrs Richmond. She's just high-spirited, that's all.'

'And you're very loyal, ducks.' Ida stepped outside, squinting in the sunlight. 'Let's hope the war ends before you get called up or have to work in the munitions factory like your sister. How old are you now, dear? I lose track.'

'I'll be nineteen in August.'

'At least you've got another year before you're called up. The war might be over by then, God willing.'

'Let's hope so, Mrs Richmond.'

'Your dad would be lost without you, Ginnie.

I dunno how he'd manage the shop if you weren't there to give him a hand.'

'I enjoy it,' Ginnie said stoutly. 'Maybe it's not what I'd set my heart on when I was at school, but I've learned how to keep accounts and I know almost as much about carpets and furniture as my dad.'

Ida patted her on the shoulder. 'You're a treasure.' She ambled across the yard and let herself out into the service lane. 'TTFN, ducks.'

Ginnie collected a dustpan and brush from the outside lavatory and hurried into the partitioned off area at the back of the shop that served as an office. She had not been lying to Ida when she said she enjoyed working for her father, but there was a part of her that wished he would allow her to enlist in one of the women's services and do her bit for her country. In a year's time she would be conscripted anyway, or else she would have to do war work like Shirley, but she did not relish the idea of slaving away in the munitions factory or volunteering as an ARP warden.

Shaking the plaster dust from her dark blonde hair, Ginnie brushed it back from her face and fastened it in a ponytail with a rubber band that she found in the bottom of one of the desk drawers along with a stick of sealing wax and an empty Fisherman's Friend tin. A stray strand tickled her nose and she secured it in place with the aid of a kirby grip, checking her reflection in the scrap of fly-spotted mirror balanced on a pile of account books, before

6

setting to work, sweeping and dusting until everything was cleaner than it had been before the bomb fell. She had just finished when she heard her father talking to their local ARP warden, Tom Adams, whose stentorian tones were unmistakeable.

She hurried through to the shop. 'Where did the bomb land, Mr Adams?'

'We was fortunate this time,' Tom said solemnly. 'It came down in the park and smashed the cricket pavilion to smithereens, but it's lucky it wasn't Saturday or it would have taken out half of the home guard and the team from the munitions factory in Dagenham.'

'That's where Shirley works,' Sidney said with a disapproving downturn of his mouth. 'That girl was top of the class in school. She'd have done well for herself but for the bloody war.' He shot an apologetic glance at his daughter. 'Excuse my French, but it makes me blooming mad.'

'Can't stay here chatting all day, Sid. Got my duties to perform.' Tom saluted and ambled towards the door. 'Abyssinia.'

'Maybe I'll see you in the King's Arms later,' Sid called after him. He turned to Ginnie with a sigh. 'The shop window's cracked. I suppose I'll have to give in and board it up, although it goes against the grain.' He bent down to heft a roll of linoleum upright. 'The blast tipped these over, Ginnie. Give us a hand to put them back up, there's a good girl, and then you'd best get home for your lunch. You

7

know how Mum worries if you're even a minute late.'

Ginnie set off at a brisk pace to walk the mile or so home. Situated in the middle of a large estate of identical 1930s semi-detached houses, Cherry Lane was a tree-lined suburban street. It was not the poorest part of town but it was on the edge of the industrial area where the gasworks sat cheek by jowl with the glue factory and the abattoir. The station with its sooty sidings and noisy shunting yard was nearby, and small businesses plied their trade beneath the railway arches.

Ginnie had been aware from an early age that the girls who lived on the other side of town, notably the posh Monk Avenue area, came from homes where they called their parents Mummy and Daddy and not Mum and Dad. Their fathers were professional men, and their mothers played bridge or socialised while charwomen did their housework. The houses in Monk Avenue were set in large gardens shielded from the road by high walls or hedges, with the golf links at the rear and the grammar school only two streets away.

Shirley might have aspirations to live in Monk Avenue, but Ginnie was fiercely loyal to her roots. There was nothing wrong with number ten, she thought as she approached the house. The exterior was pebble-dashed and the lounge and master bedroom had the benefit of curved bay windows.

There was a good-sized garden at the rear and a smaller one at the front, separated from the pavement by a low brick wall. Ginnie paused at the gate, looking up at the small triangular window behind which was her personal domain, cluttered with her most prized possessions, including a silver-backed dressing-table set that her paternal grandparents had given her on her sixteenth birthday. They had been killed in the Blitz, although it was still hard to believe that Hitler had got the better of Granny Travis. Ginnie still missed the old lady, with her acerbic tongue and wicked sense of humour. Her maternal grandparents had succumbed to heart attacks within weeks of each other when Ginnie was twelve years old, leaving her with nothing but happy memories of Christmases and summer holidays spent in their bungalow at Frinton-on-Sea.

She took her front door key from her handbag and let herself in. 'Mum. Hello, it's only me.'

Mildred Travis bustled out of the kitchen, wiping her hands on her floral pinafore. Snail-like pin curls had escaped from the scarf tied turban-fashion around her head, and her cheeks were flushed. 'Did you hear that doodlebug go over, Ginnie? I was in the Anderson with Mrs Martin from next door, and when it stopped my heart was beating so fast I thought I was going to pass out with fright. Thank God you're all right. D'you know where it landed?'

'In the park, Mum. Mr Adams said the cricket pavilion copped it, and the shop window's cracked, but Dad's going to board it up.'

'About time too. I keep telling him that he should have done it years ago, but will he listen to me? No, of course he won't. Your father is the most stubborn man I've ever met.' Mildred shot back into the kitchen, reappearing a moment later with a saucepan in her hand. 'Just caught the spuds before they boiled dry. I'll serve up right away.'

Ginnie tossed her handbag and gasmask case onto the hall stand and peeled off her gloves. Although it was a hot day she would have been nagged to death had Mum seen her less than immaculately turned out. War or no war, standards had to be maintained. Ginnie took her seat at the table and waited for her mother to bring in a steaming plate of Woolton pie. It was Wednesday and meals were served on a strict rota, so at least she knew what to expect, although a salad would have been more welcome.

'Flaming June,' Mildred said as she brought the plates to the table, placing one in front of her daughter. 'It's too hot to spend the day slaving away in the kitchen, but your dad likes his midday meal, and I've never let him go one day without a proper cooked lunch since we were married.' She nodded, sighing. 'That'll be twenty-four years ago in July.'

'Yes, Mum.' Ginnie picked up her knife and fork. 'You've done wonders. This looks really tasty. I'm sure Dad will love it. I'll go back early and relieve him so that his dinner won't be dried up.' She sampled a mouthful and swallowed manfully. It was stodgy and salty with an overriding flavour of onions, but it was hot and filling and she would not have hurt her mother's feelings for the world. 'Lovely.' She washed it down with a sip of water.

'At least you've got a good appetite, not like your sister.' Mildred pushed a piece of potato round her plate, eyeing it with distaste. 'She's been looking very peaky recently. I blame the chemicals in the munitions factory.'

'Yes, Mum.' Ginnie continued to plough her way through the plate of food. Shirley was probably eating in the works canteen and listening to *Workers' Playtime* on the wireless, surrounded by her friends and colleagues. It was impossible not to envy her sister's independent spirit. Shirley had refused to help their father run the shop when she left school and had made a feeble and unsuccessful attempt at job-hunting. She had spent most of her time at the tennis club, but this had ended abruptly when the government decreed that single women over the age of twenty would be compelled to enlist in one of the armed forces or take up war work. The munitions factory had not been Shirley's idea of a perfect job, but she had chosen not to enlist, stating that all the uniforms were hideous and unflattering and she would not be seen dead in any of them. Ginnie smiled to herself. Blessed with impossibly good looks and irresistible charm, Shirley could probably commit murder and get away with it.

'Are you listening to me, Ginnie?'

Her mother's voice cut across her thoughts and Ginnie looked up. 'Yes, Mum.'

'I was saying that I'd have taken you girls to stay with your Auntie Avril in Shropshire at the start of the war if it weren't for your dad and the perishing shop.' Mildred sighed and pushed her plate away. 'But I couldn't leave him to look after himself. He can't boil an egg, let alone cook a decent meal.'

'But I thought you didn't get on with Auntie Avril, Mum? You've always said she was no better than she should be.'

'I never did.' Mildred dabbed her lips with a gingham table napkin. 'I just said that Avril's way of life wasn't my cup of tea, but at least she's calmed down a bit since her last husband died.'

'She's only had two, Mum.'

'And both of them dead before their time. That's what comes from living the high life, but she's still my sister and it would be her duty to take us in.'

'You wouldn't enjoy living in the pub. You don't even like the smell of beer.'

Mildred sniffed and set her knife and fork down at a precise angle on her plate. 'Anything would be better than waiting to be blown to bits by a buzz bomb. Anyway, it's a lovely part of the world. Your dad and I spent our honeymoon in Shropshire, only Sid took to fishing and I spent most of my time standing on the riverbank being bitten by gnats.'

'Poor you.'

'Why are you grinning?' Mildred demanded,

eyeing her suspiciously. 'It wasn't funny, and we had to eat fish for dinner every night. I hate trout and I've never touched it since.'

Ginnie dabbed her lips with her napkin. 'That was delicious, Mum. I'd better get back to the shop now and let Dad come home to enjoy a feast.'

'But you haven't had your dessert.'

'I'll have it for tea, Mum.'

'But it's strawberries from the garden. I picked them this morning.' Mildred pursed her lips. 'You'll suffer from dyspepsia like your dad if you're not careful.'

'I'll take them to work with me, Mum. I'll have time to enjoy them later.'

'Shirley's bringing a young man home for tea, so make sure that you leave the shop on time, and tell your dad not to stop off at the pub. We don't want to create the wrong impression.'

'Which boyfriend is this?'

'Don't say things like that, dear. It makes it sound as if Shirley's flighty. She's a very pretty girl and she can't help it if she attracts a lot of attention.'

'She's had more boyfriends than I've had hot dinners. Anyway, I thought she was going steady with Charlie Crisp.'

'Charlie's a lovely fellow, but I think Shirley deserves more in life than to marry a man who works for the water board.'

Ginnie knew very well that in reality Charlie's job was at the sewage works, but to mention it at the table would offend her mother's delicate sensibilities. 'So who is she bringing home today?'

'Olivia Mallory's brother. Shirley was at school with Olivia and the family are very well-to-do. Olivia introduced Shirley to the tennis club.'

'I remember her,' Ginnie said, frowning. 'I always thought she was a snooty cow and she treated Shirley like dirt.'

'Her father is a solicitor and he's on the council. He's a magistrate too, so I believe, and they have a house in Monk Avenue. I've seen Mrs Mallory in church, but I've never spoken to her. She has some lovely clothes, Ginnie. I daresay she bought them in posh shops up West.' Mildred sighed and smiled. 'Some people have it all. Anyway it's Olivia's brother, Laurence, who's coming round tonight. He's in the Navy. He's an officer.'

'That must make him a very nice chap.'

Mildred shot her a suspicious look. 'Are you laughing at me, Virginia?'

'Of course not, Mum.' Ginnie rose from her seat and dropped a kiss on her mother's turbaned head. 'Bye. See you later.'

At six o'clock that evening Ginnie was standing outside the bathroom, banging on the door for a second time. 'Hurry up, Shirley. I want to wash the plaster dust out of my hair before tea.'

'I won't be long.' Shirley's voice was accompanied by the sound of running water.

'Are you washing your hair, Shirley Travis? If you've used the last of my precious Amami shampoo I'll never forgive you.' Ginnie waited anxiously until at last the door opened and Shirley breezed out of the bathroom with a towel wrapped round her head.

'I think I might have used the last drop. Sorry, love, but I'm sure your friend Fred Woollies will let you have another bottle.' Shirley sailed past her, leaving a waft of Amami shampoo and Lifebuoy soap in her wake.

Speechless and knowing that it was useless to argue, Ginnie took a deep breath and counted to ten. Even so, she was still angry and she followed her sister into the large, airy back bedroom. 'You selfish beast. You might have asked first.'

Towelling her hair, Shirley looked up and smiled. 'I know, I'm a cow sometimes, Ginnie, but you are a sweet little sister and you wouldn't begrudge me my big night, would you?'

'What are you talking about?'

Shirley let the towel fall to the ground and stepped into her parachute silk camiknickers, fastening them at the waist with a single mother-of-pearl button. 'I want you to be nice to my new chap.'

'It's only Olivia's big brother. I never liked her; she's stuck-up and she used to get you in trouble. What's so special about Laurence Mallory, anyway?'

'Don't say nasty things about Olivia. She was my best friend at school and I had a bit of a crush on Laurence. We met again at a tennis club dance a couple of weeks before Easter when he was home on leave. He made me feel like one of the Monk Avenue set and it was lovely.'

'Don't, Shirley. You sound snobby, just like Mum.'

'I'm not a snob. Laurence is super and I know he really fancies me, but his leave is up tomorrow and he has to return to his ship, so I want him to take fond memories of me back to sea.'

'But what about poor Charlie? He's totally devoted to you.'

'I know, and I'm very fond of him too, but it only takes a moment to fall in love, Ginnie. You'll know when it happens to you.' Shirley made a moue and tossed her head so that her strawberry-blonde hair formed Medusa-like curls around her face. 'You'll love Laurence, but only in a sisterly fashion because he's mine.'

Ginnie rose to her feet. 'Well, good luck. That's all I can say.'

'He's tall and blond, and he has deep blue eyes with little crinkly lines at the corners from constantly staring out to sea.' Shirley reached for her bra and put it on, struggling to do up the hooks and eyes. 'Give me a hand, Ginnie. This wretched thing must have shrunk in the wash or else my boobs have got bigger. Come to think of it they've been a bit tender recently. Perhaps I should see a doctor.'

Ginnie clipped the two ends together. 'Mum said you'd been looking a bit peaky.' She let the elastic go and it snapped against her sister's back, making her yelp.

'Ouch, that hurt.'

'Sorry.' Ginnie stood back, eyeing her sister thoughtfully. 'You haven't had any other symptoms, have you, Shirley?'

'I hope you're not insinuating anything improper, my girl.' Shirley snatched the dress she had laid out on her bed and slipped it over her head. She tugged at the zip fastener, pulling a face. 'I'm definitely putting on weight. It's all that hateful stodgy food we're forced to eat in the works canteen.'

'Are you sure about that?' Ginnie gazed at her sister's voluptuous figure with a sinking heart. 'You haven't done anything silly, have you, Shirley?'

'I don't know what you mean. Ouch.' Shirley's eyes filled with tears. 'I've pinched my skin in the blasted zip. That really hurts.'

'Breathe in.' Ginnie held the material together with one hand and eased the fastener into place. 'Just don't eat much at tea or you'll burst the seams.'

'It's not funny.' Shirley did a twirl, examining her reflection in the mirror on the front of her wardrobe. 'I'm getting fat.'

'How long is it since you had the curse?'

'That's none of your business.'

'It will be if you're up the creek without a paddle.'

'I can't be. Charlie took care of that side of things and with Laurence it was . . .' Shirley clapped her hands to her flaming cheeks. 'I mean, it's simply not possible.'

Ginnie shook her head. 'It might be a false alarm. You'll have to make an appointment to see the doctor.'

'Yes, I will.' Shirley dashed her hand across her eyes. 'The last thing I want is to have to beg Charlie to make an honest woman of me.'

'At least he won't get blown out of the water by a U-boat torpedo,' Ginnie said grimly. 'I hope you know what you're doing.'

Shirley moved swiftly to her dressing table and seized a hairbrush, dragging it through her tangled curls. 'I'll be all right. I know what I want out of life and it isn't a terraced house close to the sewage works.'

'I feel sorry for Charlie. He's crazy about you. Isn't that enough?'

'I can hear Mum calling you,' Shirley said, pointing to the door. 'I expect she wants some help with the meat paste sandwiches or whatever she's laid on for tea. Let's hope we don't have to eat them in the Anderson shelter. That would be the last straw.'

'I haven't had time to wash and change yet,' Ginnie protested. 'You're nearly ready. You go down and help with the food. It's your chap who's coming, not mine.'

'That would be difficult considering you haven't got a boyfriend.' Shirley slumped down on the dressing-table stool, turning her head with an apologetic smile. 'Sorry. That was bitchy. I didn't mean it. Please go downstairs and keep Mum happy, and I'll shift heaven and earth to find you another bottle of Amami.'

'I'll do it, but only if you promise to see the doctor tomorrow.'

'Cross my heart and hope to die, although not literally, of course. It's just a false alarm. It's got to be.'

Ginnie had just reached the foot of the stairs when the doorbell rang.

'Answer that will you, Ginnie?' Mildred called from the kitchen. 'I'm just taking the scones out of the oven.'

Ginnie opened the door. She had not seen Laurence Mallory since she was a child, but the smiling young man in naval uniform simply had to be her sister's latest conquest. 'Hello,' she said, smiling. 'You must be Laurence. Do come in.'

'And you must be Ginnie. You were just a kid when I last saw you.' He took off his peaked cap and tucked it under his arm as he stepped over the threshold. He handed her a bottle wrapped in brown paper. 'It's gin. I'm afraid I couldn't get anything else, but perhaps I should have got some fizzy pop for you. I'm not very good at this sort of thing.'

She frowned. 'How old d'you think I am?'

His cheeks reddened beneath his tan. 'I'm awfully sorry. Have I put my foot in it?'

She caught a glimpse of herself in the hallstand

mirror. Thanks to Shirley, she had not had time to change out of the open-neck blouse and slacks she had worn to work, and her face was innocent of make-up. With her hair still tied in the ponytail she realised that she could have passed for a schoolgirl and it was her turn to blush. 'I'm older than I look, but thank you for the gin.' She ushered him into the front room. 'I'll call Shirley. She won't be long.'

'I am sorry if I embarrassed you just now.' He smiled, and Ginnie noticed that his eyes did crinkle rather attractively at the corners, just as Shirley had said.

'That's all right. I don't always look such a mess, but the blast from the doodlebug brought some of the ceiling down at the shop and I haven't had time to change.'

'You look fine as you are. I was afraid you might all be dressed up and it was going to be terribly formal.'

'What would you like to drink, Laurence?' She opened her parents' much prized cocktail cabinet and realised her mistake when she saw the row of empty shelves. 'Oh dear, I'm afraid there's no choice. It's going to be gin and water or just gin.'

He grinned appreciatively. 'I'll take gin and water, but only if you'll join me.'

'Thanks, I will.' She selected two glasses and poured a measure of gin in each. 'I'll fetch some water.'

In the kitchen she found her mother red-faced

from the heat as she took the second batch of scones from the oven. 'What's he like, Ginnie? Where's Shirley? She should have been the one to greet the poor man.'

'She's getting dolled up, of course. He's nice, Mum. You'll like him and he's brought a bottle of gin. I just came to get some water.'

'He's obviously a gentleman. Shirley could do worse.'

'She's only been going out with him for a short while.'

'I'd only known your dad for three days and I knew he was the one for me. That's all it takes sometimes, dear.' Mildred tipped the scones onto a cooling rack. 'Mrs Martin gave me her last jar of strawberry jam so that we could have a proper tea. Take the water and keep him company, while I finish up here. Your dad should be home soon.'

Ginnie filled a jug with tap water and took it to the front room where she found Laurence looking at a framed photograph of herself and Shirley on the beach at Frinton. 'I was nine there,' she said, adding water to their drinks. 'And Shirley was twelve.'

'This is how I remember you,' he said, grinning. 'You've both changed quite a lot since then.'

'Shirley said that you're going back to your ship tomorrow. That's a pity. I mean it would have been nice to get to know you properly.'

He raised his glass to her. 'I'll drink to that, Ginnie.'

The door opened and Shirley swanned into the room, arms outstretched. 'I'm so sorry I wasn't here to greet you, Larry darling.'

He put his glass down and stood up to give her a brief embrace. 'That's quite all right, Shirley. Your sister has kept me entertained.' He met Ginnie's amused gaze with a hint of a smile. 'I'm afraid I was a bit early.'

Ginnie was about to offer Shirley a drink when a movement in the front garden caught her eye and she saw her father running up the garden path. 'Here comes Dad, and he's in a tearing hurry.'

'Is that gin?' Shirley said, eyeing the bottle. 'I'd love a drink, Ginnie. Pour me a stiff one, there's a dear.' She sent her a warning glance. 'Please.'

Ginnie was about to pour the drink when the door opened and Sid burst into the room. He came to a sudden halt when he saw Laurence. 'Oh, you're here already, son. I'm afraid you've arrived at a bad time.'

Mildred had followed him into the room and she clutched his arm. 'Not now, Sid. Whatever it is can wait until after tea, can't it?'

'I don't think so, love.' Sid patted her hand. 'This concerns you mostly, Shirley. During the air raid this morning a buzz bomb fell on the sewage works. I'm afraid there were casualties.'

Chapter Two

'Casualties?' Shirley stared at her father in disbelief. 'Not Charlie?'

'I'm afraid so, love.'

'Is he badly hurt?' Mildred demanded, clutching her husband's arm. 'Is he in hospital?'

'I'm sorry, but it's worse than that.' Sid cleared his throat. 'There were seven killed, and Charlie was one of them.'

Ginnie's hand flew to her mouth as she stifled a gasp of horror. No one moved and it seemed as though time itself had stood still. The colour drained from Shirley's face and her eyes were wide with shock as she crumpled to the floor. Mildred uttered a shriek and slumped down on the nearest chair while Sid looked on helplessly. Ginnie and Laurence moved at the same time to help Shirley to the sofa, where she lay amongst the cushions with her forearm covering her eyes.

'I should go,' Laurence said in a low voice. 'This isn't the time for entertaining guests.'

'I'll see you out.' Ginnie followed him into the hall. 'I'm so sorry about this. Charlie was a good friend.'

He took his cap from the hallstand. 'I understand. You don't have to explain.'

'I'm sure that Shirley will tell you so herself when she's feeling better. It was a shock.'

He laid his hand on her arm. 'Of course it was. Tell Shirley that I'll call in tomorrow on my way to the station.'

'Yes, of course. I'm so sorry, Laurence.'

'Don't apologise, Ginnie. It's just one of those things.'

She opened the front door and watched him as he walked to the gate. He paused, turning to give her a sympathetic smile and then he was gone. She leaned against the door jamb, taking deep breaths of the warm summer air. The fragrance of mock orange mingled with the sweet aroma from the bed of night-scented stock that her mother had refused to turn over to vegetables. The front lawn had been dug up and planted with potatoes, but there were some things that were sacrosanct and her mother's favourite flowerbed was one of them. The Germans, should they ever cross the Channel, would find that Mildred Travis was equal to Boadicea when it came to protecting her own. Mum might criticise and grumble about small things in life, but when it came to her family and her cherished home and garden, she would give her life's blood to protect them.

In an uncertain world some things never changed, but Ginnie wondered how her mother would react at the prospect of increasing their family number with an illegitimate child whose father had died at the sewage works. It was a prospect that was almost as terrifying as the moment when the engine of a flying bomb had cut out overhead. She closed the door, hoping against hope that Shirley had kept her mouth firmly shut. Tomorrow she would take time off work and make certain that her sister sought medical advice. She was about to enter the front room when Shirley blundered past her. 'I'm going to be sick,' she said, heading for the kitchen.

Next morning they had just arrived home from the surgery when Ginnie spotted Laurence walking towards them with a bunch of flowers clasped in one hand and a rather battered leather suitcase in the other.

'Oh, God,' Shirley groaned, thrusting the gate open. 'I can't face him, Ginnie. Tell him I'm dying of something horrible. Tell him anything but the truth.' She ran up the path and let herself into the house, slamming the door behind her.

Ginnie waited by the gate, wondering what she could say to explain her sister's odd behaviour. 'Hello, Laurence.'

'I just wanted to see how Shirley was this morning, but I can see she's still very upset.' He pressed the bouquet into Ginnie's hand. 'Will you give her these from me?'

'Of course, but won't you come in?'

'No, thanks all the same, but that would be intruding.'

She met his candid gaze with a feeling of chagrin. 'I'm really sorry it's worked out this way. Shirley isn't quite herself.'

'It's all right. I understand. My family has lost friends too.'

She nodded her head, struggling to think of an excuse for Shirley's apparent rudeness and failing miserably. 'Yes, war is ghastly.'

To her astonishment this made him smile. 'That's one way of putting it.' He glanced at his watch. 'Look, I know this sounds a bit cheeky, but would you like to walk to the station with me? I'm a bit early so perhaps we could have a cup of tea in the buffet or something.'

She knew that she ought to go to the shop or at least go inside and utter words of comfort to Shirley, but she had a sudden need to do something for herself, and Laurence obviously wanted company. 'I'd love to, if you could just wait a moment while I take the flowers indoors. I don't want them to die on me.' She hesitated, realising what she had just said. 'I'm afraid that sounded a bit crass in the circumstances.'

'If I had a pound for every time I said the wrong thing I'd be a rich man,' he said with a sympathetic smile. 'Go ahead, Ginnie. I'll wait here.'

Entering the station buffet was like stepping into an old-fashioned sepia tint. Everything in it seemed to be painted in shades of brown and beige, including the tea and the toasted teacake that the woman behind the counter slapped in front of them. 'My old man was a submariner,' she said grimly. 'He left from this platform and that was the last I saw of him. Torpedoed by a U-boat, he was. No survivors.' She waddled back to her position behind the tea urn.

'That wasn't very tactful, considering your uniform.' Ginnie glanced anxiously at Laurence but the twinkle in his eyes made her smile for the first time that morning.

It had not been a good start to the day. The time she had spent with Shirley in the doctor's waiting room had been nerve-racking, with small children creating chaos, and elderly people grumbling about the absence of discipline in the younger generation coupled with lack of respect for their elders. It had been even worse in the surgery when the doctor confirmed the fact that Shirley was two or three months into her pregnancy. She had collapsed in tears and then there had been an embarrassing few moments when they had had to make their way out between rows of curious patients. Ginnie returned to the present with a start as she realised that Laurence was speaking to her.

'It's all right, Ginnie,' he said cheerfully. 'I'm used to people saying things like that. Don't look so worried.'

'I don't suppose she meant anything by it, but

you haven't had a very good send-off, especially where my family are concerned.'

'I'm sorry that I didn't get a chance apologise to Shirley for leaving so abruptly yesterday. She's obviously very upset.'

'She is, but then she's a very emotional person.' Ginnie felt a sudden need to reassure him. 'She's an extremely loyal friend, and she's really sorry that your last evening ashore was ruined.'

'She asked you to tell me that?'

Ginnie could not look him in the face and lie. She concentrated on stirring her tea, even though she did not take sugar. 'Yes, words to that effect.' It was untrue, of course. Shirley had forgotten all about Laurence until she had seen him that morning.

'I wouldn't upset her for the world. Shirley's a lot of fun and we had a good time; it's just a pity it had to end so abruptly.' He pushed the plate towards her. 'Would you like half the teacake? I don't think I can face eating the whole thing and I wouldn't want to offend Lady Macbeth over there.' He jerked his head in the direction of the woman who had served them.

Ginnie suppressed a giggle. 'Shh. She might hear you.'

'Not a chance. She's got her hooks into a young chap in army uniform. She's probably telling him that her father was blown to bits at Mons or Ypres.'

Ginnie giggled and received a disapproving look

from Lady Macbeth. 'You'll get us thrown out of here, Laurence.'

'And I'd have to trot out the corny old line – I've been thrown out of better places than this.' He glanced at his watch. 'I can hear a train coming. I think it's time I made a move anyway.' He rose to his feet. 'Will you see me off? It would be nice to have someone waving to me as the engine pulls out.'

She stood up and slung her gasmask case over her shoulder. 'You really are a romantic, aren't you?'

'I suppose I am.' He left a tip in the saucer and went to open the door. A gust of steam blew into the buffet as the train belched into the station. Ginnie followed him onto the platform. Carriage doors were flung open and passengers alighted while others waited to take their place. She held her hand out. 'Good luck, Laurence.'

He hesitated, gazing at her intently. 'Say cheerio to Shirley for me.'

'Of course.'

He leaned forward and kissed her on the cheek. 'You're a great girl, Ginnie.'

The guard's whistle shrilled and Laurence leapt into the carriage just as the train began to pull away from the platform. He leaned out of the open window and waved. Ginnie raised her hand and returned the gesture, waiting until the train was out of sight. Taking her hanky from her pocket she dabbed her eyes. It was ridiculous to feel sentimental about a man she hardly knew, especially when he was her sister's boyfriend, but there was a chance that he might never return and genuine tears of regret spilled from her eyes. She blew her nose, squared her shoulders and started walking.

She went straight to the shop but found it closed, which was unheard of mid-morning on a weekday. She hurried next door to the china shop and found Fred sitting disconsolately on a stool behind the counter. His expression brightened for a moment when she walked in and he stood up. 'Is everything all right, ducks?'

'I was about to ask you the same question, Fred. Why did Dad close the shop?'

'He had a phone call from home. Dunno what your mum said, but he put the closed sign on the door and told me he'd be back later. That's all I know. I've had Ida down here asking the same question. What's going on, Ginnie?'

She backed towards the doorway. 'I'd better go home and find out.'

Number ten Cherry Lane was in a state of uproar when Ginnie arrived. Her mother was shouting down the telephone and her father was upstairs, hammering on Shirley's bedroom door.

Mildred put her hand over the mouthpiece, glaring at Ginnie. 'You knew about this, miss. Why didn't you tell us?' She uncovered it quickly. 'No, I wasn't speaking to you, Avril. This is a terrible line.

I'll have to call you back later.' She slammed the receiver down on its cradle, standing arms akimbo. 'Well, I want an explanation. You took Shirley to see the doctor so you know all about it.'

'I only found out last night, Mum. There wasn't any point in telling you until she was sure.' Ginnie slipped past her, heading for the kitchen. 'I'll put the kettle on.'

Mildred followed her. 'A cup of tea isn't going to sort this out, young lady. Your sister has disgraced us all. I suppose Charlie is the father, and not the young man who was here last night.'

'You have to ask Shirley, Mum.' Ginnie filled the kettle at the sink. 'It's got nothing to do with me.'

'You'll change your tune when no one will speak to you. We'll be a laughing stock in the neighbourhood and I'll never be able to attend another Mothers' Union meeting.'

'She's been unlucky, that's all. It happens in wartime.' Ginnie lit the gas and put the kettle on the ring. 'It's done now and poor Charlie isn't here to do the right thing. Shirley will need all the help we can give her.'

Mildred paced the floor. 'I've already made arrangements. Shirley will have to go to Shropshire and stay with Avril until the baby is born. Then she can come back with a wedding ring on her finger and we'll make up some story about a wartime wedding and tell everyone that she's a widow.' She spun round to face Ginnie, pointing her finger. 'And you'll go with her. Your dad will just have to find someone else to help in the shop. We'll say that we're sending you both to safety because of the doodle-bugs. That will be much more believable. I'd come with you but I can't leave your father. He'd be lost without me.'

The station at Lightwood Common was deserted apart from an aged porter who tottered up the platform to help them with their luggage. It had been a long and tortuous journey with several changes of train and many stops along the way. Their carriage had been packed with servicemen and women when they left Paddington, and when passengers alighted at stations along the line they were immediately replaced by yet more travellers. Older women wearing ugly felt hats grumbled incessantly about rationing and shortages, while young squaddies shared bawdy jokes until sharp reprimands from their elders silenced them and left them red-faced and resentful. Young babies wailed in their mothers' arms, and the mere sight of them made Shirley groan and turn her head to stare blankly out of the window.

The train had reduced speed several times during air raids and this had added to the seemingly never-ending journey. They had eaten their packed lunch at midday with no hope of getting any more food until they arrived at their destination, and the buffet car had long since run out of tea.

'Follow me, ladies.' The porter piled their cases onto a trolley and set off along the platform.

'It's the back of bloody beyond,' Shirley said grimly. 'I'll die of boredom in this godforsaken hole.'

'Don't be such a pessimist.' Ginnie gazed round appreciatively. It was several years since her last visit to Shropshire, but she had never forgotten the sweet smell of newly mown hay and damp earth combined with the scent of honeysuckle and dog roses. The mild air that caressed her cheeks was fresh and untainted by carbon monoxide fumes from cars and buses, and she remembered the countryside as being lush and gently rolling. She was a Londoner at heart but she had always had a soft spot for this part of the world and had looked forward to the brief holidays she had spent with Auntie Avril, who was the complete antithesis to their mother.

Where Mildred was spiky, snobbish and very much aware of her status in the community, Avril could not give two hoots what people thought of her. She lived, loved and dressed to please herself and had buried two husbands, both dead from natural causes, and was rumoured to have had at least half a dozen lovers in her misspent youth when she was an artist's model in Paris.

'I suppose we'll have to walk to the pub,' Shirley said crossly. 'I'm sure my ankles are swelling already. I'll be like a whale by the end of the nine months.'

'Come on. You'll feel better when you've had a nice hot cup of tea and something to eat. Auntie

Avril is a wonderful cook, or she was before rationing came in. I can remember her chocolate éclairs – they were absolutely scrummy.'

'This way, ladies.' The porter trundled his cargo through the ticket office. 'Mrs Parkin's sent someone to meet you.'

'Thank God for that.' Shirley uttered a sigh of relief. 'A chauffeur-driven car would be heaven.'

Ginnie was nearest to the exit and she could see the form of transport that their aunt had laid on and it was most definitely not a limousine. She followed the porter out into the leafy lane where a pony and trap was waiting to take them to the Ferryboat Inn. The driver had a battered felt hat pulled down over his forehead and a pipe stuck in the corner of his mouth. He gave them a cursory glance and then continued to stare absently into space. The pony, a sturdy Welsh cob, pawed the ground and snorted as if eager to be off.

'Give us a hand with the baggage, Percy.' The porter tossed Shirley's dressing case into the trap, followed by the pigskin valise which had been their father's twenty-first birthday present and much valued by him even if it was a bit worse for wear.

'That's your job,' Percy muttered, grinding his teeth on the pipe stem. 'I'm just doing Avril a favour. I ain't no taxi driver.'

Grumbling beneath his breath the porter hefted the last of their bags into the back of the cart and stood, holding out his hand. 'There you are, ladies. All stowed safely.'

Ginnie fumbled in her bag for her purse and gave him sixpence. He did not seem impressed as he hobbled back into the ticket office muttering something about mean Londoners.

'Hop in then, unless you want to walk alongside,' Percy said impatiently. 'I ain't got all day. I got pigs to feed and a thirst on me that's a proper torment.'

Ginnie climbed up to sit beside the driver and held her hand out to help Shirley, but it was brushed aside.

'I can manage, thanks. I'm not helpless.' Shirley hauled herself up to sit beside Ginnie, squashing her against Percy. 'Stop fussing,' she hissed. 'I don't want everyone to know.'

Ginnie made herself as small as possible. There was a strange smell emanating from their driver and she could not tell whether it was the coating of mud and something nasty on his boots, or the fact that his personal hygiene left much to be desired.

Shirley turned to him with a wave of her hand. 'Drive on, my man.'

'I ain't your man, lady. I'm me own person as you'll find out in due course.'

'I can't wait,' Shirley said in a stage whisper. 'I'm going to be out of here on the first train tomorrow morning. I refuse to be buried alive in a place where the driver stinks of eau de pig.'

'Shut up, he's not deaf. He'll hear you.'

Shirley tossed her head. 'I don't care, and if the jolting of this foul contraption doesn't bring on a miscarriage, nothing will.' She clung to the side rail as Percy flicked the whip and the pony jerked into action.

The Ferryboat Inn nestled amongst the trees on the riverbank, lazing in the late afternoon sun as though it were posing for a photograph which would adorn many chocolate boxes and calendars. The building itself comprised of two seventeenth-century cottages built of mellow golden stone with Welsh slate roofs. Stone steps led down from the gravelled terrace to a grassy bank, where the hand-operated chain ferry was at rest, bobbing idly on its moorings close to the shore. Percy drew the trap to a halt outside the main entrance. 'Get out here,' he said gruffly. 'I got to see to the animal.'

Shirley leapt to the ground like a parachutist bailing out of a burning plane and Ginnie followed more slowly. 'Thank you, Mr Percy,' she said, trying hard not to wrinkle her nose as the breeze wafted his body odour her way.

'Just Percy, miss.' He tipped his hat. 'I'll bring your bags to the bar, save you carrying them.'

'That's very kind. Thanks again.' She moved aside as he clicked his tongue against his teeth and encouraged the pony to walk towards the stable.

'There's Auntie Avril,' Shirley said, waving enthusiastically. 'Thank goodness she's still the same. I was beginning to think we'd stepped into the pages of *Cold Comfort Farm*.'

'Don't be such a snob, Shirley. You sound just like Mum.'

'Shut up.' With a toss of her head, Shirley hurried across the gravel forecourt to meet their aunt.

Ginnie hesitated, gazing downriver where the trees bowed to its stately progress towards the sea, their green foliage reflecting in the sun-dappled water. She gasped with pleasure at the sight of an otter breaking through the glassy surface as it reached the opposite bank and slid sinuously into the undergrowth. The river had always held a special fascination for her in all its moods, from lazing along as it was now on a hot June day to rushing past in a foaming torrent as it had one Christmas when they had come to stay. The noise and bustle of the city seemed a million miles away and she felt as though she had stepped into another world where war and destruction did not exist, and time slowed down so that it was endless summer.

'Ginnie, darling. Are you going to stand there all day or are you coming in?' Avril waved a silk-clad arm to attract her attention. 'I've made a jug of Pimm's in honour of your arrival. Unless, of course, you're like your mother and would prefer a cup of tea.' She disappeared into the depths of the pub with Shirley hot on her heels.

Ginnie needed no second bidding. It was cool inside the building and nothing seemed to have changed since their last visit. The taproom was dominated by the large inglenook with its cast-iron fire basket and ornate andirons. The low beamed ceiling was tarnished by years of tobacco smoke and the walls were hung with gleaming horse brasses. Roses spilled from a posy bowl on the bar and either by chance or by design their colour was reflected in the chintz curtains and seat covers.

Apart from the fact that a bar counter had been built across one corner of the room, nothing much had changed in the three centuries since the first cottagers moved into their new home. The roughly plastered walls were covered with framed oil paintings done by Avril's first husband, a noted artist in his day, and some charcoal sketches of the locals executed by Avril herself. She had slipped behind the bar and was holding up a dust-encrusted bottle. 'I've been keeping this hidden from view since 1940,' she said triumphantly. 'I'll just pop into the kitchen and get some ice and the trimmings. I've had everything ready for hours because I didn't know when you'd arrive. Sit down and make yourselves comfortable. You can unpack later.' She opened a door at the back of the bar and went into the kitchen.

Shirley took off her hat and gloves and laid them on a table by the window. 'I'm still not staying,' she said mutinously. 'I adore Auntie Avril, of course, but that doesn't mean that I want to spend the next six months in the backwoods.'

'You're jolly lucky to be here.' Ginnie peeled off

her once white gloves which were now a disheartening shade of grey. 'If you'd kept your legs crossed this would never have happened.'

'Don't be vulgar. It wasn't like that and now I'm a widow before I was even a wife, or at least I think it's Charlie's, but I can't be sure.'

Through the open doorway Ginnie could see their aunt struggling with a tray of ice cubes. 'Auntie's gone to a lot of trouble for us, Shirley. You'd better start thinking about other people.'

'What d'you mean?'

'This is a small village. It might be better if you pretend that you are married. You don't want to embarrass Auntie Avril.'

'Did I hear my name mentioned?' Avril breezed into the bar carrying a glass jug filled with ice and slices of cucumber, apple and a sprig of mint. 'I can assure you that there's very little that would embarrass me, my dears.' She splashed Pimm's into the jug and topped it up with soda water, tossing in a few strawberries at the last moment. 'It would be so much nicer with lemonade, but I haven't been able to get any for ages.' She filled three glasses and raised one to her lips. 'Welcome to the Ferryboat Inn, my darlings. It's lovely to have you here.'

Ginnie passed a glass to Shirley, who had collapsed onto the wide window seat and was fanning herself with her hand. 'Drink this. It'll make you feel better.'

Avril patted her immaculate victory roll, flicking back an invisible tress of sleek auburn hair. 'Are you feeling queasy, darling? I've never been in the pudding club so I wouldn't know how it feels, but it's beastly bad luck.'

Shirley took a mouthful of her drink and swallowed. Her eyes brimmed with tears. 'It is rotten, Auntie. No one seems to understand how I feel. Mum and Dad were absolutely furious and made me feel this big.' She demonstrated by squinting through a minuscule gap between her thumb and forefinger.

Avril leaned on the bar, her brightly coloured kimono sleeves trailing on the counter. 'Well, darling, we have to be practical. People are very narrow-minded, especially round here. I've kept your grandmother's wedding ring for sentimental reasons, but now I see a perfectly good use for it. Mildred insisted that you're to be widowed at the earliest opportunity, so we might as well make a drama of it.' She sipped her drink and her green eyes sparkled mischievously. 'It will be fun. Besides which, some of the residents in this village are so self-righteous they would have a field day if they knew the truth.'

Ginnie swallowed a mouthful of her drink, trying hard not to pull a face. It might be nicer sweetened with lemonade, she thought, hoping that Avril would not be offended if she did not drain the glass. Shirley, however, did not seem to have a problem. 'May I have a refill? That was most refreshing. I feel much better now.'

'Why not? You've had a terrible time recently. Just

one though, I don't want to lead you into bad ways. I'll go upstairs and root through my jewellery box to see if I can find the ring. We'll be open soon and I think we ought to start as we mean to go on.'

'I'll look after Shirley, Auntie.' Ginnie seized her sister's empty glass before she had a chance to get a refill.

'Thank you, darling. You were always such a helpful little girl. I'm sure I can find lots of things to keep you occupied while you're here with me.' Avril hurried through to the kitchen and moments later her light footsteps pattered overhead.

Ginnie passed what was left of her own drink to Shirley. 'I don't like this stuff, but you'd better go easy or you'll be squiffy.'

'I want to be drunk,' Shirley said, pouting. 'I want to blot out the whole horrible mess, but I meant what I said earlier, Ginnie. Tomorrow I'm leaving on the first train for London, even if I have to find lodgings in East Ham or Hackney. I'm not staying here any longer than I can help. I hate the bloody countryside . . .' She broke off as the door opened and a young man wearing the uniform of an American army officer looked into the bar.

'Is it opening time?' he asked anxiously. 'I'm afraid we might be a bit early.'

Ginnie glanced at her watch. 'I'm not sure. What time does it normally open?'

'About now,' he said, grinning. 'May we come in, ladies?'

Ginnie glanced through the door to the kitchen but there was no sign of her aunt, and anyway the lieutenant and his two companions were already in the bar. One of them took a seat at a table next to Shirley. 'Good evening, ma'am. Lieutenant Tony Petrillo, US Army Medical Corps, at your service.'

Shirley blushed and fluttered her eyelashes. 'Shirley . . .' she hesitated for a heartbeat. 'Shirley Mallory. My husband is in the Navy.'

Chapter Three

Ginnie stared at her sister in horror. Pretending to be married to an imaginary person was one thing, but to involve someone like Laurence Mallory was quite another. She could see all kind of complications rearing their ugly heads, but Shirley was looking happy and obviously relishing the attention of the good-looking young American officer.

The lieutenant who had asked if the pub was open turned to Ginnie with a friendly smile. 'Are you staying here, ma'am?'

She met his candid gaze and her heart warmed towards him. Ever since she could remember she had lived in the shadow of her older sister, and at the shop she was still Sid's little girl who used to help out after school and in the holidays. Laurence had thought she was a schoolgirl until she had put him right, but this good-looking American officer, whose smart uniform made him look more like a film star than a soldier, had seen her as an adult. She returned his smile, holding out her hand. 'Yes, I'm Ginnie Travis. My sister and I are staying here with our aunt.'

'Nick Miller.' He shook her hand. 'Tony has just

introduced himself, and the big guy on my right is Danny Flynn.' He slapped his comrade on the shoulder. 'We're both from LA, and Tony is from New York. We're stationed at the US military hospital in Lightwood House.'

'Nice to meet you, ladies.' Danny bowed to each of them in turn.

'It's a pleasure to meet you,' Shirley said graciously. 'Are you doctors as well as soldiers? How thrilling.'

Ginnie felt the blood rush to her cheeks with embarrassment and she willed her sister to stop making a complete fool of herself, but the Americans did not seem to mind. In fact Tony appeared to be hanging on her every word. 'Yeah, we're medical men. We put the poor guys back together again when they come from the battlefield.'

'You're surgeons,' Shirley said in an awed voice. 'That's so interesting.'

'I guess that's not a local accent, Mrs Mallory.'

'Actually we're from London.'

'Is that so, ma'am? I went there once. It's a great city.'

'It's Shirley,' she said, leaning towards him. 'And, yes, London is a wonderful place, what's left of it after the German bombs have done their worst.'

Nick reached for the brass hand bell that stood on the bar and rang it. 'Hey, Avril. You've got thirsty customers waiting.' He gave Ginnie a wry smile. 'I'm getting used to drinking warm beer. May I buy you ladies a drink, or would that be inappropriate as we've only just met?'

Shirley held out her empty glass. 'I'd love one, thank you.'

'We've only just arrived and we really ought to unpack,' Ginnie said hastily. 'Maybe another time?'

'Are you planning to stay long?'

She nodded, casting a covert glance at Shirley. 'For quite a while.'

Nick grinned. 'Then we'll have plenty of time to get to know you better.'

'Yeah,' Tony said eagerly. 'We're stationed in one of your stately homes just outside the village. I could get used to living like a lord.'

Ginnie was wondering whether to drag Shirley off the window seat before she became too tipsy to move when Avril hurried in from the kitchen. She leaned on the bar. 'Good evening, gentlemen. I see you've met my lovely nieces.'

'Yes, ma'am.' Danny gave her a mock salute. 'And how are you today, Mrs Parkin?'

'My, we are formal.' Avril bobbed a curtsey. 'You don't have to worry about the girls. We might be in old England, but the days of high-button boots and chaperones have long since gone. Women are doing men's work and doing it well.'

'Somehow I don't see you as Rosie the riveter, Avril.' Nick winked at Ginnie.

'You'd be surprised what I can do when I put my mind to it.' Avril took a mug from the shelf beneath

45

the bar. 'The usual, gentlemen?' She worked the beer engine with the expertise of long practice. 'I've been known to throw a drunken chap out of the door for behaving badly, Nick. I may look as fragile as a fairy but I'm a tough cookie when necessary. You see, I've even picked up the lingo, dealing with you boys from across the pond.'

Danny took some coins from his pocket and laid them on the counter. 'This one's on me. Will you have one yourself, Avril?'

She gave him a brilliant smile. 'Thank you, darling, but not now. It wouldn't do to get squiffy this early in the evening.' She pulled two more pints and counted out Danny's change. 'I've laid supper in the kitchen for you girls,' she said, staring pointedly at Shirley and Tony who were in deep conversation. 'You must be tired after your long journey, Shirley, love. There's the item of jewellery we were talking about on the kitchen table. You might want to take a look at it.' She lifted the hatch in the bar counter. 'You'll have plenty of time to chat with the boys; they're some of my best customers.'

'That makes us sound like drunks,' Nick said, laughing. 'We just like to soak up the atmosphere in this quaint old inn, and enjoy the scenery on such a warm and pleasant evening.'

Danny took a swig of his beer. 'And the beer is good too. I'm developing quite a taste for your English bitter.'

'I like Pimm's,' Shirley said, holding out her glass. 'This is the last of Auntie Avril's private stash.'

'And you've had quite enough for a woman in your condition.' Ginnie moved swiftly to her side and helped Shirley to her feet.

Tony leapt up and put his hand beneath Shirley's arm. 'Gee, I had no idea. I beg your pardon, ma'am. You really shouldn't be drinking alcohol.'

Shirley wrenched her arm free with a spirited toss of her head. 'I'm perfectly fine, thank you, lieutenant. My sister fusses like an old maid.' She glared at Ginnie as she marched past her. 'Goodnight, gentlemen.'

'That didn't go down too well,' Avril murmured as Ginnie walked past her. 'Keep an eye on your sister, dear. She seems a bit edgy.'

'She'll be okay, Auntie.' Ginnie hurried into the kitchen, closing the door behind her.

'Well, thank you very much.' Shirley pulled up a bentwood chair and sat down, resting her elbows on the pine table. 'You've just ruined any chance I might have had with Tony. Couldn't you see that he was interested in me?'

'You were the one who told them you were married – and to Laurence of all people. Couldn't you have invented a name?'

'Why? Do you want him for yourself?'

'Is Laurence the baby's father?' Ginnie demanded angrily. 'Did you cheat on poor Charlie?'

'I wasn't married to Charlie, or even engaged.

I had a tiny fling with Laurence, that's all.' Shirley held her hand to her mouth. 'I think I'm going to throw up.'

Ginnie went to the sink and filled a glass with water. She put it down in front of her sister. 'Sip that and stop acting like an idiot. You got yourself into this mess. What were you playing at out there?'

Shirley sipped the water, avoiding Ginnie's anxious gaze. 'I don't know what you mean.'

'Yes, you do. You were flirting with that chap as if you were still available.'

'I am available, as you put it. It's just that there's a bit of a complication.'

'And it will get bigger every day. There's another human being growing inside you and it'll be your responsibility. It's not a puppy or a kitten that you can give away.'

'Stop going on about it. D'you think I don't know all that? I'm scared, Ginnie. I don't want to do this on my own.'

'You're not on your own. You've got us, your family. Whatever Mum and Dad said they'll change their minds when you take the baby home. They'll love it because it's their grandchild, and we'll all help you.' Ginnie stared at her sister's bent head and experienced a rush of sympathy. Despite the normal sibling rivalries she loved Shirley and she wanted to see her happy. She patted her clumsily on the shoulder. 'You'll feel better when you've eaten something.' She went to the stove and lifted the lid of a saucepan that was simmering on the hob. 'This smells delicious.' There were two bowls warming in the rack and she ladled the savoury-smelling soup into them. She placed one in front of Shirley. 'Eat up. I've no idea what's in it, but Auntie Avril is a magician in the kitchen.'

Shirley stared at it, shaking her head. 'My life is such a mess. I don't know how I'm going to cope, Ginnie. I really don't.'

Ginnie took a seat opposite her sister. She tasted a spoonful of the soup. 'This is really good,' she said appreciatively. 'Do try and eat something, Shirley.' She caught sight of a gold ring placed on a table napkin and slid it towards her. 'Look. It's Granny's ring. Try it on and see if it fits.'

Reluctantly, Shirley picked up the ring and slipped it onto her finger. 'Perfect,' she muttered. 'It might have been made for me.' She met Ginnie's encouraging look with a hint of a smile. 'When can we decently kill off poor Laurence? I look rather fetching in black.'

'I thought you'd fallen for him. You said it was the real thing.'

'Making a joke of things is the only way I'm going to get through this, Ginnie. I'm going to need your help. I really am.'

Their bedroom, which they had shared in the school holidays, overlooked the terrace and the gentle curve of the river with its tree-lined banks and the chain ferry, which had been used daily during peacetime, ferrying the locals across the water to their jobs in the coalmine on the opposite side. The mine, so Avril said, was still in use but operated now by the men who were too old to be conscripted into the forces and the Bevan boys who were billeted in the village. Occasional calls were made from the far bank and Avril would trip daintily down to the winch and haul the ferry across with surprising strength for a lightweight. Ginnie tried it once but found that even hefting rolls of linoleum and large pieces of furniture had not prepared her for such a feat.

Sharing a room with her sister was not Ginnie's idea of heaven, but there were only three bedrooms in the pub and Avril kept one for paying guests, who before the war would usually have been fishermen, but now were mainly young couples on honeymoon or older people wanting to get away from the destruction in the towns and cities.

Gradually, as the summer progressed, Ginnie became more and more involved in the running of the pub, waiting on tables in the dining room and working in the kitchen. She helped out in the bar occasionally, although at first that was Shirley's domain and she was in her element, sitting on a stool behind the bar, chatting to customers. As an expectant mother she was now exempted from war work, but by the beginning of August she was becoming increasingly tired and lethargic. On the days when the temperature climbed she lay on her

bed refusing to come downstairs, and Ginnie began
to take over Shirley's duties as well as her own.

Early evenings were the best time of day for
Ginnie. She grew to enjoy the quiet moments before
they were invaded by thirsty customers. The summer
weather was, as always, temperamental. One day
might be warm and sunny and the next one cool
and cloudy, but even in the rain she loved to watch
the river whatever its mood, whether calm and
serene or angry and turbulent. There was the dis-
tinctive scent of the wild flowers that rampaged
along its banks, mingling with the perfume from the
roses that climbed the walls of the pub, reaching as
far as her bedroom window. She could have leaned
out and plucked one to toss to an ardent lover who
serenaded her, had there been such a person. She
could only dream.

Even so, there was always a hint of excitement in
the air before opening time, as if they were on stage,
waiting to perform for an audience that had yet to
arrive. But as the weeks went by it was Nick whose
appearance made her heart beat that little bit faster,
and it was his company that raised her spirits so
that the world seemed a brighter and happier place.
He made her laugh and he made her feel that she
was the only woman in the room. It took her a long
time to admit it to herself but she realised that she
was falling slowly, deeply and irrevocably in love.
It was exciting and it was frightening. She knew he
liked her and sometimes she caught him looking at

her with a warm glow in his dark eyes, but her inexperience in the art of romance left her confused and uncertain whether her feelings were reciprocated.

Every evening was mystical and sweet and a definite challenge. She was always down early to open up and she waited, hoping that Nick would be the first to walk through the door, but it was usually the less than fragrant Percy who called in every day on his way home from work. Straight from the pig pens of the home farm on Lord Thurston's estate, he took his seat in the inglenook and sipped his pint of mild while reading the newspaper. His lips moved as he studied the accounts of the Allies' continued drive into Normandy, from which he would suddenly read a paragraph in a booming voice that startled anyone who happened to be in the bar at the time, including Ginnie.

'They're starting the trial of them who tried to blow up Adolf. They should give the perishers a medal,' he announced one evening as Nick entered the bar.

'You don't say?' Nick smiled at Ginnie who had already pulled a pint of bitter and placed it on the counter.

Percy glared at him. 'I do say so, mate. It's here in black and white.'

'Will you have the other half?' Nick suggested, grinning. 'You see, Ginnie, I've learned the lingo too.'

'Don't mind if I do.' Percy held out his glass,

which was almost empty. 'A top-up then, please, Ginnie.'

Nick took it from him, handing it to Ginnie with a wry twist of his lips. 'It's more like a pint than a half, but that's okay by me.'

She filled it from the appropriate pump. 'You're very generous.'

He grinned. 'And one for yourself?'

'I'm not old enough to drink in a pub.'

'Sorry, I forgot that you're just a kid.'

She gave him a playful swipe with a tea towel. 'It's the law, silly.'

'And you shouldn't really be serving in a bar.'

'I don't think the local constable will arrest me.' She topped up Percy's glass and placed it on the bar. 'Would you give that to your new friend, please?'

Nick handed it to Percy. 'Here you are, buddy. Cheers.'

Percy took it with a grunt that could be interpreted as anything from thank you to something less polite.

Nick sipped his drink, eyeing Ginnie thoughtfully. 'You know, you're wasted here. We always need staff at the hospital, especially now. There was a huge influx of guys who were wounded during the D-day landings and many of them are still with us. '

'But I'm not a nurse. I've only ever worked in my father's furniture shop.'

'The men are mostly convalescent so it's not too gory. We've got army nurses, of course, but we need more help. Would you be interested? You'd be well paid.'

The offer, coming out of the blue, was both startling and exciting. She had never imagined herself as an angel of mercy, and even if the job turned out to be that of a glorified ward maid she would have jumped at the chance of working closely with Nick. She looked into his eyes and the warmth in his gaze took her breath away. 'I'd love to, but I'd have to ask my aunt. I'm not sure if she can spare me.'

'She managed for years without you, honey. I guess business is pretty quiet these days.'

'It's different though, with Shirley being pregnant and not able to do much.'

'She's fit enough to go to the dance on Saturday night with Tony.'

'I didn't know that.'

He laid his hand on hers as it rested on the bar. 'I like your sister a lot, Ginnie, but I think she's taking you for a ride.'

Ginnie frowned. She had suspected as much herself, but she was not going to admit it. 'You don't know all the circumstances.'

'I guess not. I didn't mean to offend you.'

'You haven't. It's all right.' She looked up as the door opened and the vicar strolled into the bar. 'Good evening, vicar.' She was quick to notice that his dog collar was slightly grubby and the cuffs of his tweed jacket were frayed, but his crooked smile was infectious and there was nothing remotely sanctimonious in his demeanour.

Everyone in the village loved the Reverend Lionel Smithers. Ginnie had heard of many instances when he had visited a parishioner's tiny cottage with a basket of treats for an invalid, or some much needed groceries for a mother struggling to raise young children while her husband was away, serving his country. A confirmed bachelor, Lionel Smithers obviously had a soft spot for the flamboyant, unconventional landlady of the Ferryboat Inn.

Nick leapt smartly from the bar stool. 'Good evening, Father. What will you have to drink?'

'How kind of you, my boy. I'd love a Scotch and soda. My throat is quite dry from taking the boys in choir practice. It's years since we had a choirmaster and my ageing vocal chords leave much to be desired.'

Ginnie measured a tot and put the glass on the counter, passing him the soda siphon. 'Do you want to see my aunt, vicar?'

'It's always a pleasure to see Avril,' he said, splashing a generous amount of soda water into his drink. 'We've been friends for many years.' He raised his glass to Nick. 'Here's to the excellent work you and your staff do at the hospital. How are the men under your care?'

'Doing as well as can be expected, sir.'

'And you and your medical team need time to relax. I hope we'll see you at the dance in the church hall on Saturday, lieutenant.'

Nick angled his head, giving Ginnie a quizzical smile. 'Do you think that Avril could spare you for the evening?'

Momentarily lost for words, she felt the blood rush to her cheeks and her knees threatened to give way beneath her. She was almost nineteen and this was the first time she had been asked out on a proper date. She was not counting the odd trip to the pictures with her best friend's brother. Spotty Tommy, the girls at school had called him, although despite his purulent acne Tommy Jarvis was a nice boy and he had bought her a bag of aniseed balls to suck during the showing of *Gone With the Wind* at the Gaumont cinema. She was about to answer when Avril breezed into the bar.

'Lionel, how lovely to see you.' She leaned across the counter and kissed him on the cheek. 'You're looking tired, my dear. Why don't you come into my parlour and put your feet up while you're saving my soul?' She gave him a saucy wink as she lifted the hatch and beckoned to him.

'You're outrageous as usual, Avril, but charming as ever.' He swallowed his drink in one mouthful. 'Actually, that would be rather pleasant, but I think your niece has something to ask you first.' He nodded to Ginnie. 'Haven't you?'

'As a matter of fact it was my idea,' Nick said before Ginnie had a chance to respond. 'I'd like your permission to take Ginnie to the dance on Saturday night. Will you give her the evening off, Avril?'

'But of course.' She threw her arms around Ginnie, enveloping her in a sweet and powdery vanilla haze of Shalimar perfume. 'You haven't had a night off since you came here, darling. Of course you must go, and you're lucky to have such a handsome partner.' She stepped back behind the bar, pausing in the kitchen doorway. 'Come through, Lionel. We'll leave the young people to look after things. I'm so lucky to have such a beautiful and capable niece to help me run my pub.'

Nick waited until they were out of earshot. 'You will come with me on Saturday, won't you, Ginnie?'

'Avril says it's all right, so – yes, I'd love to.'

'That's great,' Nick said, smiling. 'For a moment I thought you might have other plans.'

A warm glow suffused her whole body, starting at her toes and making her feel quite light-headed. She could hardly believe that he had chosen her to accompany him to the dance when he had the pick of the young nurses at the military hospital as well as the village girls. 'I'll look forward to it, Nick.'

'Me too, honey.' He downed the rest of his pint. 'I've got to go now, but think about what I said about working at the hospital. I won't be in tomorrow as I'm on duty, but I'll call for you at seven on Saturday evening.' He leaned over the bar and kissed her on the cheek. 'See you soon.'

'Goodnight, Nick,' Ginnie murmured as he stepped outside, leaving the soft touch of his lips imprinted on her skin. She heard the roar of the jeep's engine and the crunch of its tyres on the gravel as he drove away.

'Don't trust them Yanks,' Percy said, holding out his glass. 'Got plenty of money to throw around but they're all talk. I'll have a half in there, please.'

She had just finished serving him when more customers began to trickle in, and by nine o'clock the tiny bar was crowded and there were people sitting out on the terrace enjoying the benefits of double summertime. Avril burst into the bar with such a theatrical flourish that Ginnie half expected her to be greeted with a round of applause, but Avril knew how to work her audience and was immediately besieged by friends eager to chat and exchange gossip.

When the door finally closed and the glasses had been collected and stacked on the draining board, Avril poured herself a stiff drink. 'That was busy for a weekday, but I suppose the nice weather brought them out. Not that I'm complaining.'

Washing glasses in lukewarm water with just a swish of household soap, Ginnie decided that this was the right time to mention Nick's offer of a job. She cleared her throat. 'Auntie Avril, how would you feel if I told you I'd been offered paid work at the American hospital?'

Avril gulped down a mouthful of brandy and soda. 'I'd be delighted for you, darling. But only if that's what you want to do. I can afford to support you and Shirley while you're staying with me. It's not as if I'm poor, and you've been a great help.'

'But you don't really need me here all day, do you?'

'I suppose not, although I do love having the company of my two favourite nieces.'

Ginnie picked up a tea towel and began drying the glasses. 'You've only got two nieces.'

'Actually, I have a niece and three nephews by marriage, but as my former husbands' families' don't speak to me, I've taken them off my Christmas card list.' Avril perched on a bar stool and reached for her silver cigarette case. 'Do you want to work at the military hospital, Ginnie? You don't have to worry about money, you know. There are far more important things in life.'

'I'd like to do something for the war effort, Auntie. Next year I'll be called up or I'll have to work in a factory, but I really don't want to wait until then to do something for my country. I love helping out here but I feel that I'm taking the easy option.'

'I don't know about that, darling. But if working at the hospital is what you want then that's what you must do. Shirley can help me and it will do her good to do something other than lying around on her bed all day, feeling sorry for herself.'

'I look like a hippo in this dress,' Shirley said, twisting round to get a better view in the mirror on their dressing table. 'I can't go to the dance looking like this.'

'You look blooming,' Ginnie said hastily. 'And I'm

not just saying that. The dress is a bit tight round the middle, but perhaps we could let out a seam.'

'I've done that, silly.' Shirley slumped down on her bed and her hair, smoothed into a slightly curly version of a Veronica Lake style, flopped artistically over one eye. 'It's all right for you; you look gorgeous in that old dress of mine, which will never fit me again.'

Ginnie glanced down at the floral patterned cotton frock with its sweetheart neckline, fitted waist and flared skirt which she had shortened so that it barely kissed her knees. 'You can have it back after the baby is born.'

'I don't want it. It's old-fashioned and I'll want something new. I can't go out looking like this.'

'Perhaps Auntie Avril has something you could wear.'

'I don't want to look as though I'm in fancy dress.' Shirley's eyes brimmed with tears. 'I hate Charlie, and Laurence too. It's all their fault and I'm left to cope on my own.'

'Wait here a moment.' Ginnie hurried from the room and went to knock on her aunt's bedroom door. 'It's me, Ginnie. Can I come in?'

Avril was sitting on her dressing-table stool, dabbing her cheeks with a powder puff. 'This is the absolute last of my Elizabeth Arden,' she groaned. 'I'll be down to using cornflour soon. My adorable American colonel won't be returning to Lightwood House, more's the pity. He brought me a supply of cosmetics from the States a year ago, but they're like gold dust now.' She turned her head to look at Ginnie. 'What's the matter, darling? You look flustered.'

'It's Shirley. She's not happy.'

'It's becoming a habit. What's wrong now?'

'Her dress is too tight. Actually it looks fine and she's a picture of health but she won't have it. I was wondering if . . .'

'If I had anything that might fit her. There's no need to look embarrassed, Ginnie. I'm well aware that my figure is more voluptuous than it was in the days when I was an artist's model – I was a sylph then but I like to think I've matured to Rubenesque.' She rose from her seat and walked over to the bird's-eye walnut wardrobe. Rifling through the tightly packed garments she tossed one after another onto the bed. 'There must be something here that would satisfy her. Ask her to come here and choose, Ginnie.'

They kept Nick and Tony waiting for a good fifteen minutes but Ginnie was quick to reassure her sister and told her that she looked stunning, which was true. One of Avril's pure silk empire line gowns was cut daringly low across the bosom and gathered above the waist so that it concealed Shirley's bump in a swirl of turquoise, lime green and navy blue. Tony's appreciative whistle was enough to bring the smile back to her face and enabled Ginnie to relax for the first time that evening.

The jeep was waiting outside to take them to the village and Nick handed Ginnie into the passenger seat. 'You look a million dollars,' he said appreciatively. 'And so do you, Shirley,' he added hastily, taking his place behind the wheel.

'That was kind of you,' Ginnie said in an undertone as he started the engine.

'It was nothing but the truth.' He drove off, sending up a shower of gravel and a cloud of dust. 'Hold tight, ladies. We're off to the ball.'

When they arrived at the village hall Ginnie was thrilled and a little overawed to see couples jiving energetically, but it was enough to convince her that her basic knowledge of dance steps was pitifully inadequate. Unless it was the polka, the veleta or an old-fashioned waltz, which had been taught at school on days when it was too wet to go outside and play netball or hockey, she was lost. She might have panicked and run if Nick had not had a firm grip on her hand, but he seemed to sense her nervousness and embraced her with a warm smile. 'Don't worry, kid,' he said softly. 'I promise not to throw you around like those guys. It's not my scene.'

Although the doors had been flung wide open the air inside was stiff with the heady mix of aftershave, cheap perfume and perspiration with overtones of cider and beer, cigarette smoke and the occasional waft of a cigar.

'There's Danny,' Shirley said, waving to him.

'Who's that blonde woman who looks as though she's going to eat him for supper?'

Tony slipped his arm around her waist. 'That's Nurse Helga Halvorsen. She has the face of an angel and the temper of someone you wouldn't want to meet. You don't get on the wrong side of Helga.'

'I doubt if our paths will cross.' Shirley pulled her mouth down at the corners, reminding Ginnie forcibly of their mother in disapproving mode.

'Let's get something to drink,' Nick said hastily. 'I think it's only beer and cider, although I suspect that there's a tea urn bubbling away somewhere.'

'I'd love a glass of cider.' Ginnie crossed her fingers behind her back, hoping that Nick would not remember that she was underage.

He gave her a quizzical smile. 'Aren't you forgetting something, honey?'

'It was worth a try. I suppose I'll have a soft drink, as usual.'

'I'd rather dance,' Shirley said before Tony had a chance to speak. 'They've changed the record to play something more my style. I just love the foxtrot.'

Tony pulled a face. 'I guess I'll have a go, but you might find that I've got two left feet.' He led her onto the dance floor and they swayed together in time to the music. Ginnie stood on her own, waiting for Nick to edge his way to the makeshift bar to get their drinks. She had never attended a function like this and she was fascinated by the way the girls had made themselves glamorous despite clothes rationing and the difficulty in obtaining any kind of cosmetics. Lips were brightened with beetroot juice and silk stockings replicated by the judicious application of gravy browning, with the seams drawn in eyebrow pencil.

Ginnie felt underdressed and insignificant compared to the local girls, who were dolled up in their best frocks and determined to have a good time. The war seemed far distant on such a balmy summer evening far away from the bomb-damaged towns and cities. Ginnie had hated every minute of the war until now, but if it were not for the conflict in Europe she would never have met Nick. She watched him making his way back to her with a glass in each hand. He moved slowly and sinuously, taking care not to spill a drop, and as he reached the open doors the rays of the setting sun caught him in a spotlight and the rest of the room seemed to fade into a blurry haze. The only person she could see was Nick. His sleek head of hair gleamed blue-black and his tanned skin glowed with health. His smile enveloped her like warm honey as he pressed a glass into her hand.

'It's cider,' he whispered. 'I won't tell anyone you're just a kid.'

'And I won't tell anyone that you're an old man of twenty-six,' she countered, taking a sip.

'Twenty-five. I won't be twenty-six until Christmas.'

'Do you think the war will be over by then?'

His smile faded. 'I don't know. I wish I could see an end to it all, but I can't. Not yet, anyway.'

'But when it's over you'll be going home to America.' The rosy glow that had made her feel like singing for joy suddenly dissipated and the reality of the shabby church hall with its tired bunting and windows criss-crossed with sticky tape hit her full force. It was overcrowded and couples were either dancing cheek to cheek in a manner which would have shocked her mother or were getting drunk at the bar. The noise was rising in a crescendo and her head was beginning to ache.

'Sure, I will,' Nick said gently. 'But that's a long way off.'

'Yes, of course.' She knew what he said was true but her evening was already ruined. She had fallen in love with a man who would one day return to his old life in his own country and he would forget all about her.

Nick took the glass from her and placed it on the windowsill amongst a sprinkling of dead flies. 'Shall we dance? "Moonlight Serenade" is one of my favourites.'

'Yes, thank you.' She was in his arms, moving in time to the romantic sound of Glenn Miller's orchestra, and the magic returned. She leaned against him, intoxicated by the scent of him and the hardness of his body as he held her close. She felt that she was floating and her feet hardly seemed to touch the floor. The steel rafters that supported the ceiling had been replaced in her imagination by a canopy of black velvet sky studded with stars. She slid her arms around his neck and they moved together as one person.

'Hey, put that girl down, Nick. You're creating a road block here, buddy.' Danny's loud voice shattered the moment and Ginnie let her arms fall to her sides. She raised her head and found herself looking into the beautiful but stony face of Nurse Helga Halvorsen.

'Isn't she a bit young for you, lieutenant?' Helga said coldly.

'What's the matter, Helga? Aren't you having fun?' Nick's tone was icy and he drew Ginnie back into the shelter of his arms. 'You should look after your lady a bit better, Danny.'

Helga opened her mouth as if to argue, but Danny took her by the hand. 'C'mon, honey. Let's get a beer.' He headed for the bar, dragging her in his wake.

Nick moved in time to the music. 'Don't take any notice of Helga.'

'Is there a history between you two?'

'We work together, Ginnie. We had a few dates but nothing serious. I guess that Helga's the possessive type. She doesn't want me but she doesn't like it if I show a preference for someone else.'

'And do you prefer me to her?'

His liquid brown eyes shone with amusement. 'I guess I do. You're cute and funny and . . .'

'If you mention my age once more I'll have to stamp on your toes,' Ginnie said with feeling. 'I'll

66

be twenty next year. I'm not much younger than you or her, if it comes to that.'

'In years maybe, but not in experience. You've led a sheltered life in your poppa's furniture shop.'

'Now you're laughing at me.'

'Never.' He bent his head and brushed her lips with his. His eyes darkened and he held her close, taking her mouth in a kiss that seemed to go on forever and she wished that it would. Her toes felt as though they were curling inside her summer sandals and her heart was thudding against the buttons of his uniform jacket. Someone cheered and slapped Nick on the back in passing and he relaxed his hold, drawing back to take a deep breath. 'I'm sorry. I guess I got carried away.'

Breathless and blushing, she flicked her hair back from her hot cheeks. 'It's all right. I don't mind.'

He took her by the hand and threaded his way through the couples on the dance floor. 'Let's go for a walk, Ginnie. There's something important that I've got to tell you.'

Chapter Four

Outside the air was cool and the fragrant smell of newly mown grass was all the sweeter after the fug in the hall. Long shadows were beginning to march across the countryside as the sun sank slowly in the west, and a fresh breeze rustled the leaves in the tree-lined lane. They were alone for the first time and Ginnie was still light-headed from the delight of their first kiss, and revelling in the thrill of simply being with him. 'What is it you have to tell me, Nick?' she asked dreamily.

He came to a halt outside the church and leaned against the stone wall. 'You don't know anything about me, Ginnie.'

His serious expression made her catch her breath. She had hoped he was about to tell her that he loved her, but now she was nervous. 'What's the matter? Have I done something to upset you?'

'Of course not, kid.' He took her hand in his. 'But there are things about me that you don't know and I really care about you, Ginnie. I have to be straight with you.'

'In what way?' She was growing more anxious with each passing second. She had never seen him look this serious and it scared her. 'What's this all about, Nick?'

'My family live in Los Angeles.'

'You already told me that.'

'I know I did, but I'm just trying to give you a picture of where I'm from.'

'Go on. I'm listening.'

'Well, I guess it's quite ordinary and nothing special. My pa owns a store and my mother and older brother work there. It's a family business.'

'A bit like my dad's furniture shop.'

'Yes, a bit. Anyway, it was a struggle for them to put me through medical school, but they managed it, although they were pretty cut up when I enlisted in the army. They wanted me to have a practice close to home and to marry and raise a family.'

'That's only natural, I suppose.' She looked into his eyes and her heart sank. 'But there's something else, isn't there?'

'I should have told you this at the start, but I didn't.' His clasp tightened on her hand as if he were afraid she might run away. 'I've known Betsy since we were children. You might say we were childhood sweethearts.'

She snatched her hand away. All her instincts warned her that this was not going to be good. 'Go on.'

He ran his hand through his hair, leaving it ruffled and unkempt. 'Everyone assumed that we'd get married one day.'

'Oh, for goodness' sake, spit it out,' Ginnie cried angrily. 'What are you trying to tell me? Are you married with half a dozen kids?'

'I'm not married.' He straightened up, shoving his hands deep into his pockets. 'I love you, Ginnie. It may sound corny but I guess I fell for you the moment I saw you.'

She swallowed hard. 'You do?'

'I love the way you look and speak. I love that tiny kiss curl on your forehead that goes every which way, even though you try to pin it down. I love the dimple at the corner of your mouth which makes me want to kiss you every time you smile. I love the way you care for the people who are closest to you, and I love you for who you are. But . . .'

Her heart was beating so fast that she could barely frame the words. 'But? There's always a but.'

'I have to be straight with you, Ginnie. I'm engaged to Betsy.' He held up his hands. 'It was a stupid romantic gesture on the night before I left for Britain. I guess I got carried away by the moment and I asked her to marry me. Guys who'd been at school who were more senior to us had lost their lives, and I didn't know if I'd ever see my family again. I want you to understand . . .'

She backed away from him. 'Of course I understand. You've been stringing me along. You say you love me but you don't or you wouldn't have played such a cruel game with me.' Her voice broke on a sob and she pushed him away. 'Leave me alone.'

'Honey, believe me, I never meant to hurt you. I didn't mean to fall in love with you, but it happened just as I said.'

'I suppose you said much the same thing to her.'

His eyes darkened. 'It wasn't like that. I've known Betsy all my life. She's a great girl but I realise now that she's not for me. I didn't know what love was until I met you.'

'Don't touch me,' Ginnie cried as he made a move to put his arm around her shoulders. 'Don't ever speak to me again. You – you bounder.' She could think of nothing worse to call him and that in itself was frustrating. She had never heard her father swear, unless he said 'damn' when he dropped a heavy piece of furniture on his foot, but then he would apologise profusely. Fred Chinashop came out with the odd expletive when he was really upset, but in her present agitated state none of them came to mind.

'You can call me anything you like, but just hear me out.'

'You've said enough.' She dragged every last scrap of self-respect from the depths of her being and held her head high. 'You're engaged to the Betsy person and that's it as far as I'm concerned. I don't want to see you ever again. You'd better find somewhere else to drink because I won't serve you.' She walked away, forcing herself to move slowly when every instinct was to run the mile or two to her aunt's pub, but she could hear his footsteps behind her and she stopped, turning her head to glare at him. 'If you follow me I'll scream for help. I meant what I said, Nick. I'm not a silly schoolgirl you can wrap round your little finger with a few well-chosen words. You had me fooled for a while, but this is it.'

'Ginnie, give me a chance to put things right.'

'Are you saying that you'll break it off with her?'

He hesitated. 'It's not that easy. I can't just send her a letter telling her that I've fallen for someone else.'

'But that's what happened, isn't it?'

'Of course it is, but I need to tell her to her face. She's a nice girl, Ginnie. I guess you two would get on well together.'

'Then you're completely stupid. She'd hate me as I hate her and I don't even know her. Go away, Nick. I never want to see you again.' It took all her strength of purpose to leave him, but somehow she managed to put one foot in front of the other and keep going. She wanted to look back. She wanted to forgive him and tell him that it didn't matter, but it did. She thought of Betsy, waiting for news of the man she loved who had promised to marry her, and she hardened her resolve. Nick should have been honest from the outset. If he'd told her from the start that he was engaged she would never have allowed herself to fall for him.

There was a bend in the lane ahead and she took the opportunity to slow down and turn her head just enough to look back. The sight of him standing in the middle of the road, staring after her with a bleak expression on his face, was enough to send daggers of pain shooting through her heart, but she did not relent and her steps did not falter. She sensed that one wave of her hand would bring him running in her direction, but she was hurt and she was angry. She would not give him the satisfaction of seeing how much he meant to her. It had to be a clean break or she would never forgive herself, and she would never forgive him either.

'It's one of those harsh lessons in life that we women have to learn, darling.' Avril stubbed her cigarette out in the ashtray. 'He's an attractive young devil, but there are plenty more where he came from, and hopefully they won't have a fiancée pining for them at home.'

'How can you be so calm, Auntie?' Shirley demanded angrily. 'That wretch was stringing Ginnie along. It's lucky it didn't go any further.' She glanced down at her swollen belly. 'It can so easily, as I know to my cost.'

'I've learned my lesson,' Ginnie said sadly. 'I was stupid to think that a chap like Nick would take an interest in someone like me.'

Avril reached across the breakfast table and slapped her sharply on the wrist. 'That's enough of that silly talk. You're a lovely girl, Ginnie. You may be an innocent, but that's what a lot of men like

Nick Miller find attractive. You'll learn through experience, as we all have to.'

'I suppose so, but I feel a complete fool.' Ginnie pushed her plate away.

'If you're not going to finish that slice of toast, I'll have it,' Shirley said, snatching it off the plate.

'You'll be the size of a house if you keep on eating for two,' Avril said, frowning. 'Anyway, we're going to show Lieutenant Miller that you're a stronger and better person than he is, Ginnie. So go upstairs, make yourself presentable and I'll harness up Duke and drive you to Lightwood House. You're going to take that job in the hospital and prove to him that you don't give a damn, as Rhett Butler said in the movie.'

'But Auntie, that's a rotten idea. I don't want to see him every day, let alone work with him.'

'Darling, you can't avoid him. I can bar him from the pub, but how would that look? His friends still come here, and Shirley seems to be getting on very well with Tony Petrillo, who's a decent enough fellow. Who knows where that might lead?'

'It's just a bit of fun,' Shirley said, blushing. 'He doesn't seem to mind being seen out with someone who's rapidly turning into a barrage balloon, and I'm not eating for two. I just hate to see waste.'

Ginnie rose from her seat. 'Tony's got good taste in women. As for me, I really don't think I want to work at the hospital, Auntie. Nick might think I'm chasing after him, and I don't think I could handle it.'

'Nonsense. To be honest, sweetie, you could do

with the money and there aren't many job opportunities in this rural area. I know I said you didn't have to worry about your finances, and I am reasonably well off, although business is not what it was pre-war. But perhaps you ought to start earning money and saving some for the future. Shirley will need to buy things for the baby and I'll help with the expense, but you've got to start planning for when you return home.'

'Yes, I'm sorry. We've sponged off you long enough, Auntie. You've been so good to us.'

Avril rolled her eyes. 'Oh, please, girls. Both of you stop calling me auntie, it makes me feel a hundred and twenty at least. Just call me Avril. Now do as I say, Ginnie. Go and change into something that looks efficient and practical and we'll leave right away. Shirley can hold the fort until we get back, can't you, darling?'

'Yes, Avril,' Shirley said, winking at her sister. 'Go on, Ginnie. What are you waiting for?'

It all happened so quickly. Next morning Ginnie was up at seven, washed and dressed, and after a quick breakfast she set off to walk the two miles to Lightwood House. Her interview the previous day had been with the woman in charge of civilian staff at the hospital, and she seemed to know all about Ginnie, although Nick's name did not crop up in conversation. She asked a few questions, but she was mainly concerned with the fact that Ginnie was young and healthy and physically able to do the work required of her. This, she said, would be the more menial tasks in the wards, which were supervised by the senior nurses, and a high standard of cleanliness was required. Avril had given her a glowing reference and before she knew it, Ginnie found herself engaged in full-time employment.

The hours were long, eight in the morning until eight in the evening, with one full day off a week, but the pay by British standards was excellent and much more than she had ever earned working for her father. Meals would be provided and she knew from conversations between Danny and Tony that the Americans ate well. Despite her reservations, she was looking forward to doing something that was completely different and also rewarding. For the first time since the war began she felt she would be doing her bit.

She discovered that much was expected of her and by the end of the first morning her back was aching miserably and her hands were sore from being immersed in hot water and the use of strong carbolic soap. Her supervisor was none other than Nurse Helga Halvorsen, and if that was not humiliating enough, Helga seemed to have taken a dislike to her. She criticised Ginnie's work and spotted minute patches of floor that she said had been missed and made Ginnie scrub the whole area for a second time. She set her to clean the ablutions and when that was done she sent Ginnie to the sluice to empty and sterilise the bedpans and urinal bottles.

She was met in the doorway by one of the more senior ward maids, a pleasant-faced girl from over the border in Wales whom she had met briefly during their morning tea break. 'What've you done to upset the old cow?' Meriel Jones demanded, pushing her unflattering white cap to the back of her head. 'You've had all the rotten jobs in one morning.'

'I don't know,' Ginnie said, shaking her head. 'But if it goes on like this I'll tell her where to go.'

Meriel patted her on the shoulder. 'Good for you, love. But this isn't a bad place to work. The pay is twice as much as we could earn anywhere else and they feed us well. Grin and bear it, that's what I say.'

'I suppose you're right. Thanks, Meriel.'

'Don't mention it. Keep your head down and don't argue with the military and you'll be fine.' Meriel picked up a bucket of hot water and marched off along the corridor.

Grin and bear it, Ginnie thought with a grim smile. It might be a cliché but it was good advice. She would not allow someone like Helga to spoil her chances of earning a good wage. She had only to think of the things that Shirley's baby would need in order to harden her resolve. She stepped inside the sluice, wrinkling her nose at the mixed odours of urine, faeces and disinfectant, and she began to empty, rinse and sterilise until the unpleasant task was carried out to her satisfaction.

She managed to survive the first day without having told Nurse Helga what she could do with her carbolic soap and scrubbing brushes, and was on her way home when she heard the unmistakeable sound of a jeep's engine slowing down behind her. She did not have to look round to know that Nick was at the wheel. She kept on walking, but he slowed the vehicle to match her pace.

'Ginnie, let me give you a lift home, please.'

She stared straight ahead and kept going.

'I know you hate me, but we need to talk.'

She came to a sudden halt. 'No, we don't. You should have been honest with me from the start, Nick Miller. It's too late now.'

He leaned over to open the door. 'What you say is true. I'm not making excuses for myself, but I didn't want to go overseas without saying goodbye.'

'You're going overseas?' His words hit her with the force of a thunderbolt.

'Get in, please, and I'll explain.'

She climbed in beside him and slammed the door. 'This is a bit sudden, isn't it?'

He drove off, concentrating on the road ahead. 'My orders only came through today. They need medics in northern France and that's where I'll be heading tomorrow.'

'But why? You're safe here and you're doing a good job.'

'I guess Helga told you that?' He glanced at her with a hint of a grin.

'No. As a matter of fact your ex-girlfriend has been a perfect bitch to me all day. She's given me all the worst jobs and made my life hell. I suppose I have you to thank for that.'

A look of genuine concern wiped the smile off his even features. 'No, honey. That had nothing to do with me. I haven't done more than pass the time of day with Helga for months. We had a couple of dates last Christmas but that's as far as it went.'

'Then why has she got it in for you and for me too?'

'Who knows what's going on in her mind? I certainly don't. I was honest with her from the start, as I should have been with you. I made it clear that we were just friends, but I guess she didn't see it that way.'

'Then why is she making my life a misery? I haven't done anything to her.'

He drew the jeep to a halt in the shade of a tall horse chestnut tree. 'I can't speak for Helga, and anyway this isn't about her. I know I've ruined my chances with you, Ginnie. You're a great girl and you deserve better than me.'

She eyed him suspiciously. 'Being humble doesn't suit you, Nick.'

'And being cynical doesn't suit you, Ginnie. I never lied to you, honey. I just didn't tell you everything about myself and I regret that bitterly.'

'I'd say that having a fiancée waiting for you at home was something you couldn't easily forget.

You didn't tell me because it suited you to keep it secret.'

He bowed his head. 'I know I was wrong, but nothing alters the fact that I'm crazy about you.' He looked up and his eyes clouded with sadness. 'I realise that you don't want to have anything to do with me now, but I didn't want to go away and leave you thinking that I'd been stringing you along.'

The sincerity in his voice was enough to convince her that he meant every word, and she wanted desperately to believe him, but a small voice in her head reminded her that he was not a free agent: he was engaged to a girl in his home town thousands of miles away. She hesitated, torn between her principles and the overwhelming desire to fling herself into his arms. 'There's still Betsy,' she said in a small voice. 'You must have loved her once.'

'And if the war hadn't brought me to Europe I would probably have married her, but then I met you.'

'And Helga.' She could not resist the dig, and it brought a glimmer of humour to his eyes.

'All right, I guess I deserved that one, but now I'm deadly serious, Ginnie.' He reached out to take her hand in his. 'I love you. I'm not asking anything of you, I just want you to believe that I meant every word I said the other night. I'd have spoken out sooner but I didn't want to scare you off.'

'When did you say you were leaving?'

'First thing in the morning, and I'm not sure exactly where we're headed for.'

She stared down at their intertwined fingers. His were tanned and square-tipped: practical hands, the hands of a surgeon. Hers were small, rough and reddened after a day of hard work, but she felt the warmth of his grasp seeping through her veins to warm her chilled heart. She raised her head to look into his eyes and as if drawn together by a magnet their lips met. He wrapped his arms around her and she relaxed against him, parting her lips and returning his kiss with unashamed passion. This was their world and they were the only two inhabitants. Nothing and no one mattered outside the close embrace that made them as one, but suddenly it was over.

She was cold and shivering as the breeze picked up, whipping strands of hair across her face and cooling her hot cheeks. Nick held her at arms' length, his mouth drawn into a thin line of pain. 'I'll drive you home.'

She felt for the handle and thrust the door open. 'No. I'll walk. I need time on my own. Goodbye, Nick.'

He caught her by the arm. 'You've had a tough day. Let me drop you at the pub, Ginnie. I won't come in.'

Her breath hitched in her throat. 'I can't do this. Leave me a shred of pride.' Wrenching free from his grasp she leapt from the jeep and walked away, keeping her gaze on the road ahead and resisting the temptation to look back. She knew that once again he was watching her walk away but this time it was final. It was not until she reached the bridge over the river that she heard the faint murmur of the jeep's engine. She hesitated with her hands clutching the parapet and allowed herself to look round in time to see the rear end of the military vehicle disappearing into the distance.

She walked on in a daze, turning the corner and following the river upstream in the direction of the Ferryboat Inn. The dark water of the millpond was eerily still and its glassy surface mirrored the overhanging trees. The mill house was unusually silent, its grindstones waiting in readiness to turn the harvested wheat into flour, and cattle grazed peacefully in the adjacent fields, oblivious to anything but their physical needs. A high brick wall on the far side of the lane kept intruders from trespassing on the squire's land, and further along she could see the gatekeeper's wife tending to her tiny vegetable plot. They exchanged polite greetings but Ginnie was in no mood to stop and chat. She slowed her pace as the pub came into view, bracing herself for a barrage of questions from Avril and Shirley, but she could not muster enough courage to face them.

She went to sit on the riverbank, gazing into the fast-flowing water, and she felt nothing. All her senses were numbed by grief and anger, but her rage was directed at herself rather than Nick. She had allowed him into her heart for a second time and that had been a big mistake.

'This is a good place to sit and contemplate, I always find.'

She looked round with a start and saw the friendly face of Lionel Smithers smiling down at her. 'I didn't hear you coming, vicar.'

He squatted down beside her. 'I'm sorry, I didn't mean to make you jump, but you looked as though you might need a friend.'

She concentrated her attention on a single blade of grass. If she mentioned Nick's name it would all spill out in a tsunami of emotion. 'I was just thinking.'

'May I join you for a while? The pub isn't open yet and I rather fancied a drop of something cheering before I took my confirmation class. I'm afraid the three girls and a boy are more interested in receiving chewing gum and the occasional chocolate bar from the American soldiers than they are in nourishing their souls.' He sat down, stretching out his long legs. 'Perhaps this was a mistake; I'll have a terrible job getting to my feet again. That's the trouble with growing older, Ginnie. One doesn't realise one's limitation until one tries to act like a young person.'

His wry grimace brought a smile to her face. 'Don't worry. I'll help you up at opening time.'

'Avril will tell me that I'm a silly old fool if she sees me from her window,' Lionel said, chuckling. 'Your aunt is an amazing woman. She's run this place single-handed since Esmond died, and I've never heard her complain about her lot.'

'Yes,' Ginnie said slowly. 'I suppose she is, but I've never given it much thought, and I don't really remember Uncle Esmond.'

'You must have been very young when he succumbed to his illness, and you live in London. It's a long way from Lightwood Common.'

'Auntie Avril always seems so capable. It never occurred to me that she might be struggling.'

'Even strong people need a little help now and then.' Lionel gave her a searching look. 'And you are in that position now, unless I'm mistaken.'

'Is it so obvious?'

'I rather think it might have to do with a certain young American officer. You two have been getting on rather well, I think.'

'He's leaving for France tomorrow. I'll never see him again.' The words tumbled out before she could stop herself.

'But you mustn't think like that, my dear. The war in Europe is almost over and he will return.'

'It's not that simple.' She hesitated. 'He's engaged to someone back home in the States. It's all over between us.'

He laid his hand on her shoulder. 'I'm so sorry, Ginnie. These things happen, particularly in wartime. I won't insult you by telling you that you're very young and that time will heal, but what I will say is that if this young man's feelings for you are genuine he'll find a way to solve the dilemma without giving his fiancée too much pain. She might even have found someone else in his absence.' He scrambled somewhat awkwardly to his knees, grimacing with pain. 'Rheumaticky joints, my dear. Would you?'

'Of course.' She stood up and helped him to his feet. 'Thank you for listening.'

'That's my job, Ginnie. But also I have great sympathy for young people in your position. I hope it works out well for you.'

'You won't mention this conversation to my aunt or my sister, will you, vicar? I mean, they know what happened between me and Nick, but I don't think I could stand a cross-examination this evening.'

'The riverbank is as good as a confessional, even though that belongs to the other department, so to speak. I would never betray a confidence, Ginnie.' He stretched and groaned. 'But I must remember not to sit on damp grass again. Now I really could do with a drop of Scotch and I can salve my conscience by telling myself that it's purely medicinal.'

They walked the short distance to the pub and arrived just as Avril was opening up. She greeted them with a smile. 'My two favourite people and you've beaten Percy to it, thank goodness. One day I'll really have to tell him about his personal hygiene problem. Come in and have a drink, Ginnie. Never mind the law; you look as though you could do with a snifter. Have they been working you too hard, darling?'

The work did not get easier, but Ginnie grew accustomed to it and with Nick out of the picture Helga seemed to have lost interest in her, or maybe she simply grew tired of trying to catch her out. Ginnie fell into a routine at the hospital and with encouragement from Meriel she made friends with the other girls, some of whom had at first viewed her with suspicion. In the beginning her London accent had set her apart and some of them seemed to think that she was too grand to stoop to menial work, but when Ginnie continued to be given the worst tasks and carried them out to the best of her ability, she gradually overcame their prejudices and earned their friendship. She was no longer that 'posh girl from London' – she was just Ginnie, the girl from the pub.

In the evenings, she served in the bar or waited on tables in the tiny dining room, and although she chatted amicably to all the customers, including the officers from the camp and the hospital, she made it clear that she was not interested in dating. Shirley and Tony had become increasingly close, although she insisted that there was nothing romantic going on between them. Ginnie suspected that for Tony this was not the case, but at least he knew the score and if he was happy to date a woman carrying another man's child that was his business. Even so, she feared that someone was going to get hurt, and she did not wish that sort of pain on anyone, but she kept her feelings to herself. She had not heard from Nick, and she was too proud to ask Tony or Danny if they had any news of him. She did her best to put him out of her mind but he remained stubbornly in her heart.

Autumn drifted into winter and November lived up to its reputation of being cold and gloomy. One evening at the beginning of December Shirley was waiting for her when she arrived home from work and she pounced. 'Tony's asked me to go to the pictures tonight; perhaps you'd like to come too.'

'Why are you asking me?' Ginnie was tired, cold and longing for a cup of tea. 'You don't usually.'

'Because Avril thinks I'm too close to my time to go out and about, but she'll stop moaning if you go with me, since you're as good as a nurse now.'

'Shirley, I scrub floors and empty bedpans. That doesn't qualify me to deliver a baby.'

'It would do you good to get away from here for an evening. It's no good moping around,' Shirley told her severely. 'Nick's gone and anyway he's engaged to that wretched girl in LA, so he wasn't serious about you, Ginnie.'

'I know, and I'm trying to move on. I am, really.'

'That's the spirit.' Shirley gave her a hug. 'This is really difficult when I've got a huge bump, but I feel for you, old thing. You're not like me: you bottle things up – I let it all out.'

'I'll never see him again,' Ginnie said sadly.

'I'm really sorry it didn't work out for you.' Shirley brushed her cheek with a casual kiss. 'But are you sure you won't come to the flicks with us? It's *Best Foot Forward* with Lucille Ball and June Allyson. It's a musical and it should be fun.'

'Thanks, but I'm not in the mood. You go out and enjoy yourself while you can.'

'I don't intend to let the baby stop me having a good time, Ginnie. It'll have a lovely auntie and a superb great-auntie. I expect you two will be falling over each other to babysit.'

'Don't count on it, darling,' Avril said, popping her head round the door. 'Are you going to help me or not, Ginnie? We've just been invaded by some rather dashing American officers. I need you now.'

'Go out and have a good time.' Ginnie picked up her sister's handbag and gasmask case and thrust them at her. 'Tell me all about it when you get home.'

'Tony's waiting for you,' Avril said, beckoning. 'Hurry up, child, or you'll miss the start of the movie.'

Shirley breezed into the bar and Ginnie followed her more slowly.

It was a hectic Saturday evening. Keeping busy was the best medicine and Ginnie forgot her tiredness and aching limbs as she served customers and put on a cheerful face, chatting and laughing at their banter.

The call for last orders had just gone out when the sound of the telephone ringing sent Avril hurrying into the kitchen. 'Who on earth can that be at this time of night?'

Ginnie did not take much notice, thinking it was probably someone looking for a room or one of Avril's friends who wanted a late evening tête-à-tête. She had just pulled a pint for an American captain when Avril appeared in the doorway, white-faced and trembling. 'There's been an accident,' she murmured. 'A terrible accident.'

Chapter Five

The corridor at the Royal Salop Infirmary was cold and draughty. Ginnie and Avril sat huddled on a hard wooden bench, waiting for news of Shirley's condition. Tony was dead. No matter how tactfully the young houseman had tried to convey the terrible news, the shock of his announcement had left them both speechless. A kindly young nurse had brought them cups of tea, sweetened with saccharin, which had left a bitter aftertaste in Ginnie's mouth, and now she was feeling slightly queasy.

Avril set her cup and saucer down on the floor. 'I can't stand this any longer, Ginnie. I'm going to see if I can find someone who'll tell us what's going on.' She half rose to her feet and sank down again at the sound of approaching footsteps, but it was the American major who had been a customer in the bar when the call came through from the hospital who strode towards them, and not one of the medical team. Major Dudley had kindly offered to give them a lift to the hospital in his staff car, confirming Ginnie's suspicions that he had a soft spot for her aunt. His brow was puckered with concern. 'I've just come from the mortuary. Is there any news of your niece, Mrs Parkin?'

'No, Major Dudley. Nothing yet.'

He nodded gravely. 'I'm afraid I have to get back to Lightwood House. I need to make certain arrangements concerning the deceased.'

'I understand, major. I'm very grateful to you for bringing us here.' Avril fished in her handbag and brought out a hanky. She dabbed her eyes. 'I'm sorry.'

He gave an embarrassed cough. 'No need to apologise. It's perfectly understandable in the circumstances, ma'am. May I offer you both a lift home?'

Ginnie shook her head. 'I can't leave while my sister's life hangs in the balance, but perhaps my aunt should go with you.'

'I'm all right, Ginnie.' Avril sniffed and tucked her hanky back in her bag. 'Thank you, major, but I'll stay here.'

'Please let me know if there's anything I can do.' Major Dudley was about to walk away when a door further along the corridor opened and a young houseman came hurrying towards them.

Ginnie leapt to her feet. 'How is she, doctor? Is she going to be all right?'

'She's in a stable condition, but the foetus is in some distress. We need to operate in order to save the baby's life, and for that we must have permission from a relative.'

'I'm her sister.'

'And I'm her aunt.' Avril stood up. 'Perhaps I ought to sign as my niece is underage.'

'But Shirley will be all right, won't she?' Ginnie's lips were so dry that she could barely frame the words. 'She's not going to die.'

'Everything possible will be done.' His tired smile reassured her to some extent, but her knees gave way beneath her and she sank down on the seat.

Avril gave her a hug. 'She'll pull through, darling. I know she will.'

They waited for almost an hour and a half. Avril was unusually silent and Ginnie stared at her watch, counting off the minutes. The hushed sounds of the hospital at night were like whispers in her head. The dull click of a catch as a door opened was followed by a muted thud as it closed again, and the soft pitter-patter of a nurse's footsteps on the stone floor was followed by ringing silence. Ginnie had an almost hysterical desire to stand up and scream at the injustice of it all. Just hours ago Tony had been a healthy young man with his whole life ahead of him, and now his corpse was lying in the mortuary, and her sister was fighting for two lives in the operating theatre. Ginnie was not particularly religious but she bowed her head and her lips moved as she prayed for the safe delivery of both Shirley and her unborn child.

Overcome with exhaustion she closed her eyes only to awaken with a start as someone nudged her sharply in the ribs. For a moment she could not remember where she was, or what had brought her to this strange place, but then it all came flooding back.

'Someone's coming,' Avril said urgently. 'It's that young doctor.' She clutched Ginnie's hand. 'Oh, God. I can't bear it. I'll never forgive myself if that poor girl loses her baby. I should have been firmer and insisted that she stayed at home.'

Ginnie squeezed her aunt's fingers. 'No one could have stopped Shirley doing what she wanted. That's my sister all over.' She rose to her feet as the doctor approached. 'How is she? Is the baby . . . ?'

'Mrs Mallory has a fractured clavicle and we think she has slight concussion, but we'll continue to assess her condition.' He relaxed visibly and smiled. 'And the baby was delivered safely by Caesarean section. He's on his way to the nursery next to the maternity ward. You can go there and see him if you want to.'

'A boy,' Avril said dazedly. 'And he's healthy?'

'He's a fine specimen. Seven pounds six ounces.'

'Thank God they're both all right.' Avril stood up, taking Ginnie by the arm. 'Come along, darling. Let's go and meet the newest member of the family.'

Ginnie hesitated, fixing the doctor with a steady gaze. 'My sister will recover fully, won't she?'

'We're cautiously optimistic, but it's impossible to assess the exact extent of her head injury as yet.'

'Shirley is as tough as old boots,' Avril said confidently. 'You worry too much, Ginnie. Now let's go and meet what's-his-name.'

A reluctant giggle rose to Ginnie's lips. 'You can't call a baby what's-his-name.'

'Well, as far as I know, your sister hadn't got round to choosing a name for her child.'

Ginnie waited anxiously for Shirley to come round from the anaesthetic. She had spent an uncomfortable night sitting in an upright chair at her sister's bedside. Nurses had been flitting in and out of the side ward all night, taking Shirley's pulse and adjusting the drip, which did not seem to disturb Avril who was sleeping soundly in a chair by the window.

The room was suffused in the cold grey light of a December morning when Ginnie roused from a fitful doze, and she was suddenly alert. She thought she had seen Shirley's eyelids flicker and she leaned closer. 'Shirley.'

Her sister's eyes opened wide, staring in an unfocused way at the ceiling and then at her. 'What happened?'

'There was an accident. You're in hospital.'

'Tony?'

'You have a beautiful baby boy, Shirley.'

'A boy,' Shirley said drowsily. 'I've got a son.'

'Don't try to talk. You had a nasty bang on the head and you've broken your collar bone, but you'll be up and about before you know it.'

Shirley's brow puckered into a frown. 'Where's Tony?'

Ginnie glanced over her shoulder in the hope that Avril had awakened at the sound of voices but she was still asleep and it did not seem fair to disturb her. This was one time when she would have been grateful for her aunt's timely intervention. 'You mustn't worry about a thing, Shirley. Just concentrate on getting better so that you can look after your baby. What are you going to call him? He needs a name.'

'Colin,' Shirley whispered. 'I'm very thirsty. I could murder a cup of tea.'

Ginnie leapt to her feet. 'I'll go and find a nurse.' She left the room and hurried to the sister's office. The aroma of hot toast and tea reminded her that she had not eaten anything since early the previous evening. Her stomach rumbled in anticipation as she knocked on the open door. 'My sister is asking for something to drink,' she said in answer to the nurse's questioning glance. 'Is it all right to give her a drink of water? Or could she have a cup of tea?'

'I'll take a look at her first.' The ward sister abandoned what she was doing. 'Is she fully conscious?'

'She's a bit drowsy, but I suppose that's normal.' Ginnie stood aside to allow the nurse to pass. 'She's asking about her friend, the young American who died in the crash. I don't know what to tell her.'

'Perhaps the least said the better until Mrs Mallory is stronger. We don't want to upset her at this stage in her recovery.'

*

Shirley and the baby returned home a week before Christmas. Major Dudley sent his aide to collect them in the staff car and Ginnie accompanied him. Shirley had recovered well from the operation but her left arm was in a sling, which limited what she could do for herself and the baby. Ginnie took charge of Colin, breathing in the sweet scent of him as she cuddled him in her arms. His shock of dark hair gave him a slightly comical appearance but when he opened his eyes they were a deep shade of violet. 'You're going to break a few hearts when you're older, Colin,' she whispered, dropping a kiss on his chubby cheek.

When they arrived home Shirley uttered a cry of delight as she walked through the door. A blazing log fire cast a warm and welcoming glow around the room and the scent of burning apple wood filled the air. Ginnie had decorated the bar with boughs of holly and had filled a copper kettle with the last of the bronze chrysanthemums that had escaped the frost. Percy had procured a Christmas tree from somewhere on the estate, which Ginnie had decorated with Avril's precious hoard of glass baubles and slightly tarnished strands of tinsel.

'It looks like a scene from a Christmas card.' Shirley's eyes filled with tears. 'It would be perfect if Tony was here to share it with us.'

Colin opened his eyes and his mouth turned down at the corners as he worked himself up to cry. Ginnie rocked him in her arms. 'I think someone is hungry,' she said hastily. 'I'll take him to the sitting room. There's a fire in there too. We've pulled out all the stops for your return, Shirley. No expense has been spared.'

'And we've got roast chicken for dinner.' Avril lifted the hatch in the bar counter. 'Actually it's an old boiler but I've used all my culinary skill to turn it into a feast. Come through, darling.'

Shirley sniffed and dashed her hand across her eyes. 'I'm sorry, Avril. I don't mean to be a wet blanket, especially when you've all gone to so much trouble.'

'We understand,' Avril said gently. 'But you've got this young man to think of now and he's telling you that he's hungry.'

Tony's funeral had taken place in the village church during Shirley's absence and after her initial outburst of grief she rarely mentioned his name, but Ginnie felt her sister's distress as if the loss had been her own. She knew instinctively that Tony's death had affected Shirley far more deeply than that of poor Charlie. Ginnie could empathise with Shirley as the pain of losing Nick had left her emotions tattered and raw-edged. To the best of her knowledge, Nick was still alive, but even if he survived the war she knew that she would never see him again. He would return to his home town and marry Betsy. They would raise their family and live out their lives in America. The worst part of it was that there was no one in whom she could confide. She could not share her feelings with Shirley, and Avril would almost certainly tell her that it was puppy love, and that there would be many more men in her life before she found the right one, if ever.

Ginnie did her best to put Nick out of her mind, but there were daily reminders of him at the hospital. It seemed Nurse Helga still bore a grudge after all, and had subtle ways of making Ginnie's life as difficult as possible while taking care not to invoke criticism from her superiors. She never overstepped the mark, but she made it plain to all that Ginnie was very much her inferior. Ginnie would have taken great delight in telling Nurse Helga exactly what she thought of her, had she not needed the wage packet she collected every Friday. But for people like Meriel and the rest of her workmates, Ginnie might not have possessed the determination to go on.

Two days before Christmas, she was sorting through the morning post when she came across an aerogram addressed to her. Avril had taken the pony and trap into town to join the queues at the shops in the hope of being able to purchase a few extras for the festive season, and Shirley was in the sitting room, giving Colin his feed. Ginnie's hand shook as she opened the envelope and her eyes misted with tears. The piece of paper, no bigger than a postcard, was from Nick. He had drawn a cartoon of a snowman with a sad expression on its round face, and beneath it the words – *I feel like this guy. Yours ever, Nick.*

She struggled between tears and laughter. He had not forgotten her and the message was in the picture, although she was not exactly certain of its meaning. Perhaps it meant that his heart was frozen like that of the snowman? She might never know, but whether or not it was foolish, it lifted her spirits and gave her hope. She was in his thoughts as he was in hers. It might be crazy but she felt happier than she had since the day he left. She took the Christmas cards and placed them on the kitchen table for Avril to open when she returned from town. There was one addressed to them with a London postmark and she took it through to Shirley who had managed to hitch Colin over her uninjured shoulder and was attempting to burp him.

'I need to be a blooming contortionist,' she said crossly. 'Poor little chap; he gets jiggled to bits by his one-armed mummy.'

Ginnie hurried to the sofa and took him from her. 'I'll swap him for a Christmas card from Mum and Dad,' she said, handing it to Ginnie. 'Come on, Colin old chap. Let's have a big burp and then I'll put you in your pram for your nap.'

'Are you sure it's not too cold?' Shirley asked anxiously. 'I mean, he's so little. I don't want him to catch pneumonia.'

'It's up to you,' Ginnie said patiently. 'Mum always said she put us outside in all weathers except fog and snow.'

'Make sure he's well wrapped up then.' Shirley

glanced at the writing inside the card. 'Mum and Dad send their love and a big kiss for Colin. Isn't that sweet? I can't wait to take him home and show him off.'

Ginnie eyed her curiously. 'Doesn't it worry you that V2s are dropping from the sky without warning? Mum and Dad are in the firing line.'

'Don't say things like that,' Shirley said, shuddering. 'I refuse to think about it.'

'Yes, you're right. I'm sorry I mentioned it.' Ginnie gave Colin an encouraging pat on the back and he uttered a satisfactory belch. 'Well done, my boy,' she said, chuckling. 'That was a corker.'

Shirley looked up, angling her head. 'You're very cheerful all of a sudden. What's got into you?'

'I'm trying to get into the Christmas spirit,' Ginnie said, hoping that she sounded convincing as Shirley was no fool and would be quick to spot a lie. 'But I'm sorry if I'm being insensitive,' she added hastily. 'I mean it's not long since . . .' Realising that she was making things worse she smiled apologetically. 'I'm sorry.'

'It's all right. I'm not going to break down every time someone mentions his name. I miss him like mad, but I've got Colin to think of now. He's the most important man in my life and always will be.'

Ginnie cradled him in her arms. 'He's adorable, even when he yells.'

'You wouldn't say that if you still shared my room.

At two o'clock in the morning he's not such a little angel, but I love him all the same.'

'It was good of Avril to let me use the spare room.'

'Well, she doesn't get many people wanting to stay in the middle of winter, and hopefully the war will be over by the spring and we can go home. I love Avril, but I don't want Colin to grow up in a pub, and I've got to think of the future. I've a child to support and I need to get a job.'

'You mustn't start worrying about that now. I'll stay on at the hospital and that will keep us for the time being. You've got to concentrate on getting fit again.'

Shirley pulled a face. 'I know, but I'm not a patient person. I want this bloody war to be over so that we can get on with our lives.'

'Don't we all?' Ginnie glanced out of the window and frowned. 'I think it's going to rain. I'll put the young master to bed in his cot and then I'm off to work. I'm on a late shift today so I won't be home until this evening. Will you be all right until Avril gets back from the shops?'

Shirley raised herself from the sofa. 'I'm not an invalid. I can open up if she's not here in time and there aren't likely to be many customers this morning. Everyone will be doing their last minute preparations for Christmas.'

'All right, if you're sure.'

'Stop fussing and go to work. It's pay day.'

*

Nurse Helga pounced on Ginnie before she had time to fasten up her shapeless and extremely unflattering overall. 'What time do you call this, Travis?'

'I'm on a late shift, Nurse Halvorsen.'

Helga's lips tightened and her pale blue eyes narrowed. 'Just because it's Christmas doesn't give you girls the right to be slack.'

Ginnie concentrated on buttoning up the starched cotton. 'Yes, nurse.'

Helga glared at her. 'Butter wouldn't melt in your mouth, would it, Travis? You can't fool me with your innocent schoolgirl act.'

'I'm sorry?' Ginnie looked up, startled by this unexpected attack so early in the day. Helga usually waited until she found something to complain about before berating her verbally. 'I'm not with you, Nurse Halvorsen.'

'You pretend to be naïve and sweet but you're a Lorelei in disguise. You took him away from me, you little bitch.'

Ginnie glanced round to see if there was anyone close enough to hear Helga's vituperative remarks, but the corridor was deserted. 'I don't know what you're talking about.'

'Yes, you do. Nick and I were an item before you sashayed onto the scene.'

'I'm not having this conversation, Nurse Halvorsen. There's nothing going on between Nick and me.'

'Not now there isn't.' Helga's lips curled in a feline snarl. 'I've just spoken to Danny Flynn and he told me that Nick has been repatriated to the States.'

Ginnie knew only too well what this meant and she clutched the door jamb for support. 'He's been wounded?'

Helga leaned forward so that her face was close to Ginnie's. 'You don't care for him, huh? Well, sister, you just let your feelings show and I know you've been lying all along. Yes, he was injured but unfortunately it wasn't fatal. The two-timing nogoodnik deserved all he got, but he's gone home to his faithful sweetheart Betsy, and that's the last either of us will see of him. Merry Christmas, Travis.' She stalked away with a backward wave of her hand, swinging her hips as she went.

Ginnie slid her hand into her pocket and pulled out the crumpled aerogram. The snowman's face seemed even sadder now, and icy fingers clutched at her heart. Helga's spiteful words echoed in her head. 'He's gone home to his faithful sweetheart Betsy.' She had known it would happen but a small part of her had hoped that he might return to England one last time. Now she knew that would never happen. Nick was lost to her forever. She picked up a mop and bucket and set off for the first ward on her list, but her mind was not on her work. She responded automatically to the cheerful banter from the patients who were patently bored and in need of company, but all she could think about was Nick. His injuries must have been severe for him to have been sent back to the States, but if Helga had been in full possession of the facts she had not been forthcoming. She had wanted to cause pain and she had succeeded.

The rest of the day passed in a blur. Ginnie exchanged compliments of the season with those who were going off duty and she managed to keep out of Helga's way until her shift ended. She had changed into her own clothes, depositing her overall in the linen hamper ready to be taken to the laundry, and had just left the locker room used by the civilian staff when she saw Danny coming along the corridor. She hurried towards him. 'Danny.' She uttered his name on a sob, and he wrapped his arms around her.

'Hey, kid. What's with the tears? Has the wicked witch of the west been getting at you again?'

She gulped and swallowed, easing away from him. 'I thought you liked Helga.'

He shrugged his shoulders. 'She's okay, I guess, and I felt sorry for her at the village hop when she turned up on her own and no one asked her to dance. But she shouldn't take her personal problems out on you.'

'I just seem to get on her wrong side.' Ginnie struggled to hold back a fresh flood of tears. 'I'm sorry, Danny. I've had a rotten day and I've been out of my mind with worry.'

He pressed a crumpled hanky into her hand. 'I guess she told you about Nick?'

'Only to gloat. She blames me for their break-up.'

He hooked his arm around her shoulders. 'It's all in her mind, honey. They were never an item, but Helga still has a thing for Nick and she's not the forgiving type.'

'You can say that again.' Ginnie blew her nose, burying her face in the soft folds of the handkerchief. 'Sorry, I'll wash this and bring it back tomorrow.'

He dismissed her offer with a casual wave of his hand. 'Don't bother, kid. I've got dozens of the things. My aunts keep the cotton industry in business and they send them to me together with socks and Hershey bars. They seem to think that I'm still five years old.'

'Thanks, Danny.'

'For what, honey?'

'For trying to cheer me up. I'm sorry I blubbed all over your uniform, but I'm so worried about Nick. Do you know anything about his injuries?'

He gave her shoulders a gentle squeeze. 'He was in a lorry convoy when it came under fire. I don't know the exact details, Ginnie, but he underwent surgery in a field hospital. They saved his life, that's for sure, but all I know is that he won't be returning to active duty. I guess we'll have to wait for more news.'

'You are telling me everything, aren't you, Danny?'

'Sure I am. I wouldn't lie to you about something as serious as this, kid. I know how much the guy means to you – to all of us. Nick's the best; he's been like a brother to me. I don't want to lose another pal.'

She tucked his hanky into her pocket. 'I'm really sorry. I wasn't thinking straight, and I miss Tony too. So does Shirley. I hate this damn war.'

'I guess it can't go on much longer, and then I'll go home to LA and take up a position in one of the major hospitals, at least that's the plan. But I'll always remember you and Avril and the pub on the riverbank. Maybe I'll come back one day with a wife and kids and show them where I spent part of the war.' Danny leaned forward and kissed her on the cheek. 'Merry Christmas, honey.'

Despite Avril's best efforts, Christmas was a subdued affair. Food and alcohol were at their scarcest, even allowing for the extras allowed by the Ministry of Food, but as Avril said, an extra one and a half pounds of sugar and eight pennyworth of meat hardly constituted a feast. But at least blackout restrictions were lifted and lights shone through the stained-glass windows of the village church for the first time since the beginning of the war.

Ginnie and Shirley had a brief conversation with their parents on Christmas morning, having booked a trunk call several days previously, but in a way this only made the separation more painful. Ginnie tried to put a brave face on things, but Nick was never far from her thoughts. She had seen men recovering from the type of injuries that he might have suffered and she marvelled at their courage and fortitude as they coped with their disabilities. She made a valiant effort to be positive but her face ached from forcing her muscles into a smile and she seemed to have a lump of lead where her heart should have been.

By nine o'clock she was exhausted and longing for closing time. There were several officers seated around the small tables close to the inglenook, and Lionel Smithers had taken his usual seat at the bar. 'It's been the busiest day of the year.' His grey eyes twinkled and he held out his empty glass. 'Is there any chance of a refill, Avril, my dear?'

She produced a bottle from the shelf under the bar and measured out a generous tot. 'This is the very last of my favourite single malt, Lionel. With the distillery mothballed until goodness knows when, I fear we'll have to drink beer or be strictly teetotal.' She beamed at him. 'And that would never do.'

He raised his glass to her. 'Here's how.' He sipped the whisky with a satisfied smile. 'And here's to an end to hostilities.'

Avril joined him in the toast. 'Amen to that.' She turned to Ginnie with a frown puckering her brow. 'You're very quiet this evening, darling. Are you feeling unwell?'

'No, I'm fine.' Avoiding her aunt's questioning gaze, Ginnie picked up a cloth and began polishing the glasses she had left on the draining board.

As if sensing her mood, Lionel leaned across the counter. 'And how is that fine young fellow Colin?'

Avril pulled a face. 'He has an extraordinarily good pair of lungs. Unfortunately my room is next to Shirley's and the walls are quite thin. I'm not getting my beauty sleep.' She smiled archly, inviting a courteous disclaimer.

Lionel did not disappoint. 'No one would know, my dear.'

'Thank you.' Avril fluttered her eyelashes. 'You always say the sweetest things.'

Their casual banter brought a reluctant smile to Ginnie's lips. 'You two are quite a double act.'

'At least we've cheered you up.' Avril patted her on the shoulder. 'Why don't you go through to the sitting room and put your feet up. You've worked hard all day and it's still Christmas. I can manage the bar and we're hardly likely to get any more customers this evening.'

Just as the words left her lips the door opened and Major Dudley walked into the bar. 'Merry Christmas, Mrs Parkin,' he said solemnly. 'That is, if it isn't too late to offer the compliments of the season.'

'It's never too late for compliments of any kind,' Avril said, beaming. 'What can I get you, major? Although I'm afraid there isn't much choice.'

'I'll take a half pint of bitter, if you please.' He took off his hat and placed it on the stool beside

Lionel. 'Good evening, vicar. I guess you've had a busy day. May I buy you a drink?'

Lionel downed the last of his whisky. 'That would be very kind, major. I'm off duty so to speak, as are you.'

'I guess that neither of us is ever completely off duty, vicar.'

Avril put a half-pint mug of bitter on the counter in front of him. 'That's on the house, major.'

He shook his head. 'I can't allow that, Mrs Parkin. Times are tough in every business.'

'Except yours, major.'

'Sadly so, ma'am.' Major Dudley turned to Ginnie. 'How is Mrs Mallory? She's well, I hope?'

'Very well, thank you, major.'

'And the baby?'

'He's thriving.'

'I'm very glad to hear it.' He took a sip of his drink, eyeing Ginnie over the rim of the glass. 'It was a bad business. Lieutenant Petrillo was a fine officer.'

'Yes, he was.' Ginnie swallowed hard. It would never do to fall apart now.

'As is Lieutenant Miller.' Major Dudley lowered his voice. 'I believe that you were friends?'

She shot a covert glance at Avril but she was deep in conversation with Lionel. Ginnie nodded her head. 'Yes.'

'Then you'll be glad to know that he is on the road to recovery. I heard this afternoon and I thought you would want to know.'

'Thank you, sir.' Ginnie felt her throat constrict and she dropped her gaze, concentrating on the glass in her hand which she had polished to a diamond shine. 'Was he badly wounded?'

'Nothing that won't heal in time, I believe. I haven't had a full report yet, but I gather that he's doing well.'

'I'm glad.' She turned away to put the glass on the shelf but it slipped through her fingers and fell to the floor where it shattered into shards. 'I'll get a dustpan and brush,' she murmured and hurried through to the kitchen before anyone had a chance to comment.

Leaning her hands on the pine table she took deep breaths. Tears of relief ran down her cheeks and a sliver of ice seemed to melt from her heart, but her pleasure was tinged with pain. Whatever the outcome, Nick was lost to her. She must face the fact and try to forget him, but somehow she knew that was asking the impossible.

'What's the matter?' Shirley stood in the sitting-room doorway, staring at her in alarm. 'What's happened?'

'Nothing. I'm just tired and I broke a glass in the bar.'

Shirley swooped on the cupboard where the cleaning materials were kept. 'Well, there's no need to cry about it. I'll clear it up.'

'I'm all right, really.'

Shirley took a hanky from her pocket and tossed

it at her. 'You never have a hanky. You used to wipe your nose on your sleeve when you were little. Mum was always telling you off for it.'

Ginnie wiped her eyes. 'The major was asking after you and Colin. He's a nice man.'

'I can't believe that made you burst into tears.'

'I'm tired, that's all.'

'Yes, you look awful. Go to bed. I'll help Avril clear up, and I could do with some cheerful grown-up company. Colin's adorable but he's not much of a conversationalist.' Shirley waltzed through into the bar and closed the door behind her.

Ginnie went to the sink and filled the kettle. A cup of cocoa would help her to sleep and blot out the memories that haunted her by day.

Unfortunately the cocoa kept her awake and when she did fall asleep she was plagued by night-mares in which Nick suffered the most terrible injuries, and she could do nothing to help him. She woke up in a cold sweat to find Avril shaking her by the shoulders. 'What's the matter?' she demanded sleepily.

'Get up,' Avril said tersely. 'I need you downstairs, now.'

In the half-light of dawn Ginnie realised that she had never seen her aunt without her customary maquillage. Avril's hairnet had slipped to one side revealing tight curls secured with criss-crossed hair-grips. 'What's wrong? Is it Shirley or the baby?'

Avril's eyes brimmed with tears. 'Just come

downstairs and I'll explain. Shirley's fainted and the baby's bawling his head off. We've just had some terrible news. I need you to be strong, darling. For all of us.' Avril's voice broke on a sob and she rushed from the room.

Chapter Six

'We've got to go home straight away,' Ginnie said dazedly. 'Mum must be in a terrible state.'

'Of course, darling.' Avril sank down on a chair at the kitchen table and reached for her cigarette case. Her hands trembled as she selected one and lit it, inhaling deeply.

'I can't believe that he's dead,' Shirley whispered, dragging herself to a sitting position on the sofa. 'Why did it have to be our dad?' She held out her arms to Ginnie, who had plucked an irate Colin from his cot and brought him downstairs. 'Give him to me. It's time for his next feed.'

Ginnie laid the sobbing child in his mother's arms. 'Poor little chap; he'll never know his grandad.'

'That's the least of your worries, Virginia,' Avril said, exhaling a stream of smoke into the beamed ceiling. 'I don't want to sound mercenary, but how will Mildred manage financially? I doubt if their mortgage was paid off and she doesn't know the first thing about business. Who will run the shop?'

Ginnie opened her mouth to protest and then closed it again. The shocking news that their father had been killed was still sinking in, but even as she struggled to come to terms with the situation she realised that Avril was simply being practical. Dad had been the main breadwinner, and she had worked for what amounted to pocket money after she had paid her contribution to the housekeeping. Mum had strong views on that score and had insisted that both she and Shirley must contribute part of their wages towards their keep, but their father had paid all the bills.

Avril's calm assessment of the situation brought Ginnie back to her senses. She went to the stove and put the kettle on the hob. 'I'll run the shop,' she said firmly. 'I've worked there since I left school and I suppose I know as much about it as anyone.' She reached for the teapot and the caddy. 'Strong sweet tea. That's what Dad would have suggested in a case like this. Not Fred Chinashop's milky concoction.' Her breath hitched on a sob and she dashed her hand across her eyes. 'Avril's right, Shirley, we've got to be practical and put Mum first. We can't let her lose the house. We just can't.'

Shirley's eyes were swimming with tears but she managed a wobbly smile. 'I'll be sorry to leave here, Avril. But we have to go home.'

Avril took another long drag on her cigarette before stubbing it out in the ashtray. 'Of course you must, but I'll miss you all terribly. It won't be the same here without you.'

'We'll come back for holidays, just like we did when we were kids.' Ginnie tried to sound cheerful, but her voice broke and she turned her attention to making the tea. She had always wondered why people made tea in a crisis and now she knew.

Avril rose from the table. 'I must get dressed.' Catching sight of her reflection in the wall mirror she uttered a squeak of horror. 'Oh my God. Just look at me. I'm an absolute fright.' She left the room with her silk peignoir flapping around her like the wings of an agitated angel and her swansdown slippers clattering on the tiled floor.

Despite her sorrow, Ginnie had to smile. 'Even if the world was about to end Avril would still insist on being dressed for the occasion.'

'Quite right too,' Shirley said, nodding with approval. 'She has standards, and I admire that.' She studied her left hand, staring at the narrow gold band on her ring finger. 'Mum's got her wish, though. Everyone will think that I'm a war widow and not a silly tart who couldn't say no.'

Ginnie almost scalded herself as she warmed the teapot. 'Don't say things like that, Shirley. You loved Charlie and you would have married him if he hadn't got killed.'

'I would, because that was what was expected of me, but I don't think I loved him. I fancied Laurence like mad, but I loved Tony, and I'll never feel that way about anyone else. I expect I'll marry some day but he'll always be second best.'

Ginnie measured tea into the pot, mindful of rationing but making it a little stronger than usual.

'What about Laurence? You told me that you fell for him and had a fling. Does that mean he might be Colin's father?'

Shirley shifted the baby to her shoulder and patted his tiny back. 'That seems like a hundred years ago. I honestly don't know which of them fathered Colin, but he's my life now and my priorities have changed.' She stroked her son's downy head. 'I just wish Dad could have seen my little boy. He'd be so proud to have a grandson. He'd have taken him to cricket matches and taught him how to play football.'

Ginnie poured the tea. 'I still can't believe he's gone. Maybe we'll get home and find it was all a mistake and he wasn't on fire watch when the V2 exploded.' She handed a cup to her sister. 'I'm on duty this morning. I'd better get ready.'

'You're not going to work, are you? Apart from anything else, it's Boxing Day. It's a bank holiday.'

'It's a hospital, Shirley. The wards have to be cleaned whatever the day, and I'll have to tell them I'm leaving. I expect there'll be forms to fill in or something like that. But we'll catch the first train out in the morning, and that's a promise. We can't leave Mum to struggle through this on her own.'

They arrived home late the next evening. It was not a long walk from the station but Ginnie had to carry their luggage, although most of it had been sent on ahead in one of Avril's trunks which bore exotic labels like *Cairo* and *Istanbul*. Shirley managed to hook Colin over her good shoulder and Ginnie had made a sling out of one of Avril's cashmere shawls so that it supported his weight, but even so it was slow progress.

As they walked down Cherry Lane it was strange to see lights in the windows of the houses for the first time in five years, and the contrast between town and country struck Ginnie forcibly. She had grown accustomed to the sounds of the river and the whisper of the breeze rustling the leaves in the overhanging trees. The scent of water and wild flowers, damp earth and even the less fragrant odours of cowpats and horse dung, were absent in the urban landscape. The smell of boiling cabbage, fried onions and chimney smoke filled the air, and even though Cherry Lane was a quiet residential area she could hear the distant rumble of traffic on the main road, and there was a sudden burst of music as a door opened further down the street and two people stood chatting on the front step.

'My feet are killing me,' Shirley moaned as she reached over to unlatch the front gate. 'And I'll swear that Colin has doubled his weight since we left the hospital.'

Ginnie's arms felt as though they were being wrenched from their sockets as she hefted the cases up the garden path, but she said nothing. She was struggling with her emotions as well as the heavy luggage as she waited for Shirley to fumble through the contents of her handbag for the door key. It was hard to imagine the state that their mother might be in when they entered the house. It was even harder to visualise what life would be like without their father.

'At last.' Shirley put the key in the lock and opened the door. 'Mum,' she shouted. 'We're home.'

Ginnie heaved the cases into the hall and let them drop to the floor. Her cold fingers had been numb but now they tingled painfully with pins and needles. Shirley was heading for the kitchen when the door opened and Mildred rushed out to greet them.

'Let me see my grandson,' she cried excitedly. 'I've been waiting all day for you to arrive.' She snatched Colin from his mother, holding him at arm's length with a delighted smile. 'Isn't he a bonny baby? Hello, Colin. I'm your granny.'

'Are you all right, Mum?' Shirley said anxiously.

Ginnie hesitated, weighing up the situation before she spoke. She had expected her mother to be prostrate with grief, but she was acting as though nothing had happened. She looked positively cheerful, and that was worrying. 'How are you, Mum?'

Mildred held the baby in the crook of her arm. 'I'm bearing up. Life has to go on, girls.' She bustled into the dining room. 'I've had supper keeping warm for ages. I hope it's not ruined.'

Shirley hurried after her. 'I should see to Colin first, Mum. He needs changing and he's ready for a feed.'

'Don't worry about the meal, Mum.' Ginnie followed them, noting with a shiver that the table was laid for four. Her father's place at the head was set as if he were about to walk into the room.

Paper chains were draped from the central light and pinned to the picture rail, but they were dusty and crumpled and might have been salvaged from one of the cardboard boxes in the attic. There were springs of holly on the mantelpiece next to the black slate clock in the shape of a Roman temple, and a red candle had been stuck on a saucer and placed on the sideboard next to a bowl of apples. The decorations put up in anticipation of the season of peace and goodwill looked sad and shabby and Ginnie had to fight back tears. She was saved from making any comment when Colin took his cue and started to whimper.

Shirley eased him gently from her mother's grasp. 'Let me have him, Mum. I'll go up to my room and see to him there.'

'Indeed you won't,' Mildred said sternly. 'I lit the fire in the front room two hours ago and it'll be much warmer than upstairs. Take him in there if you must, but then we'll eat. I'm not letting good food go to waste.'

Ginnie exchanged anxious glances with her sister. 'Why don't you sit down and let me do the work, Mum? You don't have to manage on your own now. We're here.'

Mildred's face crumpled and tears spurted from

her eyes. 'I have to carry on as normal, Ginnie. If I stop I have to face the fact that my Sidney's gone forever. That bloody V2 took him away from me. I'll never forgive Hitler. Never.' She buried her face in her hands and sobbed.

Shirley backed towards the door. 'I'll be in the lounge if you need me.'

It was an odd sort of homecoming. Mildred's moods seemed to alternate between desperate attempts to appear normal and a downward spiral into tears and depression. After an uncomfortable meal that included the dreaded Woolton pie, Shirley was pale and exhausted and Mildred insisted on doing the washing-up, shooing them off as if they were still schoolgirls. 'You look worn out, Shirley,' she said as she piled up the dirty crockery. 'Go to bed. I'll see to everything down here.' She held up her hand as Ginnie opened her mouth to protest. 'No, honestly, I must keep to my routine.'

Reluctantly, Ginnie left her to cope on her own and she followed Shirley upstairs to her room, where Colin had been put to bed in a drawer taken from the tallboy. Swaddled in a shawl he lay on a pillow like a tiny mummy stolen from an Egyptian tomb.

'Will Mum be all right?' Shirley slumped down on her bed and slipped off her shoes. 'She's fine one moment and then she collapses.'

'It'll take time,' Ginnie said softly. 'We've got to be supportive.'

'I'll have to get a job. D'you think that Mum is capable of looking after Colin?'

'We'll have to wait and see.' Ginnie lifted Shirley's case onto the bed and opened it. 'You'll have to wait until you're fit enough to work.'

'But we haven't got any money. I don't know how Mum is fixed.'

'We can hardly barge into her room and ask how much cash she's got in the bank,' Ginnie said with a wry smile. 'Anyway, tomorrow I'm going to open up the shop. It'll be business as usual. That's what Dad would have wanted and that's what I'm going to do.'

Walking into the shop for the first time in six months felt like entering a foreign country. Without her father's cheery presence the retail area seemed dark and oppressive. The tall rolls of linoleum towered over her and the smell of linseed oil and hessian was evocative of happier times, but that was little comfort now. The utility furniture was practical but dull, and the stock was sadly depleted. There were a few carpet squares set out on the floor and rolls of broadloom stacked against the walls. Whether it was the cold grey December day or the gloom that hung above her in a dark cloud, Ginnie felt a shiver run down her spine. No wonder trade had dropped off if this was what prospective customers found when they entered the shop.

She took off her hat and peeled off her gloves as

she marched down the aisle that separated the displays. She switched the light on in the office and her heart sank as she took in the chaotic scene. Without her there to keep order her father had allowed the paperwork to pile up, and the filing baskets overflowed with bills, dockets and receipts. Dirty crockery littered the desk and the wastepaper bin was exploding with rubbish. She took off her coat, rolled up her sleeves and set to work, starting with the cups and saucers. She wrinkled her nose at the smell of sour milk and a rancid half-eaten cheese sandwich that she found hidden beneath an order book. A trip to the dustbin in the back yard was her first priority and then she unlocked the outside lavatory where there was a small hand basin and a gas geyser, which of course had gone out and needed to be relit.

Eventually she found a box of matches hidden in one of the desk drawers together with a packet of Woodbines, which was her father's guilty secret. Mildred had refused point blank to allow him to smoke at home, and he used to light up the moment he sat down at his desk. Ginnie could still smell a hint of tobacco smoke and the walls were yellowed with nicotine. She hurried back to the geyser and after a few attempts she got it going again, and the water gurgled and burped its way through the pipes to splatter into the small sink. Having left the cups to soak she went back inside to find Fred Chinashop waiting for her with a mug of tea in his hand.

He held it out to her and his bottom lip quivered. 'I'm so sorry about your dad, Ginnie.'

'Thank you, Fred.' She took it from him with a grateful smile. 'That was a kind thought.'

'He was the best. Sid Travis was the finest man I ever knew.'

She stared at the milky liquid, knowing that it would be horribly sweet and sickly, but she took a sip anyway. 'I needed that,' she said diplomatically. She looked round for a space where she could put the cup down and there was none. 'It's a bit of a mess in here.'

'You're not going to open up, are you?' Fred peered at her and his eyes looked enormous behind the pebble lenses of his spectacles. 'I mean, people would understand if . . .'

'I'm carrying on where Dad left off,' Ginnie said firmly. 'He spent half his life building up this business and I don't intend to let him down.'

'But it's not the business for a young woman to cope with alone.'

'Why not? I've worked here since I left school. I know as much about it as my dad did.'

Fred shuffled his feet and stared at a point some-where above her left shoulder. 'I – er – well, I mean you're a slip of a girl. You couldn't lift a heavy piece of furniture or a roll of lino on your own.'

'I'll take on someone who can do the things that I can't manage on my own. I'm here to provide a service and that's what I'll do.'

'Well, good luck, Ginnie. If there's anything I can do to help, just bang on the wall and I'll pop round.' Fred cocked his head on one side. 'That was the shop door if I'm not mistaken. I think you've got a customer.'

That morning Ginnie sold a doormat and a kitchen stool. It would not make their fortune but it was a start, and as Mrs Richmond pointed out when she brought down a cheese scone hot from the oven, it was too soon after Christmas to expect people to go shopping for anything other than food. There were the usual queues at the butcher's shop, the grocer's and the greengrocer's, but that was to be expected. She stood over Ginnie while she ate the scone. 'That'll keep you going until lunchtime,' she said with a nod of approval. 'You're a brave girl, Ginnie. Your dad would be proud of you.' Her eyes misted with tears and she kissed Ginnie on the cheek before bustling out of the shop, taking her plate with her.

Ginnie stood in the middle of the aisle, gazing round at the practical but unimaginative displays. She had often made suggestions in the past, but her father was conservative in his outlook and unreceptive to her ideas. 'It's dull,' she said out loud. 'Sorry, Dad, if you're looking down at me, but this shop needs a woman's touch and that's what it's going to get.' She hurried through to the office and made a space on the desk, digging the telephone out from beneath a bundle of receipts. She found the telephone directory on the floor under a pile of show cards. She flicked through the pages, found the number and dialled.

'Hello.' A woman's voice quavered at the other end of the line.

'Hello, Mrs Fitzwilliam. It's Ginnie Travis here.'

'Oh, I'm so sorry, my dear. Jimmy told me about your poor father. It's a tragedy.'

'Yes, it is, but I'm going to keep the business going. I wondered if Jimmy was free to come round and see me today.' Ginnie heard a sharp intake of breath and waited for Mrs Fitzwilliam to recover from her surprise.

'Yes, dear,' Mrs Fitzwilliam murmured after a long pause. 'I'm sure he'd be only too pleased. He's just gone to the shops for me but I'll tell him as soon as he gets back.'

'Thank you.' Ginnie replaced the receiver with a sigh of relief.

Jimmy Fitzwilliam had worked part time for her father since he was a boy. Sid Travis had taken him under his wing because he had seen something in Jimmy that other people seemed to miss. Jimmy had always been a big fellow and a bit slow when it came to school work, but he had shown an aptitude for both carpet and linoleum laying and could measure a room accurately, even though he had difficulty in working out the yardage required for each specific job. In the past this had been Sid's domain and he had also submitted the estimates, leaving it to Jimmy to carry out the physical work. Jimmy had learned to drive and when he was called up had been given a job as an army driver, but his weak chest had caused him to be invalided out after the first winter of the war. He had returned to his old job with Sid and had joined the Home Guard.

He arrived just as Ginnie had finished tidying the office and was sorting the work into relevant piles. His big face beamed with pleasure on seeing her but this was replaced almost immediately by a look of consternation. He dragged his cap off and grasped it in front of him, stuttering an apology. 'I – I'm sorry about your dad, miss.'

'Thank you, Jimmy.' She guided him out into the shop and pointed out the items of furniture and floor coverings that she wanted him to move. While he was doing this a woman came in to enquire about a coffee table and went off with a price list. Another woman wandered in wanting to purchase a tablecloth and Ginnie explained patiently that she would have to go to a haberdashery or visit one of the big stores in Oxford Street. 'But I've been saving my coupons,' the woman said angrily. 'I don't want to travel up West to buy a single item. You should think about what people want, young lady.' She marched out into the street, casting disgruntled looks over her shoulder, but she had given Ginnie an idea.

*

At home that evening, supper was fish pie made with tinned snoek, which Mildred had previously scorned, saying that it was only fit for cat food, but with everything in short supply she declared that they were the beggars who could not afford to be choosers. Ginnie ate hers, barely registering the taste as her mind was buzzing with ideas for the shop. Shirley pushed her portion around her plate but eventually hunger got the better of her. 'I'm only eating this because I'm breast-feeding,' she said grudgingly. 'Colin must come first, but if it poisons me I'll never forgive you, Mum.'

'Oh, eat up and stop grumbling,' Mildred snapped.

Shirley stared at her in surprise. 'Mum?'

Mildred pushed her plate away, leaving her own portion half eaten. 'I know it's horrible, love, but there's nothing I can do about it. We're broke, girls. Your dad didn't have any life insurance and there's the funeral to pay for as well as the mortgage and the costs of running a house. Sid did all that and now I've got to take over. I don't know how I'll manage.'

'What about your savings?' Shirley said, frowning. 'Dad was always telling us to put our pennies in the bank.'

'We've been dipping into them when business was bad. There's not much left.'

'You should have told us, Mum.' Ginnie laid her hand on her mother's shoulder. 'We'd have stayed here and helped out and never mind what the gossips said.'

'It's all right for you, Ginnie. You wouldn't have had to live with the disgrace,' Shirley said crossly.

'I'd have had more sense than to get pregnant.'

Shirley's eyes welled with tears and her mouth drooped at the corners. 'That was mean.'

Ginnie sighed, wishing that she had not spoken so hastily. She moderated her tone. 'Look, it's happened and you've got a lovely baby boy. Dad's dead and gone and we've no choice but to keep going.' She turned to her mother. 'I'm sorting out the books at the shop, but it will take a few days. Dad left them in a bit of a mess, but if you and I go over your bank statements we might be able to make some savings.'

Mildred raised her head, glaring at Ginnie. 'What do you know about money matters, miss?'

'I've done the books for Dad for the last two years. He was hopeless at keeping accounts and he'd never chase people who hadn't paid up on time. I won't be so lenient. I've got ideas for the shop and the war can't go on much longer. When it ends people will need to rebuild their bombed-out houses and they'll have to furnish them. I'm going to make the business pay and I'm going to make a success of it. And that is a promise.'

'And I'll go back to work as soon as I'm able,' Shirley added hastily. 'We'll look after you, Mum. You mustn't worry.'

Mildred wiped her eyes on her pinafore, which normally she would have taken off before sitting down to dine. She looked from one to the other. 'You're good girls. I'm lucky to have you.'

Sid's funeral was supposed to be a quiet affair but when they arrived at the church, having left Colin in the capable hands of Mrs Martin's fifteen-year-old granddaughter, Ginnie was amazed to see that the church was packed with mourners. Mildred had expected a few friends to turn up, but the meat paste sandwiches they had prepared earlier that day would not go far, and neither would the sponge cake made with liquid paraffin and filled with a concoction of cornflour, milk and a minute amount of sugar, which was somewhat grandiosely named mock cream in the government recipe leaflet. Ginnie gave her mother an encouraging smile. 'It's wonderful to think that Dad was so popular.'

Mildred's bottom lip trembled but she bore up bravely until the last minute at the graveside when she broke down in floods of tears, Ginnie and Shirley were at a loss as to what to do next, but Mrs Martin, the woman who had spent most of her widowhood tittle-tattling about her neighbours, suddenly came to the fore and escorted Mildred into the church hall. There was little that Ginnie could do other than hurry after them and to her consternation she realised that everyone was following her. She shot an anxious glance at Shirley but she was deep in conversation with Olivia Mallory. That was a concern in itself but Ginnie was too anxious about her mother to waste time worrying about what Shirley would say to Laurence's sister, or whether she would admit to having given birth to an illegitimate baby and had been masquerading as Mrs Mallory. It would be interesting to find out, but not now.

Ginnie burst into the church hall and was met by the ladies of the WVS who were manning the tea urns and trestle tables which appeared to be groaning beneath the weight of plates piled high with cucumber sandwiches and a selection of home-made cakes. Mildred was sitting on a chair being ministered to by Mrs Martin and another lady who was pressing a cup of tea into her hands. Ginnie hurried over to them. 'Are you all right, Mum?'

'Yes, dear. I'm sorry to make such a show of myself, and I wasn't expecting all this. I don't know what to say, but I'm very grateful to everyone.'

'Quite so,' Mrs Martin said briskly. 'There are a lot of people who have reason to be grateful to your Sidney. Drink your tea, dear.'

The WVS lady beamed at Ginnie. 'You don't remember me, Virginia, but I was Brown Owl when you were in the Brownies.' She held out her hand. 'Eudora Fox. How do you do?'

Ginnie shook her hand. 'Very well, thank you, Mrs Fox. I do remember you now.'

Eudora threw back her head and laughed. 'My dear, you were very young and you would have thought I was positively ancient, which of course

I am now, but the WVS has been a lifesaver. I love to feel useful.' She drew Ginnie to one side. 'And your father was an amazingly kind man. He was generous in the extreme both with his time and with his financial assistance. There are many people here today who have him to thank for helping them through hard times, but I'm sure you know that.'

'Hmm,' Ginnie said vaguely. 'Of course.' This was news to her but it might explain the parlous state of her father's bank account. She moved aside as people jostled to offer their condolences to her mother, and was immediately pounced upon by Shirley who grabbed her by the arm.

'You didn't tell me that you'd invited Olivia,' Shirley hissed. 'How could you?'

'I didn't invite her. She must have seen the notice in the local paper.'

Shirley released her with a dissatisfied grunt. 'She caught me on the hop. She wanted to know where I'd been all this time.'

'You didn't tell her?'

'How could I? She'd pass the news on to Laurence and I'll never see him again.'

Ginnie angled her head, puzzled. 'But I thought you were in love with Tony. You said . . .'

'I know what I said and I meant it, silly. I did love Tony but he's gone and Colin needs a father. I like Laurence and his family are well off, besides which . . .' She hesitated, blushing furiously.

131

'What have you done?'

'Well, you know I told everyone in the pub that I was Mrs Mallory.'

'Of course I do, and I thought it was a stupid idea.'

'Maybe, but now I'm stuck with it. When Avril took me to register the birth I had to give Colin a name, and I didn't want the world to know that he was a little – you know what.'

'Whose name did you give him?' Even as the question left her lips, Ginnie knew the answer.

'Colin Mallory.' Shirley's lips trembled and she glanced round nervously, lowering her tone to a whisper. 'I know that it might have been better to use Charlie's surname, but I couldn't bear to have a kid called Colin Crisp.'

'You didn't put Laurence down as the father, did you?'

'No, I'm not that stupid. I left that blank. You don't have to put the father's name, and I suppose some girls don't know who it was anyway.' Shirley's eyes filled with tears. 'And I suppose I'm one of them. Anyway, I gave my name as Shirley Mallory. I'll go to prison and you'll have to bring my son up for me.'

Ginnie shook off her restraining hand. 'You're an idiot, but I don't think it's illegal to use an alias. You're going to have to be Shirley Mallory from now on, although I don't know how Olivia's family will like that, let alone Laurence.'

'He'll never speak to me again,' Shirley said, hanging her head. 'I deserve everything I get for being such a silly snob, but I don't know how to tell Olivia.'

'Tell me what?'

Ginnie spun round to see Olivia Mallory standing at her side.

Chapter Seven

There seemed to be little point in prevarication. Shirley's stricken expression was a complete giveaway, and Olivia had the tenacity of a bull terrier. She was smiling but her eyes were alight with curiosity. 'Do tell,' she said in a tone that brooked no argument. 'What secrets are you keeping from me? You were always a terrible liar so you'd better own up, Shirley Travis.'

Ginnie glanced over her shoulder, hoping that her mother was not within earshot. 'I think you'd better make a clean breast of it, Shirley.'

'Now I'm intrigued. Did you elope with my brother? Is that the big secret?' Olivia folded her arms. 'Spit it out, old thing. It can't be that bad.'

Shirley turned to Ginnie for support. 'You tell her. I feel such a silly ass.'

'You're that all right,' Ginnie said with feeling. 'You got yourself into this fix. You're the one who needs to give Olivia an explanation.'

'This is getting more interesting by the minute.' Olivia leaned against the ancient ice-cold radiator, pulling a face. 'You'd think they could allow a little bit of heating in this weather. It's freezing in here.'

'I'll get you a cup of tea. That'll warm you up.' Shirley started to walk away but Ginnie caught her by the wrist.

'No, you don't. I'll fetch the tea. You stay here and sort things out.'

Olivia held up her hand. 'I don't want a cup of tea. If you don't spill the beans, Shirley, I'll have to shake it out of you as I did when we were in the fifth form.'

'You wouldn't.'

Olivia grinned. 'It always worked at school.'

'Well, all right then.' Shirley took a deep breath. 'I went to Shropshire because I was pregnant.'

Ginnie patted her on the shoulder. She knew how much it had cost Shirley to make such an admission, especially to someone she had always looked up to and had tried to emulate. 'Good for you,' she said softly.

'Really?' Olivia's eyes lit up and she leaned closer. 'You've got a baby?'

'Yes,' Shirley said simply. 'A boy.'

'I don't quite know what to say in the circumstances. I take it you're not married.'

'No.'

Ginnie held her breath, waiting for Olivia to digest this piece of information. She half expected Olivia to walk off in disgust but after a moment's pause, she threw back her head and laughed. 'Oh my God. Now I need something stronger than tea. I could absolutely murder a gin and tonic.' She was suddenly serious. 'I'm sorry, I shouldn't laugh. I mean I don't know whether to congratulate or commiserate. It's a bit of a devil, isn't it? Who's the father, or don't you know?'

Visibly offended, Shirley drew herself up to her full height. 'Of course I know who it is.'

Olivia narrowed her eyes. 'It wasn't my brother, was it? Not Laurence, surely? He's so awfully prim and proper about things like that.'

'What's the matter, Olivia? Don't you think I'm good enough for him?' Shirley's cheeks flooded with colour. 'What would you say if I told you that you have a nephew?'

'Steady on,' Ginnie whispered. 'People are looking. Don't make a scene.'

'I'd think it was frightfully funny,' Olivia said carelessly. 'But I don't think that Mummy and Daddy would approve.' She flicked her ash-blonde hair back from her face.

'Then they'll just have to get used to it,' Shirley said angrily. 'Laurence is the father and we're going to be married. I'm surprised he didn't tell you.'

Ginnie stifled a gasp of dismay. She had not seen this coming. 'Shirley,' she said urgently. 'This has gone far enough.'

'Come on, then, Shirley.' Olivia struck a pose. 'Admit that it's a pack of lies. I'll bet the father is that chap from the sewage works. That would be about your mark.'

'Charlie worked for the water board,' Shirley said

through clenched teeth. 'He was a decent bloke and now he's dead. But my son's birth certificate gives his name as Colin Travis Mallory and I've changed my surname to Mallory so that it doesn't matter whether Laurence marries me or not. You and I are very nearly sisters-in-law, Olivia. We're equals now so you can't patronise me like you did when we were at school.'

Olivia's face paled to ashen. 'I don't know what you're talking about. And you hardly knew Laurence. How dare you take his name?'

'Of course I know him. He was always there in the background while we were growing up, even if he didn't take any notice of me then, but that all changed at the tennis club dance last April.'

'It was just a fling before he returned to duty,' Olivia said slowly. 'I wouldn't have thrown him your way if I'd known that beneath the boring working-class mantle of respectability you were really a man-eating shark. Besides which, you were always the class clown and no one ever took you seriously, let alone my brother.'

Ginnie fisted her hands at her sides. She might tease her sister but she was damned if she was going to let Olivia speak to her in such a manner. 'That's enough. There's no need to be mean.'

'She's making it all up,' Olivia said, scowling. 'Laurence would never tie himself to a girl from Cherry Lane.'

'That's what you think.' Shirley leaned towards

Olivia with a martial light in her eyes. 'Laurence and I got on like a house on fire at the dance and he took me home afterwards. He's not a stuck-up snob like you and he didn't think I was a clown. We had a cosy half-hour snogging in the back seat of your father's car, only it went a bit further than that. Do I have to spell it out for you, Olivia?'

Ginnie grabbed her by the arm. 'That's enough, Shirley.'

'It's the sort of talk she expects from a common working-class girl,' Shirley said with a defiant toss of her head. 'What else can I say?'

'I think you've said too much already.' Olivia picked up her handbag and slung it over her shoulder. 'I don't believe a word of it. Larry's far too honourable to behave like that, and anyway he wouldn't want to tie himself to a family like yours. He's got better taste.'

Shirley raised her hand as if to strike Olivia but Ginnie stepped in between them. 'I think you'd better leave. You've gone too far this time, Olivia. That was a cruel thing to say.'

'It's the truth, but don't worry, I'm going. I'll tell Larry about your little plan to trap him into marriage, Shirley. It won't work.' She stormed off, pushing her way through the crowd of mourners.

'You've done it now,' Ginnie hissed. 'What on earth possessed you to make up a story like that?'

'I wasn't making it up.' Shirley hung her head. 'Anyway, it was Olivia's fault. She's always treated me like an inferior. I'm sick of being patronised by her and her family.'

'But you like Laurence. You asked him to our house for tea.'

'Yes, I did. I do like him, a lot, but I know he's too upper class for a girl like me. I suppose it was wishful thinking that a chap like him would want to marry me.'

'Don't be silly. You're as good as the next person and you don't need to have a name like Mallory to prove it.' Ginnie enveloped her in a hug. 'Forget them. They're not worth worrying about, but Mum is and she needs our support to get through this.'

In the days that followed Ginnie was too busy assessing the needs of the shop to worry overmuch about her sister's private life. Laurence was away at sea and unlikely to get shore leave for a while at least, and Olivia had made it clear that she wanted nothing to do with Shirley or the baby. Ginnie could only hope that Olivia did not mention the conversation to anyone, but she did not hold out much hope. It would be awful if Laurence returned home from sea and heard the rumours that were bound to circulate, as discretion had never been one of Olivia's virtues.

But there was no point worrying about things over which she had no control, and Ginnie spent long hours at the shop, sorting out the chaos in the office, and making the retail area look as attractive as possible. There was still the threat from the V2s, but as the weeks went by it seemed that Kent was suffering the worst of these attacks and London was being spared. Even so, there was a definite demand for furnishings, as Ginnie explained to the bank manager when he granted her a brief interview in the New Year.

'As you know, sir,' she said tactfully, 'the Assistance Board has a scheme for giving grants for essential furnishings and household articles to people who have lost everything in bombing raids and whose incomes fall below a certain level. I would like to increase the range of items that were previously sold in the shop.'

'Really? And what had you in mind?' Mr Walton leaned his elbows on his desk, steepling his fingers and regarding her with a steady look. His expression was not encouraging and she was beginning to feel that she was being interrogated as if she were a spy or a hardened criminal who had come up before a particularly stern judge. She took a sheet of paper from a rather battered file she had taken from the office and handed it to him. 'I've been doing a random survey of shoppers on the High Street, asking them what they would need in such circumstances. I've made a list.'

He set a pince-nez on the end of his nose and studied it. 'This seems quite comprehensive, and I see that you've worked out your costings. Are these accurate, or simply an educated guess?'

'I've been to the wholesalers, Mr Walton. I've studied their price lists and worked everything out to the last penny. I've written down how much I need to restart the business and I'm confident that I can make a go of it.'

'Really?' He slid the sheet of paper across the desk. 'You're very young, Miss Travis. Do you mind telling me how old you are?'

'I'm almost twenty.'

'You're still a minor.' His frown deepened. 'I would be taking a huge risk if I agreed to this loan.'

Ginnie clasped her hands tightly in her lap. This was going to be tougher than she had thought, but she needed the money or the shop would fail and with her mother, Shirley and the baby dependent upon her failure was not an option. 'I am determined to succeed in this, Mr Walton. I've worked in the shop since I left school and I know the customers and I know what they like and what they don't like. Everyone says that the war is almost over and then people will want to rebuild their homes. Men will return from battle whether it's on land, sea or in the air, and they'll get jobs in the local factories and earn good money. Some of that will be spent in my shop.'

For a brief instant she though she saw a flash of humour in Mr Walton's brown eyes, but it was momentary and his expression remained guarded. He looked down at his notes. 'You're extremely confident, Miss Travis, and you seem to have done your homework.'

141

She smiled for the first time during their meeting. 'I studied hard at school, but this is the first opportunity I've had to prove myself. I know I can do it; I just need a helping hand at the start, but I'll go on to bigger and better things.'

He was silent for what seemed like an eternity and he tapped his fountain pen slowly and rhythmically on the blotter, perhaps in time with his thoughts. His deadpan expression gave no clue as to what he was thinking, but the constant drumming might be the death knell of her hopes. She crossed her fingers and her palms were damp with perspiration. She glanced at the Art Deco mantle clock and suddenly its ticking seemed to fill the room, drowning out the tap-tap-tap of the pen on the desk. The sounds echoed in her head and she was beginning to feel faint when Mr Walton cleared his throat and she realised that she had been holding her breath.

'Agreed.' He took the cap off his pen and signed a form with a flourish.

'You mean you'll give me the loan?' Ginnie murmured on a gasp of air.

His lips sketched a smile. 'That's what I said. You do understand the terms of repayment and the interest that you will be charged?'

'Yes,' she said dazedly. 'I understand.'

He rose from his seat and extended his hand. 'Good day to you, Miss Travis. And good luck.'

It was snowing when she stepped out of the bank door into the High Street, but in Ginnie's mind the sun was shining and life was filled with endless possibilities. She had already made out the orders for the various wholesalers and now she was in a position to stick stamps on the envelopes and put them in the red pillar box on the corner of Cherry Lane. It was no greater chore than sending Christmas cards but the effects would be long lasting and if she had made the right choices she would achieve a modest success. She did not expect to make a fortune in the first year, or even the second, but she was determined to earn enough money to provide a decent living for herself and her family. When Shirley was fit enough to return to work she might even give her a job as a saleslady. Shirley would charm the customers into buying things they might not have chosen until she put the thought in their heads. Shirley had always been good at getting her own way.

Ginnie hurried back to the shop to relieve Mrs Richmond, who had volunteered to keep an eye on things while Jimmy took over the shop floor. He might be a bit slow on the uptake but he knew the cost of each item of stock without consulting the price tag. His fresh-faced boyish looks and diffident manner endeared him to the older ladies, and his cheerful disposition made him a hit with everyone. He had been dealing with a customer when Ginnie walked through the door, but he abandoned his task and bounded over to her like an eager puppy. 'Well, did you get it?'

'Yes, I did. Go and put the kettle on and I'll finish serving the lady.' She hurried over to the woman who was staring at her in astonishment. 'I'm so sorry, madam. Jimmy is a bit over-enthusiastic at times. That's a very fine rug, and I'm afraid it's the last of our pre-war stock. I don't know when we'll be able to get more in.'

'Well, dear, I do like it, and a live coal fell out of the fire and burned a great big hole in our rug at home. I know we should make do and mend, but it's gone past that and my daughter is getting married on Saturday and everyone will be coming back to our house for tea.'

'How exciting!' Ginnie thought for a moment, trying to decide whether to forgo a little bit of profit in return for goodwill. 'As it's such a special occasion I'll let you have it at sale price.'

The customer's eyes lit up and she opened her handbag. 'I'll take it, and I'll recommend you to my friends. I usually go all the way to Leytonstone and shop at Bearman's, but you're much nearer.'

'And I'm branching out. I'm going to stock items of household linen that don't require coupons, and some kitchen utensils too.'

'Then I most certainly will use your shop in future. Thank you, my dear, and good luck to you.'

The new stock started to arrive and Ginnie spent her evenings at the shop unpacking crates and displaying the items to their best advantage. Despite the crack in the plate glass she had the boarding taken down from the window, and she sought advice as to whether it was likely to shatter or if it was safe to wait until she could afford a replacement. The glazier took a look at it and said that in his opinion the damage was minimal and unlikely to be a danger to the public. 'The war,' he said, 'is almost over. I listen every night to the BBC Home Service and that chappie Alvar Lidell who reads the news said the Allies were advancing on Berlin and the Jerries were virtually beaten. We're winning, ducks. We've almost beaten that bloody Hitler.'

Ginnie could only hope that he was right as she arranged a window display to resemble the sitting room of a comfortable home. She placed easy chairs around a coffee table and a tea trolley, complete with paper doilies and a china tea set borrowed from Fred Chinashop. She completed the scene with a wireless she had on loan from the electrical shop further along the parade, putting a placard to this effect on the top together with a photograph of a young man in uniform. She went out into the street to examine her work, but it lacked colour. It needed something else to make people stop and stare. Mrs Richmond provided the answer when she came down from her flat half an hour later with a fish paste sandwich for Ginnie's lunch.

'You don't eat enough, my girl,' she said sternly. 'You're too thin. It's not attractive. You'll never catch a husband if you look like a stick bean.'

Ginnie turned her head away so that Mrs Richmond would not see that she was close to tears. Her careless words, no doubt meant to be jocular, had brought back memories of Nick that blotted out everything other than the pain of parting and the knowledge that she would never see him again. She took the plate. 'Thank you, but you shouldn't waste your rations on me.'

'What's the matter, ducks?' Mrs Richmond peered into her face. 'You're not crying are you, Ginnie?'

She shook her head. 'No. I've got something in my eye.'

'I've heard that before.' Mrs Richmond took off her glasses, huffed on them and polished them on her apron. 'You've been overworking. I've seen the lights on late at night when you should be out enjoying yourself like other young girls, or home in bed getting your beauty sleep.'

Ginnie took a bite of the sandwich and realised that she was extremely hungry. She took another. Despite the fact that she was heartily sick of margarine and fish paste, she ate it with relish. 'I'd like your opinion on the shop window,' she said, changing the subject. 'Come outside and tell me what you think.'

Mrs Richmond followed her outside and stood at the edge of the kerb with her arms folded across her ample bosom. 'Colour,' she said firmly. 'Cushions are what's needed. Those utility chairs look a bit plain and boring in that beige uncut moquette. I've got just the thing in my flat. You don't have to sell them but they'll brighten up the display. You could do with a bit of fancy glass or a china ornament on the coffee table. I'll have a word with Fred and see what he's got tucked away in his back room.'

'But he's already loaned me the tea set.'

'Think of all the cups of tea your dad gave Fred over the years. I'll bet if they was laid out in a straight line they've stretch to Southend and halfway back again, not to mention the pints of mild and bitter that Sid treated him to in the pub of an evening. I love Fred to bits, but he's a mean old sod.' She patted Ginnie on the arm. 'Leave it to me, ducks. Go back inside and finish your sandwich and I'll do the rest.' She marched into Fred's shop, leaving Ginnie standing on the pavement feeling slightly dazed. She glanced once again at the display and decided that Mrs Richmond was right. A splash of colour here and there was all that was needed to bring the window to life. Maybe she ought to scatter some women's magazines on the coffee table, and perhaps an overflowing ashtray. She giggled at the thought. That would definitely be going too far.

She had barely finished her sandwich when Mrs Richmond returned with a large blue glass vase and a china fruit bowl. 'I've got some wax fruit upstairs,' she said triumphantly. 'My Norman gave it to me for our twentieth wedding anniversary, the silly old fool. What I really wanted was a posh silver cigarette case like the sort that Paul Henreid had in *Now,*

Voyager. You remember the scene when he lit two cigarettes and gave one to Bette Davis. I always wanted Norm to do that but he only smokes a pipe.' She gave a throaty chuckle. 'You're looking less peaky now, dearie. You've got to remember to eat or you won't be able to lift a spoon and fork, let alone a roll of lino.'

'Thank you for the sandwiches,' Ginnie said, laughing. 'And the vision of Mr Richmond lighting two pipes and handing one to you. That'll haunt me for the rest of the day.'

'At least I've cheered you up. I'll go upstairs and get the cushions and the imitation fruit. We'll make your window display the best outside of Selfridges.'

As soon as Shirley was fit enough to consider taking a job Ginnie asked her if she would like to help in the shop. With the new and improved range of goods on sale trade was gradually picking up, and when Jimmy was out delivering furniture or laying carpets and lino Ginnie needed someone to serve the customers. Shirley was reluctant at first. She had been snubbed by several of Olivia's friends when she had ventured into town, pushing Colin in a second-hand pram that Mildred had bought from one of Mrs Martin's daughters. It was clean and serviceable, but it had seen better days and could hardly compare with the coach-built Marmet or Silver Cross prams that the mothers in Monk Avenue bought for their offspring.

'I wish I'd never made up that silly story about me and Laurence,' she said tearfully when Ginnie broached the subject again one evening after a meagre supper of bread and dripping. Shirley emptied the washing-up water into the kitchen sink. 'How can I work in the shop with everyone believing that spiteful gossip put about by Olivia?'

'The Monk Avenue crowd aren't likely to give us their custom. Most of them wouldn't be seen dead in Collier Lane. They patronise the big department stores up West. We don't get a look in.' Ginnie did not add that she was determined to change their habits and attract a wider clientele. That would come in time, but for now she needed an assistant whom she could trust.

'I must start bringing in a wage,' Shirley said doubtfully. 'But I was thinking of going back to the munitions factory.'

'You could try there, but I don't think they'd be as flexible about hours as I would and they might not take you as you've got a baby to look after.'

Shirley shook her head. 'I've really messed up my life, haven't I?'

'No. Never say that. You've got a gorgeous little boy and you've got Mum and me solidly behind you.'

'But I'll never live down this business with Laurence. What will happen when he comes home and Olivia tells him what I said?'

'You'll have to face that when it happens, but he's

a decent chap. I really liked him and he's got a sense of humour. Maybe he'll see the funny side.'

'There isn't one,' Shirley said sorrowfully. 'I've lost Charlie, who loved me to bits, and the man I really adored is dead. Sometimes I wish that I'd died with Tony in that car crash.'

Ginnie bit back a scathing remark. They had both fallen in love with men who were now far beyond their reach and she understood the agonising pain of loss only too well. She reached out to cover Shirley's hand with her own. 'You've got another bloke in your life now, and he's bawling his head off.' She hung the damp tea towel on the rail above the hot water boiler. 'Start on Monday. Do a couple of hours in the morning and a couple in the afternoon, and we'll see how we go. You can't hide away forever, and people will soon find someone else to talk about.'

Shirley wiped her hands on her apron. 'I'll give it a try.'

Despite the war and the privations of strict rationing it felt as if spring had come at last to Cherry Lane. The ornamental trees were in full bloom, and the air was filled with the heady scent of wallflowers as Ginnie walked to work early one April morning. She liked to be in the shop long before opening time in order to make everything ready for the day ahead.

She went through the order book to make certain that Jimmy had loaded the correct items in the old field ambulance that was now their delivery van. Strict petrol rationing was still in place, making it necessary to plan deliveries carefully and where possible to get customers to collect their purchases in person. Stock had to be reordered and availability checked. Shortages were a problem, but wherever possible she tried to visit wholesalers and deal with them face to face, which she found produced the best results. She had discovered that being young and reasonably pretty was a great advantage in a male-dominated business, and she was soon on first name terms with her suppliers. But the basic problem remained that utility furniture was only available to newly-weds and civilians who had lost everything in bombing raids. With this in mind she made a detour to the newsagent's shop to purchase a copy of the local paper, which she bought every week in order to study the *For Sale* column. Selling second-hand furniture would have been totally against her father's principles, but to Ginnie it made good business sense.

She took the newspaper to the office and was about to set it to one side when one of the headings on the front page caught her eye. 'Local naval officer fights for life in hospital.' But it was the sight of the photograph beneath that wrenched a gasp of horror from her lips.

Chapter Eight

After many successful missions escorting convoys across the Atlantic, the destroyer HMS — was sunk by a mine in the southwestern approaches. Amongst the survivors is Lieutenant Laurence Mallory, son of much respected local solicitor and Justice of the Peace Councillor Colin Mallory and his wife Isabelle. Lieutenant Mallory is receiving treatment in the naval hospital, Gosport. His condition is said to be critical.

Ginnie's hands shook as she put the newspaper down. Memories of their brief time together in the station buffet came flooding back. The faded old photograph image of the tea room and the aroma of toasted teacakes and hot tea filled her head with snapshots of frozen moments in time. She could hear the shriek of the guard's whistle and the roar of the steam engine as it pulled away from the platform. She could feel the damp caress of the steam in her hair and smell the smoke from the glowing coals in the firebox that sent sparks and cinders flying as the train picked up speed. She could picture Laurence's smiling face as he leaned out of the carriage window waving to her until he was out of sight.

She took a deep breath. She would have to break the news gently to Shirley. She picked up the telephone receiver and was about to dial home when she had second thoughts. Perhaps it would be better to wait until Shirley arrived for work, and then she would sit her down with a nice strong cup of tea and let her read the article in the local rag. It was probably exaggerated in order to make a good story.

Shirley studied the newsprint, saying nothing.

'Are you all right?' Ginnie asked anxiously. 'I mean it's not as if he was your steady boyfriend or anything.'

Shirley raised her head and her expression was stark. 'I treated Charlie so badly, but I really thought I was in love with Laurence. He was so sweet and kind and I was very drunk that night after the tennis club dance.'

'But you can't be sure that he's Colin's father.'

'You know I can't, but I want it to be him.'

'So that's why you called your son after his father. I didn't realise that Mr Mallory's first name was Colin until I saw it in the newspaper.'

'The name just popped into my head. I suppose I must have heard Mrs Mallory call her husband by his Christian name, but I don't remember. Anyway, everything was a blur after the accident.' Shirley shook her hair back from her face. 'Stop asking all these questions. I'm confused enough as it is.'

The shop bell jingled. 'We've got a customer.' Ginnie opened the office door. 'I'll serve her. You'd better sit here until you feel calmer.'

'I must go and see Laurence in hospital,' Shirley said urgently. 'I can't let that bitch Olivia get to him first with a pack of spiteful lies.'

'What lies? If she tells him about Colin he's bound to think that the kid is his. He's too much of a gentleman to think the worst of you.'

Shirley reached for her handbag and fished inside for a hanky. 'Don't be cruel. Can't you see that I'm upset?'

'Why? Is it because the lies you told have come back to bite you on the rear end? You said you loved Charlie and then Tony was the light of your life and your heart was buried in the grave, and now you're worried because Laurence might die before you can get a real wedding ring on your finger.'

'That's a rotten thing to say. I do care for Laurence. I do.'

'It's not me you have to convince, Shirley.' Ginnie's patience was stretched to the limit and she hurried onto the shop floor before she could say something she would regret.

Minutes later, having explained that the imitation bananas and oranges were for display purposes only, Ginnie returned to the office to find Shirley leafing through the telephone directory. 'What are you doing?'

'I'm going to speak to Olivia or her mother. I don't

care who's at home but I must find out if they've been to see Laurence.'

Ginnie snatched the directory from her hands and closed it with a snap. 'That would be a big mistake. You've already told Olivia that Laurence is Colin's father and she's not likely to have kept that to herself. You'll just have to tough it out, as Nick would have said.' She stopped short. The mere mention of his name left her breathless with longing, quickly followed by despair. She put her arm around Shirley's shoulders. 'Maybe the least said the better at this stage. Wait until he's better and then go and see him.'

'But he might not recover.' Shirley jabbed the article with the tip of her finger. 'It says here that he's in a critical condition. What if Olivia tells him that I'm a lying bitch who's trying to blackmail the family into supporting me and my little bastard?'

Shocked, Ginnie dropped her arm to her side. 'Why are you talking like this? Olivia didn't say anything of the sort.'

'It's what she accused me of when I happened to bump into her in town. She was with her snooty pal, Bernice Fuller. I was going to walk past them but Olivia made a pretence of bending over the pram to admire Colin. Then in a loud voice she told Bernice that I'd lied about Laurence and me so that I could claim maintenance for my illegitimate baby. She called me a tart and said I'd slept with so many men that I didn't know who the father was.'

'Why didn't you tell me before now?'

'I didn't say anything because I was embarrassed and totally humiliated. It never crossed my mind to ask the Mallorys for anything. I wouldn't do a thing like that even if I was certain that Laurence was Colin's father.'

Ginnie shook her head. 'What a mess, but you've only got yourself to blame, Shirley. If you hadn't mixed with the Monk Avenue crowd none of this would have happened.'

'What are you saying? Do you think I'm too common to attract a top bloke like Laurence?'

'No, of course not.'

'Then do something for me, Ginnie. Help me, please.'

Ginnie hesitated, torn between pity and a desire to shake some sense into her wayward sister. 'All right,' she said reluctantly. 'What do you want me to do?'

'Go and see Laurence in hospital. Get in there before Olivia has a chance to spread her poison. Tell him the truth.'

'Why me? You're the one he seduced, or maybe it was the other way round given your track record. You're the one who ought to visit him and put things straight.'

'I can't. For one thing I can't leave Colin, and for another I'd fall apart if I saw him in a hospital bed. It would bring it all back. Losing Tony was the worst thing that ever happened to me and I'll never forget the way he looked after the crash.'

Startled by this admission, Ginnie sank down on the desk chair. 'I thought you didn't remember anything about the actual accident.'

'I must have passed out before the police and ambulance arrived on the scene, but I remember the skid on the icy surface of the road and Tony yelling at me to hold tight. I remember screaming as he struggled to regain control of the car and then the crash as it hit the tree. He slumped forward and then his head fell back – there was blood everywhere and his eyes were open, but he wasn't breathing. I couldn't move. I couldn't help him – he was dead.' Shirley buried her face in her hands and wept.

Ginnie turned round to see Mrs Richmond standing in the doorway. 'Be a love and put the kettle on, please, Ida. Shirley's had a bit of an upset.'

'Course I will, ducks.' Ida Richmond plucked the key to the outdoor lavatory from its hook. 'Be back in two ticks.' She whisked out of the office and a gust of wind rustled the papers on the desk as she opened the back door. Ginnie stared in horror as the front page of the newspaper undulated in the breeze, causing Laurence's photograph to move gently as if he were trying to attract their attention.

Shirley slammed her hand down on the page with a gasp of horror. 'It's a sign. He must be told the truth before that evil sister of his gets to him. I simply can't go, but you could do this for me. Please, Ginnie.'

Ginnie had a sudden vision of Betsy sitting at

Nick's bedside in a Los Angeles hospital, holding his hand as they discussed their marriage plans. He was lost to her forever, but Shirley deserved a second chance and Colin needed a father. 'Okay. I'll go to Hampshire, but I can't promise anything, Shirley. He might not be in a fit state to see anyone.'

'Just don't let Olivia get to him first.'

'That might be difficult, but I'll try. What do you want me to tell him?'

'The truth. Don't varnish it – tell him everything.'

It had not been easy to persuade the sister in charge of the ward to allow her to see Laurence, but Ginnie explained, without resorting to an actual lie, that she had come to give him news of his baby son. The sister's stern expression melted into a genuine smile. 'That's just what he needs. Lieutenant Mallory is on the road to recovery but he tires easily and you mustn't stay long.'

Ginnie entered the side ward half expecting to see Laurence in an oxygen tent, but to her surprise he was fully conscious and propped up on pillows. His expression lightened when he saw her and he held out his hand. 'Ginnie. What a wonderful surprise.'

She hesitated in the doorway. His warm welcome was unexpected and she was suddenly at a loss for words and inexplicably shy. It had seemed so simple on the train journey from Waterloo. She had had it all worked out in her head, but she had not been prepared for the look of genuine pleasure in his eyes, or for the leap of sympathy she experienced on seeing him looking pale and vulnerable in his hospital bed. 'Hello, Laurence.'

'Pull up a chair and take a seat. It's good to see you again.'

'How are you, Laurence?' She knew it was a silly question, but she could think of nothing else to say.

He grinned. 'I'm getting there, but how are you? You look absolutely splendid.'

Her hand flew to pat her windblown hair into place. 'I'm fine.'

'And Shirley? She was a bit under the weather when I last saw you.'

'Yes, she's fine too.' Ginnie sat down and began peeling off her gloves. She wanted to tell him about the baby, but she didn't know how to start.

'It's good of you to come all this way,' Laurence said easily. 'I certainly didn't expect you to. Tell me what's been going on in Cherry Lane. How are your parents? I hope they're well.'

She stared down at her hands clutching the well-used leather bag that had once belonged to her mother. 'Dad was killed in an air raid.'

'Oh, Ginnie, I'm so sorry. I had no idea.'

'Of course not. You've been away at sea for months.' She raised her eyes to meet his sympathetic gaze. 'It's hard, but we're coping as best we can.'

'I only met your father once, but Shirley worshipped

159

him. It must have come as a terrible blow to both of you.'

'Everybody has lost someone in this beastly war.'

He nodded silently, allowing her time to compose herself.

'At least you survived,' she said, forcing a smile. 'I read about the sinking of your ship in the local paper.'

'Livvie tells me that I'm a local hero, which is absolute nonsense. I was lucky, that's all.' He raised himself to a sitting position. 'What is Shirley up to these days?'

So he really didn't know. Ginnie smothered a sigh of relief. 'We spent six months in Shropshire with our aunt. She owns a lovely old riverside pub on the edge of a small village.'

'It sounds idyllic.'

She pulled a face. 'I suppose it was before the war, but the whole place had been taken over by the US army. Not that they were any trouble,' she added hastily. 'Most of them were quite charming, and I worked in the American hospital for a while.'

'I didn't know you were a nurse.'

'I was a ward maid. It wasn't very glamorous.'

'But essential. I'm truly grateful for everyone who slaves away in this hospital. I was in a pretty bad state when they brought me in here.'

'I'm really pleased to see you looking so well. You were at death's door according to the local rag.'

He chuckled. 'I'm sorry to disappoint you.'

'Don't be silly.' She hesitated, eyeing him thoughtfully, wondering if this was the right time to break the news. She decided that it was. 'Actually, Laurence, I did come here with a purpose.'

'I guessed as much. I mean, I'm delighted to see you, but I don't flatter myself that you came just to hold my hand.'

She took a deep breath. 'It was Shirley who asked me to come and see you.'

'Why didn't she come herself?'

'She wanted to, Laurence, but she was afraid you might have heard things.'

'I'm not with you. What things?'

There was nothing for it now but to tell him the truth and the words came tumbling from her lips. 'She was pregnant when you last saw her. That's why we went to Shropshire.'

'And she wanted you to come here to tell me that?' The colour drained from his face. 'Am I the father?'

So he was not going to deny all knowledge. A wave of relief flooded over her. 'Shirley had a beautiful baby boy.'

'I have a son.'

'His name's Colin.'

'That's my father's name.' Laurence stared at her dazedly and then a slow smile spread across his handsome features. 'I'm a father. I can't believe it.'

She could not bear to deceive him. 'Shirley wanted to be absolutely honest with you, Laurence. She was virtually engaged to Charlie, a chap she'd known for years, but he died during an air raid.'

'So the boy could be his?'

She nodded her head. 'I'm afraid so. It sounds awful when you put it like that but Shirley isn't a bad person. If anything she's too generous. She'd give you her last penny if you were in trouble.'

'I know that, Ginnie. You don't have to defend her to me, but I still don't understand why Shirley felt she couldn't come here and tell me to my face. It's not as if I'm an ogre.'

'She made the mistake of falling out with Olivia. They were like that when they were in school, if you remember.'

He grinned. 'I seem to recall Livvie falling out with everyone in her class, and next day they'd be the best of friends.'

'This is different, Laurence. Your sister is telling everyone that Shirley is trying to extort money from your family, which is totally untrue.'

'That sounds like Livvie in a strop. My dear sister has a devil of a temper when she's roused, and she's inclined to exaggerate. I wouldn't have believed what she said, but I'm very glad you came here to put me in the picture.'

Ginnie rose from her seat, light-headed with relief. 'That's all that matters. Shirley will be so relieved when I tell her that you've taken it like this.'

'Hold on a moment.' Laurence raised himself on his elbow. 'Don't run away, Ginnie. Please don't go.'

'But I've done what I had to do. I just wanted to reassure you that we don't expect anything from you.'

'I understand, but of course I'll stand by Shirley and the boy. You mustn't worry about that. Won't you stay a while longer?'

She sat down again. 'There is something else,' she said cautiously. 'Shirley shouldn't have done it, but to stop people gossiping she pretended that she was married, and the first name that came into her head was yours.'

'I'm flattered.'

'And she registered the baby with your surname, but she didn't cite you as the father.'

'So the boy is Colin Mallory.'

'You don't mind?'

'I daresay the birth certificate can be amended to show that I am the father.'

'You don't have to do that, Laurence. Shirley doesn't expect anything from you. I'm running the shop now and she's working with me. We're doing quite well.'

'You don't understand, Ginnie. I won't renege on my responsibilities. Whether Charlie was his biological father or not is purely academic as the poor chap is dead. I'm very much alive and I won't allow Shirley to struggle on alone. I'll marry her and make the whole thing legal.'

'You'd do that, even knowing that Colin might be another man's child?'

'Of course. There's no question about it.'

'Do you love Shirley?'

His blue eyes darkened to the colour of slate and he turned his head away to gaze out of the window. 'I like and admire your sister. I'll do the right thing by her, Ginnie.'

'You could ruin both your lives by marrying someone you don't love.'

'And what about the boy? He might well be mine and he deserves to be brought up in a family with a mother and a father. Money doesn't come into it and Livvie was wrong to spread such an unkind rumour.'

'Shirley might have other ideas, Laurence. I haven't told you the full story yet.'

He shot her a puzzled glance. 'What else could there be?'

She had been endeavouring to keep the memories of their months in Shropshire filed in a secret place, wrapped in tissue paper like precious mementoes to be stored and taken out occasionally for a brief dusting and then stowed away for safe keeping. It was impossible to mention Tony without involving Nick and Danny. The happy times were deeply enmeshed in the net created by pain and separation, but she felt that Laurence deserved to know the whole story before committing his life to Shirley and her child.

She related the incidents leading up to the fatal accident and Colin's birth as succinctly and unemotionally as possible, but her voice broke when she mentioned Nick's name and Laurence reached out to give her hand a comforting squeeze.

'Thank you,' he said softly when she finishing speaking. 'That must have been hard for you, Ginnie. It's obvious that you cared deeply for Nick.'

'I never said so.'

'You didn't have to. It was written all over your face, and I'm sorry it didn't work out for you both.'

'It's all over,' Ginnie said hastily. 'He went back to the States and he'll marry his fiancée and I'll never see him again. But that's my problem, not yours. I'm only telling you all this because I don't want you to marry my sister out of misguided loyalty, only to find out later that it was a huge mistake.'

'You're a great girl.' Laurence released her hand with a wry smile. 'If things had been different, maybe . . .' He shook his head. 'Tell Shirley that I'll come and see her as soon as I'm fit enough to leave hospital, although I think I'm being sent to a convalescent home for a week or two after this.'

'I'll tell her, but you'd better sort things out with your family, Laurence. I don't think they're going to be too pleased with your decision.'

'Father will understand; he's an honourable man. As to Mother and Livvie, they'll get used to the idea.'

The door opened before Ginnie had time to think of a suitable answer, and the ward sister marched purposefully into the room. 'That's quite enough excitement for one day, Lieutenant Mallory. Visiting time is over.'

'I was just going,' Ginnie said, rising to her feet. 'Goodbye, Laurence.'

'Wait a second.' He attempted to sit up straight but fell back against the pillow with an exclamation of annoyance.

'You've overdone it, lieutenant,' the sister said severely. 'No visitors for you this evening.'

'Send me a photo of Colin,' Laurence said urgently. 'Will you do that for me, Ginnie?'

She nodded and blew him a kiss. 'Of course I will.'

It was late that evening when Ginnie got off the bus at the bottom of Cherry Lane. She was exhausted physically and mentally. She had had plenty of time to mull things over during the train journey to Waterloo and the subsequent ride on the tube, but she was tired and perhaps she was not thinking straight. Laurence had said all the right things and he had behaved like a perfect gentleman, promising to stand by Shirley and her baby, but she had a nagging feeling that he was driven more by his sense of honour and duty than by any deep emotional attachment to her sister. She walked slowly, burdened by the knowledge that Shirley might be making a huge mistake if she married Laurence in order to gain respectability. The garden gate swung open at a touch, screeching on rusty hinges, and the front room curtains twitched. A sliver of light illuminated the concrete path and just as she was about to open her handbag to look for her key the door was wrenched open.

'Well? Did you see him? What did he say?' Shirley stepped aside to let her into the hall. 'Don't keep me in suspense.' She closed the door. 'Go into the lounge. Mum's kept some supper for you.'

'Give her a moment to catch her breath, love.' Mildred emerged from the room resplendent in a cherry-red candlewick dressing gown, with her hair in curlers and Sid's old carpet slippers on her feet. 'I'll make the cocoa.' She hurried along the hallway, waddling like a duck in footwear that was several sizes too large for her but which she insisted on wearing because they had been her beloved husband's favourites. She flicked on the kitchen light. 'Don't tell her anything until I bring in the hot drinks.'

'Tell me now,' Shirley hissed, taking Ginnie by the arm and dragging her into the living room. 'I've been going crazy all day.'

Ginnie shook off her restraining hand. 'Stop being an idiot. I'll tell you everything when Mum comes in because I'm not going through it twice.' She tossed her bag and gloves onto the sofa and sat down, kicking off her shoes. 'I'm absolutely whacked, so don't expect me to go into too much detail.'

'But did you see Laurence?' Shirley perched on the arm of the settee.

'Yes, I saw him.'

'And you told him about Colin.'

Ginnie bent down to rub her sore feet. 'Yes.'

'And how did he react? If you don't tell me I'm going to scream.'

'He's an out and out gentleman, Shirley. If you've got any sense you'll grab him with both hands and hang on.'

'He wasn't furious? Olivia hadn't told him?'

'No, she hadn't said a word. And this will surprise you, because it astounded me – he wants to marry you and bring Colin up as his son.'

Mildred had come into the room unnoticed and she almost dropped the tray she was carrying. She slammed it down on the coffee table, spilling some of the hot cocoa. 'No! Really?'

Shirley leapt to her feet and danced her mother round the room. 'He's going to make an honest woman of me, Mum. What have you got to say to that?'

'Laurence Mallory wants to marry you?' Mildred slumped down on the nearest chair, fanning herself vigorously. 'You're the luckiest girl alive, Shirley Travis. Not many men would be so willing to do the right thing.'

Ginnie stared at the plate of Spam sandwiches with curling edges that had been kept for her supper and her appetite deserted her. 'Thanks, Mum, but I bought a pie from the station buffet. I'll wrap these up and take them to the shop for my lunch.'

'You should come home at dinner time,' Mildred said, frowning. 'Your dad always made a point of shutting up the shop from one until two. He said it was more important to have a good meal than to stay open.'

'Yes, Mum.' Ginnie picked up a mug and took a sip of cocoa, but she put it down again as she heard the sound of a car pulling up in the street outside. She rose from the sofa and went to peer out of the window. 'There's someone coming up the path.'

'No.' Mildred's lips formed a circle of surprise. 'Who do we know who's got enough petrol to go visiting, especially at this time of night?'

'I'll go,' Shirley said eagerly. 'Perhaps Laurence has discharged himself from hospital and come to see me and the baby.'

Ginnie made for the door. 'I can't see who it is but I'd better go. You're in your dressing gown, Shirley.'

'It's a negligee,' Shirley said sulkily. 'I made it from parachute silk and it's a copy of one that Carole Lombard wore in *My Man Godfrey*.'

'Sit down, you silly girl,' Mildred said peevishly. 'Let your sister answer the door. It can't be good news. No one uses their precious petrol ration unless it's a dire emergency, and nobody makes social calls at eleven o'clock at night. It can't be the ARP warden because all that's finished now.' She jumped visibly as someone hammered on the door knocker. 'For goodness' sake go and see who it is, Ginnie. And tell them to go away.'

Chapter Nine

Ginnie opened the front door to find Colin Mallory standing in the porch. He took off his Homburg hat. 'I realise that it's rather late to call on you, Miss Travis, but my wife had a very disturbing telephone call from the hospital in Gosport. May I come in?'

Ginnie was too astonished to refuse. 'Please do.'

He crossed the threshold, gazing round the narrow hallway with the stairs rising directly opposite the front door, and she had the feeling that he was comparing it unfavourably with his own house in Monk Avenue. She had only been there once and that was when she was ten and Shirley was supposed to have been keeping an eye on her while their mother went up to the West End to buy a new dress.

Shirley had wanted to go out with Olivia and had threatened Ginnie on pain of death not to tell their parents that she had disobeyed instructions to stay at home. Shirley and Olivia had gone into town, abandoning Ginnie. She had been left on her own in the imposing entrance hall with its highly polished parquet floor and a sweeping staircase leading to a galleried landing. The furniture had been equally grand, its surfaces glowing with the sheen of ripe conkers and its brass handles gleaming like pirate gold. She remembered large flower arrangements, their heady perfume vying with the cloying smell of Mansion Polish and Brasso, and there had been a cream Bakelite telephone on a half-moon table, above which was a framed print of a duelling scene. Standing in front of a waiting carriage, the wounded victor was being supported by his seconds. She had stared at the picture for so long that the horses in between the shafts had begun to move their legs, and she had huddled on the bottom step of the Turkey carpeted staircase, hiding her eyes.

She had been found an hour later by the maid who had come from the nether regions of the house to answer the doorbell, and having sent the caller round to the tradesmen's entrance the maid had marched Ginnie to the drawing room to be interrogated by Mrs Mallory. Olivia's mother had not been pleased to learn that her daughter and Shirley had gone to meet their friends at the ice cream parlour, and she had telephoned Mildred that evening, telling her what she thought about the lax discipline in the Travis household. Shirley had been punished and Ginnie had had her pocket money stopped for a month for being party to her sister's escapade. She sighed. It had not seemed fair then and did not seem fair now.

'Where is your sister?' Mr Mallory said angrily. 'I want to see her and I'm not leaving here until I've had words with that young woman.'

Ginnie was no longer a frightened ten-year-old and she stood her ground. 'As you said yourself, it is very late. Can't this wait until morning?'

He drew back his head so that his chin rested on his starched Gladstone collar and his eyes narrowed to slits. 'No, it can't. Not only have we had a telephone call from our son, but Olivia has told me about a conversation she had with your sister not so long ago.'

'Your daughter has got it wrong, Mr Mallory. I've been to see Laurence today.'

'So it was you who went to the hospital. I thought it was your sister, but that's neither here nor there.' His dark eyebrows snapped together over the bridge of his nose. 'My wife said he sounded feverish on the telephone and all because of you. He's been seriously ill and he needs rest and quiet. You took a lot on yourself, young lady.'

The sitting-room door opened and Mildred emerged, curlers bristling. 'Who are you, sir? And why are you calling on us at this time of night?'

'This is Mr Mallory, Mum. Laurence's father,' Ginnie said hastily.

'It's Councillor Mallory actually, and I'm here on a very personal matter, Mrs Travis.'

Mildred folded her arms across her chest. 'This is a fine time of night to come calling.'

'It's not from choice, madam. My daughter tells me that . . .' He broke off as Shirley wafted out of the front room. The creation in parachute silk clung to her voluptuous figure, leaving little to the imagination.

'I'm Shirley,' she said, holding out her hand. 'We've met before, Mr Mallory, but it was a long time ago. I was at school with Livvie.'

He barely touched the tips of her fingers before dropping his hand to his side as if an electric shock had passed between them. 'My daughter told me that you were a trollop,' he said, glowering. 'You won't get a penny out of me for your little bastard.'

Mildred utter a gasp of horror, but Shirley appeared to be unmoved by the insult. 'Livvie was lying,' she said firmly. 'I'm sorry to say it, but Livvie made it all up. She's always been a troublemaker.'

Mallory took a step towards her. 'Are you denying that you have a child?'

As if on cue, Colin began to cry and Shirley's lips curved in a proud smile. 'I have a son and he's ready for his feed, if you'll excuse me.' She ascended the stairs, leaving them staring after her in an awkward silence.

'I blame you for this, madam,' Mallory said in a voice that throbbed with suppressed anger. 'Your daughter is trying to blackmail my son into marriage.'

Mildred shook her head. 'It's nothing of the kind. This is a matter between Shirley and her young man. We should leave them to sort it out.'

'My son has been accused of fathering your daughter's illegitimate brat, and your daughter is after maintenance for her little mistake.'

'Indeed she is not.' Mildred's tone was icy. 'My daughter is the one who has been wronged. It's always the man who gets off scot free. I thought you were a respectable man, Councillor Mallory. I thought you were a fair man, but I can see that it's all a front. You're just as bad as the rest of them.'

Ginnie stared at her mother, seeing her suddenly in a new light. She had not expected her to take on someone as important and overbearing as Mr Mallory and it was obvious that he too was taken by surprise, but he was also angry. He clenched his hands at his sides and she stepped in between them. 'Livvie is mistaken, Mr Mallory. Shirley hasn't asked for maintenance. She hasn't asked Laurence for anything, and that's what I told him when I saw him today.'

'You had no right to poke your nose into matters that don't concern you, young lady.'

'It does concern me when my sister is accused of something she hasn't done. That's why I went to see Laurence and told him that he may or may not be Colin's father.'

'She named the brat after me? How dare she do a thing like that?'

'There's no law against it.' Mildred padded over to the front door and opened it. 'I think we've said all we have to say for now, Mr Mallory. Go home and tell that meddling daughter of yours to watch her tongue in future or we might have to see our solicitor and have her up for slander.'

Mallory's face darkened to a dangerous shade of purple. 'How dare you!'

'You'll burst a blood vessel if you're not careful,' Mildred said smugly. 'Goodnight, Mr Mallory.' She held the door open.

Ginnie moved to her mother's side. 'You'd better go, Mr Mallory. Laurence was absolutely fine with the news. In fact he was delighted to think that Colin might be his and he genuinely wants to marry Shirley.' She had the satisfaction of seeing Mallory at a loss for words as he stormed out of the house.

Mildred slammed the door. 'That put him in his place, Ginnie. Let's go and finish our cocoa and you can tell me exactly what Laurence said.'

Laurence telephoned Shirley next day and told her that he was to be transferred to a convalescent home in Surrey, which was considerably nearer home than the hospital in Gosport. Despite opposition from his family, he was adamant that he wanted to marry her and to raise Colin as his own child. Shirley was radiant and Ginnie was pleased for her sister's sake, but she was worried that his decision had been made too quickly, and that he might live to regret his chivalrous action.

After a week of indecision Shirley finally plucked up the courage to accept Laurence's invitation to spend a weekend at a small hotel near the convalescent home. 'He might change his mind when he sees me again,' she said, gazing critically at her reflection in the dressing-table mirror as she secured the perky little pillbox hat she had bought in a jumble sale with a pearl hatpin. 'He might have been under the influence of drugs when you saw him in the hospital and now he's afraid to tell me the truth.'

Ginnie took the pin from Shirley's trembling fingers. 'Here, let me. You'll do yourself a mischief if you stab yourself in the head.' She slipped it through the soft felt, feeding it carefully through a lock of hair. 'Stop talking nonsense and get a move on. You've been speaking to him on the phone almost every day, so you know he's sincere.'

Shirley rose to her feet. 'Do I look all right? My boobs are enormous after breast-feeding the baby. Thank goodness I've got him on the bottle now, but Laurence might think I look fat and blowsy.'

'You look absolutely smashing. Stop worrying and go get him, sister.'

'You spent far too much time hobnobbing with the Yanks.' Shirley's smile faded and she clapped her hand to her mouth. 'I'm sorry, Ginnie. I didn't mean to say that.'

'It's okay and I'm fine with it now, but what about you? I know how much you cared for Tony.'

Shirley's eyes glittered diamond-bright and she shook her head. 'There'll never be anyone like Tony. I've had to accept that, but I swear to God that Laurence will never suffer for it. What I felt for Tony is buried here.' She clutched her hand to her heart. 'And that's where he'll stay forever, but I've got to go on living and I have to bring up my son. I'll do anything it takes to give Colin a good start in life. Absolutely anything.'

'I don't know whether you're being terribly brave or really stupid,' Ginnie said, dashing tears from her cheeks. 'But good luck, Shirley. I hope it works out for you and Laurence.'

Shirley took a final look in the mirror. 'It will. It has to.' She picked up her handbag and headed for the door.

Ginnie sank down on the edge of the bed, listening to the sound of Shirley's footsteps as she ran down the stairs, followed by the thud of the front door closing behind her. The room seemed oddly silent and empty, but the scent of Shirley's favourite perfume, Evening in Paris, lingered in the air and the pile of discarded clothes strewn all over the place was testament to her frantic search for an outfit that would have the desired effect on Laurence. Ginnie stood up and went to the window. She could see the pram in the back garden with its canopy raised to protect Colin from the sun, and she could just make out one chubby leg where the crocheted blanket had been kicked aside. He was a contented baby, and although it worried her that taking care of an infant was too much work for her mother, Mildred seemed to enjoy looking after him.

Ginnie glanced at her watch. It was time to go to work and she checked her appearance with a brief glance in the mirror as she hurried from the room.

She did not want to be late opening the shop. It was her life now, and she was determined to make a success of it. Business was improving slowly and although she was not making a fortune she could earn enough to make the mortgage repayments on the house and pay the bills. There was little enough left for luxuries, but they had a roof over their heads and food on the table. It gave her a feeling of intense pride to be able to support her family, and the shabby shop was her own personal empire.

On Monday evening Shirley returned engaged and triumphant, although the ring she wore was a gold band with a gypsy-set diamond that was several sizes too large for her finger. She had secured it with a piece of chewing gum, which was a habit she had acquired from Tony.

'Are you absolutely certain that this is the right thing for you?' Ginnie asked anxiously when they were alone in Shirley's room after a supper of Spam salad.

'Yes, I am. We had a wonderful weekend,' Shirley said happily. 'Laurence was allowed out of the convalescent home and we stayed in the hotel. It was fun.'

Ginnie gave her a hug, but she could not help worrying. Shirley seemed certain that she could keep Tony's memory in the sacred shrine of her heart, but Ginnie was not convinced. As for herself, Nick was never far from her thoughts and she was resigned to staying single. She had convinced herself that a career and marriage seldom went together, but she knew that Shirley thought differently. 'I don't want to be a wet blanket,' she said tentatively. 'But you don't have to get married if you don't want to. The shop is doing well and I've got plans for expansion. Fred Chinashop is thinking of retiring next year, and if I can make enough money to take over the lease and pay the ground rent, I might be able to persuade the landlord to knock through and make one large retail area, and I'll be on my way to owning a department store. Bodger's and Bearman's look out, Ginnie Travis is on her way up.'

'Good for you,' Shirley said, holding her hand up and admiring the tiny diamond. 'Laurence is going to buy me a proper ring as soon as he's fit to leave the convalescent home, which could be as early as next week. He's so looking forward to seeing Colin, and I know he'll be a wonderful dad.'

'Has it occurred to you that Colin might grow up to be the image of Charlie?'

Shirley frowned. 'Don't say things like that. I meant to say that I'm even more convinced that Colin's his son now.' She glanced at the sleeping baby in his cot beside her bed. 'He's got Laurence's blue eyes.'

'Don't all babies have blue eyes?'

'They might when they're newborn, but Colin is almost five months old and they won't change now, and he's going to be fair, just like Laurence.'

'Charlie had fair hair too, and blue eyes.'

'His hair had a reddish tint and his eyes were paler blue. Why are you being like this, Ginnie? Don't you want me to be happy?'

'Of course I do. That's why I want you to be absolutely certain that this is right for you and for Colin. You're going to have a hard time from the Mallory family. They're not likely to come round and give you their blessing.'

'I don't care, and if Laurence doesn't mind, then why should I? We can do without the snooty Mallorys and their big house in Monk Avenue. Laurence is going to stay in the Navy and I'll be a naval wife and go to all the cocktail parties and balls. We'll probably live on the base and I won't see an awful lot of you.' Her happy smile faded. 'You will be all right – running the shop on your own, I mean? I don't want to leave you in the lurch, so to speak.'

'I'll try to manage,' Ginnie said, smiling. 'You have your own life to lead, Shirley. If what you'll have with Laurence makes you happy then I'm happy too.'

'And the war's nearly over. It's just a matter of weeks, so Laurence says. We're going to get married in June. I want to be a summer bride so we'll have to start looking for dresses. Maybe Avril could help because I haven't any coupons left.'

'We'll manage something,' Ginnie said, chuckling. 'You'll be a lovely bride.'

*

It was official. The war in Europe was finally over and people danced in the streets. Miles of bunting were resurrected from storage and bonfires blazed on common land throughout the country. Impromptu street parties were organised and the new era of peace began with jubilation and optimism, but that did not seem to have infiltrated as far as the house in Monk Avenue. The Mallory family declined their invitation to attend their son's wedding at the register office in the middle of June.

Avril had travelled down from Shropshire the previous day bringing with her a creation in oyster slipper satin that had been made for her in Paris before the war. It might not have been the latest fashion now, but with a few minor alterations it fitted Shirley perfectly. Ginnie did her hair for her, twisting her sister's blonde locks into a perfect victory roll and securing the tiny straw hat with a diamond hat pin on loan from Avril as the 'something borrowed'. The hat, trimmed with cream silk roses and a wisp of a veil, had been an extravagance that Ginnie could justify on the grounds that it was gorgeous and might have been designed especially for Shirley to wear on her special day. Ginnie had squandered the last of her clothing coupons on it and paid the eye-watering price with a smile, even though she would have to forgo having her own shoes soled and heeled.

Mildred had been up early on the day, getting her slippers soaked with dew as she made a foray into the back garden to pick rosebuds for the wedding bouquet. Mrs Martin had baked a sponge cake using her entire week's fat ration and powdered egg. She had borrowed a cardboard cover from the cake shop which looked like real icing, except that it was a little battered and worse for wear, having been used for almost every wedding in the parish since icing sugar became unobtainable. The cake, splendid in its near pristine whiteness, had been taken to the King's Arms where the party were to have the wedding breakfast. Ginnie suspected that the sandwiches and sausage rolls had probably been left over from one of the local street parties, but she hoped that no one would notice.

Laurence and Steven Carter, his fellow officer and best man, both resplendent in their uniforms, were waiting at the register office in the High Street when Ginnie arrived with Avril, having left Shirley to follow on with their mother who had insisted that she was going to take Sid's place. 'I know you don't need to be given away in a civil ceremony, Shirley,' she had said at breakfast. 'But I want to walk you down the aisle so to speak. Your dad would be so proud of you if he could see you now.'

As they entered the room set aside for the nuptials, Avril nudged Ginnie in the ribs. 'He's a smashing-looking chap,' she said, nodding in Laurence's direction. 'Shirley's done well for herself.'

'He's lovely,' Ginnie said sincerely. 'I just hope they're doing the right thing.'

'It's up to Shirley to make it work, but it's never easy. Relationships are difficult at the best of times, and this one has had a shaky start.'

Ginnie glanced at Laurence and he smiled, but she knew intuitively that he was nervous. She murmured an excuse and left Avril to settle herself on one of the Rexine-covered chairs next to Ida and Fred Chinashop. She hurried over to him. 'How are you, Laurence?'

'Bearing up.' He turned to his best man. 'Steven, you haven't met my future sister-in-law. Ginnie, this is my good friend Steven Carter.'

She smiled and shook his hand. 'Nice to meet you, Steven.'

'How do you do? I've heard a lot about you, Ginnie.'

'Good or bad?'

'All good.'

'I don't think that Laurence has known me long enough to discover my bad points.'

'He sang your praises,' Steven said easily.

She decided that he had a nice smile and candid brown eyes. He looked like the sort of man you could trust to take you home after a party without fear of being leapt upon in a dark alley. Not that that had ever happened to her, but Shirley seemed to have experienced several such encounters in her colourful past.

'Never mind flirting with the maid of honour.' Laurence glanced anxiously at the door. 'Is she going to keep me waiting, Ginnie?'

'She was ready when I left the house. Jimmy should be there now, that's if he's finished tying white ribbons on the furniture van. Ida spent all yesterday cutting an old sheet into strips, but I'm afraid it will look more like bandages than anything.'

'This is more nerve-racking than steering a ship through a minefield.' Laurence took Ginnie's hand in his and looked deeply into her eyes. 'I am doing the right thing, Ginnie. I want to make her happy; you know that, don't you? But I worry that I'm rushing her into it, and I'll be back at sea in a week's time. Perhaps we ought to have waited.'

'It's pre-wedding jitters. I expect Shirley feels exactly the same.'

'Where's Colin?' he asked, lowering his voice. 'I hoped he would be here.'

'We thought he might yell through the ceremony and drown out the registrar's voice. He's got a fine pair of lungs. Mrs Martin's going to bring him to the reception.'

He tightened his grasp on her hand. 'Thank you.'

'For what? I haven't done anything special.'

'For being you. That American chap was out of his mind when he made his choice.'

She thought for a moment that he was teasing her but one look at his face and she knew that he was deadly serious. This was not the sort of conversation a man about to be married ought to have with his future sister-in-law. She withdrew her hand gently. 'He was being honourable – just like you.'

'At what cost?' Laurence looked up as the doors opened and Shirley entered the room on her mother's arm.

Ginnie hurried back to her seat, but for her the day was spoilt. It was cruel of Laurence to remind her of what she had lost. She had told him about Nick in the strictest confidence and he had chosen to mention him in front of Steven, who had turned away tactfully, but the damage was done. She felt that her private life had been dragged into the open, and, like a cut freshly exposed to the air – it hurt.

She took a deep breath and forced her lips into a smile as Shirley teetered past her on a pair of Avril's high-heeled sandals, which were a couple of sizes too small. Like the Little Mermaid in Hans Andersen's fairytale Shirley was smiling bravely, despite the pain she must be suffering. She walked up to Laurence and his serious expression softened as she whispered something in his ear.

The registrar cleared his throat. 'Ladies and gentlemen, we have come here today . . .'

His voice droned on, rich and treacly as he enunciated each syllable in every word with the aplomb of a Shakespearean actor, but Ginnie was finding it hard to concentrate. Laurence's casual mention of Nick had shaken her more than she cared to admit and she found her mind wandering during the brief ceremony, and she barely heard the responses.

And then it was over. Laurence kissed his bride and everyone applauded dutifully. Mildred shed a few tears and Avril clapped enthusiastically. Ginnie was not sure how she felt, but she managed a smile.

As soon as the formalities were over everyone trooped out of the building and walked the hundred yards down the street to the King's Arms. Ginnie glanced anxiously into the shop window, resisting the temptation to go inside and find out how Jimmy was coping on his own. Fred Woollies had promised to look in on his way to the pub, but Ginnie could not help being concerned. She managed to contain her worries during the speeches and the inevitable toasts, and then Myra, who worked in the tobacconist's shop next to Woolworth's, sat down at the piano and began playing her rendition of Glenn Miller's 'Moonlight Serenade'.

Laurence and Shirley took the floor and everyone clapped them as they danced, keeping perfect time and moving as one person. 'That's a good sign,' Avril whispered in Ginnie's ear. 'They're physically simpatico, which bodes well for the wedding night.'

Ginnie glanced round, hoping that her mother and Mrs Martin were out of earshot. 'You're incorrigible, Avril.'

'I know I am, but someone needs to liven up this dreadfully dreary crowd. You'd think this was a wake.' She gripped Ginnie's arm, jerking her head in Steven's direction. 'Why don't you go and ask that dreamy naval officer to dance?'

'I hardly know him.'

'All the more reason to go and talk to him. The poor young man looks lonely standing there by the wedding cake, and he's frightfully good-looking.'

'I'll have to leave soon. I promised Jimmy that he could come and join in the party before closing time, and to be honest I don't trust him to lock up properly.'

'Darling, it's one thing to be a good businesswoman but don't let that little shop become an obsession. You're not twenty yet and you need to have some fun.'

'All right. You win. I'll go and talk to Steven, but then I'm going to the shop. I can't swan off and leave my business as you obviously can.'

Avril pulled a face. 'I've left Lionel in charge. Who could be better than a man of God to be left in charge of a pub? Anyway, I'm going home tomorrow, so he'll be free to do the Lord's work on Sunday, as usual.'

'I hope there's plenty of Scotch in the cellar,' Ginnie said, grinning. 'I seem to remember that Lionel was fond of a dram or two.'

'I'd be a mean woman to begrudge him a little drink after closing time. Anyway, he'll only have old Percy and a couple of locals to serve. Business has dropped off enormously since our American friends left.'

'They've all gone?'

'They packed up camp and left. Lightwood House is being refurbished at the US government's expense and the owners will soon be back in residence.' Avril sighed and shook her head. 'The village will never be the same, although there are quite a few new additions to the population, and they won't have an easy life coping with the stigma of illegitimacy.' Realising what she had said, Avril gave a self-conscious giggle and patted Ginnie on the arm. 'Obviously I'm not including Colin in that category. Shirley has found herself a good man and the boy will have a stable background. He's one of the lucky ones.'

'Yes, he is,' Ginnie said, turning her head to look at her mother who was dandling Colin on her knee. 'Shirley deserves to be happy.'

'As you do, Ginnie. Now go and speak to that poor young officer who looks quite lost amongst your shopkeeper friends.'

'All right, but don't start match-making, Avril. I'm not interested.' Ginnie made her way through the crowd to where Steven was standing with a glass of beer in his hand. 'We're neglecting you,' she said apologetically.

'Not at all. I like watching people when they don't know that anyone is looking.'

'Like animals in the zoo?'

He threw back his head and laughed. 'No, not at all. If you'd spent as much time at sea as I have then you'd appreciate mixed company too.'

'So you're actually spotting the totty,' she said, smiling mischievously.

'Who could blame me for that? There are some very pretty girls here.'

'Would you like me to introduce you to some of them? That's Myra playing the piano, and that girl over there, the redhead, is her sister Doris. They're both unattached as far as I know.'

'And what about you, Ginnie? Are you involved with anyone?'

'No, I'm too busy to think about things like that. The shop takes up all my time.'

'Everyone needs a break now and again. May I have this dance, Miss Travis?'

She had intended to palm him off on tall, athletic Doris, or toothsome Pearl who served on the sweet counter in Woolworth's, but his smile was genuine and she had not the heart to refuse. 'Thank you, I'd love to.' To her surprise she meant it, and it was pleasant to feel a man's arms around her as they joined the couples on the dance floor. When the music stopped he kept hold of her hand.

'Thank you, Ginnie.'

'I enjoyed dancing with you, Steven, but I really should go and check on Jimmy. He's not used to being left on his own in the shop.'

'How would it be if I came with you?' He glanced at the clock above the bar. 'You could close up for the day and then we'd be able to come back and see the happy couple off on their honeymoon.'

'Yes, of course. But shouldn't you stay here as you're the best man?'

'I don't think I'm needed at present. Laurence and your sister are doing very well without either of us.'

They left the pub together and walked arm in arm along the parade of shops, most of which had already closed for the night. 'I should have left earlier,' Ginnie said, quickening her pace. 'I need to cash up.'

'How far is it?'

She came to a sudden halt as she saw Jimmy rush out of the shop, waving his arms and shouting. 'Something's terribly wrong.' She broke into a run.

Chapter Ten

Jimmy ran towards her, flapping his arms. 'Come quick. There's a mad woman in the shop.'

Ginnie came to a halt, staring in horror at the shop window, which was covered in white paint. A small crowd had gathered and she pushed through them with Steven and Jimmy following close behind. She thrust the doors open and the sight that met her eyes wrenched a gasp from deep within her. Olivia Mallory stood in the middle of the shop floor with a paint can in her hands. She was shaking it and spraying droplets onto furniture that was already iced white as if there had been a sudden snowstorm. The strong smell of gloss paint pervaded the whole area and Ida's wax fruit floated on a slowly moving glacier as it slid from the coffee table onto the carpeted floor.

'Stop it.' Ginnie's voice broke on a sob. 'What have you done to my dad's shop, you crazy bitch?'

Olivia's eyes glittered with malice. 'You've destroyed my family – I've returned the compliment.'

Ginnie made a move towards her but Steven caught her round the waist, holding her back. 'Don't,' he said firmly. 'This is criminal damage.' He turned to Jimmy, who was weeping openly. 'Call the police.'

'No.' Ginnie stopped struggling. 'Not yet. I want Mr Mallory to see what his daughter's really like. Let me go, Steven.'

'Promise me you won't do anything silly.'

'I'm not going to touch her. I'm going to use the phone in the office. Don't let her leave the shop.' He released her and she strode past Olivia, ignoring her taunts and using every last scrap of self-control to keep calm. In the office she searched for the Mallory's home number, picked up the receiver and dialled.

Colin Mallory's car screeched to a halt outside the shop, where the crowd of onlookers had doubled in size. He stormed into the building but came to a sudden halt when he saw his daughter. Spattered with white paint, Olivia stood in the middle of the destruction, pale but defiant. 'Daddy,' she cried. 'Take me home.'

'Did you do this, Livvie?' Her father gazed round in horror. 'Tell me it's not true.'

'Of course she did.' Ginnie walked slowly towards him. 'I wanted you to see exactly what sort of person your daughter is before I called the police.'

'You might have done this yourself,' he said defensively. 'Can you prove that Livvie had anything to do with it?'

Steven indicated the damage with a sweep of his

hands. 'Come off it, sir. You can see for yourself that she's covered in paint and she's still holding the tin.'

Olivia uttered a shriek and tossed the can into the window display. 'Of course I did it, Daddy. I did it for you and for Mummy and for that stupid brother of mine who's allowed himself to be taken in by that tart, Shirley Travis. I wanted them to suffer for tricking Laurence into taking on another man's child.'

Ginnie clenched her fists, digging her fingernails into her palms. With her mind concentrated on the pain she was less likely to lose her temper and stoop to their level. She raised her hand as Steven opened his mouth to speak. 'It's all right. I'm not going to let her get to me. Call the police, Jimmy. Dial 999 and let's get the law to sort this out.'

Sniffing and wiping his eyes on his sleeve, Jimmy had begun to shamble towards the office but Colin Mallory barred his way. 'There's no need to be hasty. I'm sure we can settle this matter between ourselves.' He took a deep breath, curving his lips into a smile that was more like a feral snarl. 'I suppose we are family now, of sorts anyway.'

Ginnie was quietly confident. She had him at a disadvantage. 'I think a charge of criminal damage would be eminently fair in the circumstances. I don't think even you could get her off this one, Mr Mallory.'

'Call her bluff, Daddy.' Olivia started towards him but he backed away.

'Don't touch me, you stupid girl. This is a Savile Row suit.' Mallory took a handkerchief from his top pocket and mopped his brow. 'All right, Miss Travis. What do you want?'

Ginnie took in the paint-spattered scene with a sweeping glance. 'I'll have to shut up shop while the cleaning up is done, and that will incur a significant loss of business. I can't tell you exactly how much it will cost to replace the stock until I've had a chance to work it out, but you won't get much change from five hundred pounds, maybe more.'

'Five hundred! That's daylight robbery.'

'She's the crook, Daddy.' Olivia stared down at her ruined clothes and paint-stained hands. 'I want to go home.'

'Shut up, Olivia.' Mallory took a cheque book from his inside pocket. 'I'll pay three hundred and not a penny more.'

'Then you leave me no choice.' Ginnie signalled to Jimmy. 'Phone the police.'

'All right. Five hundred it is, but I want your word that none of this will become public knowledge.'

'If it does it won't have come from me. And there's one other thing.'

'I guessed as much. Don't push me too far, young lady.'

'It's not money. I want you to go to the function room at the King's Arms and give Laurence and Shirley your blessing.'

He recoiled as if she were a hissing cobra about to strike. 'Never. I won't acknowledge your sister or that brat of hers in public.'

'Don't let him goad you into something you'll regret,' Steven said softly.

'It's all right; I'm not going to do anything silly.' Ginnie faced Mallory with an unblinking stare. 'You will go there and shake both their hands, and you'll tell your snooty wife not to snub my sister if she meets her in the street.' She turned her head to glare at Olivia. 'And that goes for you too. If I hear that you've said anything untoward to my sister or my mother, I'll take the story to the papers and let's see how they deal with it.'

'That's blackmail, you vicious little bitch,' Mallory said angrily. 'You're going too far.'

Steven cleared his throat. 'I'd advise you to moderate your language, sir.'

'Who d'you think you are?' Mallory demanded angrily. 'You're not on the bridge now, sailor boy.'

'Actually I'm a qualified solicitor, Mr Mallory. But for the war I'd have been practising for several years.'

'Then you should know that I too am a solicitor, a member of the local council and a Justice of the Peace, and I don't accept insolence from juniors.'

Ginnie turned to Steven with a shadow of a smile. 'Thanks, but I can fight my own battles, and I'm not budging on this. Either he acknowledges Shirley as his daughter-in-law or I'm prosecuting Olivia for malicious damage to my property.'

'Oh for goodness' sake do as she asks, Daddy,' Olivia said crossly. 'I'm soaked to the skin and the smell of the paint is making me feel sick.'

'And whose fault is that, you stupid girl?' Mallory pondered for a moment, and then nodded his head. 'Very well. I'll do as you demand, but that doesn't mean that I'll welcome Shirley and her child into my home.'

'I don't suppose she'd want to visit you anyway.'

Olivia stamped her foot. 'Daddy! I want to go now.'

'You're not getting in my car in that state. You can walk home and if you're a laughing stock then it damned well serves you right.' Mallory rested his cheque book on a table that had escaped the paint frenzy, and taking a pen from his pocket he wrote the amount and signed it with a flourish. He tore the cheque off and handed it to Ginnie. 'Don't think you can extort more from me. This is in full and final payment.'

'I can't go out like this.' Olivia's voice rose in a wail and tears poured down her cheeks.

Ginnie stared at her and felt nothing but pity. 'You're a sad cow,' she said slowly. 'Jimmy, you'd best take her home, but put her in the back of the van on a pile of sacks so that she can't spread paint all over the floor.'

'Daddy,' Olivia gasped. 'You can't let her do this to me.'

'You should think yourself lucky, my girl. And go out the back way. I don't want people to see you looking like that.' He opened the door and stepped outside. 'Move along. There's nothing to see.'

Olivia stared after him, her bottom lip trembling. 'I can't go in a furniture van.'

Jimmy sidled past her. 'C'mon, miss. The van's parked in the yard.'

Shooting a malevolent look at Ginnie, Olivia followed him towards the back of the shop. 'You haven't heard the last of this.'

Left alone with Steven, Ginnie experienced a sudden sense of panic. All her hard work had been destroyed in a few minutes of malicious vandalism. 'This is awful. I'll have to shut the shop and I'm going to lose so much trade. People will just go to the big stores locally or even up West.'

Steven slipped off his uniform jacket and hung it on a coat stand near the door. 'You've got friends, Ginnie. What we need is some elbow grease and several gallons of turps or white spirit.'

'Where am I going to get that sort of thing at this time in the evening?'

'I was introduced to your friend Fred Woollies at the pub. He's bound to have a stock of the stuff. Why don't you go back to the reception and have a word with him and anyone else who's up for a night of hard work. We can't perform miracles and these soft furnishings have had it, but we could get the place shipshape and Bristol fashion in time to open up tomorrow.'

Ginnie stared at him in amazement. 'Why would you do this? You hardly know me.'

'I'm a sucker for a maiden in distress, and Laurence

is my friend. We've been through some tough times together and I don't see why his spoilt brat of a sister should be allowed to ruin his big day.' He rolled up his sleeves. 'Go on, Ginnie. Chop chop.'

She reached up to plant a kiss on his cheek. 'You must be the best pal anyone ever had. I'll be as quick as I can.'

'You might want to pop home and change into something more suitable,' he said, grinning. 'You look stunning in that dress but it's not very practical.'

She felt the blood rush to her face as she met his appreciative gaze. She had not been able to afford a new dress for the wedding, and they had pooled their clothing coupons to buy Shirley a going-away outfit. This had left Ginnie with little alternative than to borrow one of Shirley's frocks that were now too tight for her, and with a few minor alterations it fitted perfectly. The delicate turquoise silk moulded to her slender figure and accentuated her small waist. It was cut rather too low at the neck for her liking but having dressed quickly that morning she had had little time to bother about minor details as she concentrated on getting Shirley ready for her big day. It was doubly flattering to receive compliments from a man like Steven and she glowed with pleasure. 'Yes. Thanks, I'll do that.' She hurried into the street and was relieved to find that the crowd had dispersed. She ran all the way to the pub.

When she arrived she almost bumped into Colin

Mallory who was about to make a hasty exit. 'Happy now?' he demanded, scowling. 'I've done my bit, but that's the end of it. Don't expect anything more from me.'

Ginnie said nothing. There was nothing left to say. She knew that she had made a powerful enemy that day, but she did not care. Shirley's future was assured and Colin Mallory had publicly acknowledged his new daughter-in-law. What happened after that would be up to Shirley and Laurence. Ginnie made her way through the bar to the room where the reception was in full swing. Younger guests were jiving enthusiastically but without much expertise and the older generation watched with benign smiles. She could see that Shirley and Laurence were about to take their leave and she paused to catch her breath before strolling up to them. 'So you're off then?'

Shirley clutched her husband's arm, smiling happily. 'We are, but I'm not sure where. Laurence has kept the honeymoon destination a big secret.'

Laurence reached out to grasp Ginnie's hand. 'Thanks for everything, Ginnie. I don't know what made my old man grace us with his presence, but I suspect you had something to do with it.'

'I don't think anyone could make Mr Mallory do anything against his will,' Ginnie said tactfully. 'Go away and enjoy yourselves. Don't worry about a thing.'

'You've been a brick.' Shirley gave her a hug. 'I

must go and say goodbye to Mum and Colin.' She wandered off, acknowledging the smiles and good wishes from the guests as she went to give her baby a loving cuddle.

Ginnie turned to Laurence with a questioning look. 'Is everything all right? You seem a bit edgy.'

'Why did my father come here just now? Are you keeping anything from me, Ginnie?'

She shrugged her shoulders. 'You're being paranoid, Laurence. I expect your father simply wanted to wish you well.'

'My father never does anything on impulse. Something's wrong and you're a rotten liar.'

'Don't be silly. This is your wedding day and everything is going to be wonderful.'

His eyes darkened and he looked away. 'Yes. I'm a lucky man.'

'Then for God's sake look as though you're enjoying yourself,' Ginnie said, torn between tears and laughter. 'This is the happiest day of her life and if you spoil it simply because you don't get on well with your father you'll have me to deal with, Laurence Mallory.'

He raised her hand to his lips. 'Why couldn't I have met you first?'

She snatched her hand away. 'Laurence!'

'I'm sorry. I shouldn't have said that.' He shrugged and walked slowly to where Shirley was rocking the baby in her arms and talking animatedly to her mother and Avril.

Ginnie stared after him, confused and at a loss. She had always got on well with Laurence, but she had never imagined that his feelings went any deeper. She watched them take their leave of the guests with a strange feeling of detachment. The whole day had taken on a surreal feeling, but Shirley's smile when she turned to her was genuine enough. She broke away from Laurence to rush over and throw her arms around Ginnie, holding her close. 'Thank you again for everything you've done for me. You're the best sister a girl could have.' She held her at arm's length. 'Are you all right, Ginnie? You look a bit flushed.'

'I'm fine. Go with your husband, Mrs Mallory, and have a wonderful honeymoon at the secret destination, wherever that may be. We'll look after Colin, so don't worry about anything. Just go and enjoy yourself.'

Shirley's eyes shone and her skin glowed. She looked so beautiful that Ginnie found it hard to believe that Laurence had any doubts. She waved them off, and as soon as the door closed behind them she headed for Fred Woollies, who was propping up the bar. 'Fred, dear Fred. I need your help.'

They worked all night. Fred Woollies supplied the turpentine, although like everything else there was a limited supply and it had to be used sparingly. Fred Chinashop helped Jimmy to lug the paint-spattered three-piece suite out into the back yard and Ida attempted to soak up the worst of the paint puddles with unsold newspapers donated by Cyril Huggins who owned the newsagent's on the corner.

It was four o'clock in the morning when Ginnie called a halt and sent everyone home. The shop reeked of turpentine and there were large empty spaces where the damaged furniture had once stood, but most of the paint had been sopped up, leaving a milky residue on the linoleum and oily stains on the floorboards. 'It's a good start,' Ginnie said, stifling a yawn. 'But it's going to take ages to get rid of the fumes.'

Steven wiped his hands on a tea towel soaked in turps. 'It's time you went home and got your head down, Ginnie. You must be exhausted.'

She gave him a wan smile. 'You too. You've been brilliant, Steven. I don't know what I'd have done without you.'

'I must say I didn't think my best man duties would involve mopping up several pints of white gloss and shifting furniture around, but I'm glad I could help. At least Livvie's outburst didn't spoil Laurence and Shirley's wedding day.'

'No. He was a bit suspicious about his father's motives for turning up unexpectedly, but I managed to change the subject.'

'He'll forget all that when he's with Shirley. I'm sure they'll make a go of things.' Steven discarded the tea towel, tossing it into a cardboard box filled with newspaper and rags. 'I'll just put this in the back yard. It's a fire hazard and we don't want the place to burn to the ground. It would only take a spark.'

Ginnie began to giggle helplessly. 'For heaven's sake don't light a cigarette in here.'

'I don't smoke.' Steven hesitated with the box in his arms. 'You're a remarkable girl, Ginnie. Most women would have been in hysterics from the start, but you just pitched in and got on with things.'

She shrugged her shoulders. 'Anything else would have been a waste of time.' She angled her head, looking at him as if for the first time and liking what she saw. 'I never thought to ask you where you were staying, Steven. You'll be locked out for certain.'

'I booked into the Limes; it's a small hotel, not too far from here. Laurence invited me to stay at his parents' house in Monk Avenue but I thought it might be a bit much for his family to cope with and now I'm glad I decided to be independent. Anyway, don't worry about me. I'll see you home and then I'll go and hammer on the hotel door. I expect someone will let me in. They'll just think the party went on all night.'

Ginnie was awakened from a deep sleep by someone shaking her. 'What's going on?' She dragged herself to a sitting position. 'What's up, Mum?'

'There's a man sleeping on the sofa in the front room. I went in to draw the curtains and there he was, curled up under a blanket. What's going on?'

Rubbing her eyes, Ginnie stretched and yawned. 'It's only Steven, Mum. We didn't get home until four thirty this morning and so I asked him to stay. Avril's in my room and I was bunking up with Shirley, so the sofa was the only place left.'

Mildred rushed to the cot and swept Colin into her arms. 'What on earth were you doing until that time? I never thought you'd be carrying on like your sister.'

'We weren't carrying on, Mum.' Ginnie swung her legs over the side of the bed and stood up, reaching for her dressing gown. 'It's Laurence's best man, Steven. I hope you didn't wake him.'

'I only saw the top of a man's head and his trousers were hung over the chair. I didn't know who it was.'

'Well if you'd be a darling and put the kettle on I'll come downstairs and tell you all about it, but try not to wake the poor chap. We had a hell of a night.'

'What's going on?' Avril poked her head round the door. 'What's all the fuss about, Mildred? Are we on fire or something?'

'I found a man sleeping on the sofa.' Mildred pushed past her. 'I want a full explanation, Ginnie. I've had enough problems with Shirley in that direction and I don't want to start all over again with you. What will the neighbours think?' She stalked out of the room, tossing her head so that the metal curlers rattled beneath her hairnet.

Avril threw back her head and laughed. 'She's just

peeved because she didn't get off with anyone at the wedding.'

'Auntie Avril! How can you suggest such a thing?'

'Your mother is human, Ginnie. She's not in her dotage yet.'

'You're a wicked woman,' Ginnie said, chuckling. 'And nothing happened. It's only Steven and we were up nearly all night trying to sort out the mess in the shop.' She held up her hand. 'Don't ask me now. I can't say anything until I've had a cup of tea and then I'll tell you and Mum together. It's bad, but I've got things under control.'

Avril's hand flew to the scarf tied turban-fashion on her head. 'It'll have to wait until I'm fit to be seen. I'm going to get dressed.' She flew from the room leaving a faint whiff of Nivea Creme and Shalimar perfume in her wake.

Following Avril's example Ginnie had a quick wash and dressed before going downstairs. She found Steven sitting at the kitchen table drinking tea. He rose to his feet and pulled up a chair for her. 'I've just been apologising for giving Mrs Travis such a fright.'

'It wasn't your fault, dear,' Mildred said, offering him a slice of toast. 'You should have woken me up, Ginnie. Steven's been telling me what happened at the shop. It's too awful to think about. That girl should be locked up.'

'It's all sorted, Mum.' Ginnie gave Steven a grateful smile as she took her seat.

'How is it sorted?' Mildred demanded. 'I call it criminal.'

'Mr Mallory gave me a cheque that should cover the damage and allow me to get some more stock.'

'That's if you can get anything from the suppliers. I don't hold with all this utility furniture; it's not a patch on the quality items your father used to stock. And what about the clearing up? Spilled paint makes a terrible mess.'

'I'd stay and help but I've got to get back to my ship,' Steven said apologetically.

'You did enough last night.' Ginnie reached for the toast rack. 'You were splendid, Steven. I don't know what I'd have done if you hadn't stepped in.'

'Anyone would have done the same.'

'I'm sure that's not true,' Mildred said, pouring tea. 'I'm sure we're all very grateful to you.'

Ginnie nodded enthusiastically. 'He was magnificent, Mum. He stood up to old man Mallory and really put him in his place. Steven's a lawyer too.'

'Not a practising one at the moment, Mrs Travis,' Steven said hastily. 'I'd only done a year as a junior solicitor before I was called up. It was a foregone conclusion that I'd join the Navy because both my father and grandfather were naval officers.'

'That's nice, dear.' Mildred turned to Ginnie with a worried frown. 'Is the shop going to be closed for long? I'm not sure how we'll manage if it is.'

'Don't worry, Mum. I'm going to pay the cheque

in as soon as the bank opens today. We'll be okay, and it might even work to our advantage.'

Mildred shook her head. 'I don't see how you come to that conclusion, love.'

'The shop was dreadfully old-fashioned. The window was cracked when the V1 landed on the cricket field, and Dad couldn't afford to replace it, so in a way having Mr Mallory's money will give us a fresh start. I'll be able to restock and modernise the shop floor. I've got plans for a big reopening and I'll see if I can get it on the front page of the local rag.'

'And you'll make a go of it,' Steven said, smiling. 'Good for you, Ginnie.'

'So your leave is over then?' Mildred refilled his cup with tea. 'Will it be long before your demob?'

'Mum!' Torn between laughter and embarrassment at her mother's cross-examination tactics, Ginnie sent him an apologetic smile. 'It's none of our business.'

He shrugged his shoulders and his eyes twinkled. 'No, I don't mind, honestly. I'm in what's affectionately known as the Wavy Navy. I'm in the Royal Naval Reserve which means that I'm not a career naval officer. I'm returning to duty, Mrs Travis, but when my demob papers come through I'll be looking for a job.'

'And you're a solicitor?' Unabashed, Mildred deposited the teapot on its stand and sat down in her usual chair. 'Where will you have your practice?'

Ginnie squirmed in her seat but Steven did not

seem at all put out by the interrogation. 'I'd started working for a firm in Southampton before the war. My parents live in a village not far from there and I was able to commute quite easily. I'll probably contact the senior partner and see if there's any chance of having my old job back.'

'Southampton, Ginnie,' Mildred said pointedly. 'That's not too far away.'

Ginnie leapt to her feet. 'I really have to go to the shop now, Mum.'

'But it's Sunday, dear.' Mildred stared at her, eyebrows raised. 'Aren't you going to have a day off? I mean, if Steven has to return to his ship you ought to go to the station and see him off.'

Her mother's blatant attempt at match-making was painful and embarrassing. 'I'm going to do as much clearing up as I can, Mum.'

'You need a break, dear. You've been working too hard.' Mildred fixed Steven with a meaningful stare. 'What do you think?'

'I haven't got the time, Mum,' Ginnie said without giving him a chance to respond. 'I intend to open up tomorrow, as usual. I'm going to show the Mallorys that I mean business.'

Steven rose to his feet. 'Thank you for breakfast, Mrs Travis. I'd love to stay longer, but I really ought to get going too.'

Mildred's mouth drooped at the corners. 'What a shame. We were just getting to know you. I hope you'll come again, Steven.'

'What's all this?' Avril breezed into the room, looking elegant as usual in a pale blue linen costume with a fashionably short skirt. 'What have I missed?'

'We were just leaving,' Ginnie said hastily. 'I'll see you both later. Are you ready, Steven? I'll walk to the station with you.'

Waiting on the platform Ginnie was reminded of the day a year ago when she had stood in the same spot, waving to Laurence as the train pulled out of the station. 'It's all goodbyes,' she said half to herself.

'Not for much longer.'

'I suppose not, but it's hard to believe that the war really is over.'

'Not for everyone.'

'No, but I'm just glad it's over in Europe. It may be selfish but we've had enough tragedy to last a lifetime.'

'Laurence told me that your father died in an air raid. I'm sorry, Ginnie.'

'It was awful and I miss him terribly, but that's why I'm so determined to make a go of the shop. Dad gave his whole life to building up the business and I owe it to him to carry on where he left off.'

'As I said before, you're a remarkable girl, Ginnie.'

She shrugged, shuffling her feet in embarrassment. 'No I'm not. I'm very ordinary, but that makes me even more determined to make something of myself.'

He raised his hand as if to pat her on the shoulder but seemed to change his mind and straightened his cap instead. 'That sounds like the train,' he said abruptly. 'Will I see you again, Ginnie?'

Taken off guard, she felt herself blushing. 'I – I don't know. I mean you'll be very busy looking for a job when you leave the Navy.'

He grinned. 'Wavy Navy – don't forget.'

'I won't.' She stood back as the engine rushed past them with a whoosh of steam and a screech of metal wheels on the iron track as it came to a halt further along the platform. 'If you're ever this way pop in and see us.'

He leaned over to kiss her on the cheek. 'Do you mean that?'

'Of course.'

'I'll keep in touch, Ginnie.' He opened a carriage door and climbed inside. 'Cheerio.'

She blew him a kiss. It seemed appropriate under the circumstances, but she had no intention of getting involved romantically. Once again she found herself standing alone on a railway station. The war years had been punctuated with goodbyes, some of them more painful than others.

The train disappeared into the distance and she set off for the shop. Business must come first. Tomorrow, as soon as the bank opened, she would be at the counter to present Colin Mallory's cheque.

Her fears that it might bounce proved unfounded. Perhaps her threat of reporting Livvie's act of vandalism to the local press had made him think twice, but Colin Mallory honoured his pledge. With the money in her bank account Ginnie was able to have a new window installed, and she hired workmen to finish the job of clearing up the mess. The pieces of furniture that had suffered paint damage were sent to be reupholstered and paint-soaked rugs had to go for specialist cleaning.

Leaving Jimmy in charge Ginnie chose a quiet day in the middle of the week to visit the warehouses in the East End. She had hoped to order new stock but there were long waiting lists and even then there were no guarantees of delivery. It would, she realised, be a long time before things returned to normal. At the end of the day she left the last warehouse feeling dispirited, and for the first time she doubted whether she could make a go of the business.

Staring gloomily out of the bus window on the homeward journey she was even more conscious of the vast craters where once there had been tall buildings, but even in the worst areas of devastation, plant life had already started to reclaim the territory. Rosebay willowherb had colonised the bomb sites, together with buddleia and dandelions. Blades of grass spiked through piles of rubble and somehow this determined attempt by nature to overcome the devastation created by man gave her the courage to fight on. If a tiny blade of grass could push its way through concrete then Virginia Travis could take on the world. She was not beaten yet.

*

Two weeks later Ginnie was in the newly glazed shop window rearranging the reupholstered three-piece suite around a coffee table that the French polisher had just delivered in mint condition. The wax fruit had sadly not survived and had been consigned to the dustbin, but she had borrowed a tea set from Fred Chinashop and this added the necessary homely touch.

She stood back, surveying her work with a nod of approval. It would be weeks before the utility bedroom furniture arrived, but the carpenter had just finished building a stand to display her newly acquired range of kitchen equipment. People setting up home for the first time or those who had lost their possessions in the bombing raids would be in need of everything from dusters to roasting pans. Ginnie was determined to supply all their requirements and she had used Colin Mallory's money sparingly, but she hoped to good effect. She was about to move forward to adjust the cushions supplied by Ida when the shop door opened and Shirley rushed in.

Ginnie stared at her in amazement. 'I thought you weren't due until tomorrow. Where's Laurence?'

Shirley dropped her suitcase on the floor and slumped down amongst the cushions on the sofa. 'He's left me,' she said on a sob.

Chapter Eleven

'What do you mean – left you?'

'He's gone back to his ship.'

Ginnie breathed a sigh of relief. She had not thought for a moment that Laurence would walk out on his bride, but even allowing for Shirley's tendency to over-dramatise she did seem upset. 'Calm down, and please get off the sofa. You're ruining my window display.'

Shirley's face crumpled and she burst into a fresh bout of tears. 'You don't understand.'

I must be patient, Ginnie thought, casting her eyes heavenwards. 'Take a deep breath, and tell me exactly what happened.'

Shirley's answer was muffled as she clamped her hands to her face, shaking her head. At a loss as to how to handle the situation, Ginnie glanced at her watch and saw that it was almost lunch time. She placed the closed sign on the shop door and locked it. 'I can't understand a word you're saying.' She helped Shirley to her feet. 'Come through to the office and I'll put the kettle on.'

When Shirley was settled in the desk chair with a cup of tea in her hands, Ginnie asked her again.

'What's wrong? You're supposed to be radiant after your honeymoon.'

'It was a disaster,' Shirley said, hiccuping and sniffing. 'I've made a dreadful mistake.'

Ginnie perched on the edge of the desk. 'What happened? You were so happy on your wedding day.'

'First of all it was the beastly hotel. It took ages to get there on the train and then we had to walk from the station because there weren't any taxis, and I was tired. My shoes pinched and my feet hurt. Then when we got to the hotel it was just a horrible old-fashioned place and we were too late to get anything to eat or even a cup of tea. The room was hideous and the bed was lumpy and I'll swear the sheets had been slept in because they smelled awful. We had our first row and I made Laurence sleep in the chair.'

'I'm so sorry, Shirley. But it can't all have been bad. It was your honeymoon.'

'Think what you like, but it was even worse next day. I was so disappointed with everything that I couldn't speak to him. I could barely look Laurence in the face and he went out soon after breakfast and didn't return until lunch time. By then I was absolutely furious and so I went out and left him on his own.'

'That might not have been the best move,' Ginnie said tentatively. 'But surely you made it up later.'

Shirley sipped her tea. 'I suppose so, but it was

too late. The honeymoon was ruined as far as I was concerned. It wasn't at all romantic and the damned hotel was filled with old people who lived there permanently, and they stared at us every time we went in for a meal. I begged Laurence to find somewhere else for us to stay but the town was heaving with troops who'd just arrived on ships from goodness knows where. It was ghastly and I missed my baby. I hated leaving Colin and although Laurence was sympathetic I knew he didn't really understand.'

'It must have been difficult for him too.'

'Don't take his side. He was supposed to make me feel that I was the only woman in the world for him. As it was I often caught him with a faraway look in his eyes and I'm sure he was thinking of someone else. You can always tell.'

Ginnie straightened up and went to look out of the window onto the desultory back yard. It was raining and Jimmy was struggling to heft a chest of drawers into the back of the furniture van. 'He adores you, Shirley. You must have been imagining things.'

In between mopping her eyes, Shirley took sips of tea. 'It wouldn't have been like that with Tony. He understood me perfectly. I hardly had to speak and he knew what I was thinking.'

Ginnie turned to give her a searching look. 'Doesn't that tell you something? Maybe you were thinking of Tony and Laurence was feeling just as you are now.'

Shirley's eyes widened. 'That's silly – I mean he couldn't have known. I never told him about Tony.'

'I did, remember, you told me to. Anyway, Laurence strikes me as a very sympathetic sort of chap. Perhaps he sensed that you weren't all that enthusiastic.'

'Oh, I don't know. Anyway it was one disaster after another. Especially when he discovered what Livvie had done to the shop.'

'Who told him? I didn't want you to find out.'

'He telephoned home to thank his dad for coming to the reception. I'm not sure if it was Livvie or their mother who spoke to him, but they gave him their version of events and he was absolutely furious. I've never seen him so angry.'

'It wasn't anything to do with him. I can understand he might be a bit upset but it's all fixed now.'

'He was worried about you, you idiot. I heard him telling whoever it was on the end of the line that he was ashamed to be a Mallory if that's how his family behaved. He said you'd worked hard and you didn't deserve to be treated that way. I think he fancies you more than he does me.'

'That's utter nonsense.'

'I saw the way he looked at you at the wedding reception,' Shirley said, frowning. 'Have you been flirting with him behind my back?'

Ginnie recoiled angrily. 'That's a rotten thing to say. I wouldn't do that, and anyway I'm not interested in Laurence. I think he's a great guy but he's not my type.'

'I seem to remember that Nick was engaged to a girl back home. It didn't stop you then so why should I believe you now?'

'That's so damned unfair. For a start I didn't know that Nick was engaged in the beginning, and when I did find out I backed down. I put a stop to it. Stop being a bitch, Shirley. Don't take it out on me.'

Shirley's lips trembled ominously. 'I'm really sorry, Ginnie. I'm so tired. I don't know what I'm saying.'

'It can't all have been bad then,' Ginnie said, grinning. 'I mean if you didn't get much sleep . . .'

'Not because of that, stupid. I was too upset and emotional to get a wink, but Laurence snored away all night in the wretched armchair.'

'You mean you never . . .'

'That's right. I'd still be a virgin bride, if I'd been a virgin in the first place.' Shirley reached for her handbag and took out a packet of Woodbines. She lit one and puffed smoke into the air.

'Since when did you start smoking?'

'I had to do something to calm my nerves. Sometimes I used to have a drag on Charlie's cigarette, although I didn't like it much. Anyway I decided to have another go and it gave me an excuse to go for a walk on my own because Laurence doesn't approve of women smoking. He made that quite clear too.'

'I am so sorry. You really have had a miserable time, but he must be feeling awful too.'

Shirley took another lungful of smoke and

coughed. 'I don't really enjoy this, and I can't say whether or not it makes me feel calmer because I'm not. My nerves are all jangly and I keep bursting into tears for no reason.'

Ginnie did some quick mental arithmetic. 'How long ago was it when you spent the weekend with Laurence? Did you . . . you know what I'm saying?'

Shirley shrugged her shoulders. 'Of course we did. How else would we know that we were in love?'

'You slept together. Am I right?'

'Yes, of course we did. Do you want me to spell it out?'

'And were you careful?' Ginnie threw up her hands. 'Stop being dim, Shirley. If you didn't take precautions you might very well be pregnant again.'

'But I was breast-feeding the baby. I couldn't be – could I?'

'You'd put him on the bottle, and anyway I think that's probably an old wives' tale. Didn't you wonder why you were in such an emotional state? Don't you ever learn?'

Shirley clapped her hand to her mouth. 'Oh, my God. I'm up the spout again.'

'At least you know for certain who the father is this time,' Ginnie said drily and was immediately sorry as Shirley uttered a throaty sob.

'You are cruel.'

'No, I'm just being practical.' Ginnie helped her to her feet. 'Now stop bawling and I'll take you home. You want to see Colin, don't you?'

'Of course I do, but another baby so soon. What will Mum say?'

'Don't imagine that I'm going to look after two nippers,' Mildred said, shaking her head. 'You're a silly girl to let it happen again.'

Shirley stared at her in horror. 'But, Mum, I thought you'd be sympathetic. I'll get a job and pay my way.'

'You've got a husband to support you, Shirley. You're a married woman now.'

'He's gone back to sea, Mum. I made a terrible mistake marrying Laurence. It's over as far as I'm concerned.'

'Stuff and nonsense. You can't walk away from your husband because the honeymoon wasn't perfect. Real life isn't like the movies, my girl. Ask any married woman and they'll tell you it's always a matter of adjustment.'

'But he's going to be away for months or even longer. I can't live like that.' Shirley cuddled her baby son, rubbing her cheek against his mop of blond hair.

'You should have thought about that before you chased after him and got yourself in the family way again.' Mildred folded her arms and glared at Shirley, as if daring her to argue.

Ginnie could see that this conversation was going nowhere. 'He's probably feeling as bad as you are, Shirley. I bet he'll be on the blower tonight, begging you to forgive him for being a pain in the neck.'

Mildred stabbed a paring knife into the potato she had been peeling. 'He'd better or I'll want to know the reason why, my girl.'

Ginnie noted the telltale wobble of her sister's bottom lip, which was a sure sign of fresh tears, and she moved towards the door. 'I'd better get back to the shop. I'll see you this evening, and don't worry, Shirley. I'm sure it will all work out in the end.' She made a hasty exit and left the house running.

'You don't normally close at lunch time.' The irate woman who had been waiting outside followed Ginnie into the shop and marched over to the display of household goods. 'My old man's just been demobbed and he expects to have his dinner on the table when he gets home from the labour exchange,' she said, picking up a saucepan. 'He's got to find hisself a job and it ain't going to be easy.' She weighed the pan in her hand. 'This isn't a patch on my old stew pan. It had some weight to it.'

'I'm sorry if I kept you waiting,' Ginnie said, making a determined effort to sound calm and courteous. 'I agree, of course, about the quality but it's all we can get nowadays.'

The customer peered at the price tag. 'Too bloody expensive. I can't pay that sort of money for a cooking pot.'

Ginnie forced her lips into a smile. 'Well, we can't allow a returning hero to go without his dinner. Would it help if I knocked sixpence off the price?'

'I ain't asking for charity, young lady.' The woman took her purse from her handbag. 'It's bloody daylight robbery, but I'll take it.' She counted out the coins. 'But I'll take advantage of the sale price,' she said smugly, thrusting the money into Ginnie's outstretched hand. 'That's what it says on the label, less sixpence.'

'Thank you for your custom, madam.' Ginnie handed her the saucepan wrapped in brown paper.

'Cheeky cow. You're glad to see the back of me.'

'Not at all. Every customer is important to me,' Ginnie said with feeling. 'It's hard for everyone these days, but I did hear a rumour that they're taking on men at the Ford factory. Maybe your husband could try there.'

'Ta, love. I'll pass it on. They're not much cop at the labour exchange. A chap could die of starvation waiting in the queue and then there's all them forms to fill in. What a welcome home for heroes.' She stomped out of the shop.

Ginnie counted the morning's takings. She could ill afford the price reduction, but she had made a sale and a satisfied customer was one who might return at a later date and make further purchases. She closed the till and was heading for the office when the telephone shrilled and she quickened her pace. 'Hello.'

'Hold the line, please. I have a trunk call for you. Press button A, caller.'

Ginnie waited, listening to the metallic clink of the coins tumbling into the box.

'Hello. Ginnie, is that you?'

'Laurence?'

'Yes. I haven't got much change so I'll have to be quick. Has Shirley arrived home?'

'Yes, she turned up at lunch time. Where are you?'

'I'm at Gosport. I expect she's told you that things didn't go too well.'

'She's upset, naturally.'

'Oh hell. Sorry, but I know I handled things badly. I just wanted everything to be perfect for her and it all went wrong.'

'Why didn't you ring her at home?'

'If she hadn't arrived it would have been awkward. I didn't want to upset your mother.'

'Well you need to phone her now. It's up to you to sort things out with your wife, Laurence.'

'I know, and I will. I'll have to get some more change and I'll call Shirley at your house.'

'You haven't left her, have you?'

'Of course not. Whatever gave you that idea?'

'Shirley thought . . .'

'I tried to explain that I didn't want to go away so soon, but I had to have a medical check-up before I was allowed to return to my ship.'

'Are you okay?'

'No, unfortunately the X-rays revealed a shadow on one of my lungs and I'm being discharged on medical grounds.'

'Oh, Laurence. I'm so sorry. Is it serious?'

'I'll have to have further tests, but a career with

the Navy is out of the question. I'll have to break it to Shirley that I'm out of work, and we've nowhere to live. I was banking on getting married quarters. It's all a bit of a mess, I'm afraid.'

More than you know, Ginnie thought, biting her lip. 'You must tell her what you've just told me, but first of all tell her that you love her, Laurence. She's very emotional and she's got it into her head that you're more interested in me, which is utter nonsense.'

There was a brief silence and then the pips went. 'Sorry, Ginnie. I'll ring—' The line went dead and then the dialling tone cut in.

She replaced the receiver in its cradle and sat down to sort through the paperwork on the desk. The bell on the street door would alert her if anyone entered the shop, and Jimmy would return soon from fitting a particularly sickly shade of pink linoleum in a customer's bedroom. He was still a bit nervous when dealing with the public, but she was always ready to step in if he was dealing with an awkward customer.

Jimmy returned but Ginnie was still finding it hard to concentrate on balancing the books. She was desperately sorry for Laurence and concerned for his health. She had very little medical knowledge but tuberculosis was a common and often fatal disease. She could only hope that the so-called shadow on his lung might have had something to do with the pneumonia he had suffered after being in a life raft for hours, and would prove to be benign. Even so, that would not be the end to his problems and she kept thinking about Shirley and wondering how she was going to break the news to Laurence that they had carelessly created another new life.

Trade was brisk in the early part of the afternoon but slowed down to almost nothing as tea time approached. There were a few window shoppers, pausing on their way home from work, but Ginnie decided that it was not worth staying open and wasting electricity and she sent Jimmy home early. She put the closed sign on the door ten minutes earlier than she would have done on a normal day and set off for home.

The house was oddly silent when she arrived. There was no evidence of food preparation in the kitchen and no sign of her mother or Shirley, but the back door was open and she stepped outside. Rounding the corner she saw Shirley sitting in a deckchair with one hand on Colin's pram, which she was rocking absent-mindedly.

'Where's Mum?' Ginnie asked anxiously.

'She's having a lie-down. She said she had a headache but I think she's cross with me.'

'Have you told her everything?'

'I've been trying to pluck up the courage to admit that I might be up the duff. It might go down better if it came from you.'

'Why me? It's your problem, Shirley, not mine. I refuse to be piggy in the middle.'

'Oh, please.' Shirley raised her head to give her a pleading look. 'Do this little thing for me and I'll work in the shop for nothing. I can't face being sent away in disgrace for a second time.'

'Don't be daft,' Ginnie said, losing patience. 'You're a married woman and this sort of thing happens.'

'I know, and Laurence will be here later, but I don't want another row. If Mum makes him feel unwelcome he'll have every reason to walk out on me.'

'Did he tell you everything, Shirley?'

Shielding her eyes from the sun, Shirley stopped rocking the pram and Colin began to murmur. 'Like what?'

'Like the fact that he's been discharged on medical grounds. That he's got a shadow on his lung, which could mean that there's something seriously wrong.'

Shirley paled beneath her tan. 'He said he'd lost his job and he'd tell me about it this evening.'

'Well, now you know and I suggest that you stop thinking about how you feel and put yourself in his place. He's out of work and he's ill. I think he deserves a bit of support and understanding.'

Shirley glared at her and then dropped her gaze. 'You're right, of course. I wish he'd told me that in the first place.'

'He was probably afraid to. Grow up, Shirley. You'd better start taking responsibility for your own actions and stop blaming everyone else when things go wrong.' Ginnie leaned over the pram and picked Colin up. She thrust him into his mother's arms. 'There you are, Colin my lad. Mummy's home now and she's going to look after you from now on. Auntie Ginnie is going upstairs to have a chat with your grandma. Although why it's always left to me to sort your mummy's problems out, I really don't know.'

'He's coming.' Shirley let the curtain fall back into place. 'I don't know what to say to him.'

Ginnie leapt up from the sofa where she had been attempting to read one of her mother's library books, Hervey Allen's epic historical romance, *Anthony Adverse*. 'I'll make myself scarce.'

'No you won't.' Shirley rushed to the door. 'Please stay for a while. It'll be easier if there's someone else in the room.'

'That's crazy. He's your husband.'

'I know and it will be fine once we get over the awkward bit. I really don't know what to say to him, Ginnie. I don't know whether to apologise or to wait for him to make the first move. I feel such a fool.'

Ginnie put the book on the coffee table. 'All right. I'll say hello and then I'm going to bed. It's up to you then.' She went to stand by the empty grate, attempting to look casual as she waited for Shirley to open the front door. There was a murmur of conversation before she ushered Laurence into the front room.

'Welcome home.' Ginnie crossed the floor to kiss him on the cheek. 'You must be worn out, Laurence. Would you like a drink? Tea, coffee, cocoa or something stronger? I think we've got some beer in the cupboard.'

He smiled tiredly. 'A cup of tea would be just the thing.' He sank down on the sofa. 'It's been a long day.'

'And you're not feeling very well.' Shirley gazed at him anxiously. 'Do they know what's wrong with you?'

'Doctors never tell you anything,' Ginnie said hastily. 'Anyway, I'll go and make the tea. I expect you two have a lot to talk about.' With a meaningful glance in Shirley's direction she hurried from the room.

She took her time and laid the tray with her mother's best china tea set, two cups and saucers and a plate of digestive biscuits which was the last of their ration for the week. She waited for the tea to brew, giving the newly-weds a little longer to kiss and make up.

They were seated side by side on the sofa, barely touching each other and Shirley had her hands folded tightly in her lap. Ginnie could tell by the whiteness of her sister's knuckles that things were still tense. She placed the tray on the table in front of them. 'Here you are. I'm off to bed so I'll see you in the morning, Laurence.'

She was about to leave them but Shirley reached

out and caught her by the sleeve. 'Aren't you having any tea?'

Ginnie snatched her arm away. 'What's the matter with you?' she hissed. 'Tell him and get it over with.'

'I'm tired but I'm not deaf,' Laurence said with a hint of a smile. 'Why don't you sit down for a few minutes, Ginnie? Shirley might feel a bit less uncomfortable if you're here.'

Reluctantly, Ginnie took a seat in their father's old chair by the fireplace. 'I don't think this is right. You two have a kid and another on the way.' She held her hand up as Shirley uttered a squeak of protest. 'I'm sorry, but someone had to tell him. You can't hide a fact like that forever.'

Laurence seized Shirley's hand. 'Is this true?'

'I didn't know how to tell you. It must have happened that weekend when I came down to Gosport.'

'I'm so sorry. I should have been more careful, but I thought . . .'

'I know. So did I. But apparently it's an old wives' tale. So Ginnie said.'

They both turned to stare at Ginnie and she held her hands up. 'Don't look at me.' She leapt to her feet. 'I'm going to bed. Goodnight.'

Next morning Ginnie was up early as usual and ready for work. She went down to breakfast and to her surprise found her mother and Laurence in the kitchen chatting amicably. Mildred rose from the table to put a slice of bread under the grill. 'There's tea in the pot, dear.'

Ginnie shot a questioning glace at Laurence. 'Is everything all right?'

'I was just thanking Mrs Travis for looking after Colin while we were away and I want to thank you too, Ginnie.'

She stared from one to the other. The dramas of the previous day seemed to have been forgotten, and her mother appeared to be happy with the situation. 'Colin's a good little boy, but Mum did all the hard work. I only helped out sometimes.'

'And another one on the way, so Laurence tells me.' Mildred took the toast from the grill pan and placing it neatly on a plate she passed it to Ginnie. 'Why the silly girl didn't tell me yesterday I'll never know. But then that's Shirley all over. Dizzy – that's what her father always called her. We'll have to say it's a honeymoon baby that arrives early. That should keep the gossips quiet.'

'Mrs Travis has been very understanding,' Laurence said softly.

'Mildred, please. You can't go on calling me Mrs Travis, you make me sound like a boarding-house landlady, and I don't want to be called Mum or Mother – that's very working class. No, Mildred will do nicely. You and I are going to be friends, Laurence.' She glanced out of the window and uttered a shriek of annoyance. 'That blooming cat from next door but one is after the birds again. Poor little things, there's not much food left to throw out for them these days, and I'm not feeding them up to provide a dinner for next door but one's moggy.' She slammed out of the kitchen and Ginnie could just see the top of her turban as she raced down the path waving her arms.

'You've worked miracles,' Ginnie said, grinning. 'You've charmed Mum all right.'

'We had a heart to heart.' Laurence pushed his plate away. 'I'm afraid I can't eat the last bit of toast. Perhaps the birds will get some breakfast after all.'

Ginnie leaned towards him. 'And you're all right about the baby?'

'How can I not be? It's mine and there's no question about it this time, but because they've discharged me from the Navy as being medically unfit I'm not in a position to keep a wife and family.'

'That's hardly your fault. What happens next?'

'I've got to see a specialist and have more tests. I'm afraid I might be very sick, and who's going to look after Shirley and the children?'

'When do you see the specialist? Did they make an appointment for you?'

He shook his head. 'I can't afford it, Ginnie. I should get a small pension from the Navy, but that might take months to come through. I just don't know what I'm going to do.'

'If it's a question of money, couldn't you ask your father? I'm sure he'd help.'

'Are you? Then you don't know him as I do.'

'How much would it cost?'

'I don't know but I doubt if you'd get much change from twenty guineas.'

'Then you'll have to go to see your father. You've got Shirley and the babies to think of now. If you won't speak to Mr Mallory, then I will.'

An hour later she was standing outside Mallory's chambers, waiting for the clerk to open the door. Her knees seemed to have the consistency of two jellies and her mouth was so dry that her tongue felt as though it was sticking to her teeth, but she was determined to do this thing for Shirley and Laurence. He was her brother now and family always came first. She could hear footsteps on the tiled floor and the bolts being shot back. The door creaked as it opened.

Chapter Twelve

Colin Mallory's office was large, plush and filled with antiques. The walls were lined with bookcases which were crammed with expensive-looking leather-bound tomes, and the floor was carpeted in best quality Axminster. Ginnie knew this for a fact as her father had won the contract for re-laying the flooring in the offices the year before the war changed their lives forever. He had talked about little else for weeks and her mother had boasted about it to her friends. Shirley had said that it was as if they had received the Royal Warrant and had been foolish enough to pass this witticism on to Livvie, who had immediately repeated it to her mother. Somehow it had travelled full circle through the grapevine and Mrs Martin had relayed it to Mildred, who had been furious and had not spoken to Shirley for a whole week.

Ginnie stood in front of the golden oak pedestal desk that would have impressed the wealthiest client, and her feet sank into the thick pile of the carpet as she waited for Laurence's father to acknowledge her presence. His clerk had shown her into the inner sanctum, but Mallory was obviously going to make her wait while he read through a long document.

He signed it with a flourish and replaced the cap on his fountain pen. With studied slowness he set it down on a silver inkstand and raised his head to give her a frosty look. 'If you've come to extort more money from me, you're wasting your time.'

'Actually that is exactly why I'm here,' Ginnie said calmly. 'But it's not for me.'

His features contorted with anger. 'I suppose that bitch of a sister put you up to this. Well, I'm not giving her anything, nor am I going to have anything to do with her or her little bastard.'

The temptation to tell him exactly what she thought of him was almost too strong to resist, but Ginnie was not going to let him get to her. She met his stony stare, refusing to be cowed. 'That's not why I'm here, Mr Mallory. I came to tell you that Laurence has been discharged from the Navy as being medically unfit and he needs to see a specialist.'

'Huh!' Mallory managed to emphasise the exclamation so that it spelled out contempt and derision. 'Do you expect me to fall for that old chestnut?'

'Laurence has a shadow on one of his lungs. He must have further tests, and he could be seriously ill.'

'If you're lying . . .'

Ginnie leaned both hands on the highly polished edge of the desk. 'D'you think I'd come here and suffer insults from you if it weren't absolutely necessary?'

'Why didn't Laurence come? If he needs my help he should be standing where you are now.'

'Doesn't that tell you something, Mr Mallory? Your son won't ask you for a penny, which is why I put myself through this embarrassing ordeal. I don't like you any more than you like me, but you are Laurence's father. Could you live with yourself if he died for want of proper medical attention?'

'What is this mystery illness? I want to know what I'm paying for.'

'This isn't a game, Mr Mallory. The doctors think it's tuberculosis.'

He was silent for a moment, and then he nodded slowly. 'All right. I'll pay his medical bills but I'm not giving him a penny in cash. I know a good chap in Harley Street who was a client of mine before the war.' He uncapped his pen and scribbled something on a notepad. Tearing off a sheet he handed it to her. 'Ring that number and mention my name. Make an appointment for Laurence and have the account sent to me.'

'Thank you,' Ginnie said simply. She slipped the paper into her handbag and left the office without another word. Colin Mallory was a hateful man but she had seen the look in his eyes when she mentioned the dreaded disease that killed indiscriminately. She had found his Achilles heel – he loved his son. Perhaps there was hope for him and for Laurence and his growing family.

Ginnie made her way back to the shop and found Olivia waiting for her. 'What do you want, Livvie?'

she demanded crossly. 'I've had enough of your family for one day.'

'I know that you went to see Daddy. I was in the office when you phoned for an appointment. So how much did you sting him for, shop girl?'

'I don't think that's any of your business, and calling me shop girl isn't an insult, which I'm sure it was meant to be.'

Jimmy had been hovering nearby but he moved swiftly to stand beside Ginnie. 'Shall I throw her out, miss?'

Livvie looked him up and down, curling her lip. 'Is this your bodyguard, Ginnie? You could have done better. This chap couldn't punch his way out of a paper bag,'

'Leave him alone,' Ginnie said angrily. 'Say what you like about me but I won't allow anyone to be rude to my staff.'

'Your staff?' Livvie glanced round the shop floor where a couple of female customers were examining a utility wardrobe while casting surreptitious looks in their direction. 'Who d'you think you are, shop girl? You're not exactly Gordon Selfridge, are you?'

Ginnie turned to Jimmy, who was sweating profusely and mopping his brow with a duster. She laid her hand on his arm. 'Go and see if the ladies over there are interested in buying something, there's a good chap.' She waited until he was out of earshot. 'Look, Livvie, I don't know why you're here but I haven't anything to say to you. If you want to make a purchase then go ahead, if not I'd be grateful if you'd go away and leave me to get on with my job.'

'I want to know what's going on. Were you trying to get more money from my father? If so I hope he told you where to go.'

'I think you'd better ask him,' Ginnie said wearily. 'I haven't got time to play these silly games, Livvie. Some of us have a living to earn, so if you'll excuse me, I'd like to get on.' She was about to walk away but Livvie stepped in front of her.

'If it wasn't about money, it must have had something to do with Laurence. Believe it or not I love my brother and if there's something wrong I want to know. Has that bitch left him already?'

'That bitch as you call her is my sister, and no, it's got nothing to do with Shirley.'

'Then it must be Laurence.' Livvie caught her by the wrist. 'I'm not leaving until you tell me.'

Ginnie looked her in the eyes and realised that her concern was genuine. 'You'll have to ask your father, or, better still, come to my house and see Laurence. Make it up with him. Life's too short to fall out with family.'

Livvie released her with an exclamation of disgust. 'Don't preach to me, shop girl. Tell Laurence if he wants to see me, he knows where I live.' She stalked off, pushing past Jimmy and the two ladies who had seemingly lost interest in purchasing anything and were openly staring at her.

Ginnie shook her head and went into the office to telephone home.

Laurence emerged from the consulting room after a long session with the consultant. Ginnie put the copy of *Country Life* magazine back on the table and rose to her feet. She had taken the morning off to accompany him to Harley Street as Shirley was suffering badly from morning sickness and felt too ill to make even a short journey. 'Well?' she said in a low voice. 'What did he say?'

He shook his head. 'The doc took a culture and a sample of my spit, only he called it sputum, but we won't know the results yet.'

'Did he tell you anything?'

Laurence plucked his trilby from the coat stand. 'He thinks it's TB.'

'Oh, Laurence, I'm so sorry.' Ginnie slipped her hand through the crook of his arm.

'It's all right. I was prepared for it. The Navy medic said much the same thing, but we'll have to wait for the tests to come back to be absolutely certain.'

'What then?'

'I'll have to go to a sanatorium far away from the city smoke. It'll mean a long stay and total bed rest, although apparently there's a new drug that they're trying out which has been very successful so far.' He opened the waiting-room door and held it for Ginnie to go out into the office where the prim receptionist sat behind her desk.

'Goodbye, Mr Mallory,' she said, smiling.

'Goodbye, and thank you.'

Laurence sounded cheerful but Ginnie sensed that he was more upset than he would care to admit and she hurried him onto the landing and into the waiting lift. It rattled and clanged its way down to the ground floor where it juddered to a halt. Laurence slid back the metal gate. 'Let's get out of here. I hate these places but I suppose I'll have to get used to them from now on.'

'You survived the war and the mine that sunk your ship,' Ginnie said, making an effort to lighten the moment. 'You'll get through this, Laurence, and we're all behind you.' She crossed the marble-tiled entrance hall and opened the front door. It was a relief to go outside and take a breath of fresh air cooled by a recent rain shower. The slightly sooty smell of the West End mingled with the pungent scent of crushed geranium petals from a flower head that had been picked or accidentally knocked off one of the plants in the window box and trodden underfoot. The scarlet petals lay like blood on the wet paving stone and Ginnie shuddered as a cold shiver ran down her spine. She glanced at Laurence and was alarmed to see how pale he looked with dark shadows underlining his blue eyes. 'Let's find a teashop and have a nice hot cuppa and a toasted teacake or a sticky bun. You must be starving because you ate hardly anything at breakfast.'

A faint smiled curved his generous lips and he

squeezed her hand. 'Always the practical one, Ginnie. I don't know what we'd do without you.'

'It's just common sense. You'll feel better when you've had something to eat. Let's go to Lyons Corner House, Tottenham Court Road. I used to love that place when I was a kid and Dad took us there for a treat. I remember having a Knickbocker Glory and feeling terribly sick as we travelled home on the Green Line bus in a pea-souper.'

'Happy days,' he said, chuckling.

The results came back positive and the consultant insisted that Laurence needed urgent admission to hospital, but this would incur considerable costs. This time it was Laurence who went to see his father. What passed between them Ginnie could only imagine but she began to revise her opinion of Colin Mallory when he agreed to fund his son's treatment, although he still refused to have anything to do with Shirley and her child. They were given a list of sanatoriums and all of them were far from London. With a view to making it possible for the family to visit Laurence, they chose one in Shropshire which was within reasonable reach of Avril's pub in Lightwood Common.

Arrangements were made and events moved swiftly. One moment Ginnie had been drinking tea and sharing a toasted teacake with Laurence in Lyons Corner House and shortly afterwards she was saying goodbye to him, but this time Shirley was travelling with him. She had been reluctant to leave Colin for a second time, but Mildred had insisted that she ought to accompany her husband on what might be his final journey. Ginnie had blenched at her mother's tactlessness, but her words had had the desired effect and Shirley set off, planning to spend the night at the Ferryboat Inn and to return the next day.

Ginnie waved them off from the front door, hoping that Laurence would soon be cured and able to return home. Even so, she realised that it would be many months before he was able to earn a living and the responsibility for supporting his family was hers and hers alone. She set off for the shop, mulling over her plans to take over Fred's business in the New Year. With extra floor space she intended to expand her stock of soft furnishings and open a linen department. She would need more staff, but she would worry about that if and when her application to take over the lease was approved by the council.

Almost without realising it she had arrived at the shop and to her dismay she found Livvie waiting for her. 'If you've come to have a row you're going to be disappointed,' she said coldly. 'I'm too busy to waste my time arguing with you.'

Livvie scowled ominously. 'I'm not here for my own benefit.'

'I'm sure this isn't a social call. What can I do for you?'

'My father insisted that I offer my services. He

said it's time I started living in the real word, and my punishment for costing him the money he gave you was to work here.'

'He didn't give me anything. The payment was to cover the damage you did to my shop.'

Livvie shrugged her shoulders. 'He hasn't forgiven me for it and now he's got to fund my brother's hospital treatment, so as usual I'm the one who's got to suffer. Laurence was always the favourite.'

'Why would he want you to work for me? He knows you hate my family.'

'It's all part of his vendetta against me. Personally I'd rather work down a sewer than serve in a bloody shop.'

'I can't afford to take on more staff at the moment, so that lets you off the hook very nicely.'

'No it damn well doesn't. He said I'd have to work for nothing if you couldn't afford to pay me, and if I didn't get a job here I'd have to move out and find myself somewhere else to live.'

Ginnie eyed her thoughtfully. 'Are you really prepared to do unpaid work?'

'It doesn't look as if I've got much choice. My father doesn't make idle promises.'

'I think I could find something for you to do.' Ginnie was beginning to enjoy herself. It was high time that someone put Olivia Mallory in her place. 'All things considered I can hardly refuse such a kind offer.'

'You bitch. You're laughing at my expense.'

'Frankly, yes, I am. But setting our differences aside, you might be of some use to me. You could bring in customers from your set who would normally go up West to shop.'

'Do you really think I'd let my friends know that I'm stuck here because it's my father's way of getting back at me for what was just a prank?'

'I wouldn't call it that. It was vandalism pure and simple.'

'All right, don't go on about it. Is it yes or no?'

'It's up to you,' Ginnie said carelessly. 'But if you're serious, you could do something to help Laurence.'

Livvie shot her a suspicious glance. 'How do you work that out?'

'I have to support his wife and child while he's in hospital and Shirley's expecting again. If you help me expand the business you'll be helping your sick brother, and you might even get something out of it yourself.'

'I won't be here long enough to make a difference,' Livvie said sulkily. 'You'll sack me soon enough.'

'And what would your father say to that?' Ginnie angled her head. 'I don't think he'd be too pleased.'

Jimmy had been serving a customer, but with the transaction completed he hurried over to Ginnie. 'Is she giving you trouble, miss? I told her she wasn't welcome but she wouldn't budge.'

'It's all right, Jimmy. This is our new assistant, Miss Mallory. Livvie, meet Jimmy Fitzwilliam, my most loyal member of staff. He'll show you what to do and how to work the till.'

Jimmy stared at Livvie as if afraid she was going to take a bite out of him. 'I'll do what I can.'

She tossed her head. 'I don't take orders from you, so get that clear.'

'Yes, you do,' Ginnie said simply. 'Now I'll put the kettle on and we'll have a cup of tea, or do you prefer coffee, being posh? I think there's a bottle of Camp coffee somewhere.'

'You're determined to make my life hell, aren't you?'

'No. Actually, I think we might do well together if you jump off that high horse. There's more to running a shop than serving customers. I've never forgotten what I saw of your house, and I know you're used to living with nice things around you. I think that you might have a talent for window dressing and setting up displays.'

Livvie stared at her in astonishment. 'Why are you being nice to me? I tried to wreck your beastly shop and I've been horrible to your sister.'

'It looks as if I'm stuck with you,' Ginnie said, smiling. 'And I've just seen Laurence off on his way to the sanatorium. Don't you think it would be better for him if we worked together? He'll have to start all over again when he's discharged from the hospital, and if we're on the same side it would be a plus.'

'You are the most extraordinary person I've ever met.'

243

'I'll take that as a compliment. Now, Miss Mallory, if you'd like to shadow Jimmy I'm sure he'll be good enough to show you how things work.'

'You gave that hateful creature a job?' Shirley stared at her sister in disbelief.

'She's working for nothing,' Ginnie said with a casual shrug of her shoulders. 'Free labour. I'd be crazy to turn that down.'

Mildred slapped a plate of food down on the table in front of her. 'I wouldn't trust her an inch. That girl tried to ruin the business.'

'And now she's making up for it, Mum.' Ginnie picked up her knife and fork. 'She might prove useful because she's got contacts. If she puts her mind to it she could bring in the class of trade we've never had.'

Mildred took her seat, eyeing her snoek fishcake with distaste. 'Your dad told me all about their sort. They come in all high and mighty, demanding this and that and thinking they're something special, but when it comes to paying that's another matter.'

'It'll be cash on the nail, Mum. I'm not allowing credit to anyone.'

'That's right, dear. But you'll have to keep an eye on that Olivia. I don't trust her.'

'She's my sister-in-law, Mum,' Shirley said, pushing her plate away. 'I'm sorry, I can't eat this, it's making me feel sick.' She jumped up from the table and ran from the room.

Mildred frowned. 'What did I say?'

'She used to think that Livvie was her friend, Mum. It must be hard for Shirley with Laurence in hospital and his family refusing to have anything to do with her.'

'I could say that she brought it upon herself, but I wouldn't be so unkind.' Mildred stared down at her plate. 'I'd give anything for a lamb chop and garden peas. I'm glad that my Sidney isn't here to see us living like paupers. He was a good provider and I miss him . . .' She broke off and left the table without finishing her meal.

Left alone in the dining room Ginnie looked disconsolately at the empty places and sighed. Their future was in her hands now and it was up to her to make a success of the business. She glanced at the photograph of her father in pride of place on the mantelpiece. 'I'll do it, Dad. I won't let you down, I promise.'

The next few months were not easy. Livvie was a reluctant member of the team and Ginnie had to have several words in her ear concerning the way she spoke to Jimmy and her off-handed treatment of Fred Chinashop and Ida. Arrogant and full of her own self-importance, Livvie brought her Monk Avenue sense of superiority to Collier Lane, but she soon discovered that this attitude would get her nowhere. Neither Ida nor Fred was prepared to put up with a prima donna and they were quick to put her in her place. Jimmy was sullen and suspicious at first but after a blazing row one Saturday morning when the shop was busy, Ginnie took them both aside and made them apologise to each other. She would have liked to bang their heads together but as that was not an option she had to content herself with making them shake hands, and extracted a promise from each of them to work together in harmony.

Things were not much better at home. Shirley was not having an easy time with this pregnancy. She suffered from morning sickness which occasionally lasted all day and she seemed to be permanently tired. She took care of Colin but did little else, leaving all the housework to her mother and lazing in a deck-chair in the garden when it was fine, or sitting on the sofa with her feet up when the weather was bad. Mildred did not complain about the extra chores but she did admit to being worried about Shirley's constant state of lassitude. The doctor shrugged it off, putting it down to the fact that she was worried about her sick husband, although Ginnie thought privately that it went deeper than that. She knew that Shirley had never come to terms with Tony's death, but there was nothing she could do or say to ease the pain of loss. Her own emotions had jagged edges that were still raw and ached miserably if she allowed herself to dwell on the past, but she forced herself to concentrate on the future. For her there was no going back, only forward.

*

The summer ended and autumn evolved into winter but Shirley had still not felt able to undertake the journey to the hospital in Shropshire. Mildred had tried to persuade her to visit Laurence, telling her that a change of scene would do her good, but Shirley had always come up with some plausible excuse. She received several letters a week from him, short extracts of which she read out to Ginnie, but she was not a prolific correspondent and sometimes it was left to Ginnie to write and send him news of Colin's first attempts at sitting up unaided, followed by crawling and his tireless efforts to stand on his own two feet. Laurence's replies were always cheerful and filled with amusing anecdotes of hospital life, but his recovery seemed to be slower than anticipated. Ginnie urged Shirley to visit him but she refused.

In the end, leaving Livvie in charge of the shop with Ida and Fred keeping an eye on her, and having extracted a promise of good behaviour from Jimmy, Ginnie travelled to Shropshire, taking with her a case filled with Christmas presents for Laurence from all his family. Included in the parcel were studio photographs of Shirley with Colin on her knee. Even in black and white she looked stunning and her advanced pregnancy only seemed to enhance her beauty.

It was obvious that Laurence was similarly impressed as he stared at the photo he held in his mittened hand. 'She is well though, isn't she, Ginnie?

I mean she's written many times to tell me that she's not finding this pregnancy as easy as the first.'

'The doctor doesn't seem to think that there's anything wrong, and she hasn't long to go now.' Ginnie shivered, clenching her teeth to stop them chattering as she huddled in her winter coat. The snow was blowing in from the open side of the ward and she had been shocked to find that open air treatment meant exactly that. Laurence and the other patients on the male ward were wrapped up in thick blankets with hot water bottles to keep them warm. 'How do you stand it, Laurence?'

He grinned. 'You can get used to anything in time. The fresh air is supposed to kill all the germs, so if we don't succumb to the cold we should get better.'

'But I thought there was a new drug that would work miracles.'

'It's not widely available, so the quacks here told me. I said I'd be glad to be a guinea pig but so far I've just had total bed rest and nourishing meals. At least we're well fed, but I'd rather be at home.' His eyes darkened. 'How is Shirley really? Tell me the truth, Ginnie. She doesn't say much in her letters.'

Ginnie clasped his hand. 'You mustn't worry about her. She's much stronger than she looks. You'll be a daddy again soon.'

'I feel awful stuck here and unable to help or even to support my wife and child. You can't imagine what it's like.'

'No, I don't suppose I can, but you mustn't worry.

We're coping well and the shop is beginning to show a profit. You know, of course, that your sister is now my best friend.' She gurgled with laughter. 'Well, almost. We rub along pretty well and to be honest I don't know what I'd have done without her.'

'Really? I can't imagine young Livvie serving in a shop, or even turning up for work every day. She was always the spoilt darling of the family.'

'Her antics with the paint can put an end to that. Your father was determined to make her suffer for her sins, and to be fair that's exactly what she's done. I pay her commission on sales; otherwise it would be slave labour. So in reality I've got a staff of two, and of course there's Ida who still bakes us cakes and brings something down for elevenses every day. She's lonely when Mr Richmond is at work, and Fred Chinashop is always popping in for his cup of sweety weaky milky tea.'

'It sounds like a bit of a madhouse,' he said, chuckling. 'But I'm glad that you and Livvie are on speaking terms. She's not a bad kid.'

'She's got quite a talent for window dressing and setting up stands. I think she has a genuine creative side that no one spotted before.'

'You're a wonderful girl, Ginnie. I can't think of many people who would have taken Livvie on after what she did.' He squeezed her fingers, but she noticed immediately that his grip was weak and a cold shiver ran down her spine that had nothing to do with the freezing temperature in the ward.

She eased her hand free with an apologetic smile. 'You mustn't over-exert yourself, Laurence. The ward sister told me not to stay too long, so I think I'd better go.'

'Must you? Can't you stay a little longer? I haven't seen you for months, and I want to hear more about home.' His voice cracked and he looked away.

She could see tears standing out on the tips of his corn-coloured lashes and she patted him on the shoulder. 'I'll come again tomorrow. I'll check on the visiting hours and I'll be here as soon as they open the doors.'

He gulped and swallowed. 'I'm sorry. I'm being an awful baby.'

'No, you're not. You're a brave man and I won't let you talk that way. After what you've been through it's not surprising that you feel a bit wobbly.'

'I doubt if I'll be able to stand when they let me get out of this damned bed,' he said with a touch of his old humour. 'I've almost forgotten what it's like to walk. But you will come, won't you? I'll count the minutes until I see you again.'

She stood up, brushing flakes of snow off her coat. 'I'll be here even if I have to borrow a pair of snow shoes or skis.'

'Are you staying with your aunt?'

'I am, and she sends you her love. She says that as soon as you're well enough you and Shirley must spend a holiday with her. You'd love the Ferryboat, Laurence. That's something to look forward to, isn't it?'

He nodded but he did not look convinced. 'Sometimes I think I'll never get out of here alive, Ginnie.' He held his hand out to her and began to cough.

A nurse rushed up with a cup, which she held to his lips. 'Visiting time is over, Mr Mallory. I think you've had enough excitement for one day.' She shot a meaningful look at Ginnie who retreated, blowing a kiss to Laurence as she went.

Outside the hospital main entrance Percy was waiting for her with the pony and trap. Hunched up in a greatcoat with his felt hat pulled down over his eyes he gave her a baleful look. 'Hurry up, miss. I'm bloody freezing and the pony should be tucked up in his nice warm stable at this time of day.'

Ginnie climbed up beside him. 'Thank you for waiting, Percy. I really do appreciate it. Can we do the same tomorrow?'

'I suppose so, but you'll have to wait until I've done me bit at the home farm. I can't afford to upset the boss.'

'No, of course not.' Ginnie huddled under the plaid blanket that Avril had thoughtfully provided. 'Let's go home.'

The lights of the pub shone out through the swirling snow as Percy dropped Ginnie off outside the door. 'Thank you again,' Ginnie said, pulling her collar up above her ears in an attempt to stop the icy flakes going down her neck. 'I'll buy you a pint when you're ready.'

He mumbled something and flicked the whip to encourage Duke to amble towards the stable. Smiling to herself, Ginnie made for the door, slipping and sliding on the hard-packed snow. She let herself in and the warmth enveloped her like a hug. A log fire blazed up the chimney and the familiar scent of burning pine mingled with the smell of beer and tobacco smoke. Avril was clearing glasses from the tables and she greeted her with a wide smile. 'Come in, darling. You're just in time.' With a sweep of her free hand she indicated a young man seated on a stool at the bar. 'Look who's come all the way from the States to see us.'

Chapter Thirteen

'Danny!' Ginnie flung her arms around him. 'What a wonderful surprise.'

He gave her a smacking kiss on the lips. 'Gee, you look like the Snow Queen. It must be pretty bad out there.'

She took off her fur hat and shook the melting snow onto the quarry tiles. 'It's practically a blizzard outside. I hope it doesn't get too deep.'

Avril placed the glasses on the bar counter. 'You look as though you could do with a snifter, darling. What will it be?'

'I promised Percy a pint or two for taking me to the hospital and bringing me home.' Ginnie slipped off her coat and laid it over the back of the chair. 'I'll have a ginger ale, please.'

Danny grinned. 'So you're still too young to drink in the bar?'

'I'll be twenty-one next August.'

Avril opened a bottle. 'How wonderful it is to be so young. You've your whole life spreading out before you like a magic carpet.'

'Put a shot of Scotch in that, Avril,' Danny said, putting his hand in his pocket and bringing out a handful of change. 'There's no one here to witness the crime being committed, and have one yourself.'

'Thank you, Danny.' Avril held a glass to the optic and added the mixer. 'You look as though you need this, darling. How was poor Laurence?'

'Still quite poorly, I think.' Ginnie took a sip of her drink. 'The ward is open to the elements. Can you believe that?' She took another mouthful.

'Hey, slow down, kid,' Danny said, grinning. 'And I'm sorry to hear about your friend.' He glanced at Avril. 'Say, honey, d'you think you could rustle up something tasty? I haven't eaten all day.'

The unaccustomed spirit was having its effect on Ginnie and she placed her glass carefully on the counter. 'I'll do it, Avril. I can scramble eggs and make toast.'

'Sounds good to me,' Danny said cheerfully.

Avril shook her head. 'You're a guest, Ginnie. I've prepared a meal and it just needs heating up, so you stay here and talk to Danny.' She disappeared into the kitchen, closing the door behind her.

Ginnie perched on a bar stool facing Danny. 'This is a lovely surprise, but what brings you here? I thought you'd gone back to the States.'

'I did return to LA, but I wanted to check out the London hospitals. I'd like to specialise in reconstructive plastic surgery and there's a hospital in Sussex I particularly want to visit.'

'But why did you come to Shropshire? It's a long way from Sussex.'

'There was another and more important reason.' His smile faded and he toyed with the handle of his beer mug. 'I wanted to find you, kid.'

'You came all this way just to see me?'

'It's not as crazy as it sounds.'

'But why me?' Her heart skipped a beat. 'Is it Nick? He isn't . . .'

'Don't look so scared – he's recovered from his injuries, or mostly.'

'I'm sorry, Danny. I don't understand.'

He met her anxious gaze with a sympathetic look. 'I know how you felt about each other. He was crazy about you and any other guy would have ditched the girl back home, but not Nick.'

'I know, and I respect him for that.'

'Well, as it turned out, it was the other way round. Betsy ran out on Nick.'

Ginnie downed the remainder of her drink in one gulp. 'She did?'

'Sure thing.'

'But why?'

'There's no easy way to say this, honey.' Danny laid his hand on hers as it rested on the bar top. 'I told you that Nick recovered from his wounds, but the truth is that the poor guy lost his sight. He's blind.'

The room began to spin in concentric circles and Danny's anxious voice seemed far away. He was calling her name but it echoed oddly in her head. 'Ginnie, are you okay?'

She dragged herself back from the edge of oblivion. 'I – I think so.'

'I'm so sorry, kid. I didn't know how to tell you, but you had to know.'

'Did he send for me?'

Danny shook his head. 'No. He doesn't know that I'm here. I told him that you'd want to know that he was a free man but he wouldn't buy it. He thinks he's washed up and he didn't want you to feel sorry for him.'

Her eyes filled with tears. 'That's not true. I mean of course I'm sorry that he's suffering but I don't care what state he's in. I love him, Danny. I always have.'

'I knew you'd say that, Ginnie.'

'Is there any hope that he'll regain his sight?'

'The head injury caused haemorrhages in both eyes. He was totally blind at first, but he's regained a little of his sight. It might improve but the doctors say it will take time and he'll probably always have blurred vision. His career as a surgeon is over.'

Ginnie opened her handbag and pulled out a hanky. 'I'm so sorry,' she said, mopping her eyes. 'It's just so awful. He must be devastated.'

Danny nodded, saying nothing. He drank his beer in silence, giving her time to recover. She put her hanky away and closed her bag with a decisive snap. 'Will he see me, d'you think?' Realising what she had said, she shook her head. 'That was a stupid thing to say, but you know what I mean.'

Danny's grave expression melted into a wide grin. 'He hasn't lost his sense of humour. He's still the same old Nick and he needs you.'

'Was he very upset when Betsy left him?'

'I think he was relieved, but he wouldn't have a word said against her.'

The kitchen door opened and Avril beckoned. 'Supper's ready. Come and get it while it's hot.' She gave Ginnie a curious glance. 'Are you all right, darling? I suppose you've heard Danny's news.'

'Yes, and I can't imagine how Nick must be feeling.' Ginnie lifted the hatch and followed Avril into the kitchen. 'I'm just trying to work out how I'm going to raise the fare to California.'

'Are you sure about this, Ginnie?' Avril asked, frowning.

'I've never been more sure of anything. I'm going to America to see Nick. I'll have to beg, borrow or steal the money but I'm not going to let anything stop me.'

'Good for you, kid,' Danny said enthusiastically. 'I knew you'd come good. I can't wait to see Nick's face when I tell him.'

Ginnie turned to him, shaking her head. 'No, don't do that. I want it to be a surprise, and it might take me some time to get the money together.'

'I can help there,' Avril said firmly. 'I've got a bit put by for a rainy day and who better to give it to than my favourite niece?'

'I can't take your savings, Avril.'

'We'll talk about it later. I've got a customer, but I'll close up early and we'll have a long chat.' Avril hurried into the bar to answer the urgent summons of the brass bell on the bar counter. She closed the door, leaving Ginnie alone with Danny.

Ginnie walked over to the stove and lifted the lid on the bubbling pan. 'That smells so good. Avril can make a gourmet dish out of almost nothing.'

'I know,' Danny said, taking his seat at the table. 'I've been here for two days and I've been fed like a king.' He unfolded a table napkin and tucked it into his collar.

Ginnie served the hotpot and sat down opposite him. 'How did you get here, Danny? I didn't think there were any commercial flights or sailings in operation.'

He took a slice of bread and dipped it in his bowl. 'You're right. I booked a passage on a freighter heading for Liverpool and took a train from there.'

'Would it be possible for me to go to the States with you? I've never travelled anywhere further than Shrewsbury.'

He swallowed a mouthful of food and smiled. 'Money talks, kid. If your aunt will be kind enough to provide the moola there's no problem, but are you sure about this?'

'I've never been more certain of anything.'

'I was planning to go south tomorrow and spend a few days checking out the possibilities before travelling home, although it might not be easy to get a passage westwards. Since Lend-Lease ended there aren't too many freighters on the transatlantic route.'

'Surely you'd want to be with your family at Christmas?'

'My folks died when I was fifteen. Nick's parents kind of took me under their wing. I used to spend holidays with them, but I'm a big boy now. I enjoy being a free agent.'

'It sounds a bit lonely to me.'

Danny helped himself to another slice of bread. 'At least I haven't got anyone else to worry about. I guess I'm a selfish kind of guy.'

'If that was true you wouldn't be here now,' Ginnie said, smiling. 'You've gone to all this trouble for Nick. That's not the action of a selfish man.'

'Maybe, maybe not. Anyway, what do you think about a trip to the States? Will you come with me?'

'I'll need a few days to sort things out at home, but yes, I will. And I want you to spend Christmas with us. It'll be a bit crowded and you'll have to sleep on the sofa, but if you don't mind that, we'd love to have you.'

'Thanks, Ginnie. That would be great, but are you sure your mom won't mind?'

'She'll be delighted to have you and so will Shirley. It will be like old times.'

The snow had settled in deep drifts overnight, making it impossible for Ginnie to visit the hospital. She telephoned and left a message for Laurence, promising to visit him again soon and to bring Shirley with her next time. It was said more in hope than in certainty. She replaced the receiver in its cradle and went to find Avril who was in the bar polishing the tables. 'I couldn't speak to Laurence, so I left a message with the ward sister.'

Avril shook the duster out and started on the next table. 'Poor boy. He must get terribly lonely without any visitors. I'd go and see him but I'm tied to this place, and he hardly knows me so it might be embarrassing for him.'

'Do you know if the road to the station is passable?' Ginnie asked anxiously. 'It's Christmas Eve on Monday and I left Livvie in charge of the shop so I really must get back as soon as I can.'

'I know, darling, and much as I'd love to have you stay here, I quite understand.' Avril attacked a sticky ring left by a beer glass. 'I telephoned the station earlier and they seemed to think we could get through with care. I've asked Lionel if he'd be an angel and take you in his Austin Seven: it's old and cranky, just like its owner, but it'll get you there in more comfort than my trap.'

Ginnie gave her a hug and inhaled the odd mix of Mansion Polish and the familiar fragrance of Shalimar. 'You're a brick, Avril. I love you.'

'I love you too, darling, but call me anything other than a brick. I know what it means but it sounds so solid and boring.'

'You'd never be that,' Ginnie said, laughing. 'And

Lionel is a dear. I'm sorry I can't stay longer and spend more time with him.'

Avril scrubbed at the remainder of the wax polish, running the duster round the inside of the tin. 'You might see a lot more of him in future, darling. We've been talking about tying the knot for ages. It's frightfully boring and middle class, but Lionel feels that it's not a good example to his parishioners if it gets around that he's having carnal relations with a pub landlady.'

Ginnie stared at her open-mouthed. 'No! I mean I'm absolutely delighted for both of you, but I didn't think you'd ever bow to convention.'

'It's not me,' Avril said calmly. 'It's the bishop. Someone sneaked to him and he's told Lionel in no uncertain terms that he disapproves, so we've decided to make it legal.'

'That's wonderful. I think you'll make an interesting and unconventional vicar's wife.' Ginnie stifled a giggle as she tried to imagine Avril soberly dressed in tweeds and a twinset but failed miserably. 'But what about the pub? Will you keep it on?'

Avril frowned. 'I haven't decided yet. I don't want to sell up so I might put a manager in, but we'll have to see.'

Ginnie kissed her scented cheek. 'You must invite us to the wedding. I wouldn't miss it for worlds.' She glanced round as the door opened and Lionel walked into the bar.

'I can see that you've told Ginnie our good news,

my dear.' He took off his hat and laid it on the counter. 'Have you got a hug for your prospective uncle, Ginnie?' He held out his arms and she walked into them.

'Congratulations, Lionel.' She had to stand on tiptoe to kiss his cheek. 'Do I have to call you uncle from now on?'

He exchanged amused looks with Avril, shaking his head. 'No, I prefer just Lionel. Nothing has changed. It's a mere formality to keep the gossips at bay.'

'Well, I'm delighted and very happy for both of you.' Ginnie released him and went to look out of the window. 'It's stopped snowing. Will you be able to take Danny and me to the station?'

'I'll have a jolly good try. My old jalopy is getting on in years but it gets me from A to B, so I hope it will struggle on for a few more miles. What time is your train?'

Ginnie consulted her watch. 'There's one in just under an hour. I'd better go and see if Danny's ready.'

Ginnie arrived home late that afternoon having parted with Danny in London. He was travelling on to East Grinstead where he had booked into a small hotel for the night, but she had extracted a promise from him that he would spend Christmas with them in Cherry Lane.

She had intended to go straight to the shop but she was tired and although the snow had not reached this far south it was bitterly cold and sleety rain made the walk home from the station seem even longer than usual. She had barely had time to divest herself of her coat and hat before she was bombarded with questions from her mother and Shirley. She tried to put their minds at rest about Laurence's state of health, and she answered their questions to the best of her ability, but Shirley did not look convinced.

'What do you mean?' she demanded. 'What sort of answer is "as well as can be expected"? Did they use those words at the hospital?'

'Shirley, I was only there for about half an hour. They wouldn't allow me to stay any longer and I didn't see a doctor, only a nurse and she wasn't very forthcoming. All I can say is that Laurence seemed cheerful enough. He was absolutely delighted with the photos but wanted to keep the rest of the presents unopened until Christmas Day. He wanted to hear all about you and Colin and he sent his love.'

Mildred leaned her elbows on the kitchen table, cupping her chin in her hands. 'But didn't they give you any idea when he'll be discharged from hospital?'

'No, Mum. It wasn't mentioned and Laurence didn't have any idea. It's obviously going to take a long time.'

'And it'll be costing old man Mallory a fortune,' Shirley said with a wry twist of her lips. 'That'll upset him more than the fact that his only son is dangerously ill.'

Mildred frowned. 'Don't say things like that,

Shirley. Show a bit more consideration for your husband.'

'I didn't mean to sound uncaring,' Shirley said tiredly. 'Everything I do and say is wrong these days.'

Ginnie could see an argument brewing and she rose from the table. 'Thanks for the tea, Mum, but I'd better go to the shop and see how things are going.'

Shirley glanced at the clock above the cooker. 'It's nearly closing time, and it's sleeting. The wretched shop will still be there tomorrow. How were things at the dear old Ferryboat Inn? There must be some good news somewhere.'

'As a matter of fact Danny was there. I'll tell you all about it when I come back.'

Shirley's eyes widened in surprise. 'Danny Flynn? But I thought he'd gone back to the States.'

'Who is he?' Mildred demanded, eyeing Ginnie suspiciously.

'He's just a friend, Mum,' Shirley said impatiently. 'Go on, Ginnie. Why was he in Shropshire? It's a bit of a coincidence that you turned up to visit Laurence and Danny had come to England. Did you know he'd be there?'

'Of course not,' Ginnie said firmly. 'He's come to England looking for work and hopes to study reconstructive surgery at East Grinstead.'

'That's nice, dear.' Mildred piled up the plates and put them in the sink. 'He must be clever if he's a surgeon.'

'Yes, I suppose he is.' Ginnie hesitated. 'Actually, Mum, I've invited him here for Christmas. He hasn't got any family, and I couldn't bear to think of him stuck on his own in a cheap hotel over the holiday.'

Mildred's pencilled eyebrows drew together in a frown. 'You asked a perfect stranger to stay here with us?'

'Shirley and I got to know him really well, Mum. Danny is a very nice chap.'

Mildred did not look convinced. 'But you'd think he'd want to return to America for Christmas. It seems a funny sort of time to come to England job-hunting.'

'Are you sure it wasn't you he came to see?' Shirley said mischievously.

'You know Danny better than that.' Ginnie made for the doorway. She paused with her fingers entwined around the doorknob, wondering whether to break the news that she was planning to go to America after the holiday, and decided against it. She knew she would face opposition from both of them, but her mind was made up and nothing they could say or do would make any difference. 'Danny is just a friend. Why do you always have to make everything into a romantic saga?'

'I was just joking,' Shirley said, pouting. She put a finger of bread and butter on the tray of Colin's high chair as he started to whimper. 'Eat that, and be quiet, there's a good boy.' She patted him on the head. 'Anyway, I like Danny and it'll make a change to have someone cheerful in the house.'

'He won't have a ration book,' Mildred said darkly. 'He'll eat us out of house and home.'

Ginnie was tempted to blurt out her plan to visit the States. Her unused food coupons for that period might compensate for having an extra mouth to feed at Christmas, but she could tell from her mother's tight-lipped expression that this argument was unlikely to find favour. With a supreme effort she managed to control the urge to confess. The Spanish Inquisition had nothing on Mum and Shirley when they got together. She opened the door. 'Must go, Mum. Won't be long.' She hurried from the room and snatched her coat and hat from the newel post at the foot of the stairs. She was still struggling into them as she left the house, ignoring her mother's demands that she should stay and tell them exactly who was going to pay for such an extravagant gesture in times of austerity.

Livvie was cashing up when Ginnie rushed into the shop. There was no sign of Jimmy, but to her intense relief everything seemed to be in good order. The stands were well stocked and there was a strategically placed Christmas tree festooned with tinsel and fairy lights. Livvie stopped what she was doing. 'How's Laurence? Is he any better? I've been so worried about him.'

There was no doubting her sincerity and the

questions that Ginnie had been about to ask about the business went out of her head. She had assumed, obviously wrongly, that Livvie was not interested in her brother's welfare, and she was suddenly ashamed of her single-minded attempt to organise her own life. 'He seemed cheerful enough,' she said, choosing her words carefully. 'To be honest, Livvie, I don't know how he's doing. I couldn't get anything out of the nurse and I was only able to see him once and that was cut short because he was easily exhausted.'

Livvie slipped a paper band around a bundle of pound notes and placed them with a small bag of cash in a bank deposit wallet. 'That doesn't sound too promising.' She sighed and her shoulders drooped. 'I should have made an effort to see him.'

'It's a long way to go,' Ginnie said sympathetically. 'And he's supposed to have complete rest and quiet.'

'Maybe I could go in the New Year. You'd give me time off, wouldn't you?'

'Of course I will. You've earned it, Livvie.' Ginnie looked round at the displays of furniture with a nod of approval. 'You've done a good job, and judging by that wad of notes you've taken a lot of money.'

A reluctant smile hovered at the corners of Livvie's mouth. 'Praise indeed. I can do well when I put my mind to it.'

'For what it's worth, I think you were wasted staying at home all day with nothing to do other than hang around with your over-privileged friends.'

'Hold on. Don't spoil it. You were being nice to me for a moment.'

'That was a compliment, even if it was a bit back-handed. I wasn't criticising you, just the people in your set.'

'Well, my set as you call them have been in the shop buying things for Christmas.'

Ginnie grinned. 'I hope they paid cash.'

'Of course. I know them better than to allow credit. I was like that myself until you coerced me into slave labour.'

'I'm paying you a wage now, so don't grumble, and I might give you a raise in the New Year. You've done really well, Livvie, and I'm grateful.'

Livvie rang up *No Sale* and closed the till. 'You'd better check the office to make sure I haven't cooked the books.'

'I'm only going to check the post. There's a letter I've been waiting for.' She left Livvie to finish up and went to the office where she found a pile of mail set neatly on the blotter in the middle of an unusually tidy desk. She rifled through it until she found what she was looking for. 'This is it,' she said, slitting the manila envelope with a letter opener. She turned to Livvie, who had followed her into the room. 'This is from the council.'

'What is it? Why all the excitement?'

Ginnie studied the typewritten page. 'They've agreed to my proposition in principle, and they're considering my application to take over Fred's lease.'

'That will almost double the floor space.'

'I know, and I plan to have a household department with bed linen, towels and china. What's more, if you're up for it, I'm going to need a manager. What do you say to that?'

Livvie gulped and swallowed. 'This is me you're talking to. Livvie Mallory. Are you sure you've got the right person?'

'Look around you. When my dad ran this shop the office was a rubbish tip. The outside lavatory was disgusting and the shop floor was old-fashioned and shabby. Between us we've done wonders. We're modernising the business and we've got a huge market out there. They're putting up hundreds of prefabs and there's a rumour that the council are building a whole new estate at Harold Hill. All those people will need to furnish their houses and we're here, ready and waiting.'

'Good God, you've really thought this through, and I called you shop girl in one of my finer moments. Maybe I underestimated you, Virginia Travis.'

'A lot of people have done that in the past, but no more. And there's one other thing I ought to tell you, Livvie.'

'Go on. I'm all ears, so to speak.'

'Actually it's another giant favour. I need you to run the shop for me on your own again for a week, or maybe two, after Christmas.'

'Why? It's a funny time of the year to have a holiday.'

'It's not a holiday exactly. It's a lot of responsibility to thrust on you, and it would mean putting off your trip to see Laurence for a while longer, but I wouldn't ask if it weren't absolutely vital.'

'Where are you going?'

'America.'

'What?' Livvie's eyes opened wide. 'Why?'

'It's a long story.'

Livvie pulled up a chair and sat down, folding her arms across her chest. 'I'll sit here until Christmas Eve unless you tell me everything. Come on, Ginnie. It's got to be something pretty earth-shattering if I'm going to take on all that responsibility.'

Chapter Fourteen

Danny arrived on Sunday. He had telephoned from London Bridge to let Ginnie know that he was on his way and she had met the train. It was wet and windy and she had to cling on to her hat as the train steamed into the station. It made a pleasant change to be welcoming someone instead of seeing them off in the knowledge that they might never return, and Danny was a link with the past and the happier moments she had shared with Nick. She waved frantically when she saw him emerge from a cloud of steam. He came striding along the platform and she ran to greet him, arms outstretched. She reached up to plant a kiss on his cheek.

'Wow! What a welcome.' Grinning broadly, he returned the embrace.

'How did it go in East Grinstead?' she asked eagerly.

'They offered me an internship which I accepted gladly. I'd work for nothing to have the chance to learn from those guys.'

'That's wonderful, Danny. When do you start?' She took his proffered arm and they made their way along the platform.

'Monday, February fourth. That gives me time to go back to LA and sort out a few loose ends.' He gave her a quizzical look. 'How about you? Are you still planning to come with me?'

'Yes. I've made my mind up and nothing's going to stop me.'

'That's great. I've looked into ways of getting back home and my plan now is to fly American Overseas Airlines from Hurn to LaGuardia, New York.'

'Really?' Ginnie stopped walking to stare at him in amazement. 'Fly in an aeroplane?'

He chuckled. 'Well I wasn't thinking of flapping my arms and leaping off the White Cliffs of Dover.'

'Very funny,' she said, laughing. 'But seriously, won't that cost the earth?'

'It won't be cheap, but if you take travelling time and meals en route into consideration I don't suppose there's much in it.'

'I can hardly believe this is happening. I'd given up hope of ever seeing Nick again and then you turn up like the genie from the lamp to grant my dearest wish.'

'You are serious about the guy, aren't you, Ginnie? He's been through a lot and I wouldn't want to take you to see him if there's a chance you'll back down.'

'There's no likelihood of that, Danny. If he doesn't want me I'll come home and that will be it, but my feelings for him haven't changed. I've never been more certain of anything in my whole life.'

'I hope it works out for you and Nick. He's a great guy and you're quite something.'

She quickened her pace as the cumulus clouds delivered a sharp shower. 'Come on. It's not too far to my house and Mum will have the kettle on.'

'I guess I'll have to get used to drinking tea again and warm beer.'

'And I'm going to fly in an aeroplane. That's one up on Livvie. She'll be green with envy and so will Shirley.'

As Ginnie had hoped, Danny was a perfect house guest. Mildred was charmed by him and at every possible opportunity Shirley brought Tony's name into the conversation. Danny did his best to satisfy her eagerness to talk about him, but Ginnie could see that her mother was uncomfortable, and despite their concerted efforts to change the subject Shirley somehow managed to steer it back to Tony.

'What's the matter with her, Ginnie?' Mildred whispered when they were alone in the kitchen washing up after supper. 'She's a married woman and her husband's ill in hospital but she's going on about that fellow Tony as if he meant more to her than Laurence.'

Ginnie busied herself putting the cutlery away. 'She was very fond of Tony, Mum. They were good friends and he died in tragic circumstances.'

'Hmm! Showing off more like. As far as I can tell he was driving too fast on an icy road and he might have killed Shirley and the baby.'

'Let her get it out of her system, Mum. Tony's dead and she'll get over him in time.'

'So there was more to it then?' Mildred pulled the plug from the sink. 'I thought so. She's a silly girl and she'll lose Laurence if she doesn't pull her socks up and start acting like a proper wife.'

'Give her a chance. She's had a lot to cope with, and getting pregnant again so quickly has taken a lot out of her.'

'Even so, she's a mother now and should start acting like one. Thank goodness I've got you to rely on, Ginnie.'

'Actually, Mum, there's something I need to tell you.'

Mildred paused with the dishcloth clutched in her hand. 'What have you done?'

'I'm taking a short break. Everything at the shop should carry on as normal and I won't be gone long, but Danny and I will be leaving for the States as soon as we can get a flight . . .' She broke off, turning to face her mother who had reacted with a sharp intake of breath.

'What? You're running away with the Yank?'

'No, of course not. Maybe I shouldn't have blurted it out like that.'

'You've got some explaining to do, young lady.' Mildred pulled up a chair and sat down at the table. 'Take a seat. I want to know what's going on.'

Ginnie had just finished a lengthy explanation when Shirley burst into the kitchen. 'I thought you were making cocoa, Ginnie.' She came to a halt, looking from one to the other. 'What's up? What have I missed?'

'Come in and shut the door.' Mildred pointed to a chair. 'You'd better sit down and hear what your sister is planning. It's madness and I blame Avril for encouraging her in such a stupid scheme.'

'What have you done, Ginnie?' Shirley sat down, leaning her elbows on the table. Her blue eyes sparkled with anticipation. 'Tell me everything.'

'I'm going to America to see Nick. He lost his sight when the bomb exploded beneath the convoy and he's almost completely blind. I have to see him again. You must understand that.'

Shirley nodded slowly. 'I suppose so, but you could be making a big mistake.'

'Exactly what I said.' Mildred rose from the table and went to fill the kettle at the sink. 'And it will cost a lot of money that would be better spent on building up the business or buying us a few luxuries. Heaven knows we've been short of everything for such a long time that I've almost forgotten what it's like to have a pair of silk stockings or a new lipstick.'

'You don't wear lipstick, Mum,' Shirley said, frowning.

'I would if I could get some, and I'd love a new dress, but that's out of the question because I let you have all my coupons.'

'I understand what you're both saying and you might be right, but this is something I have to do.' Ginnie said firmly. 'I'm desperate to see Nick even if it's just to make certain that he's coping with his disability. His feelings for me might have changed, but if they have I want to hear it from him.'

'Couldn't you write a letter?' Mildred struck a match and lit the gas. 'Or send him a cable?'

'Yes, you're being a bit selfish,' Shirley said crossly. 'It's not fair using Avril's money for a jolly when we're stuck here. If I had that much cash I'd move out into a place of my own.'

'You never would.' Mildred stared at her aghast. 'You couldn't cope without me and your sister. What would you live on and how would you look after two babies?'

'I'm not helpless, Mum.'

Ginnie could see that this was going to escalate into a full-blown row and she rose to her feet. 'Let's stop this, shall we. I'll repay Avril as soon as I'm able and I don't intend to stay away for more than a week or ten days.'

Shirley eased herself from her chair. 'Well, I think it stinks, but I can see that nothing will change your mind. I'm going to join Danny in the living room. He's the only person round here I can talk to.'

Ginnie and her mother exchanged meaningful glances as Shirley marched out of the room. 'The sooner that young man leaves the house the better.' Mildred reached for the tea caddy. 'Shirley needs to

276

forget the American soldier and concentrate on Laurence. The same goes for you, miss.'

'There isn't anyone else for me, Mum.'

'What about that nice young naval officer who stayed here after the wedding? Steven, wasn't it? Now he was lovely and he's got a profession to go back to when he's demobbed. You could do a lot worse, Ginnie. A lot worse.'

'Thanks, Mum. I'll bear that in mind, but whether you and Shirley like it or not, I'm going to the States with Danny.'

Business was brisk on Christmas Eve and Ginnie worked late, making certain that everything was in order before she took time off. She had given small bonuses to Livvie and Jimmy, although she could not really afford to do so, but they had worked hard while she was in Shropshire and she felt they deserved a show of appreciation. She took a last look round the office to make sure that she had not forgotten anything, and satisfied that she had done all she could she went to lock the back door. She unplugged the fairy lights on the Christmas tree and was about to turn off the main switch when the telephone rang. She hesitated, unwilling to get involved in a request from a customer who had left their Christmas shopping until the very last moment, but she could not simply let it ring. She hurried into the office to pick up the receiver. 'Hello.'

'Ginnie, you've got to come home right away.'

Her mother sounded panicked and breathless. 'What's the matter, Mum?'

'Shirley's had a fall and gone into labour. I can't get hold of the doctor or the midwife.'

'Is Danny there?'

'No. He went out. He said something about taking you for a drink after work.'

'Someone's hammering on the shop door, Mum. It could be him.' A quick look into the depths of the shop confirmed that Danny had arrived and was waiting for her in the street. 'We're on our way.'

It was all over by the time the family doctor arrived. After a few words with Danny he went upstairs to check on mother and baby, and apparently satisfied with what he found he left to make another house call.

Ginnie raced up the stairs two at a time and found Shirley looking pale and exhausted but smiling happily as she cuddled her baby daughter. 'Isn't she beautiful, Ginnie?'

Ginnie smiled and nodded. 'She's gorgeous, Shirley. What are you going to call her?'

'Antonia,' Shirley murmured. 'Toni for short.' She closed her eyes.

Ginnie gently prised the baby from her mother's arms and laid her in the Moses basket at the side of the bed. Colin's cot had been temporarily moved to Mildred's room and Ginnie went in to check on him. She was relieved to find that by some miracle he had managed to sleep through everything, and she leaned over to drop a kiss on his baby curls. Closing the door softly she made her way downstairs.

Mildred jumped up from her chair as Ginnie entered the front room. 'Is she all right?'

'Mother and daughter doing well,' Ginnie said, grinning. 'Thank you, Danny. I don't know what we'd have done if you hadn't been here. I wouldn't have known where to start when it came to delivering a baby.'

'And I wouldn't have been much help either.' Mildred sank back onto her seat. 'Is there any sherry left in the sideboard, Ginnie? I think we should drink to the baby's health.'

Danny reached for his jacket which he had hung over the back of a chair and produced a half-bottle of whisky from one of the pockets. 'I think we could all do with a drink. I couldn't get a full bottle, so I guess this will have to do.'

Ginnie crossed the floor and threw her arms around him. 'Happy Christmas, Danny.'

Mildred peered at the clock on the mantelpiece. 'I'd no idea it was so late. It's Christmas Day.'

Ginnie went to her father's cocktail cabinet and selected three glasses. 'I think this is going to be the best Christmas for years. Happy Christmas, Mum.'

Ginnie awakened next morning with a dry mouth and the hint of a headache. She vaguely remembered drinking a couple of large whiskies and after that it was a blur. She peered at the alarm clock on her bedside cabinet and saw that it was almost eight o'clock. She could hear movement in her mother's room and she could only guess that Colin had awakened early and was playing with the teddy bear that Santa Claus had thoughtfully left in his cot for him to find on Christmas morning. She sat up and slid her legs over the side of her bed, reaching for her dressing gown and pushing her feet into her slippers.

She left her room and listened outside her mother's door, smiling as she heard Colin's excited cries and the cooing tones his doting grandmother used when she thought no one was listening. All was quiet in Shirley's room and Ginnie tiptoed past heading for the staircase. She reached the hall just as the phone rang. She picked up the receiver hoping that it hadn't awakened Danny who deserved a rest after his heroic actions the previous evening. 'Hello.'

'I have a trunk call for you from Shropshire. Hold the line, please.'

Ginnie thought for a moment that someone must have told Laurence and he was calling to enquire after his wife and child, but she realised that was impossible as they had decided to leave it until morning to telephone with the good news.

'Hello.' A male voice boomed in the earpiece. 'Am I speaking to Mrs Mallory?'

'No, I'm her sister, Virginia Travis.'

'This is Dr Hollister. May I speak to Mrs Mallory, please?'

The solemnity of his tone sent shards of ice coursing through her veins. 'Is it about my brother-in-law?'

'I really need to speak to Mrs Mallory.'

'I'm afraid that's out of the question at the moment. My sister gave birth to a baby girl last night.'

The line crackled and there was a slight pause. 'I'm afraid I have bad news, Miss Travis.'

The air seemed to have been sucked from her lungs and she could hardly form the word. 'Laurence?'

'I am very sorry to inform you that Mr Mallory passed away in the early hours of the morning. He suffered a severe haemorrhage and despite all our efforts we were unable to save him.'

There was no question of leaving until after the funeral. Shirley had taken the news badly and the doctor had given her a strong sedative, but she could not be kept in a drugged state forever, and when the pills wore off she was inconsolable. Ginnie knew that her sister had been fond of Laurence, but she suspected that his death, coming when Shirley had just given birth to their child, had revived memories of the fatal car crash in which she had lost the one person who had genuinely touched her heart. Tony and Shirley had been soulmates, of that she had no doubt.

Ginnie had had the painful task of informing the Mallorys of their son's death, and she had given a grief-stricken Livvie the rest of the week off. Mr Mallory met the situation with cast-iron stoicism, but Ginnie could only imagine how Laurence's mother must be feeling. Shirley was in no state to make the necessary arrangements and Ginnie was relieved when Mr Mallory insisted on taking over and organising everything as though it were a state funeral.

Avril and Lionel travelled down from Shropshire and booked into the Limes Hotel. Mildred greeted them enthusiastically but she made her feelings plain when she discovered that they were sharing a room. 'They're sleeping together,' she said, checking her appearance in the hall mirror and rearranging the feathers on her black toque, which was supposed to be an exact copy of one the dowager Queen Mary had once worn when in mourning for a distant relation. 'I know she's wearing a flashy engagement ring, but he's a clergyman. What is the world coming to? And what will the neighbours say?'

Ginnie had no answer for that. 'I'll go and see if Shirley's ready, Mum. Could you check that Mrs Martin is still okay to babysit?'

'In my day we had a two-week lying-in period and we stayed in bed. Shirley should be resting.'

'This is different, Mum. Shirley needs to say goodbye to Laurence.'

Mildred sniffed and tossed her head. 'It seems to me she cared more for that Yank than she did for her husband.'

Ginnie said nothing. Her mother's acid comment was too close to the truth to deny with any conviction. She went upstairs to help Shirley put the finishing touches to her borrowed black outfit.

The first person Ginnie saw as she entered the church was Steven. There was no doubting his sincerity as he embraced Shirley and offered his condolences. He shook Ginnie's hand. 'It's good to see you again, even though I could wish the circumstances were different.'

'It's good to see you too, Steven.' She turned round to introduce Danny but he was already halfway down the aisle, escorting Shirley to the front pew to join Mildred, Avril and Lionel.

Steven followed her gaze. 'Your boyfriend?'

'No, he's just a friend. I'd better join my family. There are refreshments laid on in the church hall afterwards, Steven. We can catch up then.' She hurried down the aisle to sit on the pew beside Shirley. She patted her gloved hand. 'Chin up.'

Shirley cast an anxious glance at the Mallorys, who were seated in the opposite pew. 'I don't know how I'm going to face them, Ginnie. They must hate me.'

'Nonsense,' Ginnie whispered. 'You mustn't think like that.' She could not resist a quick look at Mrs Mallory who was heavily veiled and clad in black, sitting straight-backed and staring ahead. Livvie seemed to sense that Ginnie was looking at her and she turned her head, acknowledging her with a wan smile, but Mr Mallory appeared to be writing something in a notebook. Ginnie wondered if he was composing the eulogy or, knowing Colin Mallory, he might have brought his work with him. She turned with a start as Shirley dug her in the ribs. 'What's the matter?'

'I'm not sure I can cope with this.'

'It'll be over soon and you don't have to stay for the wake or whatever they call it. You've got two good excuses to go home after the committal.'

'I don't feel anything now, Ginnie. It's as if I'm frozen inside and I can't grieve any more. What's wrong with me?'

'We're all different. It's just your way of coping.'

'I didn't deserve him,' Shirley whispered. 'It was you he really wanted, but I was desperate and I threw myself at him. Poor Laurence. It's my fault he's dead.'

Ginnie slipped her arm around her sister's shoulders. 'Nonsense. You mustn't think that way, and you're wrong. There was never anything romantic between me and Laurence.'

'Not on your part maybe, but I knew.' Shirley buried her face in her handkerchief.

Ginnie opened her mouth to argue but the congregation shuffled to their feet as the pall-bearers brought the coffin into the church. The service was about to begin.

*

When it was all over Steven caught up with Ginnie in the church hall. He handed her a glass of sherry. 'You look as though you need this.'

She took it with a grateful smile. 'I'm not too keen on sherry, but it will give me Dutch courage so that I can face Mr and Mrs Mallory. I know I shouldn't say it but they aren't my favourite people.'

'I didn't think much of Mr Mallory when I met him after Livvie vandalised your shop, but you've obviously made it up with her and I think Laurence would have been pleased about that.'

She took a sip of the drink and pulled a face. 'I don't think this stuff has ever seen a grape. But you're right, Steven. Laurence never wanted there to be a rift between our two families.'

'I take it that there haven't been any more paint attacks?'

'Livvie is my right-hand woman now. We work really well together.'

'And how are you, Ginnie? You seem to have taken responsibility for everyone and everything.'

'I'm fine. I like working hard and I'm beginning to make a go of the shop. One day it'll be Travis's Department Store and will rival Selfridges or even Bloomingdale's.'

He shot a suspicious glance in Danny's direction. 'I sense the American influence again, Ginnie.'

'As I told you before, Danny is just a friend.'

'Have you known him long?'

'What is this? The third degree?'

'No, I didn't mean it to sound that way.'

He looked so crestfallen that she took pity on him. 'Shirley and I met Danny when we were staying with my aunt in Shropshire. The Americans were based in Lightwood Common and we became friends with some of the officers at the military hospital. I worked there for a few months.'

'I sense there was more to it than that.'

She looked him in the eye and the temptation to talk about Nick was overwhelming. 'Do you really want to know, or are you just being polite?'

'I'd like to think you could confide in me, Ginnie. Laurence was my best friend and I know he was fond of you too.'

She spotted two chairs set apart from the main body of the hall in what was possibly the coldest and draughtiest spot near the outer door, and they sat side by side, on the edge of the proceedings. It was like watching a play and Ginnie felt an odd sense of detachment. Steven spoke first. 'I'm a good listener, if you feel like talking.'

She had not intended to unburden her troubles on a virtual stranger, but once started the suppressed emotions bubbled to the surface and she found herself telling him everything from the first moment she met Nick until the day she walked away from an impossible situation. Her voice broke when she spoke of Nick's terrible affliction, but she managed to hold back the tears. 'That's the story so far,' she said with a rueful smile. 'Danny and I are flying to Los Angeles next week.'

'Thanks for confiding in me. It can't have been easy.'

'Thank you for listening.' She stood up. 'I'd better check on Shirley. She might be feeling a bit tired by now and she'll want to get home to the baby.'

He rose hastily to his feet. 'I'm staying in the same hotel as your aunt and her fiancé. Can I see you again before you go away?'

'I'm going to be frantically busy at the shop.'

'You have to eat. Maybe I could take you to lunch tomorrow?'

'Maybe . . .'

'That's fine. I'll pick you up at one.' He smiled apologetically. 'I don't mean to be pushy but I enjoy your company and we were both fond of Laurence. I'll miss him.'

'And so will I. He was one of the good guys.' She met his amused glance with a shrug of her shoulders. 'Sorry for the Americanism, but it has more to do with Saturday mornings spent at the Odeon watching cowboy films than anything I picked up from Nick or Danny. I had a crush on Gene Autry.'

'I was more a Tom Mix and Tex Ritter fan myself.' Steven glanced over her shoulder and frowned. 'I can see Laurence's father glaring at me. I think I'd better go over and offer my condolences. It's not going to be easy but I can't put it off a moment longer.'

287

'Of course you must, but if I were you I'd avoid Mrs Fuller, the big lady with the tiny hat perched on her blue rinse. She's been eyeing you like a blackbird spotting a juicy worm, and she's heading this way with her unmarried daughter Bernice in tow. I'm not saying anything against Bernice but she's one of Livvie's old set – the Monk Avenue bitches. Best avoided, Steven.'

'Thanks for the warning. See you tomorrow, so don't forget.' Steven cast an anxious look at the redoubtable Mrs Fuller and the equally reluctant Bernice and fled. Satisfied that she had saved him from an embarrassing few moments, Ginnie went to look for Shirley with a view to taking her home.

'She left ten minutes ago, darling,' Avril said, making an extravagant gesture with her left hand. 'Poor girl, she looked exhausted and Danny offered to take her.' She waved her hand beneath Ginnie's nose. 'What do you think of my ring?'

Lionel seized her hand and raised it to his lips. 'Hardly appropriate, my dear. I don't think a wake is the right time to flaunt your diamonds.'

Unabashed, Avril caressed his cheek. 'I'm proud to be engaged to a man of the cloth, and this is a church hall. Maybe I ought to get up on the stage and announce our good news to the world.'

'No!' Ginnie and Lionel cried in unison.

Lionel slipped his arm around Avril's waist. 'Time and place, my dear. Time and place.'

'I was just joking.' Avril chuckled mischievously.

'Isn't he just adorable, Ginnie? This time it really is for keeps. I'm going to nurture my darling Lionel as if he were a hothouse flower. Nothing is too good for him.' Her smile faded. 'Uh oh! Here comes my dear sister. Now I'm really in for it.'

Mildred advanced on them, looking majestic in her toque, but her expression was thunderous. 'Avril Parkin you're showing me up again.' She turned to Lionel with a pleading look. 'Can't you make her behave like a woman of forty-eight instead of acting like a silly schoolgirl?'

'Forty-seven, darling,' Avril said, frowning. 'You always add an extra year on to my age.'

Lionel gave her a hug. 'You don't look a day over thirty-five, my love.' He turned his smile on Mildred. 'And you are obviously the younger sister, Mildred. By the way, that's a splendid hat. I'm sure I saw Queen Mary wearing one quite similar.'

Mildred's scowl was replaced by a smile. 'You did. This is an exact copy. The shop assistant in Ann Paget's on the High Street told me so, but now I must circulate. That's what you should be doing, Ginnie. I saw you having a tête-à-tête with Steven Carter. It won't do. This is not a church social.' She sailed off to speak to one of her Women's Institute cronies and Ginnie heaved a sigh of relief.

'Well, go on,' Avril said, winking. 'Do what your mother says, Virginia.' She caught her by the hand as she was about to walk away. 'Come and have dinner with us tonight, darling. We can't impose on

Mildred and I'm sure that your sister will be worn out by then and will need to put her feet up, so please say you will.'

'Yes, do,' Lionel added eagerly. 'The other guests are all commercial travellers or ageing spinsters who live there permanently. We would really enjoy your company.'

'And I can tell you all about our wedding plans,' Avril added, dimpling. 'You must come, and Shirley too, if she's not too tired. Maybe she could bring Danny as he seems to be very attentive and I gather he's going to work here for a while.'

'Danny and Shirley?' Ginnie shook her head. 'No, Avril, you've got it all wrong. He's just a friend.'

'If you say so, darling. Now you must promise to have dinner with us. I want to hear all about your proposed trip to the States. Mildred told me you were planning to go and see Nick, and personally I'm delighted. Aren't we, Lionel?'

His lips twitched. 'Are we? Yes, I suppose so, Avril my love. Nick is a good chap but you need to think very hard before you devote your life to a blind man, Ginnie. It won't be easy and you're still very young.'

'He might not want me,' Ginnie said simply. 'But I have to find out for myself. I understand what everyone is saying, but it's between him and me.'

Chapter Fifteen

Juggling a complicated emotional crisis at home and making certain that the business ran smoothly in her absence tested Ginnie's patience to its limit. Livvie was to manage the shop and Ida volunteered to help out when necessary, even if it was only to act as cashier and answer the telephone. Jimmy promised to carry out Livvie's instructions without arguing, but Ginnie asked Fred Chinashop to keep an eye on things and step in if there was any bickering.

Having risen from her bed to attend Laurence's funeral, Shirley had chosen to ignore her mother's dire predictions that she would suffer long-term consequences if she refused to take an adequate amount of rest. When she had a spare moment to give it any thought it seemed to Ginnie that her sister had undergone a complete metamorphosis. Almost overnight Shirley had changed from a fun-loving flirt to a devoted mother who protected her infants with the ferocity of a tigress. She shunned any attempts to help her and the daily routine in Cherry Lane revolved around the children's needs. Ginnie was secretly looking forward to getting away from a house where it was difficult to get into the bathroom because Shirley was bathing one or both of her babies. The kitchen was as hot and humid as a tropical rain forest with nappies hanging from the clothes airer, and it was impossible to walk into the sitting room without treading on a teddy bear or knocking over a pile of wooden bricks. When the baby slept everyone had to speak in a whisper and tiptoe around in case she awakened, and the moment Toni uttered the smallest whimper her mother was at her side, snatching her from her cot to check that her nappy pins had not come undone and examining her tiny body in case she had suddenly developed a rash.

Colin observed all this frantic activity with his thumb plugged firmly in his mouth, and his first tottering steps were applauded by his grandmother and Ginnie, but largely ignored by his mother who was fussing over the baby. Mildred compensated by resurrecting the old wooden ladder from the garden shed and clambering up into the attic. Ginnie had followed her upstairs, wondering what on earth had caused this sudden desire to explore the roof space. 'Mum, are you all right up there? For goodness' sake be careful.'

Mildred poked her head through the open hatch. 'Help me down with this box. It's full of your old toys. I've kept them all these years.' She passed a large and extremely dusty cardboard box down to Ginnie. 'I'll leave the doll's house until Toni's old enough to appreciate it, but we might find some things in there for young Colin. Poor little chap, he's had his nose put out of joint and it's not fair.' She climbed down, pulling the hatch cover back into place. 'Take it downstairs for me, there's a good girl.'

Ginnie took the box to the sitting room where Shirley was resting on the settee. They sorted through the items one by one, and Ginnie resurrected her old jack-in-the-box, which made Colin crow with laughter, and a clockwork celluloid duck riding a tricycle that skittered about the floor. Her rag doll, Sally-Anne, lay crumpled and grubby in the bottom of the box, her yellow wool hair matted and in need of a wash and her gingham dress sadly faded. Sally-Anne had been the only doll that Ginnie had played with, and that was only on rainy days when it was too wet to go outside to race around with the local children, playing tag or hopscotch. Even though she had been three years her senior Shirley had been happy to stay at home and have tea parties with her dolls seated on the floor around her. 'Now I know why you used to spend all your time dressing and undressing your dollies,' Ginnie said, grinning. 'You were in training to be a mum.'

Shirley looked up from changing Toni's nappy. 'Don't be daft.'

'Think about it, Shirley. You're a born mother. It must have been obvious to the grown-ups from the start, if they ever stopped to think about it.'

'I didn't plan to get pregnant,' Shirley said indignantly. 'It just happened.'

'Twice to be exact. That's no coincidence.'

'Keep your amateur psychology for someone who likes to listen to you talking rubbish. I love my kids, but I'd give my right arm to be flying off to America tomorrow.'

'I know it's tough for you, but I've got to do this just as you had to go and see Laurence in the convalescent home.'

A wry smile twisted Shirley's lips. 'Well, don't come back with a bun in the oven like I did.'

Ginnie gurgled with laughter. 'Don't let Mum hear you talking like that. You'll get a slap round the legs with a wet floor cloth and I can remember how much it hurt.'

'I think I'm a bit too big for that now.' Shirley wrapped the baby in her shawl and tucked her in the crook of her arm. 'Well, good luck, Ginnie. You're the bestest sister a girl could have and I hope it goes well for you, I really do.'

'And you're a fantastic mum. I'm proud of you too.' She scrambled to her feet. 'I'm off to the shop one last time to make sure that Livvie knows exactly what she's doing.'

'You and that shop,' Shirley said, laughing. 'I bet you've got *Travis's Furniture Shop* engraved on your heart.'

Shirley's words echoed in Ginnie head as she stood beside Danny in the airport lounge, waiting to board the aeroplane. Her palms were moist and her heartbeats quickened when the call came for their flight, and she had to force herself to act nonchalantly as she followed Danny towards the gate. She wondered if the other passengers felt the same, but they were chattering amongst themselves and sauntering across the tarmac as though taking a flight across the Atlantic was like catching a bus. As they drew closer to the waiting DC-4 Ginnie was overawed by the splendour and size of the four-engine propeller-driven aircraft. She had seen aeroplanes flying overhead but faced with one on the ground she was amazed at the size and beauty of the machine. It was almost impossible to imagine that anything so large could take off and soar into the sky. In a few moments she was going to find out. She clutched Danny's hand. 'I'm a bit nervous.'

He gave her an encouraging smile. 'There's nothing to it. We'll be touching down at Shannon and then Gander, Newfoundland, and on to LaGuardia.'

'And then another plane to Burbank. Yes, I know, but I still can't believe I'm going to see Nick again.'

He stood back to allow her to climb the steps into the aeroplane. 'Better believe it, honey. We're on our way.'

Ginnie's heart was pounding as she entered the cabin and was shown to her seat. She sat back and closed her eyes, opening them as the stewardess offered her a boiled sweet. She took one, not wanting to offend the woman, who was smiling graciously.

'Thank you.' She glanced anxiously at Danny. 'What's this for?' she whispered. 'We aren't at the pictures.'

'When we take off you and gain height your ears will pop,' he said, chuckling. 'Sucking a sweet helps.'

She clutched it tightly in her hand. 'Anything else I should know?'

'No, honey. Sit back and enjoy the flight. It'll take seventeen hours plus to get to the Big Apple.'

'I can't believe I'm doing this. Does Nick know that I'm coming?'

'No. I guess he's going to have the surprise of his life.'

Exhausted, feeling grubby and in desperate need of a change of clothing, Ginnie followed Danny out of the airport building in Burbank. According to her watch it was elevenses time in England but it was the middle of the night in California, and it was cool. She had imagined stepping out into blazing sunshine and blue skies but the street lights were reflected in puddles as though there had been a sharp shower of rain. She glanced up at Danny. 'It's not how I thought it would be.'

'Wait until it gets light. This is the coolest month of the year but I can promise you sunshine most of the time.' He took a step forward as a pick-up truck drew to a halt at the kerb.

The driver opened the door and climbed out. 'Hi, Danny. Right on time.' He held his hand out to Ginnie. 'Hi, you must be Ginnie. I'm Bob.'

Danny picked up their luggage and tossed it into the back. 'This is Nick's brother, Ginnie. In case you hadn't guessed.'

Despite exhaustion and the disorientation of being in another time zone, Ginnie managed a smile. 'I can see the likeness.' She shook his hand. 'Hello, Bob.'

'Hop in. You must be worn to the bone with all that travelling.'

Too tired to argue, Ginnie climbed in beside him, followed by Danny. It was a short drive to the Millers' house on the outskirts of Eagle Rock, but Ginnie slept all the way and awakened only when the pick-up pulled into the drive outside the Millers' home. It was too dark to see much detail but the house seemed enormous, gleaming whitely in the moonlight. Bob lifted their luggage from the back of the truck and led the way up a flight of stone steps. He ushered them into a spacious entrance hall. The starkness of the whitewashed walls was offset by the colourful Moorish design of the tiled floor, and the earthy tones of terracotta pots spilling over with Boston ferns.

'Everyone else is asleep,' he said in a low voice. 'So I'm the welcoming committee. Can I get you guys anything to eat or drink, or would you like to catch up on some sleep?'

Ginnie rubbed her hand across her eyes. 'I'd like to go to my room, if that's okay.'

'Sure, honey. I'll show you where it is.'

She followed him up a wide staircase with an ornate wrought-iron balustrade, and once again she was struck by the size of the house compared to her home in Cherry Lane. He opened the door at the far end of the landing and ushered her into the room. 'See you later, Ginnie. Sleep well.' He placed her suitcase on a carved cedar chest and left the room, closing the door behind him.

She was physically exhausted but she doubted if she would be able to sleep, and she needed to get her bearings before she went to bed. Unsurprisingly her room was at least four times larger than her bedroom at home. Glassed doors led to a balcony with views that were no doubt spectacular, but she would have to wait until morning to appreciate them. She peered into the darkness outside, wondering where Nick might be sleeping in this rambling house. He could be in the adjacent room for all she knew, and it was hard to believe that she would see him again in just a few short hours. She caught sight of her reflection in the dressing table mirror and her hand flew to her face. Dark shadows underlined her eyes and her skin was the colour of sour milk. Her hair hung in lank strands around her shoulders and she was in desperate need of a wash. Bob had forgotten to tell her where to find the bathroom and she never went to bed without first cleaning her teeth.

She opened her case and began to unpack, but there did not seem to be a wardrobe, just a row of louvred doors on the wall opposite the colonial-style four-poster bed. There was nothing for it but to try each in turn. Three doors opened to reveal a fitted wardrobe and behind the fourth was the sort of bathroom she had only seen in expensive magazines. Even better, there was a shower attachment in the bathtub. She would have such a lot to tell them back home, but now all she wanted to do was take a quick shower and climb into bed.

She was awakened by someone tapping on the door which opened slowly to admit a plump dark-haired lady who crossed the floor to place a small silver tray on the night stand. 'Good morning, Ginnie. I'm Nick's mom.'

Ginnie struggled to a sitting position. 'I'm sorry. Have I overslept?'

Mrs Miller perched on the edge of the bed. 'Of course not, honey. It's nine thirty but I thought you might be hungry and breakfast's ready when you are.'

Ginnie picked up the cup and saucer and sipped. 'Tea,' she said, smiling. 'I thought you only drank coffee in America.'

'Some of us like our tea and Danny told me that's what you Brits drink first thing in the morning, so I wanted to make you feel at home.'

'You're very kind, Mrs Miller.'

'Call me Barbara, honey. There's no need to be formal.'

'Thank you – Barbara.' Ginnie took another sip

from the cup. 'How is Nick this morning? Does he know I'm here?'

Barbara rose swiftly to her feet. 'Not yet. Bob took him to the hospital to see the ophthalmologist. Nick has regular visits to see how he's doing.'

'Has he regained much of his vision?'

'Some, but we continue to hope.' Barbara moved towards the doorway. 'Come downstairs when you're ready. I'll be in the kitchen.'

Ten minutes later, having stopped for a few seconds to admire the view of distant mountains from the balcony, Ginnie had a quick wash in the luxury of her own bathroom and dressed in a cotton summer frock and sandals. She brushed her hair and made her way downstairs to search for the kitchen.

The tempting aroma of hot pancakes wafting through the house made it easy to find, and she paused on the threshold, gazing around the room in awe. It might have been a set from a glamorous American movie. Built-in units lined the walls and a refrigerator the size of a small wardrobe stood in one corner vying for pride of place with the range cooker, large enough to cater for a small army. Gingham curtains draped the window, framing a view of the garden filled with fan palms, trees that were different from anything she had seen at home and exotic plants set against a backdrop of the foothills. Ginnie stood transfixed. She had stepped off the plane into another world far from the austerity of cold, foggy, war-torn England and she might at any moment wake up and find it was all a dream.

Barbara lifted a pan from the hob and flipped a couple of pancakes onto a plate. 'I hope you're hungry, honey.' She opened the oven and took out a tray of crispy bacon rashers, serving them onto the same dish. She placed it on the polished oak table where the centrepiece was a ceramic bowl filled with oranges.

'Take a seat, and eat up, honey. There's fresh orange juice in the jug, so help yourself. Would you like more tea or would you like to try our coffee?'

'I'd like to try your coffee, please. We haven't been able to get proper coffee for ages, and to be honest I can't remember seeing this much food on one person's plate for a very long time.' Ginnie poured the freshly squeezed juice into a glass and tasted it with a sigh of pleasure. 'This is absolutely gorgeous. I haven't tasted fresh orange juice for years.'

Barbara abandoned the pans and took a seat at the table, resting her chin on her cupped hands. 'Nick and Danny told us that it's been difficult over there, but I had no idea it was so bad.'

'Where is Danny? Is he still in bed?'

'No, dear, he went with Bob and Nick. He's been such a good friend to my boy both before and after Nick was wounded. Sometimes I think I've got three sons and not just two.' She passed a jug to Ginnie. 'Try some maple syrup on your pancakes.'

Ginnie cut into the soft buttery pancake and took a bite. The syrup was deliciously sweet with a slightly nutty flavour and added to the saltiness of the crisp bacon it was a wake-up call to her taste buds that had become accustomed to plain and frankly boring food.

'I do like to see a girl with a good appetite,' Barbara said with a nod of approval. 'Some young women are so finicky; it makes me cross to see them pushing a pea around their plates as if it's going to choke them.' She cocked her head on one side. 'I can hear the pick-up engine. I'd know that sound anywhere, and Earl is at the store so it must be the boys.'

Ginnie's appetite deserted her and she leapt to her feet as the door opened and Danny walked into the kitchen, closely followed by Nick. He came to a sudden halt, as if sensing her presence. Ginnie could neither move nor breathe. He looked the same but although he might appear outwardly unchanged the light had gone from his eyes. His lips were set in a hard line and deep lines of suffering were etched on his face. She took a deep breath. 'Hello, Nick.'

He recoiled at the sound of her voice. 'Ginnie? It is you.'

'Yes, Nick. It's me.'

He rounded on Danny. 'You brought her here? You did this in spite of what I said? Why would you do this to me?'

Barbara rushed towards him, arms outstretched. 'Come and sit down, honey. We thought it would be a wonderful surprise.'

'You should have known better, Mom.' He turned

to Danny, scowling. 'What the hell did you think you were doing?'

'For God's sake, calm down,' Danny said angrily. 'Ginnie's come all this way to see you.'

She took a step towards Nick but he held up his hands. 'Don't. Please, Ginnie, go home. This isn't the place for you. Danny was wrong to bring you here.' He walked towards the door with a measured tread as if counting the number of steps needed to make his escape.

Danny made a move to follow him but Barbara shook her head. 'Let him go.' She laid her hand on Ginnie's shoulder. 'That's not like Nick. He'll come round, you'll see.'

'I'd better make sure he's okay,' Danny said anxiously. 'This is my fault, Barbara. I should have warned him.'

'I shouldn't have come.' Ginnie found her voice at last but even to her own ears it sounded strange and strangled. 'I'm sorry.'

Barbara moved closer, giving her a sympathetic hug. 'Don't be sorry. We're the ones who handled it badly. Give him time.'

Ginnie shook her head. 'He's made his feelings clear. I was stupid to think that I could just turn up and everything would be all right.'

'Maybe it was a mistake,' Barbara said slowly. 'But you're our guest, and we're delighted to have you stay with us. Now sit down and finish your breakfast.' She went to the table and refilled her cup with coffee, spilling some in the saucer as her hand shook.

'Maybe I ought to go and speak to him. At least I can tell him I'm sorry. I wanted to see him so much and I thought he'd want to see me.' Ginnie made a move towards the door but Danny barred her way.

'Bad idea, Ginnie. It wasn't just you turning up out of the blue that made him flip his lid. The ophthalmologist told him that there hasn't been any significant improvement in his vision, although I guess Nick knew that.'

'But it's early days yet,' Barbara murmured.

Danny nodded. 'Sure it is. Now why don't I take Nick a cup of coffee?'

'Yes, Danny. Do that, please.' Barbara filled a cup and handed it to him. 'He'll come round. We just have to give him some space.'

It was one of the worst days of Ginnie's life. Despite the show of kindness from Nick's mother, she wanted to crawl away and hide. Nick's outright refusal to speak to her was agonising and humiliating. She wished with all her heart that she had stayed at home. She had crossed the Atlantic chasing a dream and that dream had turned into a nightmare. She felt like a trespasser in the Millers' luxurious home. Danny had returned to his own apartment and would be fully occupied for the next few days sorting out his own affairs, and Ginnie was left to entertain herself as Barbara had an appointment at the beauty parlour and Nick had shut himself in his room.

She sat in the den and read magazines and when that palled she went outside to walk round the garden, pausing every now and again to stare at the upper floor windows, wondering which room was Nick's. It was torture to be this close and yet so far away from him. She wanted desperately to be near him if only to hold his hand and tell him that her feelings had not changed. She could only hope that he might relent when he had recovered from the initial shock of her sudden arrival, and that they could at least talk to each other like friends.

It was even worse that evening when Earl and Bob returned home accompanied by an attractive young woman, who greeted Ginnie with a warm smile. 'Hi, I'm Bob's fiancée, Marilyn.'

Earl stepped forward, holding out his hand. 'And I'm Earl. Welcome to our home.'

'I'm sorry it hasn't worked out as you hoped, Ginnie,' Bob said in a low voice. 'Danny telephoned the shop and told me what happened this morning. It was our fault. The truth is we've been pussyfooting around him as if he was still an invalid instead of treating him like a responsible adult, but that doesn't excuse the way he treated you.'

Even more embarrassed than before, Ginnie acknowledged his apology with a vague wave of her hand. 'It was nothing, really.'

'I don't buy that for a moment. Maybe we were in the wrong, but Nick's acting like a dope.'

'That's not fair, Bob.' Barbara emerged from the dining room. 'Nick just needs time to adjust.'

'You always take his side, Mom,' Bob said angrily. 'Sure we all know he's a war hero and he's still suffering, but he's behaving like a jerk.'

Earl stepped in between them. 'Go upstairs and tell your brother that I expect him to come down to dinner.'

'That's not fair, Earl,' Barbara said anxiously. 'Let Nick work this out in his own time.'

'You always did spoil that boy, Barbara.'

'I'll go,' Bob said, making for the staircase. 'But I can't promise anything.'

'I am so sorry,' Ginnie said, fighting back tears. 'I shouldn't have come.'

Marilyn reached out to grasp her hand. 'Don't say that. It's great to have you here.'

'We're forgetting our manners,' Barbara said stiffly. 'I'm sorry, Ginnie. What must you think of us?'

'Why are we standing here when we could be out on the patio having a drink before dinner?' Earl glanced at their glum faces with an attempt at a smile. 'I need one after the day I've had at the store.'

'Earl mixes the best cocktails in LA, and I can stretch ten into fifteen minutes if it helps everyone to unwind and relax.' Without waiting for a response Barbara hurried off in the direction of the kitchen.

'Let's go through,' Marilyn said, slipping her arm

around Ginnie's shoulders. 'Papa Miller is the king of the martini makers. You must try one and see.'

Bob returned after an unsuccessful attempt to persuade his brother to join them for dinner. There was a strained atmosphere in the dining room when everyone sat down to eat, and despite the mellowing influence of a martini Ginnie could barely swallow a morsel of the huge steak that was served up to her. She toyed with the creamy mashed potato and hot biscuits, which she discovered were nothing like Rich Tea or Digestives, but more like scones served straight from the oven. She managed to eat a few of the crisp green beans, but it must have been obvious that she was struggling and Barbara removed her plate without comment. The family had tried to make light of Nick's refusal to join them for dinner, but it was an uncomfortable meal and when dessert was finished Earl rose from his seat. 'I'm not having this, Barbara. The boy might be suffering but we brought him up with better manners than this.' He strode towards the doorway.

Barbara jumped to her feet. 'Please don't upset him, Earl.'

'It's time someone told him straight. Okay, he's had it tough, there's no denying the fact, but he's got to face up to it sooner rather than later.' He stormed out of the dining room leaving an awkward silence in his wake.

Barbara began clearing the table and Marilyn leapt to her feet. 'Let me do that, Mom.'

'I can manage, thank you, honey. Why don't you take Ginnie into the den and I'll bring coffee when I'm done in the kitchen.' She shot a meaningful look at Bob. 'But you can help if you've a mind to.'

He obeyed without hesitation and as they left the room Ginnie could imagine the agitated conversation taking place over the washing-up. She shot a wary glance at Marilyn. 'I'm really sorry to have caused so much trouble.'

'It's not your fault, Ginnie. You weren't to know and Danny thought he was doing Nick a favour.'

'But it hasn't worked out that way.'

Marilyn pushed back her chair and stood up. 'Not yet, but don't give up. Nick's a great guy and he's had a hard time.'

'And I've made it even worse.'

'Maybe – maybe not.' Marilyn angled her head. 'Tell you what, Ginnie. Tomorrow you and I will have a girls' day out. I'll show you all that Eagle Rock has to offer.'

'But don't you have to work?'

Marilyn tossed her blonde curls. 'Sure I do, but what's the point of being engaged to the boss's son if I can't take a day off when I want to?'

'You are so lucky,' Ginnie said sincerely. 'Bob seems such a nice chap and Barbara has been kindness itself. All I've done is upset everyone.'

'You mustn't blame yourself. Tomorrow we'll hit the stores and spoil ourselves. How does that sound to you?'

'That sounds lovely, and perhaps Nick might have a change of heart and agree to see me.'

'Maybe, honey. We'll have to wait and see.'

A morning spent shopping with Marilyn was an experience that left Ginnie breathless and open-mouthed. After years of austerity and clothes rationing it was incredible to enter a shop and realise that she could have anything she wanted, if she had the money to pay for it. Marilyn bought a lipstick and some mascara, handing over the money without bothering to count her change. She was about to walk on when she stopped, turning to Ginnie with a questioning look. 'Don't you want anything from this department?'

'I don't wear much make-up. Actually it's so hard to come by in England that women have been using other things.'

Marilyn's eyes sparkled with sudden interest. 'Like what?'

'Beetroot juice on their lips. Soot on their eyelashes and used matches to emphasise their eyebrows.'

'No, really?'

Warming to the subject, Ginnie nodded emphatically. 'My sister used to smooth gravy browning on her legs and I had to draw a line up the back of her calves in eyebrow pencil because she couldn't get silk stockings.'

'You poor girl.' Marilyn pulled out her purse. 'Let me treat you to something that you don't need but would love to have.'

Ginnie shook her head. 'No. Thanks a lot, but I couldn't.'

'Nonsense. You might be my sister-in-law one day and then we'd be family, so what will you have?'

'Perhaps you could lend me the money to buy a lipstick for my mum. She'd really love that.'

'For your mom? Okay, if that's what you want then that's what you'll have.'

They spent some time choosing the right colour and Marilyn pressed the package into Ginnie's hand. 'I hope your mom likes it, but I'm still going to get you something, and don't start by telling me what your sister would like or that girl who helps out in your store. Today is about you, Virginia Travis.'

Recognising a spirit akin to her mother's forceful nature, Ginnie could only smile and hope that Marilyn would tire of her attempts to make up for Nick's hurtful behaviour. She gave in a little when Marilyn bought several pairs of nylons and insisted that Ginnie must take them home. 'Think of it as a present from Los Angeles,' Marilyn said, smiling.

Ginnie had an image of day trips to Southend-on-Sea and the sticks of pink rock with the name of the town printed all the way through. Perhaps the stockings had Eagle Rock embroidered on the heel?

'What's funny?' Marilyn eyed her warily. 'Are you okay, Ginnie?'

Realising that she was grinning idiotically and probably on the verge of hysterical laughter, Ginnie pulled herself together and tried to explain, but

Marilyn seemed to find it difficult to appreciate the joke. She shook her head. 'I guess that all you Brits are crazy. I could use a coffee. How about you?'

Ginnie was about to ask if it was possible to get a cup of tea when she realised that she had lost Marilyn's attention. 'What's the matter?'

'Keep walking. No, it's too late, she's spotted us.' Marilyn came to a halt, curving her lips into a smile. 'Hi, Betsy.'

Chapter Sixteen

'Hi, Marilyn. It's been a while.'

One look at Marilyn's flushed cheeks and apprehensive expression was enough to convince Ginnie that this was Nick's ex-fiancée. She turned slowly, preparing herself to hate the woman who had thrown Nick over for someone with better prospects, but it was hard to hate someone who had such a charming smile and seemed genuinely pleased to see them. Marilyn did not seem to be impressed. 'It sure has, but we were just leaving. Maybe we can catch up another time?'

Betsy did not appear to be listening as all her attention was focused on Ginnie. She held out her hand. 'I don't believe we've met. I'm Betsy Novak.'

'Ginnie Travis. How do you do?' Ginnie shook her hand.

'So you're Ginnie?' Betsy cocked her head on one side, eyeing her critically. 'You're even prettier than I thought you'd be. But then Nick always had good taste.'

Marilyn nudged Ginnie in the ribs. 'We'd better get going. Great seeing you, Betsy.'

'Don't rush off.' Betsy laid a gentle but firm hand

on Ginnie's arm. 'I've heard such a lot about you from Nick. We're still good friends in spite of the break-up.'

'That's nice, but I think we have to leave now.' Ginnie glanced anxiously at Marilyn who took her cue and stepped in between them.

'How's Brad? I heard that you'd moved to Pasadena.'

'He's just fine, and yes, we've bought a property. We'll be moving in soon and you must come to our housewarming party.' She turned to Ginnie, smiling. 'And you too, if you're still around. Are you staying with the Millers?'

'Yes, she is,' Marilyn said, grabbing Ginnie by the hand. 'But we really are in a hurry.'

Betsy closed her fingers even more tightly on Ginnie's arm and for a wild moment she thought they were going to have a tug of war, pulling her limb from limb. Marilyn was obviously agitated but Betsy had a steely look in her eyes. 'I guess you came in that old pick-up truck of Pop Miller's,' she said in a saccharin-sweet voice. 'So why don't you go and get it from the parking lot, honey? We'll follow you.'

Marilyn hesitated, frowning. 'We'll be late if we don't leave right away.'

'There you are then.' Betsy made a walking motion with her fingers. 'We'll be right behind you, Marilyn.'

'We'll catch you up,' Ginnie said firmly. She was growing tired of being piggy in the middle and she wanted to find out more about Betsy. This might be her one and only opportunity. She waited until Marilyn was out of earshot. 'Well, go ahead, Betsy. Spit it out.'

Betsy's eyes widened. 'Excuse me?'

'You obviously want to tell me something that you didn't want Marilyn to hear, so go on. I'm listening.'

'No, honey, you've got me all wrong. I wouldn't say a word against Nick or his family. I mean losing his sight is just the most terrible thing that could have happened to him, but that wasn't why I broke off our engagement.'

'You didn't love him enough to stand by him?'

'That's not fair, Ginnie. I've known Nick since kindergarten and we went through high school together. I guess everyone assumed we'd get married one day, but he was away at med school and then overseas. A girl gets lonely.'

'I can see that it must have been difficult.'

'It was okay until he met you.' Betsy's eyes narrowed although her lips were still firmly set in a smile. 'I knew from his letters that something had changed.'

'So when did you meet Brad?'

Betsy shrugged and turned her head away. 'It was love at first sight. I know that sounds corny, but I wasn't sure where Nick and I were heading.' She shot a sideways glance at Ginnie and there was a hint of malice in her baby-blue eyes. 'I knew that Nick had found someone else and I was hurt.'

Ginnie glanced towards the glass doors but there was no sign of Marilyn. 'But you'd fallen for Brad so you'd lost interest in Nick.'

'I'd had the rug pulled out from under me for the last time.'

'What do you mean by that?'

'You don't know Nick as I do. He's had quite a few affairs in the past, but he won't find it so easy to break hearts now.' Betsy leaned closer, lowering her voice. 'Take my tip, honey, and don't get involved. That family will chew you up and spit you out when they've taken all you have to give.' She glanced over Ginnie's shoulder and her expression changed subtly. 'Well, got to go. Good luck, kid. You're sure going to need it.' She lifted her hand and waved to a woman on the far side of the cosmetic counter and a smile transformed her face. 'Hi, Julie.' She rushed off, leaving Ginnie trying to decide whether there had been a grain of truth in her words, or whether she was acting out of spite. She walked slowly towards the exit where the Millers' pick-up had just pulled up at the kerb.

'What did she say to you?' Marilyn asked anxiously as Ginnie climbed into the passenger seat.

'I'm not sure what to believe.'

'I wouldn't take anything she said seriously. The girls at school used to call her Poison Ivy.'

'She said that Nick was always cheating on her.'

'If anything it was the other way round. She kept poor Brad dangling for years and we all knew that she was seeing him when Nick was in med school, but he always believes the best of people and she's a manipulative bitch. Sorry, Ginnie, but you were bound to come across her sooner or later. Forget what she said and don't let her twist the truth so that the break-up was your fault, because it wasn't. When she realised that his prospects weren't so good she was off. Poor old Brad didn't stand a chance.'

Ginnie sat in silence, mulling this over. Betsy had been convincing, but she trusted Marilyn to tell her the truth. Poor Nick, she thought sadly. No wonder he had lost his faith in women if that's how his childhood sweetheart had treated him. She made up her mind to face him and challenge his decision, which affected both their lives. She hardly noticed the scenery as Marilyn drove along the wide boulevard until a yellow trolley car trundled past, clanging its bell to warn the unwary to get out of its way.

'We call it the galloping goose,' Marilyn said, grinning. 'It sways and rocks and occasionally jumps the tracks. My pop told me that the kids in Ellenwood used to grease the tracks so that the car slid back down the hill. I guess you haven't got anything like that in London.'

'We have trams in Ilford, but they're not the same.'

'Are you okay, honey? I mean you didn't believe Betsy's lies, did you?'

'Of course not,' Ginnie said stoutly. 'It's obvious that she wanted to make trouble, although I can't

316

think why when she seems to have got everything she wanted.'

'Except Nick.' Marilyn pulled into the Millers' driveway. 'Betsy had her heart set on being a surgeon's wife. I guess she couldn't forgive Nick for letting her down.'

Ginnie opened the door and was about to climb out when she realised that Marilyn was still behind the wheel. 'Aren't you coming in?'

'I'd better get back to work, honey. I'll see you at dinner tonight.'

Ginnie stood on the drive watching Marilyn expertly reverse into the street and drive away. She turned slowly to gaze at the white stuccoed frontage of the Miller residence, which was even more impressive when seen in daylight. She walked slowly up the steps to ring the bell and when no one answered she went round to the back and let herself into the kitchen. 'Hello? Barbara?' Her voice echoed eerily but there was no response and she was about to go in search of her hostess when she saw a notepad on the table and her name written in block capitals.

GINNIE. Have some errands to do in town. Make yourself at home. Back soon, Barbara.

She gazed round the kitchen, wondering what to do. Should she help herself to food from the giant refrigerator? Or should she wait for Barbara's return? There was no mention of time on the note and it might have been written minutes ago or soon after she had left with Marilyn. She walked through the ground floor, pausing at the foot of the stairs and listening for sounds of movement. Nick might have gone with his mother or he could be in his room, brooding over his disability. Suddenly she was angry. She was shaking with rage as she thought of Nick giving up on life without giving her a chance to tell him that she would stand by him no matter what. Betsy might have thrown him over for upwardly mobile Bradley, but he ought to have known that she, Virginia Travis, was not shallow and fickle. She was loyal and trustworthy and if that made her sound like a faithful Labrador she did not care.

She took the stairs two at a time, shouting his name. 'Nick. Nick, where are you? I'm coming in so you might as well open the door.' She ran along the landing, banging on each door in turn. She was just about to crash her fist against the panelling of the last door when it was flung open and she came face to face with Nick. For a breathless moment they stood motionless, staring at each other, and then he turned away and walked over to a chair by the window. She entered the room, closing the door behind her. 'Why won't you talk to me?' All the opening gambits she had been composing during the flight from England had gone from her head. She knew she sounded like a fractious child, but the words had tumbled from her lips before she could stop them. 'Why, Nick? Why are you treating me as if you hate me?'

'You know why, Ginnie.' He sat down, turning his head away. 'I didn't want you to see me like this.'

She crossed the floor to kneel at his side. 'Look at me. I know you can see something although I haven't a clue how much, but it doesn't matter to me. I mean, of course it's awful for you to be suffering like this, but I still love you. I love you for who you are and not what you are. Can't you understand that?'

He turned his head slowly to meet her gaze with a hint of a smile, and he raised his hand to smooth her tumbled hair back from her forehead. 'I believe you, Ginnie. But it's not enough. To all intents and purposes I'm a blind man and I can't support myself, let alone a wife. Betsy was right to throw me over for Brad. She's a practical girl and I guess she knew that my heart wasn't in it.'

'And was hers? I met your ex-fiancée in one of the shops in town. She tried to tell me that you'd ditched her because of me, but I didn't believe a word of it.'

'She knew I'd fallen for you. I told her because she had to know the truth. If she'd insisted on going ahead with the marriage I would have gone through with it, but we both knew that any feeling we'd had for each other as kids had fizzled out long ago. She did the right thing by marrying Brad.'

'So where does all that leave us, Nick?' Ginnie clasped his hand in hers. 'I haven't changed. Have you?'

319

'It doesn't matter how I feel or what I want. You've got a future and I haven't. It's as simple as that.'

She raised his hand to her cheek. 'I won't let you talk like this. You're still the same man I fell in love with. I want to spend the rest of my life with you.'

A tender smile lit his eyes. 'How old are you, Ginnie? No, don't tell me. I know the answer, and you won't be old enough for me to buy you a drink in a pub for another seven months.'

'You remember.'

'Of course I do. Every moment we spent together is fixed in my mind. I can see everything clearly but only if I close my eyes and travel back in time. The present isn't for me, Ginnie. I'm useless as a surgeon and a physician and all those years at med school have been wasted. I couldn't even take a job in my father's store.'

'But you're alive, Nick. You can't just give up. I won't let you.'

He leaned towards her, grasping both her hands. 'I want you to go back to England and forget all about me, Ginnie.'

Wrenching free from him, she leapt to her feet. 'No. You can't make me do that. I won't.'

'If you care about me at all that's exactly what you'll do. You'll go back home and concentrate on building up that store of yours. You'll meet someone else and you'll put all this behind you.'

'How can you think I'd do that?' Her voice broke on a sob. 'I don't want anyone else. I want you.'

He rose to his feet and faced her angrily. 'You sound like a spoilt kid. I've told you how it is, Ginnie. You've got to respect my wishes and get the hell out of here.'

She had never heard him use that tone of voice, nor had she seen him lose his temper. She backed towards the door. 'That's so cruel. You don't mean it.'

'Go home, kid. Go back to England and give my folks some peace. They've been through enough without you coming here and stirring things up. The Nick Miller you knew is long gone. Let him rest in peace.'

'That sounds as though you're burying yourself alive. I won't let you do that.'

He slumped down again, turning his head away. 'I'm tired. There's no more to say.'

'There's a lot more to say. I'm not giving up on you, Nick. This isn't the end.' She wrenched the door open and stepped outside, almost colliding with Barbara.

'What's going on? I could hear you shouting as soon as I walked into the house.'

'Ask your son,' Ginnie said, pushing past her. 'He's a stubborn idiot and he won't believe that I love him.' She ran down the corridor to her own room and gave way to the tears that she had been holding back. She did not hear the door open and it was not until Barbara sat down on the bed beside her that she realised someone else was in the room.

'I know it's hard, honey,' Barbara said gently. 'But you must do what Nick wants.'

'He talks as though it's all over for him, but I won't have that. He's still the same man, he just can't see very well.'

Barbara placed her arm around Ginnie's shoulders. 'Of course he is to those who love him, but to the outside world he's a wounded war veteran who relies on his family to do everything for him. And that's not going to change, Ginnie. I hoped that your visit would cheer him up but it's only made things worse, and that is our fault. Earl and I should have known better and we should have told Danny that it was a bad idea, but we hoped – we really hoped – and now you see what it's done. It's made it harder for Nick to come to terms with his disability.'

'But there's always hope. Mr Miller told me that Nick might regain more of his sight, and even if he doesn't I don't care. I'll look after him. I'll be his eyes.'

'That's so sweet, but it's not going to happen.' Barbara held her at arm's length, giving her a gentle shake. 'Be realistic, Ginnie. You're little more than a kid yourself. I only know what Danny told me about your home life but it seems to me you've got enough hassle supporting your mother and your widowed sister and her two babies. You're trying to build up a business and look after your family. How could a girl like you cope with a disabled husband?'

'Nick isn't helpless, but living like this is making

him believe that this is all there is. There must be some schemes that help men like him.'

'He gets a pension from the government, but that wouldn't be enough for him to keep a wife. And would you leave everything in England and come to live here?'

Ginnie recoiled in surprise. 'I don't know. I never considered it.'

'Well consider it now, honey. Would you leave your mom and sister and her little ones to fend for themselves? Would you be happy to live in this house with us? Nick wouldn't be able to afford to buy or even to rent a property, not for a long time. Even if his father gave him a job in the store, there isn't much that a blind man could do in the commercial word, and Nick is too proud to take charity, even from his own family.'

'I hadn't thought about it like that.'

'No, honey, I guess you hadn't thought it through at all. We all want what is best for Nick, but he has to find his own way. We can stand by him and offer help, but none of us can fight this particular battle for him. He has to do it himself.'

'Are you telling me to go away and leave him alone?'

'Yes, Ginnie. I believe I am.'

That evening after dinner Ginnie was alone in the den. It was late and she was tired but the row with Nick had upset her more than she had thought possible. She did not relish the prospect of a sleepless night, tossing and turning in her bed or sitting by the window gazing out into the darkness and waiting for the first light of dawn.

Bob and Marilyn had gone out for the evening and Barbara and Earl had been invited to a card party in a neighbour's house and were unlikely to return before midnight. They had asked Ginnie if she would like to accompany them, but she had declined the invitation, admitting ruefully that she had not progressed further than Snap and Beat Your Neighbours. Anyway, she needed time on her own. She wanted to think and to get things straight in her head. If she could have caught the next plane home she would have done so, but Danny was not yet ready to leave and he had made their travel arrangements for the end of the week. She would have to accept the Millers' hospitality for a few days longer, even though Nick had made it plain that she was not welcome in his home. She sat on the banquette staring out into the darkness. It was raining.

Sensing that there was someone else in the room, she spun round to see Nick standing in the doorway, his hand clutching the side post. 'Ginnie?'

She jumped to her feet and hurried to his side. 'I'm here.'

'I wanted to talk.'

'Come and sit down.' She tried to take his arm but he jerked it away.

'I can find my own way.'

'I'm sorry. It's impossible to know how much you can see.'

'Enough to know that I made you unhappy and I couldn't bear that.' He made for the banquette beneath the window and sat down, patting the empty space beside him. 'Come and sit by me.'

She went to him, sitting close but not touching. 'I didn't think there was anything left to say. I'll be going home at the end of the week.'

He felt for her hand and held it in a firm grasp. 'I just wanted you to know that I love you, and I always will.'

'Then why . . .'

He laid a finger on her lips. 'For all the reasons I gave you this afternoon. It wouldn't work, Ginnie. My eyesight might improve or it might not. Even if it does I won't be able to operate again.'

'But you're still a doctor.'

His lips twisted into a wry smile. 'Physician heal thyself. That's ironic in the circumstances.'

She curled her fingers around his in an attempt to ease his pain, but there was little she could say that might comfort him. 'I love you too, Nick. I'd do anything for you.'

'Then go home and get on with your life. That's the best thing you could do for me. If I know you're happy and successful I can take what's coming to me, but I'm damned if I'll be a burden to you.'

'But you still love me?'

'I do.'

She leaned forward and kissed him on the lips. He made a half-hearted attempt to push her away but she slid her arms around his neck and he responded, kissing her hungrily and hard; making no excuses. Her lips parted and she gave herself up to the overwhelming desire that robbed her of reason. Nick drew away first, looking deeply into her eyes. 'I can see you,' he whispered. 'And even if I was stone blind I could still see your face. I'll never forget you.'

'Don't. That sounds like goodbye.'

He twirled a strand of her hair around his finger, smiling sadly. 'I guess it is, my darling.'

'But we have a few more days.'

'No, we don't. I've booked myself into a rehabilitation centre. It's time I did something for myself. You've made me see that.' He brushed her lips with a kiss. 'I'll be leaving early in the morning.'

She watched from an upstairs window. Earl carried Nick's suitcase to the waiting cab and Barbara hugged her son, waving him off with a smile that faded the moment the taxi pulled away. She leaned against her husband and Ginnie could only guess at the words of comfort that passed between them. Theirs was a solid relationship, the sort that Ginnie had always hoped might be hers one day, but now she knew that could never be. If she could not have Nick she would remain single and devote herself to making a success of her business. If only she had a magic carpet that would waft her back to England right away, but that was the stuff of fairytales. Her prince would not ride on a white charger to claim her hand, and for them there would be no happy ending. Nick wanted her to forget him, but it would not be easy to put him from her mind and impossible to banish him from her heart.

She crossed the landing and made her way downstairs. Earl was in the entrance hall studying the headlines on the newspaper. He looked up and smiled. 'Hi, Ginnie. Did you sleep well?'

'Yes, thank you. It's a very comfortable bed and a lovely room.'

He nodded appreciatively. 'We thought you might be at a loose end today, so I wondered if you'd like to come to the store and see how we run things here in Eagle Rock.'

'I'd like that, if it's no trouble.'

'You might even pick up some tips from us, or you might give us some.'

'I don't think I could offer anything useful, but I'm sure I could learn from you.'

'Then that's settled. Let's get some breakfast first. I always say you need a good meal to start the day.'

Miller's Hardware store sold everything from horse tack to dry goods, building materials and seed. Ginnie shadowed Marilyn, who seemed to be the chief cashier and book-keeper as well as serving behind the counter if the other assistants were fully occupied. Bob was in charge of the lumber and building materials and Earl ran the whole business, and as far as Ginnie could see ran it very successfully. She did her best to help, but there was a limit to what she could do as the trade in this up and coming town was quite different from that in East London. Eagle Rock, she discovered, had only been a town since 1911 and seemed set to expand rapidly now that the war was over. Marilyn was just as enthusiastic about the town's prospects and those of the store as Bob and his father, and Ginnie could imagine the three of them going on to even greater success. She wondered if she would be able to do the same at home, but America was a much larger and wealthier country and Britain was on the verge of bankruptcy, if not already bankrupt. She knew that it was not going to be easy, but the time spent in Miller's store gave her plenty of ideas for modernising the shop in Collier Lane.

When the day finally came to return home, Ginnie had mixed feelings. She might be leaving her heart here in California, but her place was with Mum, Shirley and the children. She was sad to say goodbye to the family she had grown to love and she knew she would never forget a moment of her time in Eagle Rock. There were happy memories as well as the painful parting with Nick, but she was making a huge effort to come to terms with the fact that he would have to fight this particular battle on his own.

Marilyn drove Ginnie and Danny to Burbank

airport and there was a tearful farewell at the check-in. Marilyn promised to write whenever she had a spare moment and insisted that she would send Ginnie an invitation to her wedding, but as she boarded the DC-3 Ginnie wondered if she would ever return to Eagle Rock. Nick had decided their future for them and she had been forced to accept his decision, but as she gazed out of the window after take-off and saw the country disappearing beneath the clouds, she knew that it was not finished. It would never be over.

Danny leaned towards her. 'Are you okay, Ginnie?' He handed her a hanky and she realised then that tears were pouring down her cheeks.

'I've got something in my eye,' she murmured, blowing her nose.

'Cheer up. I've got something for you.' He put his hand in his pocket and pulled out a small package.

'A present?'

'It's not from me. Open it and see.'

Her fingers trembled as she tore off the wrapping paper to reveal a small box. She lifted the lid and saw, nestling on a bed of midnight-blue velvet, a small golden eagle brooch. She took it out and laid it in the palm of her hand.

'It's from Nick,' Danny said in a low voice. 'I went to see him at the rehab centre and he said he wanted to give you something to remember him by.'

'I could never forget him, not in a million years.'

She pinned the brooch to her cotton blouse. 'It's beautiful. Will you thank him for me?'

Danny took a slip of paper from his pocket and placed it in her hand. 'You can write and tell him what you think of it. I wasn't supposed to give you the address, but I know you'd want to drop him a line or two.'

'Just to say thanks,' Ginnie murmured, tucking the slip of paper into the box and stowing it safely inside her handbag. 'I really love the brooch. Thank you.'

'Don't thank me. I can't take the credit. Nick described what he wanted but it was Marilyn who chose it.'

'I'll thank her too.' Ginnie leaned back in her seat and closed her eyes. 'This doesn't feel like the end, Danny. I'm not giving up on him, ever.'

Chapter Seventeen

After the comparative warmth of California, returning home to an English winter and the bomb sites of London was enough to dampen even the most optimistic person's spirits. Cherry Lane, with its front gardens dug over ready for planting potatoes and the bare branches of the trees dripping rainwater onto sodden pavements, was a depressing sight. Ginnie tried not to make comparisons but the house seemed even more cramped and shabby than it had before she made the trip to America. Shirley was tired and crotchety and Mildred spent most of her time grumbling about the untidy state of her home. If Ginnie had been missed neither her mother nor her sister was letting on, although she suspected that they might have noticed her absence more if the housekeeping money had not been forthcoming. They enquired politely as to Nick's progress, but Mildred remained tight-lipped whenever his name cropped up in conversation and Ginnie had the feeling that Shirley considered she had had a lucky escape.

After her mother and sister's initial curiosity about the way of life in California and even more questions about what it was like to fly high above the clouds, Ginnie realised that their interest had waned, especially when Shirley discovered that the population of Los Angeles did not consist entirely of movie stars. She seemed to have the idea that idols like Errol Flynn and John Wayne might be seen moonlighting at the pumps in gas stations, and that Ava Gardner and Lauren Bacall worked in diners waiting on tables while resting between movies. Neither her mother nor Shirley mentioned the cost of Ginnie's travels, but it was obvious to her that they thought the money could have been better spent.

Ginnie missed Nick more than she dared to admit and in her heart she knew that her feelings for him would never change. It would have been easier if she had had someone to confide in, but Danny had moved into a shared house in East Grinstead and was fully occupied with his new job at the hospital. She was beginning to feel like a visitor in her own home and she was glad to escape to the shop every morning. At least Livvie seemed to have coped while she was away and no crises had developed during her absence.

Fred Chinashop was pathetically pleased to see her. 'No one makes a cup of tea quite like you do, Ginnie,' he said, clutching her hand. 'I'll miss you when I retire later this year, but at least I know that my shop will be in safe hands.'

'Is it all settled, Fred? I can take the lease over and I've got planning permission to knock the two shops into one?'

He nodded, sipping his tea. 'It came through while you were away.' He pulled out a grubby hanky and mopped his eyes.

Ida thrust a plate of Rich Tea biscuits under his nose. 'Stop snivelling you big baby and have something to eat.' She offered them to Ginnie. 'I haven't had time to do any baking because I've been working full time in the shop.'

'No, thanks,' Ginnie said, smiling. 'Mum made me have a bowl of porridge before I came to work. Maybe later.'

'I'll have one.' Livvie reached out and snatched a biscuit. 'There's the bell now, Ida. You can serve the customer while I bring Ginnie up to date.'

Ginnie cringed inwardly. She did not care for the tone Livvie had used and it would not have hurt her to say please.

Ida did not seem to have taken umbrage. 'You see?' she said, smiling proudly. 'I'm indispensable.' She put the plate on the desk and hurried out of the office.

'And I'd better get back to my shop.' Fred downed the last of his tea, smacking his lips. 'That was just the ticket. I'll see you later, ladies.' He left with a cheery wave of his hand.

'Well, I see nothing's changed,' Ginnie said, looking round at the tidy office with a smile of approval. 'How are the takings? It's always quiet in January and February but hopefully things will pick up soon.'

Livvie flipped the account book open. 'Take a look for yourself. It's not been too bad, but we could do better. Anyway, now you're back we can really begin to make changes. I've got plenty of ideas but of course they've got to have your approval.'

'Since when did you bother what I thought?' Ginnie examined the rows of figures, nodding her head. 'This seems pretty good. We're on the right track, and I picked up some good tips in Eagle Rock.'

'So how did it go? Or shouldn't I ask?'

Ginnie slumped down at the desk, pulling a face. 'I must invest in new office furniture. How Dad put up with this uncomfortable old chair for so many years, I'll never know.'

'If you don't want to talk about Nick, I quite understand.' Livvie glanced out of the window. 'There's Jimmy. He's just come back from a delivery. Hold on a moment. Don't go away.' She hurried out through the back door and Ginnie could hear her rattling out instructions to Jimmy, but there was a harsh note in her voice that made Ginnie rise swiftly to her feet. She went to stand in the doorway. 'Hello, Jimmy. Everything okay?'

A wide grin almost split his face in two as he barged past Livvie and lumbered towards her. 'Welcome home, Miss Ginnie.'

He looked so much like a happy schoolboy that she was moved to give him a brief hug. 'It's good to see you too. I'm pleased to see that things are going well.'

His smile dimmed. 'She's not like you,' he muttered. 'I wouldn't stay working here if you was to sell up to the likes of her.'

Ginnie stared at him in surprise. 'There's no question of that, Jimmy. I'm expanding the business and I've no intention of selling to anyone. Who gave you that impression?'

'Is he grumbling about me?' Livvie strolled up to them and Jimmy backed away.

'I ain't said nothing. It was just what I heard.'

Livvie took a small pad from her pocket and tore off a leaf, thrusting it into his hand. 'There's a measuring-up job to do now. That's the address and don't stop for endless cups of tea and a chat. I want you back here by midday. Is that clear?'

Jimmy nodded wordlessly and shambled over to the van. He climbed in without a backwards glance and drove off.

'That's no way to speak to him,' Ginnie said coldly. 'And what's this about someone buying me out?'

'He has to be kept in order. If you don't spell things out he doesn't understand.'

'I've never had any trouble with Jimmy and neither did my dad. He's a bit slow on the uptake but he's a good worker and he's loyal.'

'Only because no one else would hire him.' Livvie smiled, but there was a calculating look in her eyes. 'Come on, Ginnie. Don't let's fall out about a trifle. I'll try to be more patient with him in future.'

'Come into the office,' Ginnie said stiffly. 'I want

to know what's been going on and I don't think you're telling me everything.'

Livvie followed her inside and closed the door. 'Don't fly off the handle, but there is someone interested in buying the shop. You could sell up and settle all your debts in one go.'

'Who said I've got debts?'

Livvie perched on the edge of the desk. 'Shirley went to see my father asking for money. She wanted him to make her an allowance.'

'Oh, no,' Ginnie gasped. 'How could she do such a thing?'

'She told him that your mother couldn't afford the rent on the house in Cherry Lane. It seems that your father left her rather badly off.'

'Shirley had no right to go begging, especially to your father. I've been keeping the family since Dad died.'

'That's a bit unfair on you, isn't it? I mean you're still a kid.'

'I'm sick of hearing that,' Ginnie said angrily. 'I've proved that I can make a go of the business. We're just starting to show a bit of a profit and when I take over Fred's shop we'll expand and do even better.'

'My father realises that, which is why he's offering to buy you out.'

'Mr Mallory wants to buy me out?' Ginnie stared at her in amazement. 'Why would he do a thing like that? He's got oodles of cash.'

'And he wants to invest some of it. He sees it as a good business opportunity, and he thinks it might be a good career for me, just in case the dearth of eligible bachelors leaves me high and dry on the shelf. Although of course we know that's not going to happen.'

'Your father wants to buy my shop so that he can put you in charge?'

'That's about it, old bean. I'll put a manager in, of course, and you might even like to apply, but—'

'Get out.'

'What?' Livvie's faced paled beneath her expensive maquillage.

'I said get out. I thought you were my friend, Livvie, but you've been scheming behind my back and planning to take away my living.'

Livvie raised herself to a standing position and her expression darkened. 'I've kept this shabby little shop going while you've been pursuing your blind Yankee boyfriend.'

'How dare you.' Ginnie faced up to her, fisting her hands at her sides. 'Nick was fighting for all of us when he was wounded and I wasn't chasing him.'

'Have it your own way, but if you sack me you'll miss the opportunity of a lifetime.'

'Get your hat and coat.' Ginnie marched out of the office and went straight to the counter where Ida was ringing up a sale. 'Excuse me.' Ginnie reached across her and snatched a handful of notes from the till. 'I'll explain later.' She turned to find Livvie standing behind her. 'Take this. It should cover your wages for the time I was away in America and a week's money in lieu of notice.'

'You can't sack me,' Livvie said breathlessly. 'I'm your business partner.'

'You most certainly are not. You were just helping out because your father made you take a job as punishment for your malicious act of vandalism. I've been paying you and Ida as casual workers, and the only person officially on the payroll is Jimmy.'

'You'll regret this, Virginia Travis. You promoted me to manager.'

'You know very well it was only a temporary arrangement.' Ginnie sighed and shook her head. 'I really thought I could trust you. I thought we'd moved on but I realise now that I was mistaken.'

Livvie glared at her with narrowed eyes. 'You bitch. You'll suffer for this.'

'Go home and tell your father that we don't want anything from him. I can look after my family and I'm not selling my shop to him or to anyone.' She walked to the door and held it open. 'Get out of here and keep away from me and my family.'

'You're forgetting that I'm Antonia's aunt. She's just as much part of my family as yours, although I have doubts about Colin's parentage. I rather suspect that his father was a sewage worker.'

'You haven't shown any interest in Shirley's children and your parents haven't acknowledged them, so don't pretend that you care. I want you and your family out of our lives for good.'

Livvie shrugged on her coat and rammed her beret on her head. 'This is all the thanks I get for slaving away in this ghastly little shop. You haven't heard the last of this. My father will sue you for every penny you've got.'

'He can try,' Ginnie said calmly. 'But he'd be wasting his time. I don't own anything of value. The shop is rented from the council and, as you discovered, our house is heavily mortgaged. But one day it will be different. I can promise you that.'

'Phooey!' Livvie marched out of the shop, pushing past bewildered customers.

Ida hurried to Ginnie's side. 'What's got into her?'

'Did she treat you well while I was away, Ida?'

'Well, she was a bit abrupt and bossy, but then I gave her a bit of leeway because I thought it might be too much for her. She's not the sharpest knife in the box.'

'She was quite rude to Jimmy.'

'Yes, well, the poor chap does need a bit of coaxing and he didn't take to Miss Mallory at all. There was a little friction there.'

'That's all at an end now, Ida. She's just informed me that her father was planning to buy me out and let her run the shop.'

Ida's eyes almost popped out of their sockets and her mouth formed a perfect circle of surprise. 'Never! Not Miss Posh Knickers!'

'Don't worry,' Ginnie said, stifling a giggle. 'It's not going to happen. I'd sooner burn the place down than let Mr Mallory get his hands on my business. We're going to make it big, Ida. We might need a bit of help from Fred Chinashop and the rest of the shopkeepers in the parade from time to time, but I'm not selling up.'

Later that morning Ginnie received a telephone call from Colin Mallory. 'Olivia could sue you for unfair dismissal,' he said abruptly.

'She was casual labour, Mr Mallory.' Ginnie took a deep breath. 'It's true that I put her in charge while I was way, but it was only temporary. I gave her a week's money in lieu of notice.'

'You can't treat my daughter like that.'

'I won't have her treating my staff like dirt. And my shop isn't for sale to you or anyone else. That's what I told Livvie and I meant it.'

'My son might be alive today if he hadn't got himself tied to your whore of a sister.'

'How dare you say things like that about Shirley? Laurence loved her and she loved him. He had TB and that's what killed him.'

'And I had to pay for his hospital treatment. If he'd been diagnosed sooner he might have recovered. You and your family are bad news and I'm going to ruin you. You won't be so cocky then, my girl.'

'Go ahead and try.'

'I can do it. I'm an important man in this town. You'll find that out to your cost.' He slammed the receiver down.

*

The first sign that Colin Mallory had carried out his threat was a letter from the planning department revoking the decision to allow Ginnie to enlarge the retail area if she took over Fred's premises. There was no reason given and Ginnie spent all morning on the telephone trying to find out why permission had been given and then withdrawn, and if she had the right to appeal. After several attempts and having been passed from one department to another, she was advised to put her complaint in writing.

Frustrated and angry, she was about to go next door to speak to Fred when he burst into the shop, red-faced and furious. 'The council have changed their minds about the leasehold,' he said, waving a sheet of paper in front of her. 'Read this, Ginnie. It doesn't make sense. Why would they do that?'

Ginnie glanced at the typewritten letter. 'I've just had something similar concerning planning permission,' she said slowly. 'Someone has got it in for me, Fred. And I know who that someone is.'

Ida hurried out from behind the counter. 'I knew it. That Livvie is a snake in the grass. I never trusted her and I always felt she was looking down on the likes of us.'

'It's her father who's at the back of this. He warned me that he'd stop at nothing to see me ruined.' Ginnie handed the letter back to Fred. 'I'm going to appeal. They can't do this to us.'

He tucked it away in his breast pocket. 'It looks

as though they can and they have, Ginnie. I can't afford to go to court over it, can you?'

She shook her head. 'Money is tight at the moment, but there must be a way. I won't be beaten by old man Mallory.'

'He's a solicitor and a magistrate and he's on the council, ducks,' Ida said, frowning. 'You'd need a good lawyer to take him on and the blooming council as well.'

'And I was hoping for a quiet retirement, spending my time on my allotment growing leeks and carrots.' Fred heaved a sigh. 'I don't mean to sound negative, Ginnie, but if you can't buy the lease I'll need to put it up for sale, and I won't be able to do that if there's an appeal pending.'

She laid her hand on his shoulder. 'I'm so sorry, Fred. But you do know that it's Mallory who wants to get hold of the lease, don't you?'

'Why would he be interested in my little china shop?'

'Because Livvie fancies herself as a business-woman and she wants to take my business from me and yours too. She had the nerve to suggest that I might apply for the position of manager.'

'I hope you told her where to go?'

'Yes, Fred. I certainly did, but apparently that was the wrong thing to do. She must have gone straight to Daddy and now he's used his position to influ-ence the council.'

Ida puffed out her cheeks. 'You're not going to let him get away with that, are you, love?'

'Indeed I'm not. In fact I'm going to his office now. Give me the letter, please, Fred. I'm going to face him with the facts and see what he has to say for himself.'

That evening Ginnie arrived home tired and frustrated after all her attempts to see Mallory had failed. He had not returned her phone calls and she had had a similar response from the council offices.

She let herself into the house and was met with a waft of warm, damp air and the smell of boiling nappies. The kitchen door was open and she could see her mother standing over the gas boiler, prodding the contents with a wooden stick. She glanced over her shoulder and her expression was not encouraging. 'I shouldn't be doing this,' she muttered crossly. 'Shirley's been out all day showing off the kids to her friends and leaving me to do all the work.'

Ginnie took off her coat and hat and hung them on the hallstand. 'Why do you do it then, Mum?'

'Because I'm soft in the head, that's why.' Mildred heaved a bundle of wet washing out of the boiler and dumped it into the sink. 'Tea will be late. I've got to finish the nappies or Shirley won't have anything to change them into tomorrow.' She stared hard at Ginnie. 'Why the long face?'

Ginnie walked through a cloud of steam scented with Persil and just a hint of Parozone. She had grown up with the lingering smell of bleach that was ever present in their kitchen. Mildred scrubbed the draining board with it, and soaked the tea towels and dishcloth in it every evening when her housework routine was completed. Some women might dab Chanel No 5 behind their ears, but Ginnie had always suspected that her mother might opt for a touch of bleach. She dragged her thoughts back to the present. 'Sorry, Mum, what did you say?'

'I said, what's wrong? Aren't things going well at the shop?'

'Where's Shirley now, Mum?'

'Bathing the little ones, and don't change the subject. I know you, Virginia, you could never hide anything from me.'

Ginnie sat down at the table. 'Old man Mallory has got it in for me because I gave Livvie the push.'

Mildred turned off the copper and sat down facing her daughter. 'Why did you do that? I thought you two were getting on so well?'

'She's got it into her head that she wants to take over the business. While I was away she persuaded her father to buy me out and she had the cheek to suggest that I could work for her as manager.'

'And you said no, of course.'

'Yes, very firmly, and I sacked her.'

Mildred nodded and her turban wobbled dangerously as if about to fall into the overflowing ashtray. She pulled a face as she picked it up and leaned over to empty it into the coke hod. 'Nasty things, cigarettes. Your sister has taken up smoking.

She says it stops her feeling hungry and she wants to get her figure back. God knows why. Even if she had a figure like Dorothy Lamour she'd find it hard to get a man who's willing to take on another chap's kids.'

'Yes, I suppose so,' Ginnie said wearily. Somehow the conversation always turned to Shirley and her children. She stood up. 'I'll put the kettle on.'

Mildred leaned back in her seat. 'So if you've got rid of Livvie and told her you won't sell up, what's the problem?'

'Mr Mallory has used his influence and I've been refused planning permission to enlarge the shop, and the sale of the lease on Fred's shop has been blocked. I've tried to get some sense out of the council office, but all they'll say is that I can appeal against the decision and that costs money.'

'Then that's what you must do, dear. That's what your father would have done in similar circumstances.'

'Yes, Mum, but I can't afford to pay a lawyer, and it would have to be someone pretty sharp to get the better of Mr Mallory.'

'And you know just the man, Ginnie.'

Ginnie paused as she was about to light the gas beneath the kettle. 'I do?'

'Of course you do. That nice Steven Carter, Laurence's best man. He's a lawyer, isn't he?'

'Yes, but I don't know if he's established in a practice. He's only just been demobbed.'

'Then you must find out. Get in touch with him

right away. His number is on the pad. I took it down when he rang a few days ago while you were in America. Now there's a charming man and English too. From Hampshire, I believe.'

'Mum,' Ginnie said, sighing. 'Don't start matchmaking. Shirley's had enough bad luck with men.'

'I wasn't thinking of Shirley, dear.'

Ginnie held up her hand. 'Don't look at me. I'm not in the market for a husband.' She poured a little hot water into the teapot, staring thoughtfully at the swirling liquid. 'But I've got a fight on my hands and Steven might be just the man to help out.'

'Ginnie. I'd love to help.' Steven's voice sounded far away and the line was crackly which made it even more difficult to hear what he was saying. 'But I've just started working for a firm of solicitors in Southampton and I can't get away.'

'I'm not asking you to do something for nothing,' Ginnie said defensively. 'It would have to be done on a business basis.'

He was silent for a moment and she thought they might have been cut off. She was about to hang up when she heard him clear his throat. 'Sorry, I was just checking my diary. Would it be possible for you to come down here to see me? I could fit you in tomorrow at about midday and then I could quite legitimately take you out to lunch.'

She thought quickly. 'Yes, of course. I'll be there. Just give me instructions how to get to you from the station. I've got a pencil and paper.' She scribbled down his address, thanked him and said goodbye, but as she replaced the receiver she wondered how she was going to keep the shop open even for a day. Ida and Jimmy could not work unsupervised and if she closed the shop it would send the wrong message to Mallory.

She ran upstairs and found Shirley putting Colin to bed in his cot. She beckoned from the doorway, not wanting to wake the baby. Shirley nodded and bent down to kiss Colin, tucking him in with his favourite teddy bear. She made her way between the cot and her double bed, pausing to check on Toni who was sleeping peacefully in her Moses basket, before joining Ginnie on the landing. 'What's the matter?'

'I need your help.'

'Mine? What could I possibly do to help the up and coming businesswoman?'

'There's no need to be sarky. I really do need you to help me if I'm going to put up a fight.'

'I don't know what you're talking about.'

'I'll explain later but I want you to manage the shop for me, just for one day.'

'You've got to be joking.'

'I'm deadly serious. Come downstairs and I'll explain.'

'I haven't said I would yet.'

'I'm counting on you not to let me down, Shirley. Our whole future depends on us all pulling together.'

*

After a great deal of talking Ginnie managed to persuade her mother to look after the children and with the greatest reluctance Shirley agreed to keep an eye on the shop, although she made it clear that she did not know one end of a carpet roll from the other and she would have to rely on Ida and Jimmy to help her out.

Finding the train fare was another matter and Ginnie had to rob the jar by the telephone in which they were supposed to put money each time they made a call, and she emptied the dried egg tin on the kitchen mantelpiece where her mother saved up sixpences to pay the gas and electricity bills. 'It's just a loan,' Ginnie assured her. 'I'll pay it back, I promise.'

Mildred raised her hand to her head to push an escaping curler back beneath her turban. 'You'd better or we'll be cut off. And how d'you think you're going to afford Steven's bill when it comes?'

'I don't know, Mum. I'm going to be honest with him and tell him exactly how we're fixed. If he doesn't want to take the case it'll be his choice. But he's our only hope.' She fingered the golden eagle brooch on her lapel and closed her eyes, wishing for good luck.

Chapter Eighteen

Ginnie alighted from the train at Southampton station and took a cab to the address that Steven had given her. The offices were situated above the General Post Office, approached through a side door in a narrow alleyway. The staircase was uncarpeted and her footsteps echoed eerily as she climbed to the first floor. Emblazoned in gold and black lettering, a half-glassed door bore the names of the three partners. She knocked, and receiving no reply she entered a small vestibule where a middle-aged woman, wearing a grey twinset and a string of coral beads, was talking on the telephone. She acknowledged Ginnie with a brief nod and continued her conversation, which as far as Ginnie could gather was about a cat with a fish bone stuck in its throat. She appeared to be talking to the vet and was growing more and more agitated. 'But I must have an appointment for Tarquin in my lunch hour. I'm Miss Golightly, a regular client.' She paused for a moment. 'No, well there must have been some mistake. I rang earlier and the young lady definitely said I could come at twelve thirty. I can't just take time off from my job whenever I want to.' She paused, cocking her head on one side and listening, although Ginnie wondered how she could hear anything with her grey hair plaited and wound into earphones. Maybe the lady suffered from the cold, or even worse had been born with bat ears that had blighted her life and left her a sad and lonely spinster with only a cat to love. Despite her own problems, Ginnie waited eagerly to learn Tarquin's fate.

'I don't care if it's your lunch time too,' Miss Golightly continued with a break in her voice. 'You're the vet and I've got an animal in distress. He had fresh herring for his tea last night, and one of the bones must have lodged in the poor darling's throat. I expect you to do something about it or my cat might choke to death, and that will be your fault. If he dies I'll have to get my employer, Mr Thorogood of Thorogood, Thorogood and Harper, to sue you for negligence.' A satisfied smile parted her lips to expose a missing molar. 'Thank you. I'll be there directly.' She replaced the receiver and stared at Ginnie as if she were to blame for her difficulties. 'Yes, miss. What can I do for you?'

'Virginia Travis. I've got an appointment to see Mr Carter.'

Miss Golightly began packing up her desk. 'He's got a client with him.' She jumped up from her chair and snatched her coat from a hook on the wall. 'I've got to go now. Just wait here, please.' She grabbed a large leather handbag from a drawer. 'I really have to hurry.'

'I hope Tarquin gets better,' Ginnie said, moving swiftly out of her way.

'Thank you.' Miss Golightly paused, peering at Ginnie through steel-rimmed spectacles. 'How kind.' She opened the door and stepped out into the corridor. The sound of her leather soles pounding on the staircase faded away and downstairs a door banged.

Ginnie looked round and found a chair beneath a pile of leather-bound books. She put them on the floor and sat down, clasping her handbag tightly in her hands.

Moments later a door opened and a bald-headed man peered at the empty desk. 'Where is Miss Golightly?'

'She – er – popped out for a moment,' Ginnie said vaguely.

'How very inconvenient. I wanted a cup of tea.' He slammed the door.

Ginnie sat watching the hands on the wall clock, but either they were stuck or time passed more slowly in Southampton than it did in London. She wondered if being this much further south could have anything to do with it. After all, time was different in other places: maybe that was the case in the dingy, dusty law office, which had a decidedly Dickensian atmosphere. She glanced round thinking that they ought to sack their cleaner, if indeed they had one. Miss Golightly did not seem to care that there was a cobweb hanging from her filing basket and her typewriter would benefit from the energetic use of a feather duster. Ginnie looked up as the door opened half expecting it to be the same man demanding his tea, but it was a middle-aged woman wearing a felt hat with a large feather stuck in the brim. She glanced at Ginnie, frowning. 'Men! They're all miserable bastards. Don't ever get married, my dear. They'll take your best years and then desert you for a younger woman.' She stamped out of the office, slamming the door behind her.

'Ah, there you are, Ginnie.' Steven appeared suddenly, making her jump. 'I hope I haven't kept you waiting.'

She stood up, tucking her handbag beneath her arm. 'I was a bit early anyway, and it's really kind of you to see me at such short notice.'

He held the door for her. 'It's good to see you, even if it isn't the most auspicious of occasions.' He led the way along a narrow passage lined with doors. His office was at the far end next to the staff lavatory. The door had been left open and Ginnie could see a washbasin with a grubby towel hanging limply from a peg on the wall. The smell of Jeyes Fluid had not quite overcome the odour of urine and carbolic soap.

Steven ushered her into his office and she noticed that the window had been flung open even though it had been raining. A yellow duster and a tin of Kleen-e-ze furniture polish sat on the top of a small bookcase crammed with leather-bound tomes.

Steven followed her gaze with a rueful smile. 'Sorry. Should have put it away but my last client caught me in the middle of my household duties. The partners refuse to employ a cleaner and I can't stand working in a mess.'

'Don't worry about it, Steven. I'm just grateful you could spare the time to see me.'

'Glad to help a friend. Anyway, do take a seat, Ginnie. You gave me a brief outline last night on the phone, but let's go through everything again.'

She remained standing. 'I have to tell you that money is a problem. I don't know how I'm going to pay you and it might take a bit of time to raise the cash.'

'I quite understand. It could be costly if we have to take Mallory to court, but I'm hoping it won't come to that. He's got a reputation to keep up and from what I know of him that would be more important than putting you out of business. I disliked the man on sight, and I don't know how he produced a son like Laurence, but that's another matter.' He went to sit behind his desk, motioning her to take a seat. 'Let's start at the beginning, shall we?'

An hour later they were sitting at a table in a crowded ABC café. The air was redolent with the smell of hot tea and toast, and hazy with cigarette smoke. It was necessary for Ginnie to raise her voice in order to make herself heard above the babel of voices. 'So do you think we've got a case, Steven?'

He stirred his tea, adding a spoonful of sugar.

'Absolutely. The shop has been in your family for more than twenty years and both you and your father have paid the rent and rates without fail. Mallory can't have you evicted as unsuitable tenants, but Fred's premises is another matter. I'll have to check the planning regulations for your particular council area, but as permission was granted initially and the sale of the lease agreed, I think we can start from there.'

'Mallory is a vindictive man. He blames Shirley for Laurence's death.'

'That's ridiculous. Laurence must have been ill for some time before the disease was detected, and I don't suppose the bout of pneumonia improved his condition, poor fellow. He was a brave man and he deserved better.'

'Mallory won't have anything to do with Shirley or the children. She's applied for a war widow's pension but there's a lot of paperwork to fill in because Laurence died after he left the Navy. She went to see his father while I was in America and asked him for financial help until the pension business was settled, but he refused.'

Steven shook his head. 'The man is a mean bastard. Apologies for the language, Ginnie, but there's no other way to describe him.'

She pushed her plate away with the cheese sandwich barely touched. 'I'm sorry. I've lost my appetite. Just thinking about Mallory makes me feel physically sick.'

'Don't worry. We'll put a stop to his little game.'

She frowned. 'It's my livelihood, Steven. I have to make a success of the shop. Mum and Shirley are depending on me.'

'I understand that, but what's happening about your American chap? Is he going to rely on you as well?'

'Nick doesn't need me.'

'I find that hard to believe.'

'I'd rather not talk about it, if you don't mind.'

'Sorry. I shouldn't have asked. You came to me for my professional opinion and I overstepped the mark.'

'I didn't mean it like that,' she said with an attempt at a smile. 'You're a good friend and I need all the friends I can get. Nick didn't want me. It's as simple as that and it's over. I have to get on with my life and that means making a go of the business.'

He glanced at his watch and stood up. 'And I'd better get back to the office. I hope to God that the vet has seen to Esther's cat or we'll never hear the end of it.'

Ginnie picked up her handbag and rising to her feet she made her way between the packed tables. A blast of cold air laced with the salty tang of the sea almost took her breath away as she stepped out of the fuggy café. The wet pavements glistened in a burst of sunshine after a heavy shower and large puddles mirrored the blue sky. Steven proffered his arm. 'Would it be possible for you to delay your journey home and have dinner with me this evening? I've been working late every night and living like a hermit. It would be great to have your company.'

She took his arm as they battled against a sudden gust of wind. 'I'd love to, but it'll take me three hours or so to get home, maybe longer if the trains are running late.'

'I understand. Anyway, I think I've got all the information I need and I'll keep you informed. If there's anything for you to sign I could always bring it over at a weekend.'

She smiled. 'That would be lovely. Shirley will be pleased to see you.'

'And what about you?'

'Don't fish for compliments, Steven. It doesn't suit you.'

'A fellow can only try.'

'You're Shirley's only link with Laurence's past. His family have made it clear they don't want anything to do with her, and you knew him better than anyone.'

'Yes, I suppose I did. Laurence was a good chap and I miss him.'

She squeezed his arm. 'I'll be pleased to see you too, but . . .' She had to let go of him in order to dodge a deep puddle.

'But what?'

She matched her step to his. 'Don't get me wrong, and I may be way off mark, but I'm not looking for a romantic relationship. I know that sounds a bit conceited, but I didn't want you to get the wrong idea.'

'It doesn't and I didn't.' He chuckled, taking her by the hand. 'But I'm sure you could do with a friend. I know I could.'

She glanced at him, smiling. 'Friends?'

He nodded his head. 'The best of friends. Come back to the office and I'll ring for a taxi to take you to the station.'

'I might walk, Steven. The fresh air will do me good and I'll be cooped up in a train for ages.'

'It's too far, and by the look of those clouds bubbling up in the west it's going to rain again. I'll sub you the taxi fare, and don't look like that. I'll put it on the bill if it will make you feel better.'

'Thanks. I really do appreciate everything you're doing for me.'

'Actually you're doing me a favour. My client list has just doubled to two.' He stopped in the entrance to the alley, where a dog had just knocked over the pig bin. Scraps of food waste were scattered on the ground and he stepped over them to open the door. 'If I was Sir Walter Raleigh I'd take my coat off and lay it down for you to walk on, but as this is my demob suit I'd better not try to be gallant.' He held out his arms. 'However, if you'd like to jump I'll catch you.'

She stared down at the glutinous mass of vegetable matter and leapt. He caught her in his arms and held her for a moment longer than was strictly necessary.

'Thanks,' she said breathlessly. 'You can put me down now, Sir Walter.'

He set her back on her feet. 'Always happy to oblige. Now let's go up and see if Esther's returned. She a very intense lady and I don't think I can face her on my own.'

'She seems devoted to her cat.'

'Tarquin is all she's got. She looked after her aged mother for many years and when the old lady passed away it left Esther with a huge gap in her life. I think that Tarquin has filled it to some extent, but I really don't want to be around when he goes to the great cattery in the sky.' He led the way up the stairs and opened the office door. 'Ah, Esther, you're back. How is Tarquin?'

'Very put out,' Esther said solemnly. 'He hates the vet and I don't blame him. That man has hands like hams and he was quite rough with poor Tarquin. A cat will naturally try to protect itself and it wasn't a deep scratch, although the vet made such a fuss you'd think he had been mortally wounded.'

'And the fish bone?' Steven asked tentatively.

'Tarquin coughed up a fur ball and the bone came with it,' Esther said with a smug smile. 'The vet tried to charge me for the consultation but I only had to remind him for whom I worked and the matter was dropped.' She shook her head. 'However,

I think I might have to register Tarquin with another practice.'

'I'm glad your cat is better,' Ginnie said, sending a warning glance to Steven who was obviously trying hard to keep a straight face and failing miserably.

Esther gave him a reproachful look. 'It's not a laughing matter, Mr Carter. Tarquin is a pedigree Persian. He's a valuable animal.'

'I'm sure he is.' Steven took a deep breath. 'Would you be kind enough to ring for a taxi to take Miss Travis to the railway station, please, Esther?'

Two days later Ginnie was in the shop window rearranging the cushions on a utility settee when she saw Colin Mallory striding along the pavement. His expression was thunderous as he barged through the door, setting the bell jangling. Ida made a move towards him but Ginnie reached him first. 'Good morning, Mr Mallory.'

'Don't you good morning me, young lady. I want a word with you.'

Ida hovered nervously at Ginnie's side. 'Shall I go and get Fred?'

'No, thanks. I'll deal with this.' Ginnie met Mallory's furious stare with an outward show of composure even though she was inwardly quaking. She was not exactly frightened of the man but she hated confrontation. 'Come to my office, Mr Mallory.' She walked off, depriving him of the opportunity to create a scene in front of curious customers, and giving him little alternative but to follow her into the office. She closed the door, facing him with arms akimbo. 'Well. What's this all about?'

He put his hand in his inside pocket and pulled out a folded sheet of paper, waving it at her. 'As if you didn't know.'

'How can I? I'm not psychic.'

He thrust his face close to hers. 'And don't try to be smart with me, miss. This is a letter from a firm of solicitors in Southampton, which leaves me with two questions.'

Ginnie stood her ground. 'And what are they exactly?'

'Where did you get the money to pay for a lawyer and what's the connection here? Why go all the way to Southampton for legal advice? As I understood it you've hardly enough money for the bus fare to Romford.'

'I don't think that's any of your business, Mr Mallory.'

'It is my business when accusations such as this are made against me.'

'I'm afraid I've no idea what you're talking about. May I see the letter?'

He put it back in his pocket. 'No, you may not. But take this as a warning. My professional reputation is at stake here and I'll do everything in my power to protect it.'

'As I don't know what the letter says, I can't comment.'

'Ask your solicitor. I assume you authorised a vicious attack on my integrity. If planning permission has been revoked it has nothing to do with me, and the same goes for the sale of the lease on the china shop. It's all slanderous lies. You'd better be careful, Miss Travis.'

'Or what, Mr Mallory? Your daughter told me that you intended to buy me out and give the business to her. I'm just surprised that you'd want Livvie to go into trade. Wouldn't that be a terrible comedown?'

'There's no talking to you in this mood, but take this as a warning. I'm a man of considerable influence and you're a nobody and your sister's a gold-digging whore.'

'Get out.' With a huge effort of self-control Ginnie managed to resist the temptation to slap his face. She lunged at the door and wrenched it open. 'Don't ever set foot in my shop again, and don't think you can bully me into selling up. My lease is good for another twenty years and there's nothing you can do about that, but I'm going to fight for Fred's shop and if it means dragging your name through the dirt, so be it.'

For a moment she thought that he was going to hit her. His face flushed a dangerous shade of puce and beads of sweat stood out on his forehead, but she stood her ground, clutching the door handle as she waited for him to make a move.

He seemed rooted to the spot but a shout from Jimmy and the sound of his heavy footsteps galvanised Mallory into action and he pushed past Ginnie. 'I'm warning you,' he hissed as he marched onto the shop floor.

Jimmy stood aside to let him pass. 'Are you all right, miss?'

'I'm fine, thank you.' Ginnie waved him away with an attempt at a smile but as she retreated into the office her legs gave way beneath her and she sank down onto her chair. 'Bloody man,' she murmured. 'Bloody, bloody man.'

Ida poked her head round the door. 'Are you okay, love?'

'I could do with a cuppa,' Ginnie murmured. 'With one sugar, please.'

Ida hesitated. 'What was all that about? I could hear him shouting and I very nearly went for help. I thought he was going to murder you.'

'I expect he'd like to, but I'm not giving in to him just because he's rich and he's on the council. He's trying to stop me taking over Fred's shop and if he did that he'd try to buy me out and give my business to Livvie.'

'He's a bugger. Excuse my French, but it's a wicked thing to do. Your dear dad worked hard all his life to make something of his business. He'd be turning in his grave.'

'I think we both need a cup of tea, Ida. And one for Jimmy too. Tell him there's nothing to worry about. I'm absolutely fine and I've put the matter in the hands of a good solicitor. He's got old man Mallory rattled, that's for certain.'

'What will happen to us? Will Mr Mallory buy you out? He's very well off and he's got friends in high places.'

'He can try, but I'd rather burn the place down than let him get his hands on it.'

'Please don't,' Ida said with a grim smile. 'My flat is just above the shop.'

Ginnie waited until Ida had gone to make the tea before dialling Steven's number. Esther answered the call and put her on hold for a few moments before putting her through.

'Hello, Ginnie. What can I do for you?'

Steven's warm and friendly voice went some way towards soothing her frazzled nerves. 'I've just had the most awful row with Mallory. He's had a letter, which I assume must have come from you. What did you say to put him in such a filthy mood?'

'I'm so sorry he took it out on you, Ginnie. If he bothers you again I could take out an injunction preventing him from contacting you in any way.'

'I don't want to antagonise him any more than necessary until I know what's happening and what my chances are of getting the lease and planning permission.'

'I quite understand, and he's overreacted. I think maybe he was trying to scare you into dropping the case, because I merely said that I was acting on your behalf and the matter was being investigated. There was nothing remotely inflammatory in the wording, but it seems to have hit home. If he hadn't been involved he would have reacted in a much more measured fashion and sent me a disclaimer. I've written to the planning inspectorate of your local council requesting the relevant form or forms. I'll submit a written representation and we'll see where we go from there.'

'I don't know how to thank you, Steven.'

'We'll need to go over the forms together and you'll have to sign them, so perhaps I could bring them over next weekend and we could have that dinner I mentioned the other day.'

'That would be lovely. Let me know when you're coming. I'd offer to put you up but there's only the settee.'

'I might take you up on that.'

'Goodbye, Steven, and thanks again.' She had just replaced the receiver when Ida bustled in with a tray of tea.

'Here you are, ducks; this will put feathers on your chest.' Ida angled her head, giving her a searching look. 'Well, you look a bit more cheerful. Who was that on the blower?'

'It was my solicitor. He thinks we've got a good case and he's going to lodge an appeal. We'll beat Mallory, I'm sure of it.'

*

364

Steven arrived in Cherry Lane with a bunch of daffodils and a bottle of wine, which he presented to Mildred with a courteous enquiry as to her health. Ginnie smiled to herself, giving him top marks for tact and diplomacy.

'How kind of you, Steven,' Mildred said, beaming. 'I can't remember the last time anyone bought me a bunch of flowers.'

'It's very good of you to put me up for the night, Mrs Travis.'

'And it's good of you to help Ginnie. That man Mallory should be shot. You don't want to know what he called Shirley, but he's no gentleman even if he does live in Monk Avenue.' Mildred laid the flowers on the draining board. 'Why don't you go into the sitting room with Ginnie and I'll put the kettle on. You won't be disturbed.'

Minutes later they were poring over the forms from the council offices. 'I've filled in the basics,' Stephen said, pointing to the pencilled answers to the questionnaire. 'But you'll need to give me the rest of the information.'

'Do you think we've got a chance?'

'I've been speaking to my colleagues and they seem to think it's most unusual for planning permission to be granted and then revoked and the same goes for the sale of the lease. Mallory must have a great deal of pull if he's gone out of his way to influence the planning department's decision.'

'He's determined to ruin me and my family,'

Ginnie said, sighing. 'I don't know what I've done to deserve such treatment.'

'You made the mistake of trusting Livvie and Laurence married your sister against his old man's wishes. Laurence was my best friend, but the rest of his family are the most terrible snobs, and they considered Shirley to be an outsider.'

'But he loved her.'

'Yes, I believe he did. He would have been a good husband and father, but he didn't have the chance to prove himself.' He looked up as the door flew open and Mildred bustled in carrying a tray of tea.

'Here you are. You can't work on an empty stomach, Steven. I've opened a packet of squashed fly biscuits in your honour.'

'You're very kind, Mrs Travis.'

'Call me Mildred, my dear. Mrs Travis makes me feel like a seaside landlady or a schoolteacher. You're practically one of the family now, Steven.' With a wink and an arch smile, Mildred left them with the best tea set and a plate of Garibaldi biscuits.

Ginnie smiled, shaking her head. 'My mother means well but she's not the soul of tact.'

'That's all right. I'm flattered that she considers me a good catch.'

'Let's get this done.' Ginnie picked up her pen and unscrewed the cap. 'Where do I sign?'

They had just completed the forms when Shirley

breezed into the room with Toni in her arms and Colin toddling along at her side. 'Steven, how lovely to see you.'

'So this is the latest addition to the family.' He rose to his feet, holding out his arms. 'May I take her for a moment? I like babies.'

'You might not be so fond of her at two in the morning,' Shirley said, with a comical downturn of her lips.

'She's beautiful, just like her mother.' Steven bent down to ruffle Colin's blond baby curls with his free hand. 'And you're a fine young man. Your daddy would have been so proud of you.'

'He would indeed,' Shirley said with a Madonna-like smile. 'But I made a terrible mistake when I named my boy.'

Ginnie held her breath, wondering if her sister was about to admit that she did not really know who had fathered Colin. 'Really?' she said faintly.

'Yes. It was stupid of me to name my little boy after that horrible man. From now on we're going to call him by his second name.'

Steven took a seat on the sofa, cradling Toni in his arms. 'His second name?'

'Travis,' Shirley said, staring at Ginnie as if daring her to argue. 'It's on his birth certificate,' she added defiantly.

Ginnie took her cue. 'Well, Travis is a good name. I'm sure that Dad would have been pleased if he'd known.'

'So how long are you staying, Steven?' Shirley sat down next to him.

'Just tonight and I'll leave in the morning.'

'A flying visit then,' Shirley said, pouting. 'We haven't seen much of you recently.'

'I've been trying to establish myself in the practice,' he said equably. 'And I'm mixing business with pleasure.' He turned to Ginnie. 'Are we still on for dinner this evening?'

Shirley looked from one to the other. 'Oh, how lovely. Where are you taking us, Steven?'

Chapter Nineteen

It was an uncomfortable meal for Ginnie. The restaurant was crowded and the menu was limited, but Shirley was in her element. She had managed to squeeze herself into one of her old dresses, showing an embarrassing amount of décolletage above a cinched-in waist. Her long blonde hair hung loose about her shoulders and she had found the stub of a Tangee lipstick in her dressing-table drawer, which she had applied with a more subtle touch than in the old days when she went out with Charlie.

Ginnie watched her sister's confident performance with a mixture of impatience and amusement. Judging by the covert glances Shirley was receiving from the men who were dining out with their wives and girlfriends, she had not lost her ability to attract the opposite sex. Ginnie was content to remain in her shadow and Steven did not seem at all perturbed to be escorting two young women to dinner. Shirley was openly flirting with him, but that, as Ginnie knew only too well, was what Shirley did best. She might have lost the love of her life in a tragic accident and been married and widowed leaving her with two young children, but she would never change.

Ginnie sat back and watched. It was good to see her sister smiling again, even if she was behaving like Vivien Leigh in *Gone With the Wind*. Shirley was Scarlett O'Hara minus the crinoline and southern accent. Ginnie had seen the film three times and read the book.

She applied herself to the menu, glancing up as someone approached the table. Thinking that it was the waiter who had come to take their order, she found herself looking into the angry face of Colin Mallory. 'This is a private party,' she said coldly.

He ignored her, directing his anger at Steven. 'What the bloody hell d'you think you're doing with these trollops, Carter?'

Steven rose to his feet. 'I beg your pardon?'

'You were my son's best man and yet you're here with this whore and her swindling cheat of a sister.'

'I'd be careful what I said if I were you, sir.' Steven towered over him and for the first time Ginnie realised that Mallory was a small man whose bombastic attitude made him appear larger than life.

'You should keep better company, son,' Mallory said, curling his lip.

'With all due respect, sir, what you've said could be construed as slanderous.'

'Are you threatening me, Carter?'

'I'm representing Miss Travis,' Steven said calmly. 'If you have any business with her in future, you will conduct it through me.' He took a wallet from his inside pocket and produced a card, which he handed to Mallory. 'You can contact me through my office, Mr Mallory, but I'd be grateful if you would return to your own table and allow us to enjoy our meal in peace.' He glanced around at the curious faces of the other diners, who instantly looked away, pretending to concentrate on their meal. 'Unless, of course, you wish to create a scene.'

'Don't threaten me, Carter. I was practising law when you were in kindergarten.' Mallory glared at him. 'I throught you were my son's friend, but I can see now that I was wrong.' He turned on his heel and walked away.

Shirley dabbed her eyes with her hanky. 'The brute. How could he speak to me like that in front of all these people?'

'Ignore him,' Ginnie said angrily. 'He's a pig and he just shows himself up.'

Steven sat down and picked up the menu. 'Ginnie's right. It was dashed bad luck that he happened to be here this evening. I'd have given this restaurant a wide berth if I'd known that the Mallorys frequented the place.'

'He's gone to sit down with his wife, and Livvie's with them,' Ginnie said, craning her neck to get a better view. 'She started all this and I'll bet she's enjoying every minute of it. I feel like going over there and tipping a bowl of brown Windsor soup over her head.'

'That's something I'd love to see.' Recovering her composure, Shirley leaned across Steven to peer at his menu. 'Sorry, they've only given us two. You don't mind, do you?' She flashed him a diamond-bright smile that would have left most men speechless, but he shrugged and handed it to her.

'You have it, Shirley. I know what I want.'

The appeal was lodged and now there was nothing to be done other than to wait, but Ginnie did not imagine for a moment that Mallory would give up without a fight. Steven had warned her that he might demand an inquiry, which would lead to a hearing, and they must be prepared for such an event. What she had not expected was a visit from an inspector from the department of public health. He strode into the shop one morning stating that a complaint had been made about a reported infestation of rodents.

Ida flew to Ginnie's defence. 'What a load of rubbish,' she said angrily. 'Do you really think that Miss Travis and I would work here if there were rats or mice in the building? My flat's above this shop, mister, and I'd have forty fits if I saw a mouse, let alone a great ugly rat.'

'I'm just doing my job, missis. I've got the authority to do a thorough investigation, starting in the yard at the back of the premises.'

'It's all right,' Ginnie said calmly. 'Go ahead. You won't find anything though. I think the report was made maliciously.'

He tipped his cap. 'I'm just carrying out orders, miss.'

Ida made a move towards him but Ginnie held her back. 'I know who's at the bottom of this, and he's just trying to make life difficult for us. Why don't you slip next door and warn Fred that he might get a visit too.' She turned to a woman who was going through a swatch of curtain fabrics, which was a new line that Ginnie had decided to try. 'It's nothing to worry about, madam. May I be of assistance?'

The next visitation occurred two days later when someone had apparently reported that the drains at the back of the shop were blocked and had caused an overflow of sewage into the service lane. The drains were duly inspected and found to be clear but Ginnie was beginning to lose patience. She was even angrier when a gas board official appeared in response to a telephone call complaining about a smell of escaping gas in the back yard. There was none and luckily it was disproved without the need for digging up the concrete, but Ginnie wondered where it was all going to end.

She telephoned Steven to ask him what she should do and he advised her to make a note of the dates and times of the inspections, but to keep away from Mallory. She was convinced that he was behind the bogus reports but she had no evidence to prove her suspicions. She was angry and frustrated, but determined not to let Mallory win. Fred Chinashop was on her side, as was Fred Woollies. Bert the tobacconist promised his support and all the shop-keepers in the parade from the chemist on the other side of the china shop to the cobbler, who had premises next to the public library, were ready to stand by her. She could, if she so wished, raise a small army of businessmen to fight her cause and this gave her confidence, but Colin Mallory seemed intent on ruining her and blackening her name. It was not going to be easy.

The inquiry proved to be inconclusive and Steven put in for a full hearing, but that entailed a wait of several weeks. Fred was anxious to sell up and retire, but the matter of the lease was out of his hands, as the council owned the freehold. Ginnie suspected that Mallory had used his money and influence to have the original decision revoked, but once again it would be almost impossible to prove. Steven kept her notified of their progress, but it was painfully slow.

Then the worst happened. It was a beautiful morning and Ginnie had walked through a snow-storm of cherry blossom on her way to work. The sun was warm on her back and the air was filled with the scent of spring flowers. Despite her difficulties she felt ridiculously optimistic as she unlocked the shop and went inside. She had managed to get a supply of utility furniture from the manufacturers and had spent a whole evening setting up the window display. It looked good, even if she said so herself, and the china stand was sparkling with blue and white Cornishware. She had placed an open cookery book on a table set with a spanking white cloth and starched napkins folded into the shape of water lilies; these alone had taken over an hour to complete. She had laid out place settings complete with a water jug and glasses and she had filled a vase with real tulips as a centrepiece. Their subtle perfume mingled with the linseed oil smell of the linoleum and the aroma of beeswax polish.

The once dingy and old-fashioned furniture shop had taken on a new lease of life under her influence, and she felt a satisfying sense of achievement. She had always lived in the shadow of Shirley's meteoric temperament and she had not particularly shone at school, but the shop was hers and its success mattered more than she cared to admit. Since parting with Nick she had flung herself into her work, but the pain in her heart remained, and she doubted if it would ever go away completely.

Taking a last look round, she went to the office to check the delivery book and make sure that the instructions for Jimmy were written out clearly so that he knew exactly where he was going that day. She was about to unlock the safe to get the float for the till when the door bell clanged. An early customer, she thought, hurrying into the shop, but it was a man in a black suit. At first glance he looked like a businessman calling in to do a spot of shopping on his way to work, but when he came closer she could see that there were shiny patches at the knees and elbows of his suit, as if it had had a great deal of wear, and his dusty bowler hat also had seen better days. He did not look as though he had come to buy a new carpet. 'Good morning,' she said in her best welcoming voice. 'Please feel free to look round, and if you need help, I'll be happy to oblige.' She was about to retreat to the office when he called her back.

'Just a moment,' he said gruffly. 'Are you Miss Virginia Travis?'

'Yes, I am. What can I do for you?'

He took an envelope from his pocket and placed it in her hand. 'I'm serving you notice to quit this premises within twenty-eight days. You are here illegally, Miss Travis.'

She stared at the manila envelope in horror. 'No. There must be some mistake. Who are you?'

'I'm a council employee, miss. I'm just here to serve notice, not to answer questions. You'll have to take that up with the department concerned.' He tipped his hat and walked out of the shop, disappearing into the crowd of people hurrying on their way to work.

Ginnie's hand shook as she ripped the envelope and examined its contents. The typewritten words seemed to dance about on the headed paper, but the gist was plain. She had four weeks to pack up and leave the premises. She brushed past Ida who had come in through the back door. 'What's up, Ginnie?' she asked anxiously. 'You're white as a sheet.'

Ginnie shook her head. 'There has to be some mistake. I'm going to telephone the council. They can't do this to me.'

Ida followed her into the office. 'For Gawd's sake, what does it say that's got you so upset?'

Ginnie picked up the receiver and dialled the number on the letter heading. 'Read it for yourself, Ida. It can't be right. It's got to be a mistake.'

Eventually, after what seemed like a lifetime, she was put through to someone who understood what she was saying. 'It's quite simple, Miss Travis.' The male voice on the other end of the line was irritatingly patronising, and she could imagine him smirking as he informed her that she was trading illegally. 'The lease is in your late father's name. You have had plenty of time to apply to take it over but you have failed to do so.'

'But the lease had twenty years or more to run. I've been paying the ground rent. You can't turn me out. This is my shop now.'

'On the contrary, Miss Travis. The lease reverts to the freeholder on the death of the lessee, unless an application is made within the stated time.'

'But I didn't know that. No one told me.'

'Did you make enquiries, miss?'

'Well, no, because I didn't realise it was necessary.'

'Then I'm very sorry, but the notice to quit stands. You have twenty-eight days to comply or the bailiffs will be sent in and your stock seized to pay for the expense incurred.'

'This is so unfair. Can't I apply to buy the lease?'

'You could put in an application, but I can't guarantee that you would be accepted and there might be other applicants.'

She could sense Colin Mallory's evil influence. 'I will apply.'

'I have to warn you that your premises is in a highly desirable location, and the take-up is expected to be instant.'

'You're telling me that you've got someone in mind? It wouldn't be Mr Colin Mallory, would it?'

'I've given you all the information I can, Miss Travis. If you have any complaints I suggest you put them in writing. Good day.' The line went dead.

Ginnie replaced the receiver and sat staring at it, unable to move.

'Are you all right, ducks?' Ida leaned over her, peering short-sightedly into her face. 'Shall I put the kettle on?'

A bubble of hysteria threatened to choke her and Ginnie nodded wordlessly.

'Right you are.' Ida scuttled out of the office calling to Jimmy. 'Keep an eye on the shop, love. Ginnie's had bad news. It looks like we'll all be out of a job soon.'

Ginnie snatched up the receiver and dialled the operator. 'I'd like to make a trunk call to Southampton, please.'

Moments later she was speaking to Esther. 'Good morning, Miss Golightly. May I speak to Mr Carter?'

378

'Who's calling?'

'Miss Travis. I visited the office some time ago. You took your cat to the vet because he had a fish bone stuck in his throat, poor thing. I hope he's fully recovered from his ordeal.'

'Ah, yes. I remember, and thank you, Tarquin is quite well now. I'll put you through.'

There was a pause and a click and then Steven's familiar voice. 'Hello, Ginnie. This is a nice surprise.'

'I'm desperate, Steven. I need your help.'

She had just finished the conversation and replaced the receiver when Ida rushed into the office, spilling tea as she slapped the cup and saucer down on the desk. 'Never mind the tea,' she said urgently. 'Look who's swanned into the shop.' She moved aside as Ginnie leapt to her feet. She stood in the doorway, staring in disbelief as Livvie strolled amongst the furniture, picking up price tags and examining them.

Ida laid a restraining hand on her arm but Ginnie shook it off. 'I might feel like throttling her,' she said in a low voice, 'but she's not worth swinging for. Don't worry, Ida. I can handle this.' Forcing herself to keep calm she marched up to Livvie. 'I suppose you think you've won.'

Livvie met her angry gaze with a mocking smile. 'I don't know what you mean.'

'You can stop pretending. You know very well that I've been served with notice to quit.'

'No!' Livvie raised her eyebrows. 'Really? But then

379

I'm not surprised. You've been having all sorts of problems lately.'

'And I know exactly who to blame for them.'

'You're becoming paranoid, Ginnie. You make a hash of everything and blame it on my father. Just the same as when you sacked me after I'd held the fort for you to go gallivanting off to the States after that American GI.'

Ginnie gasped as her breath hitched in her throat. 'Leave Nick out of this. He's a war hero and he was a medical officer, not a GI.'

'Oh dear! Have I hit a nerve?'

'Get out of my shop.'

'But it's not yours, is it? You're going to be evicted and then the shop will be mine to do with as I please. Not that I want to be in trade, it's frightfully vulgar, but it will amuse me to see you signing on the dole and finding your proper place in life with your tart of a sister.'

Ginnie seized her by the shoulders and propelled her towards the door. An astonished female customer scuttled out of their way. 'Get out and stay out. We'll see who wins this battle, and I'm not giving up without a fight.'

Livvie stumbled out onto the pavement. 'You'll be sorry you did that.'

'What will you do? Go running to Daddy and tell him that I've been beastly to you? Grow up and get a life of your own instead of trying to ruin mine.' Ginnie slammed the glass door. She turned to see the customer staring at her open-mouthed. 'A shop-lifter,' she said, shrugging. 'They come in all shapes and sizes. May I help you, or are you just browsing?'

The woman gulped and swallowed. 'I was looking at the blue and white china. It would go very nicely in my kitchen.'

'My assistant will be pleased to help you, madam.' Ginnie beckoned to Ida who hurried to her side with an anxious frown.

'Are you all right, Ginnie?'

'I'll be okay in a minute. Could you help the lady? She's interested in the Cornishware.'

Ginnie managed to reach her office before her knees gave way beneath her and she sank down onto her chair. Any doubts she might have had as to Mallory's influence with the council had been dispelled by Livvie's spiteful words. She leaned back in her seat, closing her eyes and picturing her father sitting at his desk with a cigarette burning away in the ashtray as he totted up the day's takings. He had struggled in the beginning and worked hard to make a success of the business. To allow it to fall into Mallory's hands would mean that she had failed her family, and that was unthinkable.

She opened her eyes with a start and found Ida standing at her side. 'Can I do anything, ducks?'

Ginnie took a deep breath. She would not break down and cry in front of Ida. They would be tears of anger but she was not about to give way to weakness at a time when she needed all her strength. She picked up the cup of tea which had cooled, leaving a thin skin floating on its surface. 'Would it be too much trouble to make a fresh pot of tea?'

'Of course not. A nice hot cuppa will set you back on your feet.' Ida bustled out of the office, calling to Jimmy. 'Shop, Jim. There's a chap looking at carpet samples. Go and see if he needs any help.'

Seconds later Jimmy poked his head round the door. 'The man said he's just looking.' He peered at her and his bottom lip trembled ominously. 'Are you okay, miss?'

'I'm fine, thanks.'

'I'm not going to lose my job, am I?'

'Not if I can help it, Jimmy. I'm not beaten yet.'

'No, miss. Good for you. Anyway, I've done the morning deliveries and I've got a wardrobe to take to Turpin Road after dinner, but if you want me to pay a visit to old Mallory, just say the word.'

The thought of good-natured Jimmy putting the frighteners on anyone, least of all a career bully like Mallory, would at any other time have made her laugh, but she forced her lips into a smile. 'Thanks, Jimmy. I'll bear that in mind.'

'You can rely on me. You know that.'

'Yes, I do, and I'm very grateful.'

His round face flushed with pleasure. 'I'd better see if the chap with the carpet samples is going to buy anything or not.' He disappeared into the shop, leaving Ginnie with silence ringing in her ears and a sense of loss in her heart. But by the time Ida reappeared with a fresh cup of tea and a sticky bun, Ginnie had recovered at least some of her fighting spirit.

Ida placed the cup and saucer carefully on the blotter. 'I went to Pat's Pantry for the bun. Young Phyllis sent it with her compliments. News travels fast round here.'

'They can't possibly know that I've been given notice to quit.' Ginnie frowned. 'You didn't . . .'

'No,' Ida protested, 'I never did. It was the Cornishware woman. She went straight to the cake shop and bought a Battenberg slice and repeated everything that Livvie said, and how you chucked her out. That got a round of applause, but now everyone in the parade knows what's going on.'

'I suppose it would have come out sooner or later,' Ginnie said, sighing. 'But I wish it could have been kept quiet until I've seen Steven.'

'What's he going to do about it?'

'I don't know, Ida. He said he'd telephone the council and see if he could get any more information about lodging an appeal and perhaps getting a stay of execution, because that's what it feels like. Giving up the shop and everything it means to me and my family would be like having my head chopped off on Tower Hill.'

Ida's eyes filled with tears and were magnified even more by the thick lenses of her glasses. She reached out to pat Ginnie on the shoulder. 'I know what you mean, ducks. It would be the same for me too. I loved your dad like he was my son, and I'm too old to get a job anywhere else. I don't know what I'd do if the shop fell into Mallory's hands.'

Ginnie jumped up to give her a hug. 'We've got to stop him. Steven's doing his best and he's going to ring me later and let me know if he's made any progress. Until then we've just got to carry on as usual.'

Ida moved away, fishing in her pocket for her hanky and blowing her nose. 'I'm a silly old fool. Don't take any notice of me.'

'But I do, Ida. You're part of the family.'

Taking her spectacles off and polishing them on the hem of her skirt, Ida gave her a watery smile. 'We've got to keep calm and carry on. Isn't that what we've been doing for the last six years?'

Ginnie waited all day for Steven's call and when he rang just before closing time he did not have any good news. 'It's like walking in toffee,' he said apologetically. 'Trying to get anyone to give me any kind of decision is almost impossible. I've been transferred from one department to another and no one seems to know anything. All they can say is to put the application in writing.'

Ginnie swallowed convulsively. 'Can they really evict me? I've paid the ground rent and the rates without fail.'

'It's a technicality. They're within their rights as owners of the freehold, but you'd think they would want to keep a reliable tenant, especially when times are tough for all businesses and the shop might remain empty for a long time.'

'But that's just it, Steven. I'm certain that Colin Mallory is behind this. He wants to see me out on the street and Shirley too. He'll give the shop to Livvie and she'll play at being a businesswoman until she gets bored. She only wants it because it's mine and she can't bear to think of a girl from Cherry Lane doing better than someone from Monk Avenue.' She broke off, her voice strangled with emotion.

'I know how much this means to you, Ginnie. Give me a day or two and I'll badger the council until I get some sense out of them. I'll come over at the weekend, if that's okay with you, and we'll go over strategy together.'

'Yes, of course. That would be wonderful. Thanks, Steven.'

'But he can't come for the weekend,' Shirley said that evening at supper when Ginnie mentioned that she had invited Steven to stay. 'You should have checked with Mum and me.'

Mildred nodded her head. 'Yes, Ginnie. It was very thoughtless of you. That nice young American is coming to spend a couple of days with us.'

For a wild moment Ginnie thought that her mother meant Nick, and then she realised that she was referring to Danny. 'But Mum, this is important. Steven is doing me a favour by representing me. I'm being threatened with eviction. I've got four weeks and then I have to move out of the shop for good.'

'Don't be silly, dear,' Mildred said, smiling. 'You always did exaggerate. The shop has been in the family for at least twenty-five years.'

'I'm telling the truth, Mum. Apparently I should have reapplied for the lease after Dad died, but no one told me. According to the council officials I've been trading illegally.'

'It's got to be a mistake,' Shirley said, cutting a slice of bread and butter into soldiers and laying them on the tray of the high chair. 'There you are, Travis. Eat up like a good boy.'

'I still can't get used to that name.' Shaking her head, Mildred reached for the jam pot. 'I don't see what's wrong with Colin. It's a perfectly good name.'

'I'm not calling my son after a man who called me a you know what.'

Ginnie smiled in spite of everything and was just about to take a sip of her tea when the telephone rang. She rose hastily to her feet. 'I'll get it. It might be Steven.'

She hurried into the hall and snatched the receiver off its cradle. 'Hello.'

'I have a long distance call for Miss Ginnie Travis.'

'That's me.'

'Hold the line, please.'

Chapter Twenty

'Hello. Ginnie?'

The voice was male and the accent American, but it was Danny and not Nick on the other end of the line. Not that she had expected to hear from Nick, but a small part of her had never quite given up hope and the sense of disappointment was acute. She licked her dry lips and made an effort to put a smile in her voice. 'Hello, Danny. This is a nice surprise.'

He responded with a chuckle. 'And I guess it would have been even nicer if it had been someone else.'

'Of course not, it's always lovely to talk to you. Anyway, you know that it's been over between Nick and me since our trip to Eagle Rock.'

'I don't believe that for a moment.'

'Can we change the subject, please?'

'I guess Shirley's just told you that I'm coming up to London this weekend.'

'Yes, she did.'

'You sound worried, Ginnie. Is something wrong?'

'I'm having a bit of a problem with the local council and my solicitor is coming up from Hampshire to try and sort it out. He's staying with us, so I'm afraid . . .'

'Don't worry. We're booked into a hotel in London.'

'We? You've got a girlfriend?'

'It's a guy. I'm meeting Nick at the airport tomorrow.'

The air seemed to have been sucked from her lungs. She could breathe neither in nor out. She was in suspended animation and it took several seconds to assimilate the meaning of his words. 'Nick is coming to London?'

'Yep, you got it, honey.'

'Is he having treatment?'

'He underwent surgery despite the risks and it was successful. He's never going to have 20/20 vision, and he's finished as a surgeon, but he's been recommended as a candidate to work in research at Moorfields.'

'Moorfields was destroyed in the Blitz,' Ginnie said slowly. It was easier to grasp a negative than a positive. Nick had been virtually blind when she left Eagle Rock. He had sent her away without giving her a chance to prove her loyalty and devotion. That was not how a man would behave to the woman he truly loved.

'It's been rebuilt, honey.' Danny's voice was gentle but insistent. 'This is a wonderful opportunity for Nick.'

'Yes, but why London?'

'His ophthalmologist has contacts over here, and he put Nick up for the job.'

'Weren't there any opportunities nearer home?'

'That's something you'd have to ask Nick, but he's been through a lot, Ginnie, and he's won through. He wants to see you, but he'll understand if you've moved on.'

Her heart was racing and her palms were damp with perspiration. What if it all went horribly wrong for the second time? The fear of losing him yet again was almost too much to bear. She needed time to think. 'I'm busy this weekend, Danny. It's the shop – I'm having to fight for survival.' She knew that it sounded as if she did not care, but the truth was that she cared too much.

'I'm sorry to hear that.' Danny's tone was cool and distant.

'It's complicated but it's true. I've been given notice to quit in less than a month.'

'That's too bad, honey. But even more reason for you to see Nick and hear him out. His main reason for coming to London is to make things right with you.'

'He could have let me know what was going on,' she said angrily. 'He sent me away, Danny. I would have stayed by him no matter what, but he didn't want me, and now he expects me to come running. Well, you can tell him that I'm in danger of losing everything I've worked for.' She broke off as the pips sounded, indicating that their time was up unless he paid for another three minutes. 'This will be costing you a fortune, so I'll hang up now.'

'But Ginnie—'

She cut him off, unable to maintain her iron-clad self-control. She rushed upstairs to her bedroom and locked the door. She needed time on her own. There were always people clamouring for her attention, whether it was family, staff or customers. She had to get things in perspective. If hearts really could break, she had had hers badly cracked several times during her relationship with Nick, but she had managed to survive. She had made a conscious decision to devote herself to her business career and now that too was being snatched away from her. She would have to reinvent herself all over again, but now she was tired. She curled up on her bed and made a determined effort to shut out the world.

She went to the shop next morning, but trade was slow and Fred came round as usual for his morning cup of sweet, weak, milky tea and a couple of Shrewsbury biscuits that Ida, as usual generous with her food coupons, had baked the previous evening. 'I'll miss all this when I retire,' he said with a bleak smile. 'But I still can't believe what they've done to you, Ginnie. Your dad would turn in his grave if he knew the half of it.'

She nibbled a biscuit to please Ida, but she had lost her appetite. She had tried to put Nick out of her mind, but the knowledge that very soon he would be within a few miles of her made it almost impossible to concentrate on her work. She had made Danny's excuses to her mother and Shirley, but she had omitted to tell them the real reason for his change of plan. She could not face the inevitable cross-examination and in-depth discussions that would follow.

Fred leaned towards her, peering into her face. 'You do look peaky, Ginnie. You need a holiday, love.'

'She'll get a long one soon.' Ida put her cup and saucer down on the desk with a thud. 'We all will, thanks to that evil man. My hubby said he'd go round and knock Mallory's block off if I said the word. But my old man's a tiger when he's roused and I wouldn't want him going down for inflicting grievous bodily harm.'

'We can't have that.' Despite the cramping feeling of helplessness and depression that threatened to overwhelm her, Ginnie had to smile at the thought of Ida's meek and mild husband committing an act of violence.

'I'd have a go myself if I was twenty years younger,' Fred said stoutly. 'But I'll have to try and resell my lease soon, Ginnie. I can't afford to keep the shop on when it's empty. There are the business rates to pay as well as the ground rent and insurance on the premises, which will all have to come out of my savings.'

'I know, Fred, and I understand.' She glanced round the tiny office, seeing not just the peeling paintwork and the worn linoleum but the hub of her small empire. She had put her whole heart into continuing her father's work, and was in danger of losing everything because of Mallory and his malicious daughter.

Suddenly it was all too much to bear and she was desperate to get away. She did not want to see Steven at the weekend, and there was little point in going over the facts they already knew. She realised that he was fond of her and she was grateful for his help, but she had no intention of allowing herself to fall for anyone ever again. It might feel like heaven when things were going well, but the hurt and despair that followed a break-up were agonising and she would not wish that on anyone. Steven was a nice, kind and honourable man and she must find a way to pay for his services so that she was not indebted to him.

'What's the matter, ducks?' Ida pushed her face close to Ginnie's. 'Are you feeling all right?'

Ginnie stared at her for a second, concentrating her thoughts with difficulty. 'How would you feel about looking after the shop for a couple of days, Ida?'

'Are you going to see your young man in Southampton again?'

'He's not my young man, Ida. And I'm not going to Southampton. Would you feel able to take charge for a while?'

'Of course I will, ducks. You need a break and business is slack all round at the moment, isn't it, Fred?'

He nodded. 'Yes, indeed. I'll keep an eye on her, Ginnie. I can always slip round if Ida needs a hand, and then there's the boy; he did well last time.'

'He'd better make the most of being in a job.' Ida took off her glasses, huffed on the lenses and wiped them on her skirt. 'We'll all be out of work soon.'

Ginnie arrived at Lightwood Common station after a four-and-a-half-hour train journey. She had run away. She had been afraid that Danny might decide to turn up, despite the fact that she had left him in no doubt as to her feelings, and she had put Steven off with an excuse. Convincing her mother and Shirley that she needed a change of scene had been more difficult, and they blamed her for Danny's change of heart, but Ginnie was past caring.

She let the window down and leaned out to open the carriage door. It was dusk, but at least an hour before nightfall, and she could see Percy sitting in the trap with a plume of blue tobacco smoke spiralling up from the pipe clenched between his teeth. It felt like coming home.

She climbed down to the platform and gave her ticket to Griff Jenkins, who doubled up as clerk, porter and assistant station master. He greeted her with his customary toothless grin. 'Come for a holiday, miss? You'll find it much quieter now them Yanks have gone home.'

'Just here for the weekend, Griff. But it's always lovely to come back to Lightwood Common.'

'Well, can't stand here chatting – I've got to wave the green flag. The train can't go unless I say so.' He scuttled onto the platform.

Ginnie walked through the ticket office and out into the forecourt. Duke pawed the ground as if he recognised her, although she suspected that was wishful thinking, but it gave her a warm sense of belonging and Percy made a grunting sound which she took to be a greeting. She tossed her suitcase into the trap and climbed up to sit beside him. 'Nice evening,' she said as he flicked the whip above Duke's right ear. 'I hope you're keeping well.'

Even as the words left her lips she realised that she had said the wrong thing. For the next mile and a half she was regaled with detailed accounts of Percy's medical complaints from rheumatics to problems with his digestive system. 'But I find a pint of mild helps,' he said pointedly as he dropped her off outside the Ferryboat Inn.

'I'll put one in for you, Percy.' She paused for a moment, breathing in the fresh country air and the sweet scent of honeysuckle and roses combined with the damp woody smell of the riverbank. It was blissfully quiet with only the gentle lapping of the water and the rustle of the leaves caressed by a warm breeze. Ginnie walked slowly across the gravel to ascend the steps. She had been happy here and also desperately sad, but this was where she had first met Nick and it would always hold a special place in her heart. Lights blazed from the pub windows

394

offering a welcome to weary travellers, and as she opened the door she was greeted by a gust of cigarette smoke laced with the smell of beer and a babble of voices.

'Ginnie, darling.' Avril's voice rang out across the bar. With a final pull on the beer engine she filled a pint mug and passed it to one of the local farmers. 'There you are, Ted. That one's on the house.'

Lionel stood up to embrace Ginnie. 'It's good to see you, my dear.'

'It's lovely to be here.'

Avril lifted the hatch in the bar counter. 'Come through, Ginnie. There's supper laid out in the kitchen. Make yourself at home and I'll join you later.'

Lionel held his hand out to take Ginnie's case. 'Let me take that.' He followed them into the kitchen.

'I don't think I've forgotten anything,' Avril said, glancing at the inviting array of food set out on the table. 'I'd better get back to the bar, but I'll shoo the locals out early and then Ginnie and I will have a nice girly chat.'

'I suppose that means I'm having an early night,' Lionel said with a rueful smile.

'Of course you are, darling.' Avril blew him a kiss. 'Girl talk might make you blush.'

'I'm sure I've heard it all before. Anyway, I'll take this upstairs to your room, Ginnie, and then I'll be getting back to the vicarage. I'll see you both in the morning.'

Ginnie waited until he had left the room. 'I thought you two were living together, Avril.'

'We have to keep up appearances, darling. The locals are frightfully old-fashioned, and if Lionel spends the night here he has to creep out at dawn and hurry home. It's quite fun, but that will all stop when we get married and it will seem awfully dull.'

'Auntie Avril, you're quite shocking.'

'I know I am, darling. But you look terribly tired and painfully thin. You need feeding up, my girl. Sit down and enjoy your meal and we'll talk later, but I want to see a clean plate.'

'You sound just like Mum.'

'We are sisters, Ginnie. Although God knows, no one would think it most of the time.'

Ginnie sat down at the table and ate as much as she could of the cold meat and salad, but she was overcome with exhaustion. Avril had obviously gone to a great deal of trouble to make the food look appealing, but Ginnie had little appetite. A bowl of strawberries and a jug of thick cream were tempting and she ate a few, but she was longing for her bed in the room with a view of the river.

She was washing the dishes when Avril breezed in from the bar. 'I thought they'd never go.' Her smile faded. 'You look whacked, darling. Never mind the chat. Auntie Avril's sending you straight to bed. We can catch up in the morning.'

Ginnie emptied the washing-up bowl. 'I am a bit

tired, but it's wonderful to be here, and it was good of you to put me up at such short notice.'

'No thanks needed. You're family and it's lovely to see you. Now go.' She flapped her hands, shooing Ginnie out into the hallway. 'Get a good night's sleep. That's an order.'

She was lulled to sleep by the gentle lapping of the river passing over the stony shallows, and the occasional hoot of a hunting barn owl. At home there was always background noise whether it was Toni crying for her two o'clock feed or the occasional motor vehicle owned by a neighbour who had enough petrol coupons to drive home after working a late shift. The milkman's horse clip-clopped down the road at dawn, pulling the float laden with glass bottles that rattled and clinked together like partygoers making a toast. In the peace and quiet of the countryside Ginnie slept well for the first time in weeks. If she dreamed she had no memory of it when she awakened refreshed and feeling much better than she had when she arrived the previous evening.

Downstairs in the kitchen Avril had set the breakfast table and the aroma of hot coffee and frying eggs and bacon made Ginnie's mouth water. Wearing a frilly apron and looking unusually domesticated, Avril gave her a beaming smile. 'Good morning, darling. Did you sleep well?'

'Very well, thank you. In fact it's the best night's

sleep I've had for ages.' Ginnie took a seat. 'It's good of you to go to all this trouble for me.'

'Nonsense. It's lovely to have you here again. I really missed you girls when you went home.'

'But you've got Lionel now. Have you set a date for the wedding?'

Avril dished up the bacon, eggs and fried tomatoes and put the plate in front of Ginnie. 'Toast will be ready in a moment.' She placed two slices of bread under the grill. 'Actually you've arrived at the right time. Lionel and I wanted a quiet wedding without all the hoo-ha that normally goes with such occasions. Shirley's nuptials are a case in point and neither of us wanted that, so as it happens we've arranged for a simple ceremony next Wednesday. You will stay for it, won't you?'

'I don't know. I'd really love to, but I said I'd only be gone for a couple of days. I've left Ida and Jimmy to run the shop and I'm not sure how well they'll manage if I'm away too long.'

Avril turned the toast over and put it back under the grill. 'So why did you decide to do a bolt?' She met Ginnie's startled look with a wry smile. 'I know you, Ginnie. You're so conscientious that you make the rest of us look like slackers. It must have been something serious to make you cut and run. It wouldn't have anything to do with Nick Miller, would it? You never told me how it went in Los Angeles, but I assumed that it didn't go too well.'

'It didn't.' Ginnie fingered the brooch that Nick

had given her, which she wore with almost every change of clothing. 'He's in London. He turned up out of the blue without a word to me. I haven't heard from him since I left Eagle Rock, and then I received a phone call from Danny to say he was meeting Nick at the airport.'

Avril only just managed to save the toast from being cremated and placed it in the silver rack. 'He's blind and yet he travelled to London on his own?'

'Apparently he had a successful operation to restore his vision. Danny said he'll never regain enough sight to work as a surgeon, but he's gone after a job in research at Moorfields.'

'And he wants to see you, quite literally.' Avril poured coffee into two cups and passed one to Ginnie. She sat down opposite her. 'But you don't want to see him.'

'I don't know, and that's the trouble. I can't face going through it all again. He'd changed and I only saw flashes of his old self when I stayed with his family.'

'But darling, he was going through a rough time. You must make allowances.'

'And I did, but he's a stubborn fool and his male pride got in the way. Now, all of a sudden, he wants to see me and I don't know if I can cope.' She toyed with the bacon on her plate. 'There's another complication. You met him at Shirley's wedding; he was Laurence's best man.'

'Steven, wasn't it? He was nice.'

'He is nice. He's lovely and he's kind and he's acting for me in my battle with the council. I told you all about that on the phone.'

'You did, and I was furious with that Mallory chap. He's an absolute sewer.'

'He wants to ruin us out of spite. Livvie started the family feud when Shirley married Laurence, but I really thought we'd sorted all that out and were friends. I realised that I'd been mistaken, and all along she wanted to take my business away from me, so I sacked her and now her father's intent on ruining me.'

'I understand all that, but why is Steven a problem? It sounds to me as though he's been a godsend.'

'I think he's getting serious about me. I've done nothing to encourage him, but I feel terrible because he's taken me on as a client even though he knows I'll never be able to repay him.' She looked up and met Avril's intense gaze. 'No, don't even think about it. You've done enough for me. You paid my airfare to the States and for that I'll be eternally grateful, but I can't take any more of your money.'

'It's mine to give, darling. Both my late husbands left me very well provided for and before the war I was doing very nicely thank you in the licensed trade, and hopefully when rationing finally comes to an end things will pick up again. Besides which, I'll soon be Mrs Vicar, as the locals put it, and Lionel has a private income as well as his stipend.'

'I really appreciate the offer, but if I lose the

business I'll have to try to get a job and my only training has been in the shop. I couldn't hope to earn the sort of money I'd need to repay a loan.'

Avril took a sip of her coffee and reached for the sugar. 'I do try to do without but I can't bear saccharin. I know the liking for sweet things is a weakness, but sometimes one just has to give in to a craving.' She stirred her coffee, staring thoughtfully at Ginnie. 'Some people are addictive too. Think about it, Ginnie. You've devoted your young life to helping your father run the shop, and now you're supporting your mother and sister and her two babies. You're going to be old before your time and you're missing out on the good things in life. Why not give Nick another chance? He must have deep feelings for you or he wouldn't have considered leaving home and taking a job in London. I'm sure they pay far higher wages in America than they do over here.'

Ginnie shook her head. 'Do you mind if we drop the subject for a while?'

'Of course not, but only if you promise to eat up. Starving yourself isn't the answer, darling. Having a nice figure is one thing, as I know myself, but the skeletal look is definitely not in.'

'I'll try, but I've got into bad habits, missing meals and eating on the go.'

'We'll soon put a stop to that, Ginnie. And you will stay for our wedding, won't you? After all, I can't expect Mildred to drop everything at home just to come up here for a register office do, and Shirley has her hands full with those two delightful babies, so you'll be my one and only blood relative.'

Ginnie felt herself weakening. The prospect of almost a week away from the worry and the pressures of work was almost too tempting to resist. 'I'll think about it.'

'Good.' Avril refilled her cup. 'And when you've finished eating we'll go into town and you can help me choose my outfit. I was going to wear one of my old Paris gowns, but now I think I'll splash out. I've saved all my coupons since you and Shirley were last here, so we can go mad. We might even find something for you.'

'Oh, I don't know . . .'

Avril raised a perfectly manicured hand. 'But I do, and it's not open to discussion. We're going to have a lovely day out. I've got a new girl from the village who helps out in the bar at lunch times. It will be good for her to cope on her own, and Saturday is usually quiet because everyone goes shopping these days, joining the queues for bread and just about everything. It picks up in the evening, but we'll be back long before opening time.'

Avril borrowed Lionel's ancient car and drove them into Shrewsbury where they spent a pleasant few hours searching for the ideal wedding outfit, but nothing lived up to her expectations. In the end it was Ginnie who came away with a fashionably short dress in peach shantung, and a matching hat trimmed with a veil and a large silk rose. 'But it will look as though I'm getting married,' she protested, gazing at her reflection in the tall mirror.

'Modom looks lovely.'

The assistant spoke as though she had a plum in her mouth and, Ginnie thought hiding a smile, as if she had a ramrod in place of a spine. 'It's a bit dressy for me,' she said doubtfully.

'It's a perfect fit, modom. It might have been made for you.'

Avril nodded in agreement and clapped her hands. 'It's absolutely wonderful. You must have it, Ginnie. I insist.'

'But what about you? I don't want to take all your coupons.'

'Darling, I've got all forty of them untouched. You could have five dresses and enough coupons left for a pair of shoes.'

Ginnie hesitated. It was tempting. She had not had a new frock since the beginning of the war and all her old clothes were too large and hanging off her. 'If you're sure, Avril.'

'I've never been more certain of anything. We'll take the hat as well and I might try on that little creation I spotted in the window. It would go wonderfully with my Balenciaga. I bought it in Paris before the war when he was just starting out, and I still adore it.' She turned to the shop assistant who was staring at her open-mouthed. 'The crimson silk hat with the veil. It's a copy of one worn by Myrna Loy, but I don't suppose she'll mind if I emulate her style.'

The assistant left the cubicle, walking backwards as if in the presence of royalty.

Avril doubled up with laughter. 'I just love name-dropping when I come up against a snobbish madam.'

'You are a dreadful tease,' Ginnie said, chuckling.

'And I've made you laugh. That's the first time you've allowed yourself to relax since you arrived last night. My therapy is working, darling. Now you simply have to stay for our wedding.'

'I'll have to let Ida know, and then I'd better ring Mum and tell her that I won't be home for a few days longer.'

'I'll take care of Mildred and you can sort it out with your helpers at the shop. My sister needs a firm hand and I know exactly how to deal with her.' Avril turned to take the hat from the shop assistant who had returned and was handling the creation as reverently as if she had just discovered the Holy Grail. 'Yes. That's the one. Myrna and I have the same good taste.' Avril placed the confection of silk, tulle and feathers on her head. 'What do you think, Ginnie? I've always fancied I could act Myrna off the stage in those Thin Man films and I adore William Powell, he's such an attractive man.'

'It's lovely,' Ginnie said, smiling. 'You look beautiful.'

*

404

She was to echo those words when she helped Avril with the finishing touches to her wedding outfit. 'Absolutely stunning,' Ginnie said, standing back to admire the full glory of her aunt's Paris gown and the perky little hat. 'You look as glamorous as any film star.'

'And you look wonderful too,' Avril said proudly. 'I knew that shade of peach would complement your colouring.'

Ginnie glanced in the mirror on Avril's dressing table and pulled a face. 'You're very kind but I'd give anything for really dark hair like yours or to be naturally blonde like Shirley, even if she does resort to a touch of peroxide now and then. But I'm just mousey and that's the end of it.'

'Golden blonde, darling,' Avril said firmly. 'The few days you've spent outside in the sunshine have given you natural highlights. I'd have to spend a fortune in the hairdresser's to get that effect. You're a very attractive girl.'

'And you're being kind. I know I was standing behind the door when good looks were given out – that's what Gran used to say. Shirley got them all.'

'My mother had an acid tongue, and she used to love putting me in my place too. Mildred was her favourite, but then my dear sister was a goody-goody and never did anything wrong and I was the rebel. Mother would be struck dumb with amazement if she knew I was marrying a Church of England clergyman.'

405

'Well, you look fantastic and I'm sure she'd be proud of you.' Ginnie ran to the window. 'There's the taxi. It's time to go.'

Avril primped in the mirror for the last time. 'I've been through this twice and yet I'm as nervous as a young bride. That's mad, isn't it?'

'I'd say it's quite natural. Now are you ready?'

'I am as ready as I'll ever be.'

Lionel was waiting for them in the vestibule of the register office. The look on his face as he greeted his bride brought Ginnie close to tears. It must, she thought, be every woman's dream to be admired and loved so deeply. For a moment she envied her aunt, but she could not begrudge Avril a single second of the happiness that she would undoubtedly have with Lionel.

Ginnie followed them into the room where the ceremony was about to take place, but she came to a sudden halt in the doorway. Avril had told her that it would be a simple affair with only a couple of witnesses but the secret must have leaked out as the seats were packed with well-wishers. It looked as though half the village had turned up, and as the congregation turned their heads to get a better view of the bride, Ginnie realised that Shirley was seated in the front row next to Steven. Surprised and delighted, she followed Lionel and Avril up the aisle between the plush-covered gilded chairs, but as she was about to sit down next to her sister she sensed that there was someone staring at her. The hairs on the back of her neck prickled as if she had seen a ghost and she was poised for flight when Avril turned and gripped her by the arm.

'If you run now I'll never forgive you, darling.'

Chapter Twenty-One

Ginnie sank down on the softly padded seat, staring straight ahead with her hands clenched around the small bouquet of roses and stephanotis that Avril had just passed to her with a warning frown.

Shirley nudged her in the ribs. 'For God's sake, Ginnie, this is a wedding not a funeral. Smile.'

Ginnie stretched her lips into a semblance of a grin. She could feel Nick's steady gaze and she knew that when the ceremony was over she would have to face him. She barely heard the registrar's words or the responses from the bride and groom. It all passed in a surreal dreamlike state, and when it was over and the happy couple were signing the register a buzz of conversation rippled round the room. She faced Shirley angrily. 'Did you organise this?'

'What are you talking about?'

'Don't look so innocent. Did you ask Danny to bring Nick all this way just to see Avril get married?'

'No, I didn't, so there's no need to look daggers at me. Danny telephoned to say that he had to work last weekend and I just happened to mention the wedding. It wasn't as though it was a state secret.'

'Avril didn't tell me you were coming,' Ginnie

whispered. 'She said it would be a quiet affair, which is why I stayed on.'

'Then she must have changed her mind. It's her day after all.'

'I know that, but it all feels like a set-up to me. Where's Mum? And who's looking after the kids?'

'She is, of course. What's the matter with you? You're acting crazy.'

'I need some air,' Ginnie said, rising to her feet. 'I'll see you later.' She walked down the aisle, refusing to look left or right, and did not stop until she was outside in the street. She leaned against the iron railings, fanning herself with Avril's bouquet which she was still clutching in her clenched fist.

'Are you running away from me?'

She looked round to see Nick making his way slowly and carefully down the steps and she had to curb the impulse to rush to his side and help him. She clung to her anger, using it as a safety barrier between her emotions and her instinctive desire to protect the man she loved. 'Why did you come here today, Nick?'

'I wanted to pay my respects to Avril and Lionel. They were my friends before I met you.'

She looked away, unable to meet his steady gaze. 'Thanks for putting me in my place.'

'You know I didn't mean it like that.'

'Do I? I don't know what you mean or what you want, Nick.'

He caught her by the shoulders, turning her slowly

to face him. 'Can't we start over, Ginnie? I was a mixed-up knucklehead when you came to Eagle Rock, but I can see clearly now in more ways than one.'

She looked into his eyes and was very nearly lost in the intensity of his gaze, but she had been this way before and it had been a disaster. 'I'm glad you've regained your sight,' she said, choosing her words carefully.

'I can see you, Ginnie. Even when I was almost totally blind I could still see you with my heart. I know that you're the one and only girl for me and I want you to believe that.'

It would be so easy to give in and throw herself into his embrace, but she forced herself to remain calm and outwardly aloof. Her instincts were telling her one thing but the warning voice in her head refused to be silenced. 'I think you mean it,' she said slowly. 'But we've been this way before.'

'And I'm sorry, honey. How many times have I got to say it?'

She laid her finger on his lips. 'Saying is one thing, keeping to it another. I travelled all the way to America to be with you, but you turned me down, so why should I trust you not to do it all over again when you suffer a setback? I've got problems of my own, Nick. I don't need this.' She steeled herself to walk past him and mount the steps, but the wedding guests were emerging from the register office, chattering and laughing. She stood aside to let them pass and out of the corner of her eye she could see Nick standing where she had left him. He was clutching the iron railings and his knuckles showed white beneath his tanned skin. He was staring up at her with a look of bafflement, but she did not relent. He had hurt her too much in the past to risk another bitter disappointment. Turning her back on him she edged her way into the building. There was someone else she needed to see.

But she did not get the chance to speak to Steven alone until late that evening. The uninvited wedding guests had followed the bridal party back to the pub, and the tiny bar was packed. Partygoers spilled out onto the riverbank, sitting at the rustic tables and enjoying the fine summer evening.

Lionel had managed to get a crate of champagne from an unknown source, although Ginnie had noticed a suspicious-looking character going into the vicarage on the previous Monday afternoon when she had been walking along the riverbank. She had seen plenty of spivs in London and this person might have stepped from a Most Wanted poster; but that was between Lionel and his conscience, and she had enjoyed a glass of champagne or two before going in search of Steven.

She found him on the river's edge, gazing into the fast-flowing water, dappled with moonlight. 'It's a lovely evening,' she said softly.

He did not look up. 'Yes, it is.'

She sensed his reserve. 'Is everything all right,

Steven? You haven't said a word to me all afternoon.'

'I didn't want to spoil the day.' He met her anxious gaze with a worried frown. 'Things aren't going too well, Ginnie.'

'I knew I should have been there.'

'Let's sit down, shall we?' He indicated a wooden bench that had just been vacated by Farmer Lewis and his wife.

'What's happened?' Ginnie took a seat beside him. 'If Ida can't cope with the shop she should have let me know.'

'The shop is running smoothly, as far as I can gather.' He reached out to hold her hand. 'It's Mallory. He's done his utmost to blacken your name. He's filed a complaint against you citing the various inspections of the property as evidence that you've let it fall into disrepair, and because of that you are an unfit tenant.'

'But that's nonsense. It was a put-up job.'

'It's difficult to prove.'

Her mouth was suddenly dry and she shivered, even though it was still warm in the shelter of the whispering trees. 'Do you mean that I'm going to lose the shop? Can't we put up a fight?'

'I'm doing everything I can, but if Mallory pulls strings in the council he might be able to block our appeal. He wants the shop regardless. It seems to have become a twisted kind of crusade as far as he's concerned.'

'What can we do?'

'I don't know. I've exhausted the legal channels and I think we might have to resort to something more drastic.'

'Like what?'

'It's a long shot, but if you could get Mallory to admit what he's being doing in front of witnesses, better still council officials, we could discredit him and clear you.'

'How on earth would I do that?'

'That's something we'd have to work on.'

She stood up. 'I'm going home tomorrow. I shouldn't have stayed away for so long.'

'I'm on your side, Ginnie.' He rose to his feet, taking both her hands in his. 'I haven't had the chance to tell you how lovely you look today. We'll do this together. I won't let him beat us.'

'Ginnie.'

She jumped at the sound of her name, jerking her hands free as she turned to see Nick standing on the bank above them with Shirley and Danny close behind him. 'It's not what it looks like,' she said hastily.

'You should have been straight with me,' Nick said angrily. 'Why didn't you tell me that there was someone else?'

'Hold on, old man.' Steven slipped his arm around Ginnie's shoulders. 'Don't speak to her like that.'

'I can stand up for myself, thank you, Steven.' Ginnie shook free from his restraining arm and climbed the steps to face Nick. 'You don't own me, Nick Miller. You think you can turn up out of the blue and everything will be forgiven and forgotten. Well, I've got news for you – it won't. I told you outside the register office and I'm telling you again now – I'm not going to let you get close only to change your mind if anything goes wrong with your job or you get cold feet.'

Steven was at her side in a moment. 'Is there still something between you two, Ginnie? I need to know.'

She spun round to face him. 'Why? Just because you're helping me out doesn't mean that you can run my life.'

Steven recoiled as if she had slapped his face. 'I'm trying to help you, Ginnie. I thought we had something going for us.'

'That was because you didn't listen to me.' Ginnie threw up her hands in despair. 'I've been straight with you all along and I did my best to convince you that there could never be anything other than friendship between us.'

'You tell them, Ginnie,' Shirley said enthusiastically. 'Just because I'm a widow doesn't mean that I'm desperate for a man either.'

'Don't get upset, honey.' Danny laid his hand on her shoulder. 'No one's accusing you of anything. I think you're great.'

She pushed him away. 'That goes for you too, Danny Flynn. You know that I loved Tony and I always will.'

'Tony?' Steven murmured. 'What about Laurence?'

Shirley shrugged her shoulders. 'Him too. I loved them both, and they're dead. Now I've got two kids to bring up on my own.' She seized Ginnie by the hand. 'Come on. Let's leave the men to sort it out between them. I want another glass of champagne.' She dragged Ginnie across the grass and up the steps into the bar, where the crowd had thinned to a few of the regulars and the happy couple. 'Is there any bubbly left?' Shirley demanded in a loud voice. She tottered over to the counter.

Avril clutched Ginnie's arm. 'What's going on?'

'It's all gone terribly wrong. Why did you invite them all up here? I thought it was going to be a quiet affair.'

'I'm sorry, darling. I thought it would be good for you to have Shirley and Steven here, but I didn't invite Nick and Danny. Somebody must have told them about the wedding, but it wasn't me.'

Ginnie shot an angry glance at her sister's back. Shirley was leaning on the bar chatting to Farmer Lewis's son, Jonathan, a strapping six-footer with a fresh complexion and expectations of inheriting the two-hundred-acre family farm. 'I know that, Avril. It was my interfering sister.'

'Perhaps she thought she was doing you a favour. After all you do still love the fellow, don't you?'

Ginnie bit her lip. 'It's not that simple.'

'And he obviously loves you or he wouldn't have come all this way to find you.'

415

'I'm about to lose my business and I've been accused of all sorts of foul things by Mallory. I need to be on my own so that I can think straight. I'm going for a walk.'

Avril stared down at the high-heeled satin shoes she had loaned Ginnie for the occasion. 'Not in my best dancing slippers. Go up and change into something more sensible and put on a wrap.'

Ginnie reached over to drop a kiss on Avril's scented cheek. 'You're a tartar, Mrs Vicar.'

Lionel had said nothing until this point but he shook his head at Ginnie. 'Less cheek, young lady. You're speaking to Mrs Lionel Smithers.'

Despite her chaotic emotions, Ginnie managed a smile. 'All right, but I think the locals will always call her Mrs Vicar.' She hurried from the bar and ran upstairs to her room. She changed her shoes and slipped a cardigan around her shoulders. It rather spoilt the effect of the dress, but she took off the hat and tossed it on the bed before going downstairs again and letting herself out of the side entrance. She headed for the riverbank but came to a sudden halt as someone stepped out of the bushes, barring her way.

'Ginnie, we need to talk to you.'

'What is there left to say, Steven?'

'Forget what happened earlier. This is important. We've been talking it over and we've come up with a plan.' Taking her by the arm he led her down the steps to the bench overlooking the water. Danny and Nick were already there and they rose to their feet.

'What is this?' Ginnie demanded. 'What sort of plan?'

'Sit down,' Steven said firmly. 'Keep quiet for once and listen. We've all got your best interests at heart, no matter what our personal feelings might be.' He inclined his head in Nick's direction.

'Sure. I agree.' Nick subsided onto the seat, patting the empty space beside him. 'We've gone into it carefully, and we think we've come up with a solution.'

It was closing time when they returned to the bar. The barmaid had been sent home and Lionel was clearing the tables while Avril washed glasses in the small sink beneath the counter. She looked up and smiled. 'I sent Shirley to bed in her old room. She's been celebrating a little too enthusiastically. I'm afraid the poor dear will have a terrible headache in the morning.'

Lionel glanced from one face to the other, eyebrows raised. 'You all look very serious. This is supposed to be a happy occasion.'

Ginnie took the cloth from him. 'I'll finish up for you, Lionel.'

'I won't argue with that.' He went to the bar and perched on a stool. 'What will you have to drink, chaps? You look as though you could do with one.'

'Yes, what's going on?' Avril asked curiously. 'Sit down and tell us.'

'It's your wedding night, and it's getting late,'

Steven said awkwardly. 'Maybe we ought to be on our way back to the hotel.'

'Just one drink.' Avril placed four glasses and a bottle of champagne on the bar counter. 'I was saving this one for you.'

Nick took the stool next to Lionel. 'That's very kind of you, Avril. It's quite like old times.' He glanced at Ginnie and she responded with a vague smile.

'Not quite. A lot has happened since then.'

Danny pulled up a chair and sat down. 'We've been hearing about Ginnie's fight to keep the business going. It seems like she's had a raw deal.'

'So what are you going to do about it?' Lionel uncorked the champagne and poured.

'We're working on a plan,' Nick said, keeping his gaze fixed on Ginnie. 'Steven thought it up and both Danny and I think it's the only way to go.'

'But you're all forgetting one thing,' Ginnie said softly. 'I'm broke and it's going to cost money. I can't even afford your fees, Steven, and I won't let you work for nothing. It's not fair to take advantage of friendship like that.'

'I thought we had something more, but I realise now it was wishful thinking.'

Lionel handed him a glass of champagne. 'You're a good man, Steven. We won't see you out of pocket.' He glanced at his wife. 'Will we, Mrs Vicar?'

Avril flicked the wet dishcloth at him. 'I get enough of that from the locals.' She was suddenly serious. 'I've already told Ginnie that I'm more than willing to pay her legal expenses, Steven. I agree entirely with Lionel. You mustn't work for nothing, especially at the start of your career. You must do whatever you have to do, and hang the expense.'

'Well said, Mrs Vicar.' Lionel clapped his hands. 'Now, gentlemen, you must put us out of our misery. What is this great plan?'

Leaving the newly-weds to start their married life with a promise to return soon, Ginnie left for London next morning. Nick and Steven were both subdued during the train journey, treating each other with polite indifference. Danny was cheerful, as always, in contrast to Shirley who was pale and complained of a headache, but received little sympathy as it was self-inflicted. Danny prescribed a couple of aspirin and a glass of seltzer before they left, and by the time they reached Paddington she was her old bubbly self.

When they parted to go their separate ways, Nick drew Ginnie aside. 'I'm taking the job at Moorfields. I'm not going anywhere and I'll prove to you that I meant every word I said outside the register office. I know I behaved like a jerk, but that won't happen again. I don't deserve you, Ginnie, and that's the truth, but I'm going to do my darnedest to win you back. I want you to trust me.'

She knew by the tremor in his voice and the agonised look in his dark eyes that he was in earnest, but she was still wary. 'I believe you mean it,' she said slowly. 'Maybe in time, Nick. Just maybe.'

'Take care of yourself, Shirley,' Danny said, giving her a hug. 'And give those kids a big kiss from Uncle Danny.'

'I will, and you must come over and see them when you get some time off.' Shirley linked her hand through Steven's arm. 'We'll see you boys soon.' She blew them a kiss and walked off towards the tube station with Steven in tow.

Ginnie was about to follow them when Nick caught her by the hand. 'Are you sure there's nothing between you and him?'

She brushed his lips with a kiss. 'Absolutely certain. Take care of yourself.' She turned to Danny with a grateful smile. 'You're a good friend. I don't know what we'd do without you.'

His face flushed at the compliment and he shrugged his shoulders. 'We were the three musketeers, weren't we, Nick? You, me and Tony.'

'Sure.' Nick nodded, keeping his gaze fixed firmly on Ginnie. 'We had some good times.'

'We were all just living for the moment,' Ginnie murmured, sighing. 'We all lost someone we loved.'

'Tony was a great guy,' Nick said as if reading her thoughts. 'And he was crazy about your sister.'

'She's never quite got over losing him.' For a moment they had regained some of their old empathy and Ginnie felt a sudden sense of panic. It would be so easy to fall back into a relationship with Nick, but this was neither the time nor the place. She turned to Danny. 'I always thought that you and Shirley might . . .'

'Not me, honey,' he said, grinning. 'To tell the truth I've met up with an old friend at East Grinstead. You'll remember Helga?'

'Nurse Halvorsen, the scourge of the ward maids?' She looked to Nick for confirmation but he was staring at his friend in disbelief.

Danny grinned. 'I know you dated her for a while and that they used to call her the Iron Nightingale at the hospital, but Helga's okay.'

'You're going steady?' Ginnie said dazedly. 'You and Helga?'

'I might get offended if you keep saying it like that,' Danny said, laughing. 'Helga's doing fine work at the hospital. She's a very competent nurse and she's not one of these women who need reassurance all the time. No offence meant, Ginnie. Just don't keep the poor guy dangling for too long.'

'Shut up, Danny.' Nick's dark eyebrows drew together in an ominous frown. 'This is strictly between me and Ginnie. You've done your bit, now leave it to us.'

Ginnie backed away. 'I've got to go or I'll lose Shirley and Steven. Call me, Nick. Give me your phone number and I'll let you know how things are going.' She hurried off before she could say something she might later regret. The conversation had become too personal and she needed time to think.

*

It was waiting for her on the hall table when she arrived home. The summons to attend a tribunal at the council offices was the final insult. Steven read it carefully and his expression was serious when he looked up and met Ginnie's anxious gaze. 'This is it,' he said, folding the sheet of paper and putting it back in the envelope. 'We've got until Monday to make our case.'

Mildred stood in the kitchen doorway, wringing her hands. 'We could lose everything. If we can't pay the rent we'll have to move out and if we're lucky the council might put us in one of those prefabs they've been building. Oh, the shame of it. I'll never be able to face the Mother's Union again, and as for the Townswomen's Guild – I'll be drummed out for sure.'

'Stop it, Mum,' Shirley said, clutching the baby in one arm and patting Travis on the head as he clung to her skirts. 'Don't talk like that. We've got a plan, haven't we, Ginnie?'

'I'd like to go round to Monk Avenue and have it out with Mallory face to face,' Ginnie said angrily. 'How dare he spread these lies about me?'

Steven handed her the envelope. 'Put this somewhere safe; we might need to refer to it. We've got three days to prepare and we must put the time to good use. We can't afford any slip-ups.'

'You're right,' Ginnie said, making an effort to sound calmer, even though her pulses were racing and her stomach was churning. What happened next would mean the difference between solvency and bankruptcy. All the hard work and hope that she had put into making the shop a going concern were in jeopardy, and all because of one man's malice.

'Are you going to stay with us, Steven?' Ever practical Mildred backed into the kitchen. 'The kettle's boiling, I'll make a pot of tea, and then I'll think about supper. I suppose you've been living like kings up there in Avril's pub.'

Steven shook his head. 'No one cooks better than you, Mrs Travis. You could have made a living as a restaurateur.'

Mildred plucked the knitted potholder off its hook and picked up the bubbling kettle. 'Really? Do you mean that, Steven?'

'Indeed I do. If you can make tasty meals using the minimum of ingredients think what you could do if there was no rationing and no expense was spared.'

Ginnie felt a smile bubble up inside her. She exchanged amused glances with Shirley. 'It's true, Mum,' she said, warming to the subject. 'Auntie Avril is a brilliant cook, but you're just as good, if not better.'

Shirley beckoned to Steven. 'Mum's laid tea out in the dining room. Come and sit down and we can go over our plan.' She shot a sideways glance at Ginnie. 'Don't look at me like that. I'm in this just as much as you are. Mallory's insulted me and

423

turned his back on his grandchildren. I want to see him kicked out of the council – that'll do for a start.'

'I'll give Mum a hand,' Ginnie said firmly. 'We'll eat first and talk later. Mum's obviously gone to a lot of trouble for us.' She went to join her mother in the steamy atmosphere of the kitchen, where an invisible tapestry of childhood memories was imprinted forever on the walls. There was still the small dent in the plaster where Shirley had had a teenage tantrum and thrown the rolling pin at her. It had missed because Shirley was a rotten shot, but it had broken their mother's favourite vase when it landed in the sink. Shirley had had her pocket money stopped for six weeks to pay for the damage. All the tears and tantrums of adolescence together with shared laughter and the small triumphs that were part of daily life were here, recorded in the brickwork. This was home, and Ginnie knew how much it meant to all of them, and their mother in particular. She watched her bustling about making tea as she had done countless times in the past, creating meals out of next to nothing, conjuring up birthday cakes like fairy castles or crinoline ladies, and making her special toffee as a treat after tea on Sundays. Seeing her through the eyes of a grateful daughter, Ginnie felt her throat constrict with tears of gratitude, and all past hurts were forgotten, because that's what love meant. 'Thanks, Mum.'

Mildred stopped what she was doing and stared at her, eyebrows raised. 'Whatever for? It's only meat and tater pie, which is mostly taters, and a bit of salad from the garden.'

'Thanks for putting up with all this. You've been a trouper, cooking and cleaning and keeping house for us while I've been at the shop, coming home at all hours. You've had nappies and babies' bottles to contend with and you've never uttered a word of complaint. It's not what you thought you'd be doing at your time of life.'

'I've only done what I've been doing for the last twenty-five years and more. I did it for your dad and now I'm doing it for you and Shirley. The babies are a bonus. It makes me feel young again to have little ones in the house.'

Ginnie leaned over to kiss her mother's lined cheek. 'You've been a brick, and I won't allow Mallory to make our lives a misery. I'm going to hold on to that shop as if I was a survivor from the *Titanic* hanging on to a life raft.'

Mildred dabbed her eyes with the hem of her pinafore. 'You are so like your dad, Ginnie. He'd be so proud of you.'

'I won't let you lose your home, Mum. I'll do whatever it takes to beat Mallory.'

'I know you will, love. You were always a determined little thing. Once you'd set your mind on something – that was it. Now take the tea tray into the dining room and I'll get the pie out of the oven. It's nicer hot than cold, I always think.'

Ginnie picked up the tray and was about to take

it into the dining room when Shirley emerged, holding her finger to her lips. 'Shh.'

'What's up?'

'Steven's on the phone. He's speaking to his office in Southampton and I think something's gone terribly wrong.'

Chapter Twenty-Two

Toni began to cry and Shirley retreated into the dining room followed by Ginnie. Travis was sitting on the floor sucking the baby's dummy and Toni was imprisoned in the wooden playpen, howling miserably. 'Naughty boy,' Shirley said, unplugging the dummy from her son's mouth and popping it into Toni's. She glanced at Ginnie with a shrug. 'It's family spit,' she said defensively. 'I can't sterilise every single thing.'

Ginnie bent down to pick Travis up and he sobbed into her shoulder. 'Big boys don't suck dummies,' she murmured into his curls. 'Big boys get chocolate if they're very good.'

Travis stopped crying to gaze into her face. 'Choc?' he said hopefully.

'He's not supposed to have sweets.' Shirley took him from Ginnie and dumped him unceremoniously in his high chair. 'You shouldn't encourage him.'

'It's only a penny bar. I bought it in the station cafeteria when we stopped for a cuppa.'

Mildred hurried into the room and placed the pie on a table mat. 'What's the matter with Travis?'

'Nothing, Mum,' Shirley said hastily. 'He pinched

baby's dummy and I scolded him, and now Ginnie's trying to bribe him with chocolate.'

Mildred shook her head. 'Never mind that. I think Steven is in trouble. I only heard the tail end of the conversation but he didn't sound too happy.'

'I'm not, Mrs Travis.' Steven stood in the doorway, his expression serious. 'I've just spoken to Esther and she told me there's a letter in the post terminating my employment.'

Ginnie sank down on her chair. 'Oh dear. It's all my fault. This wouldn't have happened if you hadn't spent so much time trying to help me.'

'I didn't fit in. The senior solicitors liked to do everything their way and they wanted a yes man. That's just not me. I'm not even sure if I want to work in the law now.'

Mildred took a seat and began serving the pie. 'I daresay the war's to blame for that, Steven. You had five years serving in the Navy and it can't be easy settling down to civilian life. There must be thousands of young men in your position.'

'I'm sorry too,' Shirley said softly. 'I shouldn't have persuaded you to come to Shropshire with me.'

Ginnie shook her head. 'No, I'm at fault. I've been obsessed with my own problems and I never gave a thought to how it might affect you, Steven. I'm so sorry, but I'll pay you for your efforts. I won't let you be out of pocket.'

'I'm afraid the money will go to my bosses, but

that's how it should be. I took the case on while I was working for them.'

'Yes, Ginnie,' Mildred said, passing her a plate of food. 'You mustn't be too hard on yourself. You've only done what you had to do.'

'Thanks, Mum.' Taking the plate, Ginnie was suddenly aware of her mother's work-worn hands, the veins standing out like cords beneath the fragile skin. They were a testament to a life spent in the service of her family, but years ago, when their father had slipped the wedding ring on her finger, her hands would have been plump and smooth, like those of a lady. Ginnie met her mother's curious gaze with a grateful smile. 'The pie looks and smells delicious.'

'That's good, love.' Mildred's face flushed with pleasure. 'It's not easy to make tasty meals. I thought that rationing would end as soon as the war was over, but it seems to be going on forever.'

Ginnie sat with her food untouched, glancing across the table at Shirley who was cutting up Travis's meal one-handed, with Toni hooked firmly in her free arm sucking on her bottle.

'The pie is excellent, Mrs Travis,' Steven said enthusiastically. 'The pastry is perfect.'

Ginnie flashed him a grateful smile. He might not be a blood relative, but he had been Laurence's best friend, and he had willingly involved himself in her affairs. That made him a part of the family – her family. No matter what problems beset her in life she was determined to protect those closest to her. She had not always seen eye to eye with either her mother or her sister, but all that was forgiven and forgotten in the face of adversity. She picked up her knife and fork. 'This is a fight,' she said, stabbing the piecrust. 'We're going to win. I won't let that man beat us.'

Later that evening, when supper was cleared away and the children were tucked up in bed, they settled down to work on their plan. Mildred had gone into the front room to listen to her favourite programmes on the wireless, the daily exploits of Dick Barton, special agent, and his doughty companions Jock and Snowy, and weekly adventures of the indomitable amateur sleuth Paul Temple and his glamorous wife Steve, who worked together to solve cases that baffled the constabulary.

'We could do with Dick Barton to help us now,' Ginnie said as she closed the door to shut out the sound of 'The Devil's Gallop', the stirring piece of music that introduced each thrilling episode. She took a seat at the table opposite Shirley and Steven. 'Any ideas as to how to trap Mallory into admitting what he's done?'

Steven tapped the tip of his pencil on the notepad in front of him. The page was blank except for a series of questions marks and a doodle. 'We'd have to get him on his own, preferably at the council offices. We'd also have to arrange for a couple of his fellow councillors to listen in to the conversation.

Mallory has a wide experience of court cases and he's no fool. It won't be easy.'

Shirley leaned her elbows on the table, cupping her chin in her hands. 'I think if he was angry enough he might forget himself.'

'He's only got to look at me and he sees red,' Ginnie said with a wry smile. 'I seem to bring out the worst in him just because I told that spoilt brat of a daughter a few home truths before I sacked her.'

'We know his Achilles heel is his daughter.' Steven wrote something down on his pad. 'But I don't see how we could involve her.'

Craning her neck to read it, Ginnie gave up as his writing was illegible especially when viewed upside down. 'Maybe we should kidnap Livvie and hold her to ransom,' she said, chuckling.

Shirley brightened visibly. 'We could cut off one of her ears and post it to her father.'

'You girls should join the Mafia.' The twin furrows on Steven's brow deepened into a frown. 'But seriously, we do need to catch him off guard. We have to put pressure on him before we get to the tribunal because the evidence against you is pretty damning, Ginnie, and without a confession from Mallory almost impossible to disprove.'

'I'll do it.' Shirley slammed her hands down on the table in a sudden burst of enthusiasm. 'I'll make Mallory as mad as hell because I hate that family. They've treated me like dirt and they won't acknowledge their grandchildren. How low can you get?'

Ginnie reached across to give her a reassuring pat on the hand. 'I know it's tough, and I agree entirely, but how do you intend to go about it?'

'All I've got to do is to turn up at the house with the kiddies in the pram. I don't have to ask for anything – just the sight of me on the doorstep is enough to make old Mallory's blood boil.'

Steven slipped his arm around her shoulders. 'What about Mrs Mallory? Surely she must want to see her son's children?'

'Apparently not. She's just as bad as him if you ask me.' Shirley's bottom lip trembled but she did not resort to tears, which surprised Ginnie. A few months ago her sister would have been sobbing on Steven's shoulder in order to gain his sympathy, but this was a different side to Shirley, and one that Ginnie had not seen before. There was a determined set to her jaw and a martial light in her blue eyes. She seemed to be prepared to do battle not only for herself but for her whole family.

'That's right. You go and get 'em, Shirley.' Ginnie gave her an encouraging smile. 'You were always top of the class in drama at school.'

'It's worth a try.' Steven wrote something in his spidery scrawl. 'If Mallory thinks you're going to ask for money that's sure to bring out the worst in him.'

'And you could threaten to go to the newspapers with your sob story.' Warming to her theme, Ginnie leapt to her feet, moving her hand slowly in front of her to indicate a headline. 'War widow's hard-hearted father-in-law refuses to help his destitute grandchildren.'

Steven threw back his head and laughed. 'You're turning it into a tragic opera, but all this will only work if we can get to him at the council offices just before the tribunal is due to start, and if we have someone on the inside who's willing to stand witness.'

'If only we could make a film of it,' Shirley said dreamily. 'I'd be the star, of course, and Ginnie could be the comic support.'

Choosing to ignore this remark, Ginnie racked her brains to think of someone they might know who would legitimately be in the council offices at the time of the hearing. 'We need someone who either works for the council or is on one of the committees. I'll ask around tomorrow when I go back to the shop. Goodness knows what I'll find there, but if we don't do something drastic there won't be a business at all.'

Steven closed his notepad with a flourish. 'And I'm afraid I'll have to leave for Southampton. I have to work my notice out, but as you are officially one of my clients I have a valid reason for returning in time for the tribunal on Monday.'

'You're such a good friend,' Ginnie said gratefully.

Shirley flung her arms around him. 'I'm not surprised that Laurence was fond of you, Steven.' She kissed him full on the lips, and when he did not resist, she kissed him again. 'You're a good kisser too.' She sighed. 'That's for nothing – see what you get for something.'

Ginnie rose to her feet. 'Put him down, Shirley. Hasn't Steven suffered enough at our hands?'

'Actually I enjoyed it,' Steven said, smiling. 'I'm not a crusty old bachelor.'

'Indeed you're not, darling.' Shirley patted him on the cheek. 'I'm going to put the kettle on. I think we all need a cuppa.' She paused for a moment, shooting a meaningful look at Ginnie. 'Isn't it time you told Steven how it is with you and Nick? I think you owe him that.'

'I'm sorry, Steven,' Ginnie said when the door closed on her sister. 'Shirley thinks that I led you on, but if I did it was unintentional.'

'I hoped that you'd got over Nick, but I realised when I saw you together at Avril's wedding that I didn't stand a chance.'

'And I'm truly sorry. I think the world of you and I wish things were different, but I did warn you from the start.'

He looked away. 'I know you did and I should have listened, but I was deluding myself.'

'I don't know why, Steven. You're a good-looking guy and you're funny and charming. You could have any girl you want.'

He gave her a wry smile. 'Except you.'

'I'm nothing special. I was always shy when it came to boys.'

'And I was never much good with women. I didn't have any sisters and I attended a boys' school. I dated a couple of girls when I was at university, but there was nothing serious, and then I was called up and joined the Navy.'

'And you had a girl in every port?'

He shook his head. 'My parents were always introducing me to somebody's cousin or sister when I had shore leave but I just wasn't interested, and then I met you at Shirley's wedding. I have to admit you knocked me for six, and I admired the way you handled Livvie and old man Mallory. But you're right; you did warn me off and if I didn't listen that's my fault.'

'I'm so sorry, Steven. I feel awful about it, and even worse now I know that you lost your job because you've been helping me.'

'I wouldn't have missed any of it, and there's still a lot to do. I'm not going to rest until I know you girls have a future to look forward to.'

Ginnie eyed him thoughtfully. 'Shirley's a good person. If she's got a fault it's just that she's too generous. When she's fond of someone she gives her all, and this business with the Mallorys has really hurt her. She's a wonderful mother, and if she meets the right man she'll be a wonderful wife too.'

He smiled. 'Are you match-making, Miss Travis?'

'No. Just making a point.'

'I don't think Laurence would be too pleased if I made a play for his widow.'

'Laurence loved Shirley and he was your best friend. He'd want both of you to be happy.' She hurried to open the door for her sister, who was carrying a laden tea tray. 'Thanks, Shirley. If you don't mind I'll take my tea to my room. I want to get an early night so that I can get to the shop well before opening time. I'm going to do some detective work of my own. I want to find an insider who's willing to speak up against Mallory.'

The small office at the back of the premises in Collier Lane was crowded with people and the air thick with cigarette smoke. Fred Chinashop had taken the desk chair with Fred Woollies standing behind him, and the rest of the shopkeepers were squashed together, attempting to sip the tea supplied by Ida. Jimmy hovered outside the door, keeping an eye on the shop floor.

Ginnie perched on the edge of the desk sandwiched in between Myra and Doris from the tobacconist's shop. Finding it increasingly difficult to breathe in the fug, Ginnie was beginning to regret inviting quite so many people to the meeting. She cleared her throat and the general buzz of conversation died away. 'You all know why we're here,' she said, trying not to cough as Fred Woollies exhaled a plume of cigarette smoke to hang in a pall above their heads. 'Does anyone here have a friend or a relation who works for the council or is on any of the committees?'

Fred Chinashop glanced round the room. 'I can't sell my lease because of the man who's lodged these false allegations against Ginnie. I want to retire but not at any price. Mallory is determined to put this girl out of business, and she's worked her socks off to build it back up after poor old Sid copped it. We all knew Ginnie's dad and he must be turning in his grave if he can see what's happening to his kid.'

A murmur of assent rippled round the room.

Fred Woollies held up his hand. 'My niece Mary works in the typing pool. She might be able to help.'

'No disrespect meant, Fred, but we could do with someone a bit higher up in the pecking order, if you know what I mean.' Fred Chinashop patted him on the shoulder. 'Nothing against Mary, of course. I'm sure she's a splendid young lady.'

Doris took a wad of chewing gum from her mouth and dropped it into her empty cup. 'My uncle Reg is on the council. He's a miserable old git, but he can't stand Mallory. He done him out of ten quid in 1935, so Uncle Reg says. Anyway, he's never forgiven him. He might be persuaded to speak up for you, Ginnie.'

'D'you really think he'd help?'

Doris shrugged her thin shoulders. 'No harm in asking.'

'Will you do that for me?'

'I don't see why not. Can I come and watch the fun?'

Ginnie eased herself to a standing position. 'I

doubt if the public will be allowed in, but if they are,' she added hastily, noting Doris's change of expression, 'I've no objections to you being there.'

'Ta, Ginnie. You're a sport.' Doris rescued the gum from the bottom of her teacup and popped it back in her mouth. 'See you in court. That's what they say in the movies. C'mon, Myra. We'd better get back to work.'

Ginnie waited anxiously outside the house in Monk Avenue. The Mallorys' maid had opened the door and would have slammed it in Shirley's face had she not put a foot over the threshold. Ginnie had heard the ensuing argument from the bottom of the garden path, and finally Shirley had been admitted after threatening in a loud voice that she would stand on the doorstep all day if necessary. She had marched into the house with Toni in her arms and Travis hanging on to her skirt. Ginnie had been left on the pavement, holding the pram. Genteel ladies had stopped to take a peek at the baby and had been mystified when they realised that the pram was empty. Ginnie had made up stories to satisfy their curiosity, but she had received some odd backward glances as they walked away.

She was beginning to grow anxious after ten minutes had passed with no sign of her sister and was about to march up the garden path and knock on the door when it opened and Shirley stepped outside. There were angry spots of colour on her cheeks when she joined Ginnie and Travis was sucking his thumb, a sure sign that he was unhappy.

'What happened?' Ginnie asked anxiously. 'Did you see him and what did he say?'

Shirley tucked the sleeping baby into the pram. 'I saw the old devil, and it worked. He's furious, and if he doesn't burst a blood vessel before he gets there he's sure to be in a filthy mood when he arrives at the council offices. I've done my bit and now it's your turn.' She lifted Travis, gave him a brief kiss and a cuddle, and strapped him in the pram next to his sister. 'I wish I could be there to see you get the better of the old bastard.'

Travis stared at his mother's lips. 'B . . .'

She shook her head. 'No, darling. Naughty word. We don't say that.'

'At least not until you're twenty-one,' Ginnie added, grinning. 'I'm off then, Shirley. Wish me luck.' She blew a kiss to Travis and ran to the bus stop in time to catch the double-decker that was about to pull away.

Steven was waiting for her in the reception area at the council offices. He gave her a reassuring smile as he clasped her hand. 'I've left a message asking Mallory to see us before the hearing starts.'

'Shirley did her bit. She said he was mad as hell, so let's hope it works.'

'Ready?' Steven squeezed her fingers.

'Ready,' she murmured. 'Let's do it.'

After making enquiries at the desk they were directed to an office at the end of a long corridor, where they were told to wait until called. Moments later the door opened and a young woman wearing a crisp white blouse and a grey pleated skirt slipped into the room, glancing nervously over her shoulder as if checking to see if she had been followed. She closed the door. 'I'm Mary,' she said in a stage whisper. 'My uncle Fred sent me to help you.'

'You shouldn't be seen talking to us,' Steven said gently. 'But we do appreciate what you're doing.'

Mary went to the interconnecting door and opened it to peer into the next office as if checking for eavesdroppers. It was all very theatrical and Ginnie had to suppress a nervous giggle, but their volunteer spy seemed to be taking it very seriously.

'Councillor Giggs is on his way,' Mary said, leaving the door ajar. 'I passed him just now, but I had to speak to you because there's something you should know about Councillor Mallory.'

Ginnie reached out to shake her hand. 'I'm Ginnie Travis and this is my solicitor, Steven Carter. What is it you wanted to tell us?'

'Councillor Mallory is trying to buy up the leases on all the shops in the parade on Collier Lane. I know that for certain because I've typed replies to his letters to the planning department. I'll get the sack if anyone finds out that I've told you.'

'We appreciate that,' Steven said solemnly. 'And

we'll do everything possible to keep your name out of it.'

'Councillor Giggs and I have worked out what we'll say to the tribunal.' Mary clasped her shorthand notebook to her bosom. 'He'll say he wanted to dictate a private letter and we just happened to be in the adjoining office.'

Ginnie frowned. 'Why would Mallory want to buy up the leases on all the shops in the parade?'

Mary glanced nervously over her shoulder as if expecting someone to leap out on her. 'My sister Betty works as a filing clerk in Mr Mallory's office and she told me that she's seen copies of the letters he sent to a firm of building contractors. He wants to buy up the leases and knock down the existing buildings to put up a huge block of flats to house people bombed out in the war. There's big money in it, so Betty says, but again no one must know that she had anything to do with this.' She opened her notebook and took out a folded sheet of flimsy, which she handed to Steven. 'It's one of the copies. Betty's had enough and she's giving in her notice today. She said use this and be damned to him.'

Ginnie stifled a whoop of glee as she read it, peering over Steven's shoulder. 'We've got him, Steven. We've got him.'

The door opened and a tall, thin man with wispy grey hair combed over a bald pate entered the room. 'I'm Reginald Giggs.' He held his hand out to Ginnie. 'You must be Miss Travis.'

441

'Yes, I'm Ginnie Travis, and this is Steven Carter, my solicitor.' She shook hands, but his grasp was limp and half-hearted and she experienced a sudden sinking feeling in her stomach. Looking into his watery grey eyes, she wondered if this man would be able to stand up to Mallory's dominant personality if asked to face him in front of the tribunal.

He nodded to Steven. 'I'm well aware of Mallory's underhand behaviour and it's time he was stopped. I'm more than willing to act as your witness.'

Steven shook his hand. 'Thank you, sir. We're more than grateful.'

Mary was suddenly alert. 'I can hear footsteps,' she said breathlessly. 'I think he's coming.' She hurried into the adjoining office, leaving Councillor Giggs to follow her.

He hesitated. 'Mallory has got this coming,' he said grimly. 'This isn't something I would do normally, but he's corrupt and he's got to be stopped.' He strode into the office, leaving the door ajar.

Ginnie stood close to Steven, taking courage from his confident posture. He caught her eye and smiled but before he had a chance to speak Mallory burst into the office, red-faced and oozing aggression. He was patently ready for a fight, but Ginnie was quick to notice that his tie was crooked and that some of the buttons on his pinstriped waistcoat were unfastened to reveal a glimpse of black braces. He might look as though he was about to declare war on them, but she could see that Shirley had done her work well. Mallory had been taken off guard and he had allowed his personal feelings to overcome his professional detachment. Anything could happen.

Steven stepped forward. 'We have something very important to say to you, councillor.'

Mallory's out-thrust chin made him look like a belligerent bulldog. He squared up to Steven, curling his lip. 'Make it quick, Carter. I'm going to enjoy seeing your client grovel in front of the tribunal.'

'Let's keep this on a professional level, shall we, councillor.' Steven's voice was ice-cold.

Mallory clenched his fists at his sides. 'I'm going to make certain that she's so discredited that she wouldn't be able to open up a stall on Petticoat Lane. I've got enough evidence to prove that she let the premises go to rack and ruin. After all, who'd put a silly kid in charge of a business?'

Ginnie held her tongue with difficulty. Hot words bubbled to her lips but one glance from Steven silenced her. There was a time to speak and this was not it. She glared at Mallory, silently daring him to continue.

'That little tart and her whoring sister have done their best to destroy my family,' Mallory continued, raising his voice. 'My son was foolish enough to marry the elder sister and give a name to her little bastards. She had the nerve to come to me today asking me for money to buy the boy a pair of shoes. I told the slut where to go and today I'm going to make certain that her sister is put out of business.

By this evening there'll be a new leaseholder in Collier Lane and very soon I'll own the whole parade.'

'And why would a successful solicitor like yourself want to become a shopkeeper?' Steven's voice cut through Mallory's rant like a wire through cheese.

Mallory blinked and drew a deep breath. 'Don't talk rubbish. I'm not going into trade.'

'So why do you want to buy up all the leases, Mr Mallory?' Ginnie took a step towards him. 'If you look down on people in trade, why do you want to join them?'

'You silly little fool. Are you really that stupid?' Mallory took a step towards her. 'I have my reasons and I'm not about to share them with you. You're ruined, Virginia Travis. I'll teach you to meddle in my family's affairs and I'll take pleasure in seeing your sister touting for business in the gutter.'

Chapter Twenty-Three

Ginnie was ready to fly at him but Steven caught her before she had a chance to make a move. Mallory threw back his head and laughed, but his mirth was cut short by the sudden appearance of Councillor Giggs and Mary.

'I think we've got enough evidence to hang him,' Giggs said with a satisfied smile. 'Miss Fielding holds a Pitman's shorthand-typist certificate for one hundred and twenty words a minute and she's taken down the conversation verbatim, which she is now going to transcribe. Off you go, Mary. Tell the typing pool supervisor that you are doing an urgent piece of work for me.'

'Yes, Mr Giggs. I'll do it straight away.' Mary scuttled out of the room as if scared that Mallory might accost her and snatch the evidence from her hands.

Steven handed the carbon copy to Giggs. 'You'd better take care of this, sir. It's proof of Mr Mallory's plans to put all the shopkeepers in Collier Lane out of business.'

Mallory paled visibly and he ran his finger round the inside of his Gladstone collar. 'There's no need to be hasty, Giggs. I can explain.'

'I think you've said enough already, Mr Mallory. Anyway, it's time to go into the hearing. I think the officials will be very interested to learn your plans for the misappropriation of council property.'

Mallory held up his hands. 'Now, now, Giggs. We're old friends. Surely we can come to some mutually satisfactory arrangement?'

'We've never been friends and I doubt if there's anyone on the council who doesn't find you an offensive upstart who just happens to have a degree in law. You may have a successful practice, but I wonder how your dealings would stand up to investigation by the Law Society. If I were in your shoes I'd be extremely careful as to how I conducted myself at the tribunal. Anyway, it's time to go in. Lead the way, Mallory. We'll be right behind you, so don't even think about making a bolt for it.'

'No,' Steven said firmly. 'I've been known to do a very creditable rugby tackle and it would give me great pleasure to bring you down, Mallory.'

'That I would like to see.' Ginnie took Steven by the hand. 'Let's get it over, shall we?'

The hearing was brief. The evidence against Ginnie was read out but instantly repudiated by Steven, who handed the chairman a list of the shopkeepers who had signed a petition in support of Ginnie. Mallory blustered and tried to discredit her, but he was obviously in no state to be objective and he subsided completely when Steven called on

Councillor Giggs to tell the tribunal what he had overheard. Miss Fielding, he said, was busy transcribing her shorthand, but Mallory's unsolicited confession of his plans would be with them as soon as she had finished.

The chairman dismissed the case, but not before calling for Mallory's resignation from the council and advising him that there would be a full investigation into his activities. Mallory left the courtroom, head bowed and shuffling like a man twice his age, but Ginnie could not find it in her heart to feel sorry for him. She suspected that his humility would dissipate like morning mist the moment he left the building and that when he recovered his temper his old self would miraculously come to the fore. She did not want to be there to see it. She was about to leave the court room when the chairman called her back.

'I want to offer you an apology on behalf of the council, Miss Travis. It's been proved beyond doubt that the real transgressor is Mr Mallory and he will be brought to book, but on behalf of the entire council I can assure you that your tenancy is secure. Permission to purchase the lease on the adjacent premises will be restored immediately, as will planning permission to expand into the shop next door. It will attract more customers, which can only be good for all the businesses in Collier Lane.' He leaned across the desk, allowing his stern expression to melt into a smile. 'I knew your father, Miss Travis.

He was a good man and he'd be very proud of you. Congratulations.'

Ginnie left the building in a daze. As she stepped outside into the hot summer sunshine she saw Shirley waiting in the forecourt and she was not alone. Ginnie's heart did a somersault. 'Nick.' She raced across the tarmac to fling her arms around him.

The kiss robbed her of her senses. Time ceased to exist and she knew that she had come home at last. She drew back just far enough to gaze into his eyes and she saw herself mirrored in his soul. All her doubts and fears were banished in a second of sheer joy. 'I won,' she whispered as she laid her cheek against his. 'But it means so much to me that you've come today. I wasn't expecting to see you here.'

He held her at arm's length, a tender smile on his lips. 'Shirley told me about the tribunal. I wanted to be near you and I'm delighted that you won your case, but whichever way it went wouldn't have made any difference to my feelings for you. I love you, Ginnie. I always have.'

She felt the past slipping away into the mists of memory. The future was all that mattered now. 'I love you too, Nick.'

Shirley slipped her arms around their shoulders. 'No bedroom talk here, kids. You're making Steven and me feel like spare parts. Let's go home and celebrate.'

Safe in a shelter of Nick's arms, Ginnie turned her

head to smile at Steven. 'Thanks for everything. I'd never have beaten Mallory if it hadn't been for you.'

'I'm glad it turned out the way it did.' Steven proffered his arm to Shirley. 'I think we ought to go back to Cherry Lane and give Mrs Travis the good news.'

'Yes, of course.' Shirley glanced over her shoulder. 'Are you two coming, or are you going to stand there like a couple of love-struck teenagers?'

Ginnie leaned against Nick, inhaling the achingly familiar scent of him. She smiled up at him. 'There's something I must do first.'

'The shop,' Nick said, smiling. 'I know, honey.'

'That's right. I must tell everyone what's happened. Do you mind?'

He raised her hand to his lips and kissed it. 'I guess that's how it's going to be from now on.'

'It's important to me, Nick.'

'I know that, Ginnie. I grew up alongside my folks' store, so it's no big deal. All I want is for you to be happy.'

Shirley took Steven by the hand. 'At least you know what you're letting yourself in for, Nick. We'll go home and tell Mum. See you later.'

Ginnie watched them walk away. 'They make a lovely couple,' she said softly.

Nick pulled her into his arms and silenced her with a kiss. 'Let them work it out for themselves. Now let's go see your store. I want to visit the place where my future wife is going to make our fortune.'

'If you think that's the sort of proposal that gets a girl going, you've got another think coming, Mr Miller.'

He fingered the golden eagle brooch on her lapel. 'You were wearing this at Avril's wedding.'

'I wear it all the time. It's my good luck charm.'

'I hope you'll wear it forever, and when the time is right, I'll propose. You'll get all the moonlight and roses you want, honey.'

'And you won't mind the fact that I'll continue working and maybe spend long hours at the shop?'

'Like I said, sweetheart, I grew up with parents who ran a store. It'll be like coming home.'

Ida, Jimmy and most of the shopkeepers in the parade were waiting for them. Mary Fielding had lost no time in telephoning her uncle to tell him the good news and now everyone in Collier Lane knew that Mallory had met his just deserts. Fred Chinashop was in tears, but they were tears of joy as he hugged Ginnie. 'Now I can retire and devote myself to my allotment,' he said, wiping his eyes on his sleeve. 'Of course I'll be on hand to help if you need me.'

'And to drink our tea ration, not to mention the sugar you put away,' Ida said, chuckling. 'You won't be able to keep away for long, Fred.' Her smile faded and she gave Ginnie a searching look. 'Will you still need me? I mean now you're going to expand you'll be taking on more staff, and they'll be younger and properly trained.'

'What about me?' Jimmy asked anxiously. 'I try hard to do me job well, Ginnie, but Mum says I'm not the sharpest knife in the box.'

Ginnie left Nick's side to give Jimmy a hug. 'You're sharp enough for my liking, Jimmy. I don't know what I'd have done without you and Ida. We're a team and that's the way it's going to be. Of course I'll take on more staff as and when I can afford to, but you two will always have a job in Travis's Furniture Emporium. I can promise you that.'

Fred beamed at her. 'I think this calls for a celebration. Put the kettle on Ida. You know how I like my tea – sweety, weaky and milky.' He followed Ida out of the office, leaving Ginnie and Nick alone for the first time that day.

'I guess I'll have to start drinking tea,' Nick said, slipping his arm around Ginnie's waist. 'You've got a great thing going here, honey. I'll help in any way I can.'

'But you'll be busy at the hospital, Nick. And I'll have to spend a lot of time working here, especially when the planning permission comes through and the builders start work.'

'I'll be busy at the hospital during the week, but at weekends I can help out in the store. It's not as if I've never done it before.'

'Would you really? Wouldn't it be an awful comedown after being a surgeon and the important work you're doing in research?'

'Honey, I'm not proud. I'm lucky to have regained

most of my sight, and I've had a long time to think and to decide what I want in life. I don't care about me – all I care about is us.'

She cupped his face in her hands, looking into his eyes. 'That goes for me to, but I'll be doing this for us and for Mum and Shirley. I've been supporting them since Laurence died, and I can't stop now.'

'I know, Ginnie, and I admire you for it. I'd do the same.'

She dropped her hands to her sides at the sound of the teacups rattling on their saucers which preceded Ida as she bustled into the office, followed by Fred who was carrying a plate of biscuits. 'Aren't you two engaged yet?' Ida demanded, dumping the tray on the desk. 'Lord knows we've given you enough time to propose, young man.'

'Moonlight and roses, Ida,' Ginnie said, smiling. 'That's what I'm waiting for.'

Later, after receiving congratulations all round for the successful outcome of the tribunal, which affected all the shops in the parade and the inhabitants of the flats above them, Ginnie and Nick walked back to Cherry Lane hand in hand.

They were welcomed by Mrs Martin who was leaning over her gate with a bunch of roses clutched in her hand. 'Well done, Ginnie,' she said, passing it to her with a broad smile. 'It's high time someone put that Mallory man in his place. I've heard nothing good about him, and now he's got his comeuppance.'

Ginnie sniffed the heady scent of the crimson roses. 'Thank you, Mrs Martin. That's very kind of you.'

Mrs Martin put her head on one side, eyeing Nick with a speculative glance. 'Is this your young man? The American soldier who lost his sight?'

Ginnie shot an anxious look at Nick, but he did not seem upset. He reached across the gate to kiss Mrs Martin's cheek. 'I'm fine now, ma'am, but in answer to your question, I am that soldier.'

Mrs Martin clapped her hand to her cheek. 'Well, I never. I can see why you're fond of this one, Ginnie. What a charmer.' Giggling like a schoolgirl she turned on her heel and hurried up the path to her front door.

Nick saluted smartly. 'Good day, ma'am.'

She paused on the doorstep. 'Such lovely manners. I do like Americans.' She went inside and closed the door.

'I'll have to watch you,' Ginnie said, chuckling. 'You'll be the talk of the town if you carry on with elderly ladies like that.'

Nick hooked his arm around her shoulders. 'I've yet to meet your mother. That's going to be the big test. She might hate my guts after the way I treated you.'

As Ginnie unlatched the garden gate she saw the front door open and her mother stepped outside. 'You're about to find out.' She clutched his hand and led him towards the house.

Mildred's stern expression melted into a smile. She held out her hand. 'Welcome to our house, Nick. I'm so glad to meet you at last.'

As he stepped over the threshold Nick was almost bowled over by Travis who rushed up to him. 'Choc?' he said expectantly.

Shirley swooped on her son and picked him up. 'Behave yourself, Travis. You don't ask people for sweets the moment they walk through the front door.' She smiled at Nick. 'Come and have a drink. Steven's managed to get hold of a bottle of gin and we've got baby orange juice. They didn't have any tonic in the shop.'

'Or there's tea, if you'd prefer it,' Mildred said, chuckling. 'Although if Fred Chinashop has had anything to do with it you'll have drunk enough tea to last a lifetime. Come in, my dear, and sit down. We're planning a party to celebrate.'

'Celebrate what, Mum?' Ginnie stared at her mother in astonishment. She had taken a chance in bringing Nick home without first warning her mother, but Shirley seemed to have taken it upon herself to pave the way.

'It's your birthday soon, dear,' Mildred said smugly. 'We've been talking it over and as it's your twenty-first and you've beaten Colin Mallory at his own game, we think we should throw a proper party. The sort we used to have before the war. We'll invite Avril and Lionel, and all your friends from Collier Lane.' She shot a sideways glance at

Nick. 'It might even turn out to be a double celebration.'

Ginnie buried her face in the posy of roses and smiled at Nick. 'Let's hope there's a moon that night.'

He nodded his head. 'I'll make sure there is.'

The official paperwork arrived and Ginnie found herself the proud proprietor of two shops in the parade. Avril transferred the necessary funds to pay the legal fees, but Ginnie insisted that Steven must draw up an agreement whereby she promised to repay her aunt at a fixed rate of interest over a set period. 'You're my first client since I decided to set up on my own,' Steven said, when the document was signed and witnessed by Ida and Fred Chinashop in the office behind the shop.

Ginnie sat back in her chair and smiled. 'We need an honest solicitor in this part of town, Steven. I'm sure you'll do well.'

'I've just got to find a suitable premises to work from, and then I'll put my brass plate on the door, and I'll be away. Shirley's going to be my part-time secretary, which will suit both of us.'

'She's done well organising this party that Mum insists on throwing for my birthday,' Ginnie said, nodding with approval. 'Shirley's got hidden depths. She'll do you proud, Steven.' She did not add that she hoped they might make a match of it. That would be going too far, but she was genuinely fond of

Steven and she could only hope that one day Shirley would find happiness again and that it might be with someone like Steven.

Ginnie had little time to think about family matters when the builders moved into the shop. She did not want to lose trade by closing down and a canvas partition was erected, but still the sound of drilling and hammering made it almost impossible to hear, and brick and plaster dust seeped into the shop that had to be cleaned up at regular intervals. A rolled steel joist was erected where support was needed and an archway into Fred's shop was constructed in a surprisingly short space of time. The bricklayers and plasterers did their work and the decorators came in to apply the final touches.

The work was completed on the morning of Ginnie's twenty-first birthday. She was now the proud tenant of an enlarged premises and it just needed the shop fitters to do their work, building the necessary stands for the new lines in chinaware and household linens that she had on order.

It was her twenty-first birthday. She left the shop at six o'clock and went home to change. The house was oddly silent as the children were both tucked up in bed and the babysitter was ensconced in the front room with a plate of sandwiches, a slice of sponge cake and a pile of magazines supplied by Shirley. There was no sign of Shirley or their mother but Ginnie realised that they were probably at the hotel, sorting out last minute arrangements. Avril and Lionel were booked into the same venue as were Steven, Danny and Helga. Ginnie made up her mind to be nice to the Iron Nightingale, and she could only hope that Helga's budding relationship with Danny might have mellowed her.

She filled the bath with water, revelling in the luxury of being able to use more than four inches of water, and she added a handful of bath salts, which were a birthday present from Mrs Martin. It was wonderful to relax and wallow in hot water after a hectic day at the shop, and afterwards when she was dressed and ready to go she waited for Nick to collect her as he had promised. She was suddenly nervous as well as excited. Tonight was her big night. All her family would be at the party as well as all her friends from Collier Lane. Nick had been with her every weekend since the tribunal but after his promise of moonlight and roses he had never raised the subject of their engagement. She knew that he loved her and she loved him, but the old shadows had not been entirely dispelled. Her palms were moist and her heart was racing as she went to answer the doorbell.

The late summer evening was surprisingly mild and there was not a breath of wind as she opened the door. Purple shadows consumed the flowerbeds and the air was filled with the perfume of night-scented stock. The evening star twinkled in a duck-egg blue sky and Nick stood there, immaculate in an evening suit with a huge bouquet of roses in his hands. He glanced up at the ghostly silver outline of the moon. 'It'll be moonlight and roses for you tonight, my darling girl.'

She accepted the flowers with a tremulous smile. 'It's what you promised me, Nick.'

He took her by the hand and led her out into the garden. 'I've even organised a full moon in your honour.' He slipped his free hand into his pocket and took out a small leather box. 'I wanted to do this now, while we are on our own. If it doesn't fit we'll change it, but I wanted to do this properly.' He flicked the box open to reveal a diamond and sapphire ring. Still holding her hand he went down on one knee. 'I love you with all my heart and soul, Ginnie. Will you marry me?'

She laid the roses gently on the step and leaned over to answer him with a kiss.

Getting to know

Lily Baxter

Read on for a letter from Lily and an extract from
The Workhouse Girl by Dilly Court

Dear Reader,

I hope you enjoyed reading *The Shopkeeper's Daughter*.
This story is very personal to me as my father, when he
was demobbed from the army in 1946, went into business
with his two brothers, opening three furniture shops in the
suburbs of East London.

I used to love visiting my father's shop as a child, and I can
still remember the smell of linoleum and hessian-backed
carpets. I remember the tiny office crammed with
catalogues and carpet samples, and the overflowing ashtray
on his desk. But that is where the likeness between me
and my heroine, Ginnie Travis, ends as I never worked in
the shop. I might have washed a teacup or two, but nothing
more arduous and I never experienced the terror of an air
raid or the life-changing events that forced Ginnie to take
responsibility for her whole family.

This story is special to me for another reason too. In a
roundabout way it was the war that inspired me to take up
writing seriously, although I never experienced the terrors
of the Blitz. My mother was a writer but the only work
she had published was a poem which was included in an
anthology of verse. It was written when she was a young
bride separated from her husband, with a baby to bring up
on her own. She continued to write into old age but was
never satisfied with her work and destroyed all her
manuscripts. When she died my brother travelled from
New Zealand to attend her funeral bringing a copy of the
anthology with him, and the deeply touching poem was
read during the service.

It was hearing the words she had written so many years ago that made me determined to honour her memory by fulfilling her ambition, even if it was second hand. If I had inherited at least some of her undoubted talent then it was up to me to work hard and learn my craft and then one day I might do what she had dreamed of doing and become a published author. Her poem is on the next page for you to read.

We all have our hopes and dreams and the only advice I would ever give is – go for it. Don't give up. You never know what you can do until you try.

With my very best wishes,

Lily Baxter

SPRING MEMOIR.

I stood on a bank bejewelled with starry, white Anemones, and gazed at the well-loved scene before me. Beneath my feet ran a stream, reflecting the youthful beauty of a peerless blue sky, and murmuring softly to the overhanging foliage, leafy tendrils of which trailed into the water.

On the opposite bank nestled clusters of Snowdrops, their delicate blossom sharply defined against a background of moss and fern.

The trees on this side stood close together, as if linked in eternal bondage. Pale-green feathery shoots were bursting forth from the dark branches ; and perched amongst the leaves was a young Starling, his black, shining chest trembling in a vain effort to produce a more pleasing note.

Beyond the trees, and stretching to the edge of a forest, lay a meadow radiant with daffodils that swayed on their short stems as a gentle breeze rippled over the pasture. With each puff of wind, it seemed as though the grass breathed softly, and lifted the golden trumpets towards the sun, thus enhancing their brilliance.

The forest beyond the meadow lay shrouded in darkness—a distant blur of pines and firs mingling with budding green trees standing on a misty carpet of deep blue.

A harsh cawing broke the stillness as a cloud of birds rose from the tree-tops, wheeling and diving. They circled overhead until the disturbance, whatever it was, ceased. Then all was quiet once more.

Before this serene beauty—this glimpse of youth, freshness and peace—how remote seemed the pain and turmoil of War, the insensate greed and hatreds of mankind !

Others may discover the secret path leading to my Paradise ; yet I feel that no succeeding season will reach such heights of loveliness as this vision of an English Spring, which lies for ever in my memory.

SYLVIA ELLIS.

Lily Baxter also writes under the name of Dilly Court

If you enjoyed *The Shopkeeper's Daughter*, why not read Dilly Court's wonderful new novel

The Workhouse Girl

Available from all good bookshops

Read on for an extract...

Chapter One

St Giles and St George Workhouse, London, 1859

'My name is Sarah Scrase, and I don't belong here.' White-faced and terrified, but defiant, Sarah clasped her small hands tightly behind her back, digging her fingernails into her palms in an attempt to control the tears that welled into her blue eyes.

'What?' Matron Trigg bellowed like a cow in calf, causing the other children in the schoolroom to huddle together in fear. 'What did you say, girl?'

'My name is Sarah Scrase and I want my ma.'

Matron Trigg turned to her husband, the workhouse master. 'Did you ever, Mr Trigg? No you did not, nor I neither. What is the world coming to when a young child speaks back to her elders and betters?'

'Shocking, Mrs Trigg. Deal with her as you see fit.' Mr Trigg beat the air with the cane he was holding, and the swishing sound sent a ripple of terrified murmurs around the classroom. 'Another peep from any of you girls and you will all feel a taste of the Tickler's anger.'

Sarah was trembling violently and a feeling of faintness almost overcame her, but she struggled to keep calm. She had already experienced the Tickler, Mr Trigg's much used method of corporal punishment, twice, and she had only been an inmate at the workhouse for a few hours. The Tickler had punished her for clinging to her mother's skirts when they were first separated, and had beaten her soundly for refusing to abandon her own clothes for the grey grogram workhouse uniform, coarse calico petticoat and blue check apron, and now she was likely to endure another assault with the fearsome instrument of torture. She glanced nervously at Matron's bulldog jaw, set in a harsh line despite her flabby jowls, but she was not going to give in. 'I'm Sarah Scrase,' she whispered, 'and I want my ma.'

'Your mother is a whore,' Matron said in a voice that reverberated like a clap of thunder. 'She is no better than she should be and at this moment is giving birth to another spawn of the devil.'

'You take that back.' Forgetting everything other than the need to stand up for her beloved mother, Sarah put her head down and charged at Matron's corpulent body, butting her in the stomach and sending her staggering backwards into her husband's arms. Sarah fell to her knees, bowing her head as if waiting for the axeman's deadly stroke.

There was a moment of horrified silence and then someone giggled.

Mr Trigg thrust his wife aside and flailed the air with his cane as he grabbed Sarah by the white cap she had been forced to wear. It came off in his hand, exposing her spiky hair, which to her horror had been cropped short when she was admitted to the workhouse. Seizing her by the scruff of her neck, he dragged her to her feet. 'You are indeed the devil's daughter,' he said, bringing the cane down across her back. 'Spawn of Old Nick. Offspring of Old Scratch.'

Sarah cried out as he beat her again and again until she crumpled in a heap at his feet. He released her with a growl. 'Let that be a lesson to you.' He turned to his wife who was leaning against the teacher's desk, clutching her large bosom and groaning. 'I'll leave this brat to you, my dear. Treat her harshly. Teach her manners in any way you see fit.' He stormed out of the classroom, slamming the door behind him.

Matron Trigg raised herself, aiming a savage kick at Sarah. 'Get up.'

With difficulty, Sarah scrambled to her feet. She faced her tormentor with a defiant toss of her head. 'I'm not the devil's daughter,' she said in a low voice. 'I used to go to Sunday school regular, and he's got no right to say things about Ma. It ain't her fault that Pa got drownded in the Thames when his wherry was run down in the fog.'

'What is your name?' Matron Trigg leaned over so that her face was close to Sarah's.

'I'm Sarah Scrase.'

'Not now you ain't.' Matron's bloodshot eyes opened wide and her nostrils flared. 'I'll tell you what it is, girl. You'll bear your demon father's name for the rest of your time in this institution. From now on you will be known as Sal Scratch.' She beckoned to one of the older girls. 'Nettie Bean. Come here.'

Sarah looked round and saw an older girl making her way between the regimented lines of wooden desks. Freckle-faced and with hair the colour of

3

gingerbread, Nettie Bean looked as though she might know how to stand up for herself. Sarah met her green-eyed gaze with a mute plea for help.

'Hurry up,' Matron Trigg said crossly. 'I haven't got all day.' Taking a sheet of paper from her desk, she dipped a pen in the inkwell. 'Can you read, Sal Scratch?'

'Yes, and I can write me name.'

Matron thrust the pen into her hand. 'Then write this – I am the devil's daughter.'

Sarah's instinct was to refuse, but her backside was still smarting from the Tickler's harsh punishment, and her ribs were sore where they had come into contact with Matron's boot.

Without waiting for the ink to dry Matron snatched the paper from her and gave it to Nettie. 'Pin it on her back. She'll wear this until she has learned her lesson.' She took a pin from her collar and put it in Nettie's outstretched hand. 'Hurry up, girl. I haven't got all day to waste on stupid and ungrateful children.'

'Sorry,' Nettie whispered as she fastened the placard to the back of Sarah's bodice.

It was barely more audible than a sigh, but the single word came as the first hint of human kindness that Sarah had encountered since she entered the fearsome building in Shorts Gardens. 'Ta,' she whispered, lifting her hand, and for a fleeting second their fingers touched. In that moment Sarah knew that she had made a friend for life.

'Get back to your seat,' Matron said, pointing to Nettie. 'And all of you write on your slates – I must not speak to Sal Scratch.' She pushed Sarah off the podium with a vicious prod in the ribs. 'Go and stand in the corner. You'll remain there until the end of the lesson.'

Sarah stumbled and only just saved herself from falling on her face, but no one laughed. Heads were bent over slates and the scrape of the girls' slate pencils and laboured breathing filled the air. Sarah stood in the corner, hands clasped firmly in front of her, willing herself not to cry. She closed her eyes, praying silently for her mother, who had been in labour for two days before desperation drove her to the workhouse door. Sarah had been present on two occasions when her mother went into premature labour, and the tiny infants had barely taken their first breaths when they had given up the struggle for life. No doubt they were in heaven with Pa, but he was buried in a pauper's grave. There had been no money to buy him a plot or even a headstone.

Sarah had loved her pa, but she had also been a bit frightened of him. Big, muscular and inclined to fits of temper, Jed Scrase had been a force to be reckoned with, but he had also been a gambling man. Drink had not been his major vice, but he would bet on anything from a bare knuckle fight to dog ratting, and the money he earned as a wherryman was often gone before he arrived home at night. They had lived mainly off her mother's earnings as a cleaner in the Theatre Royal, Drury Lane, which was close to the rooms they rented in Vinegar Yard. Sarah's education had been gained from watching the actors during rehearsals, and she

5

had learned to read by studying the programmes and billboards. The theatrical folk had taken her to their hearts, and by the time she was five years old she could recite whole passages from dramas by Boucicault without faltering. She had also been quite a favourite with the ballet dancers, especially when as a toddler she had climbed onto the stage during rehearsals and attempted to copy their graceful movements.

None of this helped her now as she stood for a painful hour, suffering muscle cramps and increasing exhaustion while the class was tested for spelling and times tables. Eventually the lesson came to an end and they were dismissed. Matron Trigg left the room, apparently having forgotten Sarah's existence, and she was left wondering what to do. Did she stand here all day and maybe all night, until someone discovered her? Or should she follow the rest of the girls?

Nettie was the last to file out of the classroom but she hesitated in the doorway and beckoned to Sarah. 'You'd best come with us. I think old bitch-face has forgotten you.'

Sarah would have giggled at this had she not been quite so scared. 'But – but she said I had to stay here.'

'You can if you like, but she'll have gone off to her office to drink tea and eat cake while we pick oakum in the yard.' Nettie held out her hand. 'Come on. I'll show you where to go and what to do.'

Sarah needed no second bidding. She ran to join Nettie and was about to rip the offending sign from her bodice when her new friend shook her head. 'I'd leave that on if I was you. She'll lock you in the cellar with the rats and spiders if you take it off. She might have forgot you now, but her memory ain't that bad, Sarah.'

Sarah smiled shyly. 'Ta, Nettie.'

'For what? I done nothing.'

'You called me by my proper name. I'm not Sal Scratch.'

Nettie grinned, revealing a missing eye tooth. 'Not to me, nipper, but if the old besom has anything to do with it you'll be Sal Scratch until you're old enough to be sold to the highest bidder.' She took Sarah by the hand and hurried down the dark corridor after the rest of the girls.

'Sold? They'll sell us?'

'They call us pauper apprentices, but it means the same. I've seen it happen often enough. You get these fat old mill owners who pay the workhouse master for boys and girls to work for them. I suppose it'll be my turn next.'

'No. You mustn't leave me,' Sarah cried, clutching her hand even tighter. 'What if Ma dies? I'll be all alone in the world.'

'Then you'll be the same as most of us in this place. Some of us, like me for instance, was dumped here as babies, and there ain't no escape unless we go to work at the mill or go into service. You just got to be brave, Sarah. Do what they tell you, but don't let them beat the spirit out of you.'

'You there. Nettie Bean.' A stentorian voice from the end of the passageway made them both jump. 'Stop talking and get to the women's yard now or you'll be on bread and water for the rest of the week.'

7

'That's Stoner,' Nettie whispered. 'He's the superintendent of outdoor labour. You don't want to fall foul of him. If you think that Matron Trigg is a dragon then he's a demon from hell.' She broke into a run, dragging Sarah behind her.

They arrived in the yard just in time to file in at the end of the line. The sight that met Sarah's eyes made her heart sink even further. Rows of women sat on wooden benches tugging at lengths of tarred rope with their bare fingers in order to extract the strands of hemp. The late autumn sun beat down on their heads and it was hot and airless in the enclosed area of the yard. Even from a distance Sarah could see that the women's fingers were raw and bleeding from picking at the salt-stiffened fibres.

'We do this until dinnertime,' Nettie whispered, seemingly regardless of the fact that the man Stoner was glaring at her beneath beetling black eyebrows. Sarah blinked, not daring to acknowledge this piece of information in case it brought his wrath down upon her head. She knew that she was an object of curiosity, if not pity, as she sported the damning sign. She had seen one of the women, who presumably could read, cross herself at the sight of the devil's child.

As she shuffled along behind Nettie towards the area set aside for the younger girls, Sarah glanced up at the building which towered five storeys above her. She had heard someone say that the lying-in ward was on the topmost floor beneath the roof. Ma was surely closer to heaven up there, but Sarah could only hope that she did not go there too soon.

'You there. Pay attention.' Stoner's loud bellow made her jump and she realised with a sinking heart that he was pointing at her. She huddled a little closer to Nettie but he reached out and grabbed her by the ear. 'So you're the devil's daughter, are you? Well, I'm Beelzebub hisself and if you don't behave yourself, little girl, I'll strike you dead on the spot.' He leaned over her and his breath stank of stale beer and tooth decay. 'D'you understand what I'm saying?'

'Y-yes, sir.' Sarah swallowed the bile that rose in her throat and threatened to make her vomit all over Stoner's dusty boots.

He gave her a shove that sent her sprawling on the bench beside Nettie. 'Show the brat what to do, Bean. I'll be round to check, so no slacking.' His cold grey stare encompassed the rest of the girls, who had already begun their onerous task. 'That goes for all of you.' With his hands clasped tightly behind his back he proceeded to walk slowly along the row and back again. Apparently satisfied with their prowess, he turned his attention to the older women.

Nettie waited until he was out of earshot before heaving a sigh of relief. 'He's a bastard, that one. We all hate him even worse than Trigg, and that's saying something.'

Sarah was doing her best to extract the fibres from the tarred rope, but her hands were small and her

9

fingers were already beginning to hurt. 'Is it always like this?'

'No, love. Sometimes it's much worse.' Nettie bent her head over her work. 'You'll get used to it.'

By midday Sarah was exhausted and her fingers were a bleeding mass of broken blisters. She had been up before six o'clock that morning and had eaten nothing since a meagre breakfast of a slice of stale bread. After three hours in the schoolroom and two hours of picking oakum, she was barely able to stand when the dinner bell rang. Nettie helped her to her feet but Sarah had to walk to the refectory unaided, and she stumbled several times before she reached the large, echoing room filled with trestle tables and narrow forms. The meal of thin soup and a hunk of bread was barely edible but she was so hungry that by this time she did not care. There was silence except for the sound of the women and children slurping the tasteless broth and slapping their lips as though it were nectar from heaven.

Despite her physical discomfort, Sarah's only thoughts were for her mother. She was determined to get to the lying-in ward one way or another, but it proved almost impossible. Their every movement was watched by someone in authority, and after the tables were cleared and scrubbed until they were bleached bone-white, and the floors had been swept clean, it was time to return to work. The women went back to the yard to continue picking oakum, but the girls were divided up and some went to the sewing room and the others, including Nettie and Sarah, were given

10

buckets and scrubbing brushes and strict instructions to clean the corridors and staircases until they were spotless.

This was something that Sarah had often done in the theatre when her mother was unwell or too far advanced in pregnancy. She filled her bucket and rolled up her sleeves. The cold water soothed her sore hands but the coarse lye soap stung when it touched the raw flesh. She did her best to ignore the pain as she made her way up five flights of stairs to the top floor. No one, it seemed, was eager to start at the top but it gave her the opportunity of sneaking into the female ward.

The heat beneath the rafters was suffocating, and the smell of blood almost knocked her sideways as she crept into the lying-in ward. The moans and screams of the women in labour filled her with horror, and she was tempted to turn and run, but somehow she forced herself to keep going. She tiptoed between the rows of iron beds, hardly daring to look at the tortured faces of the women as they struggled to give birth. The midwives were too busy to notice one small child in their midst, and Sarah was able to get to the far end of the room without being apprehended. She found her mother lying white-faced and still amongst blood-stained sheets. Her eyes were glazed and her lips moved silently as if in prayer.

Sarah went down on her knees at her mother's bedside, taking her hand and holding it to her cheek. 'Ma, speak to me.'

Ellen Scrase turned her head slowly, focusing her eyes on her daughter. 'My Sarah.'